Praise for Cheryl Williford and her novels

"A breath of fresh air."
—*RT Book Reviews* on *The Amish Midwife's Courtship*

"Well done and will have you rooting for a [happily-ever-after]."
—*RT Book Reviews* on *The Amish Widow's Secret*

Praise for Debby Giusti and her novels

"The active pace becomes more engaging as the drama intensifies."
—*RT Book Reviews* on *The Agent's Secret Past*

"Plenty of suspense, a captivating mystery and fast pacing make this a great read."
—*RT Book Reviews* on *Protecting Her Child*

"It flows…and the characters' inner struggles are relatable."
—*RT Book Reviews* on *Stranded*

Cheryl Williford and her veteran husband, Henry, live in South Texas, where they've raised three children and numerous foster children, alongside a menagerie of rescued cats, dogs and hamsters. Her love for writing began in a literature class, and now her characters keep her grabbing for paper and pen. She is a member of her local ACFW and CWA chapters, and is a seamstress, watercolorist and loving grandmother.

Debby Giusti is an award-winning Christian author who met and married her military husband at Fort Knox, Kentucky. Together they traveled the world, raised three wonderful children and have now settled in Atlanta, Georgia, where Debby spins tales of mystery and suspense that touch the heart and soul. Visit Debby online at debbygiusti.com; blog with her at seekerville.blogspot.com and craftieladiesofromance.blogspot.com; and email her at Debby@DebbyGiusti.com.

CHERYL WILLIFORD

The Amish Midwife's Courtship

&

DEBBY GIUSTI

Plain Truth

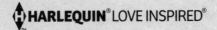

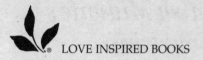

LOVE INSPIRED BOOKS

Recycling programs
for this product may
not exist in your area.

ISBN-13: 978-0-373-20975-0

The Amish Midwife's Courtship and Plain Truth

Copyright © 2017 by Harlequin Books S.A.

The publisher acknowledges the copyright holders
of the individual works as follows:

The Amish Midwife's Courtship
Copyright © 2016 by Cheryl Williford

Plain Truth
Copyright © 2016 by Deborah W. Giusti

www.Harlequin.com

Printed in U.S.A.

CONTENTS

THE AMISH MIDWIFE'S COURTSHIP

Cheryl Williford

This book is dedicated to my husband, Henry, who's always there when I need him, and to Clare Naomi, our youngest granddaughter. Your smile makes the sun shine brighter. Much thanks goes to Barbara Burns and Susan Cobb, my daughters and two of my biggest fans, and to ACFW's Golden Girls critique group. Without you ladies I'd still be editing my own weak verbs.

The Lord is good and does what is right;
he shows the proper path to those who go astray.
—*Psalms* 25:8

Chapter One

Pinecraft, Florida
November

Molly Ziegler gave the dust mop one last shove under the bed and hit a mahogany leg. Unexpected movement under the bed's mound of sheets and wedding-ring quilt caught her unaware.

She froze.

Something swung toward her head. Instinctively she launched the mop high into the air, warding off the coming blow.

The mop's handle connected with something solid.

A satisfying *clunk* rang out in her *mamm*'s tiny rental room. Her heart thumped in her chest as she stepped back from the bed, lost her balance and hit the floor. Her feet tangled in the folds of her skirt as she pushed away.

His dark brown hair wild from sleep, a gaunt-faced, broad-shouldered man gazed down at her, his dark green eyes wide with surprise. He dropped the wooden crutch he'd been holding. "Who are you?" His hand gingerly touched the bump on his forehead. His eyes narrowed in a wince.

The bump on his forehead grew and began to ooze blood.

He wasn't supposed to be in the bedroom at this time of the day. The door hadn't been locked.

In a stupor of surprise, she blinked. She had no brothers, and with the exception of her father who had passed away in his sleep five years earlier, she'd never seen a man in his nightclothes. There were dark shadows under his eyes. Thick stubble on his chin and upper lip told her she was dealing with an unmarried man.

Annoyed by his words, she scowled. "I was about to ask you the same thing. Cover yourself. There's a woman in your midst. You might be visiting Pinecraft, where rules are often bent and broken, but my *mamm*'s dress code is very strict and must be followed by all renters."

"It wonders me why you're showing off those lovely stockings to a man if your *mamm*'s dress code is so strict."

Molly's face burned as she swiftly straightened her skirt. She clambered to her feet, an already sour mood making her wish she stood taller than five foot nothing in her stocking feet.

She controlled the urge to stomp as she stepped away from the bed with all the dignity she could muster. Her hands brushed down the skirt of her plain Amish dress and cleaning apron. With eyes narrowed, she sliced the man with an icy glare. "My *mamm* and I run a decent boarding *haus*. Our ways are Plain, but we keep high standards."

"Anyone ever tell you that you're a bit grumpy in the morning?"

Molly tried to ignore the man's uncalled-for comment and smirk, even though she knew he was right. She had woken up grumpy, her sleep cut short by Frieda Lapp's early-morning call and delivery of a beautiful baby girl, who they planned to call Rachel after John's recently departed mother.

She inched toward the closed bedroom door. Her *mamm*'s rule was firm and told to every renter who stayed in their boardinghouse. "This room was to be vacated by noon. It's now past one. Didn't you see the sign when you paid your deposit?"

"I saw the sign, but I made other arrangements with Mrs. Ziegler late last night. I'll be staying for several days, perhaps a month until I can find a permanent place, now that I've bought the bike shop. Didn't she tell you?"

A thick line of blood trickled down the man's forehead, threatening to drip on the bed linens.

He must be Isaac Graber, the stay-over Mamm mentioned this morning, and now I've struck him.

She turned on her heel and shoved back the plain white curtains blowing at the window. A crutch lay by her foot. She found an identical crutch leaning against the bedpost.

Molly dug into her apron pocket and pulled out a clean tissue and thrust it into his hand. "Here. You need this. *Mamm* won't want blood on the sheets."

He pressed the tissue against the bump, then gazed down at the blot of scarlet blood. "You cut my head!" His coloring turned from primrose to a sickly mossy green.

"I wouldn't have hit you if you hadn't taken that swing at me with the crutch." She leaned in to hand him a wastebasket and then stepped back fast, inching her way toward the closed bedroom door. The man behaved like a brute, but she had to admit he was an attractive one. She'd never seen eyes so green and sparkling.

And such thick, glossy nut-brown hair. Dark strands jutted at every angle in the most unusual way.

Molly realized he was talking, and she tried to drag her attention away from his face and back to his words.

"I was asleep and you startled me awake. You could have been a thief, for all I knew."

"A thief!" She sucked in her breath and then chuckled. "That's rich. I was doing my job and *you* attacked me."

He kept talking as if she hadn't spoken. "I grabbed the closest thing I had to defend myself." He looked at the plastic trash can she'd placed on the edge of the mattress and gazed at her, befuddled, his forehead creasing. "What's this for?" he asked, swallowing hard.

"In case you vomit. Some people do when they see blood and turn that particular shade of green."

"Green? I'm not green. It's more likely I'm red from all the blood." He offered her the can, leaving his bloody fingerprints on the rim. "Take this thing away. I don't need it."

If Mamm *hears about all this, she'll rant for hours.* Her eyes glanced at the small alarm clock on the bedside table and was shocked to see that time had gotten away from her. It was almost two. *I'll be late for singing rehearsal if I don't hurry.*

She snatched the can, her gaze on the impressive bump growing on the man's forehead. The cut was at least a half-inch long, blue as the sky and still dripping blood. "Does it hurt?" Her anger cooled and she began to feel contrite. "Maybe you could use some ice…a cloth?" She spoke softer "Maybe a doctor?"

He looked heavenward, rolling his eyes like a petu-lant teenager. "Oh, *now* the woman shows concern, and here I am thinking her a heartless thief." He pulled the sheet up and covered his thin sleeping shirt in mock alarm.

"Think what you will. Men usually do. Now, do you want a damp cloth or not, because I'm busy and don't have time for this foolishness."

"A cloth would be good if you're not too busy."

His sarcasm didn't go unnoticed. Her bad mood darkened. She grumbled to herself as she went into the old-fashioned, minuscule bathroom just off the bed-room. She didn't resent being told to clean the sparsely furnished back bedrooms when their last two renters left, but she'd already had her day planned.

She was used to hard work during their peak win-ter season, but holding down a job at the local café as a waitress and birthing babies as the local midwife kept her busy. Sometimes too busy. She liked the whirl of her demanding life, but she did resent her *mamm*'s at-titude. Just because she was still single didn't mean she didn't have anything better to do on her day off than mop floors and strip down beds. She'd miss singing practice again this afternoon thanks to her *mamm*'s un-reasonable demands on her time.

Her lip curled in an angry snarl as she pushed back a wayward strand of hair behind her ear, then ran a clean washcloth under cold running water.

Lifting her head, she caught a glimpse of herself in the mirror and scowled. Dishwater blonde hair that had been neatly pulled back in a tight bun now ran riot around her head. Remembering the renter's good looks, her cheeks flushed pink. What must he think of her appearance?

Her brown eyes flashing with frustration, she looked away, reprimanding herself for behaving like the frustrated twenty-year-old spinster she was.

With a jerk, she tugged her prayer *kapp* back into place and then squeezed the water out of the cloth. She was in enough trouble for hitting the man. Now wasn't the time to start ogling the guests and worrying about how she looked. The sin of vanity brought only strife into the life of a Plain person. She had to pull herself together.

The worn but well-polished hardwood floor squeaked as she hurried back to the bedroom and handed the cloth to the man. Their hands touched and she pulled away, not about to admit she felt anything.

But she had.

He ran his fingers through the dark spikes on his head and brought a semblance of order to his wild hair before wiping at the cut above his eyebrow.

"Here, let me do that. All you're doing is making it bleed again." Forgetting her own stringent proprieties, Molly moved to the bed, pulled her full skirt under her and sat as far away from him as she could and still touch him. She jerked the cloth from his fingers before he could object and dabbed lightly around the seeping wound.

"A butterfly bandage should take care of any further bleeding and keep the wound from scarring," she said. "The bandages and antibiotic cream are in the kitchen. I'll be right back."

She ran for the door, then skidded to a halt. "While I'm gone, please get out of bed and put on proper clothing." She bounded away, her skirt swirling around her legs as she hopped over the trash can and slipped out, letting the bedroom door bang behind her.

Isaac Graber's head hurt. He wiped the sticky blood off his fingers with the damp cloth the petite blonde-haired housekeeper had left behind and found himself smiling, something he hadn't done since the accident and his painful recovery.

The tiny woman had put him through sheer misery trying to keep up with her rapid-fire conversation. She taxed his patience and his temper, but he couldn't wait for her to come back into the room.

With a tug, he threw back the tangled covers and slid out of bed. The same white-hot agony that kept him up most nights stabbed down his leg. Angry red lines of surgical stitching laced up the puckered skin near his left knee and calf, his leg pale where the cast had covered it for several months.

He struggled to get into a pair of clean but well-worn trousers and a wrinkled long-sleeved cotton shirt he'd pulled from his suitcase, and then put on a fresh pair of socks and his scuffed boots, as he tried to forget the fresh ache in his head.

He'd taken his last pain medicine in Missouri, weeks before, and now had nothing to dull the ache in his leg or his heart. Not that he deserved the mind-numbing pills that helped him forget what he'd done and the tragedy he had rained down on his best friend's family.

Isaac dropped his chin to his chest and forced himself to breath slowly. He shouldn't have been driving that day, especially since the country road was slick after a sudden hard rain. He had no license. No insurance. Someone else could have taken Thomas home from the multi-church frolic when he'd wrenched his ankle. Why had he offered to drive? It wasn't like him to break Amish laws, even if Thomas's ankle was swollen after the rough game of volleyball.

With his eyes squeezed shut, his mind went back to the horrific day. The memory of Thomas lying on the ground next to him was seared in his mind.

The first police officer at the scene had assumed Thomas, who was Mennonite, had been driving. In shock and bleeding profusely, Isaac had been too confused to speak. He'd been rushed to the hospital and then into surgery.

But days later, when his thoughts had cleared, he'd heard the police were blaming the dead-drunk man in the other vehicle for the accident. Isaac knew they were wrong. Surely he was the one at fault and needed to make it right.

In the hospital, Isaac had confessed everything that day to his *daed*, but his father had railed at him, "We are Amish and will manage our own problems. You are to ask *Gott* for forgiveness and then be silent. I will not have the truth known to this community just to make you feel less guilty. Nothing can be gained by your confession. It was *Gott*'s will that Thomas die. You are to keep all this to yourself, do you hear, Isaac? You must tell no one. The shame you carry is yours, and yours alone. It is *Gott*'s punishment. You must learn to live with it. Your *mamm* and I will not be held up to ridicule because of your foolish choices. This kind of shame could kill your *mamm*. You know her heart is weak."

And like the coward he was, he'd run to Pinecraft, desperate to get away from his *daed*'s angry words, his mother's looks of shame. Isaac would spend the rest of his life dealing with things he could not change.

His hands braced against his legs, he looked down at his scuffed brown boots, at the crutch at his feet. He deserved to be crippled. If the police in Pinecraft ever found out the truth, he knew he'd be arrested, thrown into an *Englischer* jail for the rest of his life.

He rubbed the taunt muscle cramping in his leg. *Gott* was right to punish him for his foolish choices.

He smoothed down his trouser leg, covering the scar. Fatigue overwhelmed him. His guilt robbed him of sleep. He and Thomas had both died that day, but he knew he had to go on living.

A ridge of stitched skin under the trouser leg sent pain burning into his calf. No more *Englischer* doctors for him. All they wanted was to make him whole again. He didn't deserve to be free of pain. The doctors in Missouri should have let him die.

He'd have to find a way to deal with the ache in his heart, his guilt and the odd way he was forced to walk. Let people stare. He didn't care anymore. Nothing mattered. Thomas was dead.

The housemaid came swinging back into the room with a tray of bandages, a bottle of aspirin and bowl of water. A steaming mug of black coffee sat in the middle of her clutter.

"I thought you might want something for the pain in your head." She set the tray on the nightstand, ruined his coffee with three packets of sugar and used a plastic spoon to stir it. With the twist of her delicate wrist, she unscrewed the aspirin bottle. "One or two?"

"None, *danke*," he said, and watched her count out

two pills and place them on the table next to the coffee mug.

"Let's get this injury seen to and then you can have some hot breakfast. I put the biscuits back in the oven to warm. The last of the renters ate their meal at seven, but I'll make an exception for you this morning." She squeezed out the white washcloth floating in warm water and approached him, her pale eyebrows low with concentration.

Their gaze met for seconds. Her whiskey-brown eyes caused the oddest sensation in the pit of his stomach, like butterflies flittering from flower to flower. He frowned and hardened his resolve. The last thing he needed was a woman trying to take care of him.

"Don't worry. I'm not going to hurt you." She smiled. Her brown eyes sparkled.

He looked away, concentrating on the colorful braided rug on the floor. Her touch was gentle, the cream she spread with her fingertips cool and soothing. She unwrapped a small butterfly bandage and pressed it down, careful not to touch his cut.

"There, all done."

Tray in hand, she backed toward the door. "Now take your pills and drink your coffee. I'll see you in the kitchen in ten minutes."

"Wait!" He realized he didn't want her to leave. It had been a long time since he'd had a conversation with anyone, much less a kindhearted woman who made him feel alive. "What's your name?"

"Margaret, but everyone calls me Molly," she said, whirled round, and then was gone.

The door shut behind her, and he stared at the spot

where she'd stood. When she left, all the life seemed to have been sucked out of the tiny room.

Molly leaned against the closed bedroom door and allowed herself to take a deep breath. She exhaled with a whoosh, then hurried back toward the kitchen. No man had ever affected her the way Isaac Graber did. She lifted her hand and watched it tremble. He had flustered her, made her pulse race. She was as happy as a *kinner* on Christmas morning and had no idea why.

Ridiculous! A man was already considering her for courtship, not that she was interested in him or ready for marriage to anyone. Still, her future had been mapped out by her *mamm*, and she really didn't have any choice in the matter.

No doubt she'd soon see the flaws in Isaac, like she did most men. She had to be practical. *Mamm* was counting on her to make a good marriage that would end all their financial problems.

She hurried through the hall and into the warm, cozy kitchen fragrant with the aroma of hot biscuits and sliced honey ham. At the stove, she turned on the gas, lit a blaze under the old iron frying pan and then added a spoon of reserved bacon fat.

Her hands still shook as she broke three eggs into a bowl and poured them into the hot oil. Crackling and popping, the eggs fried but were forgotten when the troublesome renter awkwardly maneuvered his way through the kitchen door, lost his balance and tripped over his own feet. He lay sprawled on the worn tile floor. Facedown. Not moving.

"Herr Graber!" Molly stepped over his crutch and kneeled at his side. The morning headlines flashed through her mind. Man Killed by Abusive Landlady. "Please be all right." She shook his shoulder.

Nothing.

She shook it again, harder this time.

"If you'd stop trying to break my shoulder, I might be able to get up."

Molly stamped her foot, angrier than she'd been since he'd called her a thief earlier. Why did this man bring out the worst in her? "You scared me. Why didn't you say something, let me know you weren't dead? I thought…"

He leaned up on one elbow. "Did you seriously think I was dead? It would take a lot more than a spill to kill me, Miss Ziegler."

She gathered her skirt around her and scooted away, not sure what kind of mood he was in, but stayed close enough, just in case he needed help getting back on his feet.

His green eyes darted her way and then over to his fallen crutches. "Your mother seemed normal enough when I signed in last night. I wonder if she knows how you treat her guests when she's not around."

"I take offense to that remark, Herr Graber. I in no way harmed you. Well…here in the kitchen I didn't. I was busy cooking your breakfast, and you fell over your own big feet." He wore scarred, laced-up boots, the kind bikers favored. Maybe that was how he'd hurt himself. A nasty bike spill, and now he was in pain and taking his misery out on her.

"You're right. I did fall over my own feet. That's what cripples do." He leaned heavily on a single crutch and pushed his way to his feet, his face contorting with pain.

"*Ach*, you're no cripple," she said, standing.

"What would you know about being crippled?"

He'd crossed the line. Molly lifted her skirt an inch and showed him the built-up shoe on her right foot. "I think I know a lot about being crippled."

He flushed, his forehead creased in dismay. He moved to straighten, and groaned.

A wave of sympathy washed over her. He had to be suffering. She'd almost been a teenager when she'd fallen out of a tree and broke her leg, damaging the growth plate. Her pain had been excruciating, but she got around fine now. He looked pale with pain. No wonder his mood was dark. "Can I help—"

He lifted his hand to warn her off. "*Nee.* I'm perfectly capable of getting myself up. I've had plenty of practice."

He rose and towered over her. He had to be at least six feet tall, with broad shoulders and a slim waist.

The smell of burning eggs reached Molly's nose. She gasped as she turned and saw smoke rising from the overheated frying pan. "Your eggs! Now look what you've made me do." She pulled the pan off the burner and then turned back, ready to do verbal battle with the wretched man.

Unsteady on his feet, Isaac Graber hobbled across the kitchen floor and stepped out the back door, waving gray smoke out of his face as he shut it behind him with a slam.

Chapter Two

A gust of wind accompanied Ulla Ziegler through the back door. She hurried into the kitchen, the folds of her once-clean apron smeared with mud and brimming with a load of gritty brown potatoes and freshly pulled carrots. Fat rain drops spattered against the kitchen window.

Finishing the last of the breakfast dishes, Molly stopped mid-swipe. To her amazement her stout little mother, who slipped and slid through the door, managed to make it across the room without dropping one potato.

Molly's brow rose in agitation. Her *mamm*'s plain black shoes had left a trail of gooey brown mud across the recently mopped linoleum floor. Naturally her mother made no apologies for the added work.

Wiping her hands dry, Molly couldn't help but smirk. The sudden morning shower had turned her *mamm*'s wooly gray hair into a wild riot of curls around her untidy, limp prayer *kapp*.

A natural trader, the older woman was blessed with the gift of bartering and had bragged at breakfast about the promise of ten pounds of freshly dug potatoes from old Chicken John, a local chicken farmer, for six jars of their newly canned peaches. Molly had a feeling the old farmer had more than peaches on his mind when it came to her mother. She'd noticed the way the widower looked at her, not that Ulla gave the man much encouragement. Her *mamm* seemed satisfied with being a widow with no man to tell her what to do.

Isaac Graber came back into the house moments after Ulla, the wind catching the door and slamming it again as he fell into the closest kitchen chair. The renter jerked a handkerchief from his trouser pocket and wiped rain from his pale face.

Sniffing, Ulla took in a long, noisy breath and coughed on the kitchen's putrid air. She dumped the potatoes into a wicker basket in the corner of the big kitchen and twirled.

"What'd you burn, *dochder*?" She jerked a dish towel off its peg and pressed it to her lips. Her watering blue-eyed gaze sliced from Molly, who stood transfixed in front of the cast iron sink, to the smoldering frying pan floating in a sea of sudsy dishwater.

Molly shrugged. She would not lie. She wanted to, but she'd never been good at weaving believable tales. Best to tell the truth. "The eggs got away from me."

She waited for her mother's reaction, her gaze slanting Isaac Graber's way, daring him to deny the truth of her words. Had he had a chance to tell her *mamm* about what had happened this morning? She looked at the bump on his forehead and then glanced away. If her *mamm* made a fuss, she surely wouldn't get to the singing practice on time.

Ulla looked in the kitchen trash and made a face, her full lips turned down at the corners. "You know it's a sin to waste good food. That dog hanging around out back would have eaten those, burned or not."

Ulla began to flap the dish towel around the room, propelling the smoke toward the slightly opened kitchen window.

"Molly didn't forget the eggs, Mrs. Ziegler." Isaac smiled and flashed his straight, white teeth. His green eyes sparkled with sincerity. "She helped me get off the floor when I tripped over my own big feet. The eggs paid the price for her efforts. Isn't that right, Molly?"

Why was he taking up for her? She put her hands on her hips and looked him over. Pale and slender, he reclined in the old kitchen chair as calm as could be, his crutches leaning against the wall behind him. He smiled at her and her stomach flip-flopped. She went back to scrubbing the frying pan's scorched bottom. Seconds later she glanced back up at him and caught him staring at her. What was he up to?

She'd expected him to be full of tales and *gretzing* to her *mamm* about this morning, and there he sat, being nice, even generous of heart. The man kept her off-kilter, and she wasn't having any of it. "*Ya*, like he said, *Mamm*. He fell and I helped him up."

One of Ulla's gray brows spiked. She mumbled, "*Ya*, well. No matter. It's *gut* you were here to help."

Molly's gaze drifted from her *mamm*'s suspicious expression back to Isaac's calm grin. He had the nicest smile.

Ulla opened the cupboard door and asked, "You two want *kaffi*?"

"*Ya*." Molly nodded and went back to scrubbing pans.

Moments later mugs of steaming coffee and plates

of buttered biscuits, with a dab of homemade raspberry jelly, appeared on the cluttered kitchen table. Molly sat next to her mother and looked at their new tenant. He gazed over his mug at her. A smile lit his face. She looked away, concentrating on spreading jam on her hot biscuit.

"Herr Graber tells me he bought the old bike shop yesterday and got it for a good price." Ulla shoved half of her late-morning snack in her mouth and began to chew.

"Did he?" Molly blew on her hot coffee.

"Please call me Isaac." He glanced at Molly, his green eyes bright.

Distracted by their shine, she took a gulp of coffee and burned her tongue, but would have died a million deaths before she let on. She would not give him the satisfaction of knowing he had once again disturbed her.

"I thought since Herr Graber had some issues with his crutches this morning, it might be *gut* if you went with him when he takes a look at the shop." Ulla drained the last of her coffee and placed the mug on the table.

"You bought the shop sight unseen?" Molly asked.

Isaac nodded. "I did."

Foolish man. She turned to her mother and tried to keep the whine out of her voice. "I'd love to help Herr Graber, but singing practice is today. There's a frolic in a few weeks. I promised I'd come this time." Molly watched her *mamm* stuff the last crumbs of her biscuit in her mouth and sighed. She knew the *mox nix* expression her *mamm* wore. There'd be no singing practice for her today.

"I'm sure I can—" Isaac tried to interject.

Ulla rose from her chair. "It is settled. No more chatter from either of you." She dusted crumbs off her generous bust and headed for the sink, not giving Molly or Isaac another glance as she continued talking. "You are a paying guest, Herr Graber, and an Amish man in good standing with the community. Molly will be glad to help you while you stay here. She has nothing better to do."

Nothing better to do! Molly held her breath, praying she wouldn't say the angry words begging to come out of her mouth. As long as she lived in her *mamm*'s *haus*, she'd never have a say in her own comings and goings.

Molly stole a look at the dark-haired tenant and was amazed to see a hangdog expression turning his bruised forehead into a deep furrow. Maybe he didn't want her to go with him. She pulled at her prayer *kapp*, content in knowing the idea of her tagging along was an irritation to the infuriating man. Molly put on her sweetest smile and purred, "*Ya*, I'll take him. I can always go to practice next week. We wouldn't want Herr Graber to fall again."

Isaac balanced himself on one crutch as he wedged himself between the peeling garage wall and the rusty old golf cart. He eyed the cart's front tire and gave it a tap with the toe of his boot. "How old is this contraption anyway?" Not completely convinced the rusty bucket would move with both their weight on board, he tossed his crutches in the big metal basket behind the bench seat and struggled to climb in. One hip on the cart's bench seat, he scooted over as far as he could, giving Molly plenty of room to drive.

Molly gathered up the folds of her skirt and climbed in on the driver's side. She kept her eyes looking forward, ignoring his questions about the cart. She started the engine. The machine sputtered for a moment, but then took off down the pebbled driveway with a roar.

Wind blew off his black hat. It dropped into the basket at the back of the cart. He held on and sucked in his breath as she took a corner too fast. Her prayer *kapp* fluttered against her head. The sound of glass breaking invaded his thoughts, the flashback so real it could have been happening again.

His breath quickened.

His heart pounded.

He practiced the relaxation techniques he'd been taught in the hospital, pushing away the memories of his leg twisted unnaturally under him.

Breathe deep and hold.

Traffic slowed, and he loosened his grip on the seat. Why were there no seat belts on these contraptions?

They drove through the tiny town of Pinecraft. Bahia Vista Street came up within a matter of minutes. Isaac thanked *Gott* for their safe arrival as Molly pulled into the driveway of a small strip mall and parked around the back of the little bike shop squeezed in between a fancy pizzeria and a Laundromat desperately in need of some paint. Isaac got out on his good leg, grabbed for his crutches as he wobbled like a toddler, fighting for balance.

"Here. Let me help." Molly shoved his left crutch farther under his arm, handed him his blown-off hat and walked across the minuscule patch of paved driveway toward the shop's wooden back door.

Determined to be independent, Isaac took a step. Pain shot up his leg. He stifled a moan and kept putting one foot in front of the other, leaning heavily on his crutches for support. The doctors said the pain would soon go away. The broken leg held together with nuts and bolts would finish healing. But he would always have a limp.

A split second in time had taken Thomas's life and turned the past two months into the most miserable period in his life. He'd expected more of himself, of the surgery that was supposed to put him back on his feet. He was lucky to be alive. Painful memories pushed their way in again. The sound of an ambulance screamed in his head. He pushed the sound away and took in a deep, shuttering breath.

"The door's locked. Do you have the key?" Molly asked, rattling the handle. She glanced his way, but seemed to avoid looking directly at him.

Isaac nodded. "The Realtor said it should be under this." He carefully shoved away a pail of murky motor oil with his good foot. He bent to grab the silvery key, swayed and then felt surprisingly strong arms go round his waist to steady him.

Molly stood against him, her breath tickling his ear for long seconds. She made sure he was stable and then gradually released his body. Without a word she stepped away, pulled back her skirt and grabbed for the key covered in muck.

"You do the honors. This is your new business." Molly handed him the key and then gave him room to maneuver closer to the door.

This business purchase had been on impulse, something he probably should have thought more about. He normally would have, but he'd been desperate for a reason to get up every morning. A reason to keep living.

His hand shook as he pushed open the door. He felt around for a light switch, found it, then flicked it on. A bare bulb lit the dark, cavernous bike shop with harsh light. Broken and bent bike parts, torn golf-cart seats and rusting tools lay strewed across a filthy concrete floor. Total chaos. He faltered at the door. Another fine mess he'd got himself into.

"Was isht?" Molly glanced around him and then said, "Oh!"

"Ya, oh." Isaac maneuvered around scattered bike wheels and seats, carefully picking his way through the rubble that was Pinecraft Bike Rental and Repair. "This is what I get for buying sight unseen. What a *zot* I am."

Molly walked around him, surveying the clutter. She looked Isaac's way, her expressive brown eyes wide open.

He knew pity when he saw it. His stomach lurched. He didn't want or deserve her pity. He'd earned everything bad that happened to him. Let *Gott*'s retribution rain down on him.

"You're not a fool, Isaac. We all act impulsively sometimes. We'll get this place fixed up in no time. You'll see." She grinned, her face flushed pink.

"We?" he asked, unable to resist the urge to tease her, to take his mind off his misery.

Molly turned her back to him and moved away. *"Ya,* we. The church. Pinecraft. This community. We always pull together. You are part of us now. You'll see. *Gott* expects us to help each other." Molly went into the small office with a half wall that looked ready to fall with the least provocation.

He watched a blush creep down Molly's neck. She was young and beautiful in her own quiet way, not that he let her good looks affect him. She had no business being nice to him. She didn't know him, know who he was, what he'd done. She'd soon lose interest when she found out the truth about his past.

"I'm good with numbers," she offered. "If you need help with the books…" She turned, a ledger in hand, her gaze steady. "I'm available."

In the past Isaac would have grinned from ear to ear if a young woman had advised she was available, but he was hearing what he wanted to hear in her words. Not what she'd really meant. There was no way someone like Molly would show interest in a man like him. "*Danke.* Let's see if I get this business going before we worry about receipts and ledgers."

"I need to tell you something," Molly murmured, seeking his gaze, her look sincere.

"*Ya?*"

"*Danke* for not telling my *mamm* about how you got the bump on your head."

"*Ya,* well. I told her it happened when I fell." He picked up a box of rubber bands and set them on a small desk in the corner of the dusty room. Brooding thoughts assailed him. He pulled off his hat and pushed the painful memories away.

"You shouldn't have lied for me." Her brow arched. "There was no need. *Gott* will be—"

"Disappointed in me?" he interrupted, finishing her sentence. "Too late, Molly. He's already more disappointed than you can imagine."

"We have only to ask and *Gott* will forgive us," Molly said, holding his gaze.

He turned away, pretending to be busy with clearing the desk of trash. He wanted *Gott's* forgiveness more than he wanted air to breathe, but did he have the right to expect forgiveness after what he'd done?

"Does it hurt?"

"What?" He turned back toward her.

"The bump."

"Nee." He flipped through a pile of papers on the desk, forcing his gaze down. The bump did hurt, but he wasn't going to tell her. Some things were best left unsaid.

"The swelling is going down some."

He grinned. "I had a good nurse."

Molly laughed out loud, her eyes twinkling with mischief. "I usually try to keep my tenants as healthy as I can."

"You mean when you're not smacking them with a broom handle."

She was a tiny woman, not much taller than his little sister back in Missouri. He didn't understand why he enjoyed watching Molly bristle so much, but the frown now puckering her forehead made him grin.

"Ya, well. You know I didn't mean to hurt you, Isaac Graber," she muttered, jerking on her *kapp* ribbons with an air of indignation and scooted out of the little office space. When he checked on her again, she was busy wiping down shelves and stacking old parts manuals the previous owner had left behind.

Isaac chastised himself as he flopped into the office chair, the pain in his leg telling him he'd have to slow down or regret it that night. "I'm sorry for teasing you, Molly. I know you didn't mean to hurt me. My leg hurts, and the pain makes me grumpy."

She walked over to where he was sitting, a dust rag hanging from her fingertips, her brows arched. She looked at the knee he was rubbing. "How did you injure it?"

He had discussed the crash with his *daed*, *bruder*, the bishop and elders of the church, but he wasn't about to tell Molly how someone had died because of his stupidity. He turned back to the desk, lifting a big sales journal out of the desk drawer. "There's not much to tell. There was an accident. I got hurt, went to the hospital for a while and had two surgeries. The doctor said the pain will go away in time."

He forced a grin as he placed the book on the desk and pushed it her way. "Look at this. Whoever owned this place cleared out in a hurry. Wonder what the rush was?"

"Leonard Lapp owned the shop for years. I heard he retired and moved back to Ohio. His son took over the business a couple of years ago. I never met him, but rumors spread like wildfire here in Pinecraft. Some said he married an *Englischer* and abandoned the church, his faith and his *daed*'s business, too." Molly looked down at the book and then at Isaac, searching his face, her curiosity about him evident in her expression. She started to speak again, seemed to think better of it and turned away. She busied herself again. He couldn't help but watch her movements. She had a way about her, something that drew him to her like a moth to a flame.

He'd have to stay away from Molly Ziegler.

Chapter Three

Wide awake at four o'clock in the morning, Molly heard the insistent ring of another late-night caller. She sat up in bed and stretched toward the tiny cell phone approved by her bishop for midwife work. Her fingers searched the bedside table, hurrying to stop the cell phone's ring before it woke the whole house.

"*Ya.* This is Molly." She pushed back her sheet, put her feet on the cool floor and rose. "Are you timing the contractions, Ralf?" She laughed, reaching for the dress she kept hanging for nights like this. "*Ya*, I guess you're right. Six kids are plenty of practice. I'll see you in a few minutes."

She slipped on her simple work dress and work apron, then slid the phone into her medical case. She brushed back her tangled hair with fast strokes and then pinned it up in a tight bun before adding her *kapp*.

There was reason to hurry. Bretta, her friend since school, gave birth faster each time she had another child, and this birth would make number seven. There was no time for much more than a quick brush of her teeth, and she'd better be out the door.

She scurried down the hall, past Isaac's door. Did his bump still hurt. She had no cause for guilt, but she still felt at fault every time she looked at the goose egg on his forehead. Grabbing her medical bag, she pulled open the back door, ran to her cart and shoved in the key. In light drizzle she pumped the gas pedal. The golf-cart engine sputtered and coughed. *Oh, no. Not now.* She'd never make it in time if she had to run all the way to Bretta's house.

Isaac repaired engines and fixed bikes, didn't he? He would know what to do.

Molly raced through the clapboard house and down the narrow hall. She tapped lightly on Isaac's door and then began to bang harder. Time passed. Time she didn't have. "Isaac. Are you awake? Isaac?"

A sound of something falling came from the room.

"Is the house burning?" Isaac asked through the closed door.

Molly pressed her cheek to the cool wood. "No, of course it's not."

"Then go away."

Persistence was called for. She banged again. "I need your help, Isaac. Please."

The door cracked open an inch.

She couldn't see much of his face, but she could hear his heavy breathing. Had he fallen again? "I'm sorry to wake you, but there's an emergency. My cart won't start."

His door opened a bit more. She could barely make out his form in the dark hallway. "What kind of emergency? Is your *mamm* hurt?"

Molly groaned. "No. Not *Mamm*. It's Bretta. She's in labor." She heard him yawn.

"Who's Bretta?"

"There is no time for foolish chatter. I need you to help me get the cart started."

"*Outen* the lights before you try to start the engine. Your battery is probably as old as the cart."

"I tried that, Isaac. All I got was a sputter for my efforts."

She could see him run his fingers through his hair in the gloom. "And tell me why you are going out in the dark, to this woman Bretta at this hour? Is she your sister?"

"*Nee*, not my sister. My patient."

"I didn't know you were a doctor." He cleared his throat and coughed, his voice raspy.

"She's in labor. I'm her midwife. Please, Isaac. I don't have time for all these questions. I need your help now. If you're not inclined to help, just tell me. I'll call Mose."

"This Mose? Is he someone you're courting?"

Molly had no patience for all this *nix nootzing*. "Look. I'm sorry I woke you. Go back to bed." She rushed down the hall and back out the kitchen door. Where was a hero when a girl needed one? The term hero certainly didn't apply to the impressive Herr Isaac Graber. *All looks and no charm.*

Flipping on the outside light, Molly rushed over to the cart, intending to give it one last chance before running the six long blocks to Bretta's home.

She listened to the sluggish effort of the engine and groaned.

"Do you have gas in this lump of rust?" Isaac appeared out of the shadows and leaned on the cart, one crutch under his arm. He breathed hard and fast.

"Gas?" Had she remembered to fill the tank after

their outing to the bike shop? *Nee.* She turned the key, looked at the tank's gauge. Empty. What a *bensel* she was. No gas and a *mamm*-to-be waiting. Worse still, Isaac grinned like he knew what a *bensel* she was. "I forgot to fill the tank. What am I going to do? I have no choice but to run all the way, or disturb Mose."

"Stop panicking and listen. Does your *mamm* keep gas around for the lawn mower?"

"I don't know. Our neighbor, Herr Zucker, cuts the grass, but he does use our mower." Molly headed for the shed just inside the fenced backyard. She pulled a long string on the wall. Light pooled a golden glow around her. She lifted a gas can off the metal shelf, shook it and then ran back to the cart.

Isaac stood barefoot next to the cart, his pajama bottoms soaking up the dampness from the grass underfoot. He had the cart's gas cap in his hand.

She avoided looking directly at him and poured the gas in the cart's tank. Isaac screwed on the cap and then surveyed her from head to toe. "You don't look like any midwife I've ever seen."

"And how many have you seen?" Molly asked, sliding into the driver's seat.

He scratched his head and yawned wide. "Only you."

She started the sluggish engine and began to slowly back up. "Thank you so much, Isaac."

"I didn't do anything. Just took off the gas cap and put it back on." He started walking toward the back door, his one crutch taking all his weight.

"You saved the day and you know it," she called over her shoulder and drove off into the night, her medical bag bouncing in the basket.

Glancing back, she watched the glow from the house

light turn Isaac into a dark shadow as he slipped into the back door, his shoulders stooped. Why did the man have such a hard time accepting compliments? Didn't he realize how important it was to have a midwife arrive before the baby? She smiled as she drove on into the darkness. Whether he wanted to admit it to himself or not, he was her hero tonight, and she'd show him her appreciation somehow.

"Food's up."

Molly scrubbed the last of the dried egg yolk off the table and headed toward the kitchen's service window. Each step was painful. The new shoes she'd bought on sale tested her patience. She couldn't wait to get home, take them off and soak her feet in a hot tub of shiny, fragrant bubbles.

Willa Mae, the owner of the popular cafe since Hurricane Katrina had displaced her, stuck a sprig of parsley on the edge of the plate of steaming home fries and perfect over-easy eggs. She pushed it toward Molly. "Table six, and make it snappy. He seems in a hurry."

Putting on her friendly waitress smile, Molly took the plate and hurried over to the lone man sitting in the front booth by the door. His back to her, she placed the large plate in front of the newspaper the dark-haired man was reading and cheerfully rattled off, "Here you go. Fries and eggs. Hope you enjoy them."

"I would have enjoyed them more ten minutes ago." The man's hand rattled his empty coffee mug to express his neglect.

"I'm so sorry, sir. We've been a bit busy and I... Isaac? *Was tut Sie Hier?*"

Pulling his plate closer, he folded his newspaper and

looked at Molly. "Why do you think I'm here? I'm hungry and want my second cup of coffee."

She hadn't seen Isaac since he'd repaired the cart for her the day before. "Why didn't you eat at home? *Mamm* made pancakes with hot apple-butter early this morning."

"I'm a solitary man. I like my own company," he grumbled as he cut his eggs into perfect bite-sized squares. He leaned over the plate to get the full benefit of a fork full of eggs and home fries. "Now, can I have some coffee to wash down my breakfast?"

"*Ya*, of course. I'll get you coffee right away."

Taking a fresh carafe of coffee off the heater, Molly hurried back, reminding herself of the café's customer service policy. *The customer is always right.* She'd agreed with the policy when she'd taken the job a year ago, but some days it took perseverance and a cool head to be friendly and courteous to certain patrons who passed through the café door.

She grimaced as the toe of her built-up shoe hit the edge of Isaac's booth, but kept a smile plastered on her face. "Let me pour you a fresh cup of coffee." She went to pour, and before she could stop him, he reached for the tiny container of milk next to his cup.

Hot coffee splashed his wrist and shirt cuff. He jerked his hand away and reached for a napkin. "Do you really work here, or are you following me around, making sure I get hurt at least once a day?"

She spoke before she thought, her temper spiked by her throbbing toes and his grumpy words. "Has anyone ever pointed out how rude you are?" She put the carafe on the table harder than necessary. Her hands on her narrow hips, she glared at him, her smile gone. "If not, let me be the first. You are no ray of sunshine, Isaac Graber, and in future I'll make sure another waitress comes to your table to abuse you."

"That's fine." He sipped at his coffee and completely ignored her.

"Fine." Molly turned on her heel and marched back to her section of the café, her fists clenched, and feeling more like a petulant child than a grown woman.

Willa Mae flipped several pancakes and then motioned Molly over to the service window. "You're as red as summer sandals. What happened? That guy get fresh with you?"

"That guy is Isaac Graber, one of my *mamm*'s new boarders. Sometimes he makes me so mad."

"Let me guess. Did he pinch your backside, child?"

"No, not at all. He's…" Molly's voice trailed off as she searched for the right word. "He's not exactly weird, you know, just kind of friendly one minute and helpful and then he goes all strange and acts the fool."

"Oh. I get it. He's not showing enough interest in you and you're mad."

Molly straightened her *kapp*, tied her apron on a bit tighter and snapped, "*Nee*, that's not it at all. He keeps accusing me of hurting him on purpose, like I spend my whole day thinking up ways to cause him pain."

"You hitting on my customers?"

"You know perfectly well I'm not. Well… I did hit him in the head with a dust mop the other day, but that was completely his fault, not mine."

Sliding a plate of golden pancakes Molly's way, Willa Mae smiled, her dark weave shiny after standing over the hot grill all morning. "This story just keeps getting better and better. Tell me everything. When are you two making your announcement in church?"

Molly shot her best friend and boss a look that said it all. "These pancakes go to your gentleman at table six. Enjoy!" Willa Mae grinned.

Four hours later a midday band of rain swept in from the coast, surprising Isaac and leaving him a prisoner in his own shop. An hour passed. Not one customer came through the shop door. His early-morning meal at the café was nothing but a pleasant memory.

He rubbed his stomach. The wonderful aroma of hot pizza mingled with the less appealing odors of grease and dirt, but still his stomach stirred. An hour later it continued to rumble loudly, begging for lunch. He downed another bottle of water and tried not to think about food, especially the pizza shop next door. He wasn't about to trust his leg and poor balance on the slippery sidewalk outside. He would wait until the rain stopped.

There wasn't much he could do to pass the time while still on crutches. He called several cleaning businesses and wrote down price quotes. Sticker shock took away some of his appetite. The amounts asked to clear out the trash from the old building was enough to buy another electric golf cart. He'd need more carts to lease to the snowbirds pouring into Pinecraft from the north. The winter tourist season would quickly pass. Every day the bike shop wasn't open he was losing money—money he needed for a permanent place to live.

A feeling of defeat swamped him as he looked around the shop, at shelves falling off the walls, trash littering the floor. An ache began to thump at the base of his skull.

The roar of a high octane engine pulling up to the curb outside drew his attention. He rose, shoving aside pieces of a dismantled blue cart in order to maneuver toward the front door. He leaned against one crutch as he wiped away some of the dried white paint swirled on the storefront windows to block out the sun.

The side door of a black van labeled Fischer Transport opened and he was surprised to see Molly jumping to the pavement, followed by several stocky Amish men. Women in tidy prayer *kapps* and plain dresses in a variety of shapes and colors followed close behind. Isaac opened the shop door and was inundated with slaps on the back, smiling faces and so many introductions he'd never remember them all.

Busy shaking hands with the men and nodding to the women, Isaac took time to glance at Molly and return her enthusiastic grin. Her warm brown eyes seemed to be saying, *you didn't think I'd leave you to clean up this mess on your own, did you?*

A tall, curly-haired blond man with powerful shoulders and a firm handshake squeezed Isaac's hand. "*Willkumm* to Pinecraft, Herr Graber. I'm Mose Fischer and this is my *bruder*'s son, Wilhelm. I've heard a lot about you from Molly. I thought I'd come see this *youngie* she speaks of so fondly, with his fine mind for motors and winning personality."

Isaac nodded at the tall man and the skinny teenage boy standing next to him and smiled his welcome as he readjusted the crutch shaken loose from under his arm. "Molly's been talking to you about me?"

"*Ya*, she has. Nasty bump you've got there."

Isaac's gaze skimmed the bland expression Molly directed his way. Had she told him what really happened? As if feeling guilty, she looked down, busying herself with a pile of magazines on the floor. *"Ya.* Like a *bensel* I fell over my own feet."

"So I heard." Mose winked, telling Isaac he knew what had really happened. "I hope you don't mind us coming to help. We may live in a tourist town, but I think you'll find Pinecraft's a strong Amish community, ready to help out in times of need." He slapped Isaac on the back. "Besides, I have an ulterior motive. One of my little girls has a bike that needs a tube replaced, and I don't have time to work on it. You'll find we do a lot of bike riding around here. There's a real need for this shop to be up and running, for the community's sake, as well as your own."

Isaac looked around at the smiling people. They all seemed ready to work. He sent a grin of appreciation Molly's way. She'd gathered this mob of workers for him, even though he'd been rude to her at breakfast this morning. He owed her a debt of gratitude. He'd find a way to pay her kindness.

Mose pulled on the arm of an *Englischer* man in jeans and a white T-shirt who was busy working on organizing parts against the wall. "Let me introduce you to one of our local police officers, Bradley Ridgeway."

Smiling, his arm full of bike tubes and tires, Officer Ridgeway extended his free hand. "Glad to meet you, Isaac. Anytime you need help, you just let me know. I've got two sons who love their bikes. They're going to be glad to hear the bike shop's opening again."

Isaac shook the man's hand, but shame made him avoid looking directly in his eyes. *"Danke,"* Isaac managed to croak out. He turned away, pretending to be looking for something in the old desk in the office.

Molly moved close to him. He watched her as she and a well-rounded, middle-aged woman navigated a cluster of men working along the back wall. She caught his eye and motioned for him to join them.

"This is Becky Esch, our local baker," Molly said, and linked her arm through the woman's.

The older Amish woman smiled up at him, her startling blue eyes reminding him of his mother. Heavyhearted, Isaac nodded, quickly pushing away the momentary sadness that threatened to overwhelm him. "Ah...you must have been the one who made those wonderful doughnuts someone was passing around," he said.

"*Ya*, well. Single men need nourishment, I always say, especially when they're working this hard. I have an idea. Why don't you come eat dinner with us some Saturday night? The girls and I could use some company. We get lonesome now that Zelner's passed on to be with the Lord. It'll be nice to have a man at the head of our table for a change."

He glanced at Molly. The people crowded into the bike shop were her friends, not his. He wasn't sure what to say, but relaxed when Molly grinned at him with a twinkle in her eyes. "*Ya*, sure," he said. "That would be fine. *Danke*."

"*Gut*. The girls and I will expect you at six next Saturday. And make sure you bring your appetite."

As the woman walked away, Molly giggled under her breath and poked him in the rib.

"What's so funny?" he whispered, his head tilting her way.

"You have no idea what you just stepped into," Molly said, laughing with all the joy of a five-year-old. "Becky Esch has two old-maid daughters and she's just set a trap for you."

"You could have warned me," Isaac scolded.

Molly's brows went up as her smile deepened. "I could have," she said, then straightened the ribbons on her *kapp* as she turned her back on him and shouldered her way through the throng of workers.

Isaac's eyes narrowed as he noticed the slight limp in her gait. He didn't know what to think of their push-pull relationship, but knew he'd better work harder at keeping his distance from her. Molly was the kind of woman he'd choose if he were looking for someone to court. But after what he'd done to Thomas, there was no chance he would risk getting married any time soon. If ever.

Chapter Four

Molly hummed as she worked for an hour in the hot kitchen, preparing rosemary pork chops, roasted new potatoes with chives and fresh green beans slathered in butter and onion sauce for later that night. A homemade cheesecake drizzled in thick strawberry syrup sat waiting on the kitchen counter. The meal begged for her *mamm* to come home with an appetite, but at 6:00 p.m. the house remained quiet and still.

Dinnertime came and went. Darkness shrouded the plain, wood-framed house, the only home she had ever known. The old clock in the front room chimed seven times before Molly rose from the kitchen table, flipped on the light over the sink and stored the uneaten meal into containers. She cleaned up the dirty pans and was wiping the last of the crumbs off the counter as Isaac walked through the back door, his face etched with tired lines from his long day at work.

"Something sure smells *gut* in here. Am I too late for dinner?"

Molly beamed, her mood lifting, glad for company and conversation, even if it was only Isaac. "*Nee*, not at all." She pulled out a kitchen chair. "Come. Sit. Let me heat some food for you."

Isaac removed his hat and tossed it on the spare kitchen chair. He ran his fingers though his hair before he sat. "No other houseguests tonight?"

"*Nee.* Our last short-term guest left early this morning. She's on her way to see her sister in Lakeland, but she'll probably stop for another night with us on her way back to Ohio. Seems everyone else went to Pinecraft Park for the bluegrass singing tonight." She pulled the containers of food out of the refrigerator and then turned back to Isaac, her curiosity getting the better of her. "Is the shop ready to be opened yet?"

"I think so. I still need some parts, but they should get here in a few days."

He flashed a grin at her that played havoc with Molly's insides. She ignored the feeling and shoved their plates into the still-hot oven. "*Gott* brought you here. He'll make sure the customers come through the doors, Isaac. We have to trust His will. Why don't you clean up a bit while the food's heating?"

He looked down at his dusty clothes and reached for his crutches. "*Gut* idea. I think I will." He rose, wincing as he put his weight on his leg. "I won't be long."

She watched him lumber out of the kitchen, his limp more noticeable than it had been in days. Her heart went out to him. Pain was a lousy friend. She knew. She'd lived with it long enough.

Turning on another light to dispel the nuance of an intimate setting, she puttered around the kitchen, putting an extra place mat on the table, then some silverware. A tub of locally made butter was set in the middle of the table.

She stood still for a moment, listening to the sounds Isaac made at the back of the house. Just as she put down the bread plates and poured tall glasses of cold milk, he hurried back into the kitchen wearing clean work clothes, his hair slicked back from his thin face.

"I hope you don't mind if we eat in the kitchen. It's just you and me tonight," Molly said. "I waited for *Mamm*, but she must have gotten held up." Her mother usually served the last meal of the day in the more formal dining room, around the big wooden table that was large enough to seat twelve for Thanksgiving and Christmas.

Isaac returned to the chair he'd been sitting in moments before and leaned his crutches close by. "*Ya*, sure. Here is fine," he said, taking a sip of milk.

She pulled the rack of reheated chops out of the stove. "I hope you like stuffed pork chops."

"I do. They're my favorite," he murmured, watching her.

She placed the largest chop on Isaac's warmed plate. "Would you like some cinnamon?" A bottle of the tangy spice hovered over the generous mound of homemade applesauce Molly had served him.

He nodded. "Sounds *gut*." He tucked his napkin on his lap.

Molly carried the two plates she'd prepared to the table and placed one in front of Isaac before sitting across from him. "Salt and pepper is on the table if you need it."

He glanced at the salt shaker close to him and then glanced back at her, a slight smile turning up the corners of his mouth. "Before we pray I want to thank you for all the help you brought to the shop today."

"I'm glad we could contribute," Molly said, not wanting to delve into her own motives too deeply. She owed him. That was all. He wasn't the only one who could be a hero.

"You did more than help. I would have never been able to get the shop as clean and organized as it is now without all those additional hands. I owe you, and the kind people of Pinecraft."

"All I did was call my brother-in-law, Mose. Once he heard about your situation, he made the calls and did the rest."

"So Mose is family?" Isaac asked.

"Ya, he was married to my sister, Greta, but she went home to be with the Lord three years ago."

"I'm sorry for your loss."

She was surprised by the sound of sincerity in Isaac's voice. Memories of Greta, her smile, the way she found good in everyone, came rushing back. Molly took a deep breath and ignored the pain prodding her heart. With a jerk of her head, she nodded. "Thank you, Isaac. I still miss her, but *Gott* had a plan. We don't always understand, but we will once we can sit down and talk with Him."

"Let's pray so we can eat," Isaac suggested, and bowed his head.

Moments later Molly lifted her chin and found herself grinning as Isaac tore into his food with the gusto of a starving man.

"That strawberry cheesecake on the counter looks special. Somebody's birthday today?" he asked, his eyes shifting back to Molly. He sliced off a large piece of pork chop and stuck it into his mouth.

"Ya. Mine."

"Happy birthday! How old are you?"

She dipped her head, ashamed to admit she was so old and still not married. "Twenty-one, but it's no big deal. *Mamm* and I usually just celebrate alone with a home-cooked meal when it's one of our birthdays." Molly clasped her hands in her lap, putting on a bright smile she didn't feel.

"Birthdays are always special, Molly. Especially when it's your twenty-first."

"*Ya*, I guess," she murmured, her appetite disappearing. "It's such a big deal, *Mamm* didn't bother to show up for the event," she muttered.

"I'm sorry."

Molly tucked into her potatoes, determined to change the subject. "*Ya*, well, it doesn't matter." *Not to* Mamm *it doesn't.*

A half hour later Ulla placed her purse on the cleared kitchen table, along with a small bag from the new bookstore in town. "I've been with John all day," she said casually. "How was your day, Molly?"

"Fine." Molly stayed quiet. Isaac had gone to bed, and she'd been left to finish the last of the cleaning up.

"Have you heard from Samuel today? He wanted to know when you two could start courting."

"I have no interest in Samuel, *Mamm*. I told you this already."

"Well, he has an interest in you, and I think it's time you begin to show an interest in him."

Molly ignored her *mamm* and left the kitchen, her head held high. It was her birthday, and all her mother could do was talk of Samuel Bawell. She had forgotten her birthday completely. Not that her forgetting was anything new or surprising. She often forgot Molly existed, unless there was a chore to be done that she didn't want to do herself. Molly was still treated like an unwanted child, and she was tired of it.

Greta had always been her mother's favorite daughter. When Greta died in childbirth, Beatrice and Mercy, Mose and Greta's tiny daughters, had taken her sister's place of importance in her mother's heart. Molly didn't blame the girls. They were beautiful, like their mother, not plain like her. The *bobbels* were blessings from *Gott*. She adored them like any devoted aunt would. They were innocent children and had no idea their *grossmammi* played favorites and made her younger daughter feel inferior.

Molly closed her bedroom door and leaned against it. Tears began to flow until her eyes burned with grit. She hated when people wallowed in self-pity, and here she was feeling sorry for herself, with a great big hole in her heart.

In the dark she walked across the small room and sat at her dressing table. With the flick of her wrist, she turned on her lamp and pulled the pins from her *kapp* and bun. She massaged her scalp, her blond hair falling like a heavy curtain down her back. Reluctantly she looked into the mirror. Her eyes were puffy, her lashes dark with tears. Her nose was red in the semidarkness of the room. She pulled her *grossmammi*'s brush through the tangles on her head and winced as it caught in her hair. She ignored the pain and lifted her hands to braid the long strands into a thick plait.

She stared at herself in the mirror. No longer a girl, but a woman of twenty-one now. An adult…limited by one leg shorter than the other, unmarried, not being courted by a man she could love, still living with her *mamm*. Failure looked back at her in the brown eyes of the woman she'd become.

She turned off her lamp, knocking over her dressing-table stool as she rose and blindly moved toward the tallboy dresser against the wall. In the dark she grabbed a nightgown from the drawer. The soft cotton gown smelled of lilacs, homemade washing soap and good, fresh air.

Tomorrow things were going to change. She'd come up with a new plan for her life. She'd learn to stand up for herself. She had to, or she'd fast find herself married to Samuel Bawell.

The next day the bell over the door rang, announcing another customer. Isaac was filled with excitement. He'd been busy selling, renting and repairing bikes all day. He'd sold his last two secondhand golf carts and left a voice mail with his supplier, telling him he needed to purchase two more used carts for repair and sale. After today he'd have no problem paying next month's bills and still have money left over to buy a few supplies.

He looked up and was surprised to find Molly wandering around the shop. Today her pale pink dress put a healthy glow to her cheeks. She looked pretty, but then she always looked fresh and tidy to him. Even last night, with her joy robbed by her mother's failure to celebrate her birthday, she'd seemed content with his company. He wasn't sure what it was about her, but he enjoyed the way she made him feel when she was around.

He usually wasn't one to be impressed with good looks. Before he'd come to Pinecraft, a good personality always got his attention first. But Molly seemed to radiate a special light from her dark eyes. And there was something about her tiny frame that made her look frail and helpless even though she was strong and capable, with a personality to match. "I'm surprised to see you here. Shopping for a new cart? The one you drive should be put in the town dump as a relic." He smiled, waiting for reaction.

Her forehead wrinkled in response to his words. "There's nothing wrong with my cart, and this is no time for teasing, Isaac Graber. I've come to talk to you about a serious matter."

He noticed her dark eyes were red-rimmed and puffy. Concern washed over him. Over the past few days, he'd seen Molly in many moods, but nothing like this melancholy state of mind. "What's wrong?" he asked, motioning for her to sit on the old couch.

She moved a few magazines and sat. "I don't know where to start. You're probably not the right person to talk to. I don't even know if you consider me a friend." Molly's expression was grim, her mouth an angry line.

Isaac lowered himself into the seat next to her. He took her hand in his, considered the fine, delicate bones that held such strength. "*Ya*, of course you're my friend. Don't be silly. This shop wouldn't be open today if it wasn't for your thoughtfulness. You talk. I'll listen."

Molly sniffed, dabbing at her nose with her handkerchief. "My *mamm* and I had a fuss this morning." Molly took in a deep breath. "She's made a ridiculous demand, and I'm not putting up with it anymore. I've made a decision, and it might be the worst mistake I'll ever make."

Isaac thought back to the mistakes he'd made the day

Thomas died. Choices that cost Thomas his life. Isaac understood regret only too well.

Hoping to cheer her up, Isaac smiled as he spoke in a teasing manner, "*Ya*, go on. Tell me about this terrible mistake you're about to make."

"It's not that easy to talk about." She looked up, and her frown deepened. "I don't know why I came here." She twisted her hand away from him. "I should go back home, take a nap. Anything to stop worrying." She tried to stand, but he pulled her back to the couch. With trembling fingers, she pushed away the wisps of hair in her face as she looked at him. "I can be such a fool, Isaac."

"You're many things, Molly Ziegler, but foolish is not one of them. I see a strong woman before me. Someone who loves deeply and has a heart of compassion. I see no fool." Their gaze held, eyes searching. Molly's brokenhearted expression tugged at his soul. He felt emotions that were foreign to him, feelings that scared and excited him. At that moment he would give her the moon if he could, anything to bring back her joy.

Molly blinked, her head turning away. "I…" She began again. "I really need your help. I know I'm asking a lot, and you can always say no, but I don't know who else to turn to, and if I don't find an answer, I could end up married to a man I don't love, maybe even be unchurched if I refuse to wed."

"Tell me what you need me to do."

Her chin dropped against her chest. "My *mamm* has plans, plans that don't set well with me."

"What sort of plans?" Isaac's stomach knotted.

"She insists I court—*nee*—marry Samuel Bawell." She tugged at her prayer *kapp* ribbon as she turned to look at him, tears pooling in her eyes. "I know everyone thinks he's such a good man, but he's not. I've seen a different side to him, one that concerns me." A single tear clung to her damp lashes and then dropped to her cheek. "He can be rough and demanding when he doesn't get his way and then go all sweet and gentle like it never happened. *Mamm* says it's just my imagination, but it's not. I won't marry him, Isaac. Not without love." Her gaze smoldered with raw, mixed emotions.

Isaac squeezed her warm hand, wishing he had the right words to comfort her. Arranged marriages still happened in his community back home, but most *youngies* picked their own mates nowadays. "She threatened to force you into this loveless marriage knowing how you feel?"

"*Ya*, and she will if it suits her purpose." She sighed deeply and slowly as she tugged at her *kapp* ribbon again, her expression grim.

"What are you going to do?" Isaac had no advice to offer Molly. He couldn't manage his own life issues. How could he help her?

"That's where you come in." She made an effort to grin at him through her tears, her cheeks flaming red. Her hand fidgeted with the handkerchief in her lap.

"Tell me," Isaac encouraged.

"If my *daed* were alive, he'd put a stop to all this nonsense…but he's not. *Mamm* has all the power. I'm just the old maid." She pushed her shoulders back and held his gaze as she sniffed. "I know it's a lot to ask of anyone, especially you, but I couldn't think of anyone else who could help." Her bottom lip began to quiver.

"I can't help if you don't tell me what you need of me," Isaac encouraged, patting her hand.

Molly took in a deep, ragged breath. "Would you

pretend to court me for a little while, act like you have a real interest in me? Between the two of us, we can consider it a joke. It would mean nothing serious or binding."

Isaac's eyebrows went up in surprise.

"I know we barely know each other, and that we don't share affection in that way, but we'd only have to go places together. Be seen in public once in a while. Nothing more. Just pretend an interest to fool my mother and the community until Samuel goes back home to Ohio in a few weeks. Once he returns home, we can end the relationship. You can just tell people I wasn't the one for you."

Isaac looked at Molly, saw expectation in her eyes. Coming to him, asking him for help, couldn't have been easy for her. He couldn't let her down, not after all the help she'd given him. He owed her that much, but was still surprised when he heard himself say, "*Ya*, sure. I can do that for you. You'll let me know when you want to start this pretending?"

Molly's stressed expression relaxed. She smiled. "There's a singing frolic in the Mennonite church tonight. All the *youngies* are going. If you're not too busy…maybe we could go together and hold hands when we get there so others would see." Molly's expression grew pensive again, her smile disappearing.

"*Ya*, that sounds okay," he said, not sure he was doing the right thing.

"Thanks so much, Isaac." Molly threw her arms around his neck, squeezed hard and then jumped off the couch. "I've got to get home before *Mamm* does. We've got a new guest, and she complains when lunch meals aren't on the table at noon."

Standing, Isaac watched Molly hurry out the shop door, a relieved smile brightening her face. He ambled back toward his chair. What had he gotten himself into?

Silence greeted him as he turned back into his office. Pain coursed down his leg, reminding him he needed to take one of the pain pills the *Englischer* doctor had given him that morning. A few days of pain medication and maybe he'd stop snapping customer's heads off just because he hurt in body as well as spirit.

He wanted to help Molly, but he didn't want to give her the wrong idea, either. She'd been nothing but good to him, but she deserved someone better to court, even if their relationship would be nothing but pretense.

Leaning forward and looking around the clean, organized bike shop took the frown off his face. He'd never experienced such kindness from total strangers before. The people of Pinecraft had been generous to a fault. Getting to know them, he found Mennonites, Amish and *Englischers* all working side by side, without pay, but with a common goal. To get his business open.

He was almost ready to flip the Closed sign over to Open, and he had Molly and the people of Pinecraft to thank for that. She'd even brought in Mose Fischer, his first real customer. And now he was about to start a fake courtship with her.

Isaac dumped his new pain pills into his hand. He looked down at the white capsules. There had been a time in his life when he'd have been tempted to swallow the whole bottle just to keep the thoughts of what he'd done to Thomas at bay, but today he singled out a pill, stuck it in his mouth and swallowed it down with a drink from his bottle of water.

Life was for the living, not that he deserved to live,

but he had a reason to go on. He set the medicine bottle on his desk and picked up the phone. Maybe a reminder to his supply house would get the carts here a few days early. He'd be glad when the shop was officially open and he had something more to do with his time than sleep and eat.

The bell above the door clattered. Glancing over his shoulder, Isaac watched a man come into the shop, his shirt logo telling him the shop's new sign was finally ready to go up.

Excitement built in his heart. The bike shop would officially be open in a few days, and he was going to the singing frolic with one of the sweetest girls in Pinecraft. He had no right to the joy that overwhelmed him, but he humbly accepted it as a gift from *Gott*.

He looked down and saw Molly's handkerchief on the shop floor. He stopped and picked it up. The scent of lavender floated up and tickled his nose. Smiling, he tucked the cloth in his pocket next to his heart and hurried toward the shop door to greet a customer. Tonight when he saw Molly he'd give the square of white linen back to her. He beamed at the thought of being with her, holding her hand, but busied himself as he reminded himself their courting was for Ulla's benefit, not his.

Chapter Five

Two hours later Molly stood silently at the thrift store's front window, pretending to flip through men's shirts hanging from a metal rack, when she was really watching Isaac's bike-shop door. She couldn't stop thinking about him, about the fake courtship she'd proposed to him.

Now that she'd had time to consider the situation, she realized Isaac must think her a complete *bensel* for asking him to go along with her foolish ruse.

Why had he agreed to fake an interest in her? They hardly knew each other. Were strangers really. What was in it for him? They had nothing in common, with the exception of living in Pinecraft and both being Amish. No one was going to believe they'd fallen in love so quickly. Her shoulders slumped. Most of the time they weren't even nice to each other.

She straightened two shirts on their plastic hangers and pondered her fate. Her mother knew her better than anyone, knew she seldom acted impulsively. Everyone in the little tourist town thought of her as good ole practical Molly, the spinster with no personal life.

She was the one everyone counted on. Her forehead crinkled with irritation as she shoved a shirt across the rack with such force the plastic hanger broke and fell to the floor. She bent to retrieve it, her mind racing. Her *mamm* wasn't going to fall for their pretense unless her and Isaac's romance was very convincing. That meant she'd need Isaac's total cooperation. He was a busy shopkeeper. He didn't have time for her childish ideas. He probably thought her a silly old maid, coming up with such grand schemes just so she didn't have to marry.

Movement across the street caught her eye. She watched with interest as a big crane carried a sign toward the roof of Isaac's bike shop. The store had been called Lapp's Bike Shop for more years than she could remember. Now it would have a new name, a new beginning.

Every bike she'd ever owned had been purchased, fixed, painted or exchanged there.

She could see Isaac silhouetted in the doorway, his stiff black hat in hand, the warm tropic breezes blowing his dark hair into his eyes.

In a few days everyone in Pinecraft was supposed to believe this dark-haired, brooding man wanted to be her husband. She was growing more and more uncomfortable with the deception in which she'd tangled Isaac. But if she tried to fight her *mamm* alone, she'd lose and be forced to marry Samuel. She sighed and leaned closer to the store window, watching the sign go up into the air.

"I thought we came to look for tablecloths. Are we going to shop, or are you going to stand there all day gawking out the window?" Ruth, tall, thin and very pregnant, called from the housewares aisle a few feet away. They'd been friends all their lives and now were next-door neighbors every November through March since Ruth had married and was living in Ohio with her husband most of the year. "I've only got a couple of hours to shop. You know when Saul starts banging on the table, dinner better be ready. You coming?"

With a smile Molly held up one finger and signaled for her friend to wait. She held her breath as the crane turned the sign around. In bold black letters, on a plain white background she read the words, THE BIKE PIT. The name described the hole-in-the-wall shop to perfection. She smiled as she scurried away, pleased for Isaac and his new adventure.

"Why are you smiling? Some *Englischer* wave at you?" Ruth picked up a lovely hand-painted cup and saucer with dainty pink roses. She set the pricy old dust catcher back on the shelf.

Molly forced the smile off her face. "No, nothing like that. Just a new sign going up across the street." Molly glanced over her shoulder and peeked at the sign again.

Ruth picked up the cup and saucer again, seemed to do a considerable amount of thinking before putting it in the shopping basket hanging from her wrist. She tucked a pair of secondhand socks around the fragile memento for safekeeping. "You think I'll break this?"

"*Ya.* Probably the first time you wash it," Molly answered truthfully.

"I don't care. I'm getting it anyway, but don't tell your *mamm*. She'll spread it around that I've gone fancy."

"Well, you have, haven't you?" Molly laughed as Ruth stuck out her tongue at her and headed toward more household items, muttering, "Yeah, but that doesn't mean everyone and their sister has to know."

Molly called after her, "I think I'll pen an article to the Pinecraft Weekly. I can see the headlines now. 'Ruth Lapp Drinks Coffee Out of Bone China and Gets in Trouble for It.'"

Ruth gave Molly a scathing look, her bottom lip half curled in a smile. "You do, and I'll write one about that mysterious bump on your new tenant's head."

Molly hurried to catch up with her friend. "I told you that was purely accidental."

"That's not what Isaac Graber said while we were cleaning his shop."

"He didn't say anything about it, and you know it," Molly fired back. She pulled out a white tablecloth, saw a red wine stain and refolded the cloth, stain side up.

Feeling eyes on her, Molly glanced up and saw Isaac enter the store. He gave her a quick nod and then shifted his gaze away as he continued to walk toward the front of the store. He leaned heavily on a cane, heading for the secondhand bike rack they'd just passed. He had a hitch in his step, but otherwise appeared as fit as he had that morning. "Oh, no. Not him," Molly said.

Ruth paused, rummaging through the tablecloths long enough to admonish, "That's not nice, Margaret Anne Ziegler."

She wouldn't have to pretend with Ruth. She'd tell her friend about her and Isaac's pretend courtship when the time was right. But not today. "You don't have to live in the same house with him or share a meal when he's grumpy." Molly tossed a used but spotless tablecloth on their stack of possibilities.

"I think we ought to be nice and see if he needs

help. It can't be easy shopping with one hand," Ruth murmured.

Too embarrassed to speak to him now that she'd realized he probably regretted his promise to her, Molly whispered, "You help him then. I'm staying right here."

"That's what's wrong with the world. No one's willing to help their neighbor anymore." Ruth lumbered off, her hands resting on the top of her bullet-shaped belly.

"Oh, all right. Wait up. But don't blame me if he doesn't want our help. He's funny like that."

Ruth kept walking but glanced back. "You mean he's independent?"

Molly screwed up her face and said, "Something like that."

Isaac perused the array of secondhand bikes lined up in a neat row, mentally calculating how many he could buy and still have enough money left over for meals and bike parts. He'd already bought several golf carts to use as rentals. Like most Amish, he didn't believe in credit cards or payment plans. It was cash-and-carry or do without. His savings were almost gone, but the shelves were better stocked. Several more rental bikes would keep the shop going, especially if the bike repairs kept trickling in.

The sound of laughter grabbed his attention. Molly came back into view. His stomach flip-flopped as he remembered their conversation that morning. Would anyone believe someone like Molly would choose a man like him for a husband?

He turned and glanced Molly's way. She was laughing with a woman he'd met, but he couldn't put a name to. "Let me guess," he said, hobbling up. "You've come to kick my cane out from under me."

Molly's face flushed red, as if he'd gone too far with his latest comment. "I don't know why you go about saying I hurt you on purpose."

"I was only joking, Molly. If you weren't so easily riled, I probably wouldn't have so much fun making you angry."

"Let me poke a hole in your theory, Isaac Graber. I couldn't care less what you say or do," she snapped back, their earlier camaraderie forgotten.

Ruth edged her way between the two of them. "We thought we'd come help you shop since you're one-handed today."

"That's very kind of you… I'm sorry. I'm lousy at remembering names. Refresh my memory?"

"I'm Ruth. Ruth Lapp, Saul's wife." The pregnant woman blushed a pretty pink. "Molly was just saying what a wonderful tenant you are."

Isaac snickered. "I imagine she was." He turned Molly's way, lost his balance and grabbed for a bike handle to steady himself.

His hip bumped the bike, and, like a row of dominoes, they began to fall, one by one, with horrific clangs of metal against metal.

Seconds later Isaac found himself on the cool concrete floor, in the middle of the jumble, his injured leg spared the brunt of the fall, but his masculine pride seriously damaged.

"I was nowhere near you. You can't blame this on me, Isaac," Molly said, her lips quivering, her laughter barely held in check. "Not this time…" Her voice trailed off as the store manager came and stood next to them, his arms folded across his broad chest.

Isaac's gaze veered away from Molly to the man frowning at him. "I'll take all six. Do you deliver?"

Molly pushed a red bike across the street, dodging several speeding cars, then trotting to the shop door Ruth held open for her. "You got me in more trouble."

"Did not," Ruth jeered. "You didn't have to offer to help Isaac, but you're kindhearted and a little in love with the man. It was you who said we'd help. Not me." She patted her baby bump. "The baby's really active today. I think he's going to like bikes."

"Did you see his face?

"Whose?" Ruth asked, looking confused.

"Isaac's. He looked grief-stricken, like the last thing he wanted to do was buy a pile of dented bikes."

"I thought you said he's always grumpy." Ruth lined up the bike Molly handed off to her.

"He is…well, not exactly grumpy. He's funny sometimes, and helpful…but he has this way about him. Sort of like he's miserable or unhappy."

"You want to fix him, that's your problem. We women love to fix our men." Ruth plopped down on an old, cracked leather couch positioned against the half wall of the office and sighed as if she'd been running a marathon.

Molly joined Ruth on the couch and picked at a piece of torn leather as she spoke. "That's not true. I don't want to fix him. I think he wants to fix me." Her words were out of her mouth before she could stop them.

Interested, Ruth asked, "Fix *you*? What do you

mean?" She rubbed a spot on her stomach, her gaze focused on Molly's face.

Molly took off her built-up shoe and flexed her toes, avoiding Ruth's scrutiny. "*Ya*, well. I asked a favor of him and he agreed to help because he knows I'm a fool, that's all."

"Help? In what way?"

"With a courting ruse." Molly worried the ribbon of her *kapp*. She wished she'd kept her mouth shut. She intended to tell Ruth, but not now, not until all the plans had been talked about between her and Isaac.

Ruth leaned in close. "What have you done, Molly?"

Isaac reappeared through the shop's door before Molly could explain herself. He used one hand to manipulate a small bike inside. He wore a smile, but was silent, almost broody.

Ruth lifted her head and sniffed. "Is that pizza I smell?" She sat forward and scooted to the edge of the couch. "How about we all go get something to eat? I can take the leftovers home to Saul." She grabbed her purse and headed for the door.

"You ladies go. Enjoy. I've got work to do. *Danke* for helping out." Isaac walked toward the desk, his limp more pronounced. Molly watched as he carefully sat, then swung around the computer chair, his face a chalky white.

The smile on his face looked forced to Molly. As she shut the shop door, she noticed his hand go to his injured leg and rub. He was in pain. *Poor man.*

Disappointment and relief battled within her as she trailed behind Ruth toward the pizza shop. She wanted Isaac to come with them, but was glad he didn't. The agreement between them had left her tense, unsettled.

She should have kept her mouth shut and not told Ruth about her and Isaac's deception. What if Ruth couldn't be trusted? She could tell someone, and the truth could get back to *Mamm*.

Amish women loved to gossip. It was something to help pass the hours as they quilted, a tasty tidbit they could share over their fences. They were all the same. Ruth was no exception. Still, she and Isaac would only be pretending for a few weeks and then would part as friends. No one would be hurt by their little deception.

The smell of hot pizza floated into his bike shop, causing Isaac's stomach to growl in loud protest. He had to count his pennies after the bicycle debacle at the thrift store. He glanced over at the six dented bikes lined up at the back of the store. At half price, the cost of the bikes had still taken a huge bite out of his food money. He'd have to tighten his belt. Miss a few dinners until he sold something.

The bell rang out. Isaac glanced toward the door. Molly came charging in, her cheeks a rosy pink. She handed over a small, square pizza box and grinned awkwardly. "Ruth and I couldn't eat the whole pie. I thought you might enjoy the last three slices while you work."

Isaac took the box from her hand. "*Danke*, but I thought Ruth was taking home the leftovers to her husband."

Molly's smile disappeared and a grooved frown replaced it.

"*Ya*, she was." She fingered her prayer *kapp* ribbons. Her voice rose an octave, just enough to let him know she was uncomfortable. "She changed her mind...well, not exactly changed her mind. I might have mentioned that you were probably hungry."

He placed the pizza box on his desk and then turned back toward her. "You didn't have to take care of me, Molly. I have some peanut butter crackers in my desk drawer reserved for busy days like this."

"Oh. I didn't know." She glanced toward the shop door, edging away, inch by inch. A red flush creeped up her neck. "I'll see you later then. Tonight. At dinner. *Mamm*'s making fried chicken." She almost smiled. "We have the singing at seven if you're still willing to come."

"*Ya*, I want to come." He did want to go with her and wished he didn't. They were just starting their courting charade, and already he regretted it. He shouldn't be taking the chance of falling in love with Molly. When she found out the truth about him, she'd back away, leave him brokenhearted.

She fumbled for the doorknob behind her. "*Gut*. I'm glad. Well…enjoy your pizza."

"Sure," he said, leaning against the low wall to take the weight off his aching leg.

The bell over the door rang wildly as Molly rushed out and down the sidewalk, leaving Isaac alone with his thoughts.

Isaac knew very little about women, but he recognized infatuation when he saw it. Molly had waited a long time to find love, but he was the wrong man for her. Somehow he had to make sure she saw that without crushing her young heart.

Chapter Six

"Don't break that," Ulla urged, her brow arched in annoyance.

Molly glanced at her *mamm*'s expression of disapproval, slowed her pace and then placed her *grossmammi*'s beloved chicken platter gently on the linen-covered dining room table.

She pushed a golden brown, perfectly fried chicken leg away from the plate's edge and then turned to head back to the kitchen.

"It makes me to wonder what all the rush is about," her *mamm* said in a low tone, straightening first Isaac's dinner plate and then stabbing a small knife into the dish of homemade butter.

Molly watched as Isaac meandered through the dining room door and joined them, his dark hair still damp from a shower and curling at the ends.

"This looks *gut*," he said, and pulled out the chair he'd been assigned to by Ulla's gesture. Molly smiled blandly at him. Ulla ignored him completely.

"*Danke*, Isaac. *Mamm* knows her way around a frying pan," Molly said, cutting a glance at her mother who was busy placing knives and forks next to three perfectly spaced plates.

Molly frowned, and fluttered her eyelashes as a warning to Isaac. Her mother didn't acknowledge Isaac coming into the room or Molly's compliment in any way. The older woman was still stewing in some kind of silent simmer, having declared she'd had a long day when she'd begun to cook an hour earlier. Ulla remained silent as Molly assisted in any way she could.

Molly breathed in deeply. She'd had a long day, too, and the last thing she needed was to be treated like some careless schoolgirl by her sullen mother.

Isaac's gaze flicked from Molly to Ulla, as if gauging the temperature between the two women.

Molly left Isaac to fend for himself. He was a grown man. Let him deal with her *mamm*'s bad mood for a few moments. She had other things to do. There was creamed corn to place on the table before they could eat, and it was already close to six.

In her haste she almost dropped the bowl of corn, and moments later she dripped a trail of water as she filled three glasses at the table. The singing frolic began promptly at seven. The Mennonite sports field would fill up quickly. It always did. She and Isaac would have to hurry if they wanted to find a good spot before the singing began.

"You have somewhere to be, *dochder*? A child to birth? A shift at the café?" Ulla lowered herself into her chair, scooted forward and then clasped her hands in her ample lap.

Molly had hoped they could get through the meal before telling her *mamm* she and Isaac were going out together. There'd be words, and in the black mood her mother was in, they'd probably be harsh and embarrassing. It was inevitable. "The frolic is at seven." She hadn't lied. She just hadn't said she and Isaac would be going together and begin their courting ruse.

They prayed in silence and then Ulla's prayer *kapp* fluttered as she turned her head and took in Isaac's freshly pressed dress shirt and clean trousers. "Will you be going to this frolic, Herr Graber?"

Isaac pulled his hand back from the table. "*Ya*, I thought I would."

"I see," Ulla said, fingering the edge of her plate. Her gaze shifted to Molly, to the clean dress she'd changed into just before they sat down to eat. Her mouth formed a hard edge.

"Will you two be going together?"

Molly bristled, realizing after tonight there would be plenty of questions to answer, but they didn't have to be answered now. Her *mamm* would be furious when she thought Molly had shoved Samuel aside for Isaac, a man who had no money.

Isaac nodded as he shoveled the last of his peas into his mouth and chewed vigorously. "I thought you'd think it best." He glanced up, his expression innocent. "We can't have you worrying that I might fall again."

Ulla smiled. "*Ya*, sure. That's fine. And will Samuel be coming, Molly?"

"*Ya*, he usually shows up if there's food at the frolic."

"*Gut,*" Ulla said with a nod, letting her daughter's comment about Samuel's robust appetite slide past. She stopped to take a sip of water, then turned back to Molly. "Don't worry about the dishes tonight, *dochder*. I'll do them. You two best hurry now. You'll want a good spot up front."

Molly didn't need to be told twice. *"Danke, Mamm."* She slipped from her chair and darted toward the kitchen, her relief visible on her smiling face. "Hurry, Isaac. I'll grab the cookies. You grab the quilt."

"Is the frolic being held at your church?" Isaac asked ten minutes later as Molly sped through the sun-filled streets, the cart puttering along at a good clip.

"Nee. Not this time." She turned down a short street and joined a group of Amish bike riders. She slowed, waving to several women her own age as they passed. "The Mennonite church is sponsoring the community frolic. Most of the singings are held during the busy part of the winter. It's not so hot, and there's a lot more *youngies* looking for something to do."

"You're sure about starting the ruse tonight?" Isaac asked.

"You heard *Mamm.* 'Is Samuel going to be there?' She's still pushing him in my face. If it's to stop, I have to take a stand."

"I just thought…"

Molly parked the golf cart next to the church's chain-link fence and then turned to Isaac. "Are you backing out, because if you are, I understand." She checked the position of her *kapp* and then picked up the cookies and slid out of the cart. "I'm not comfortable about lying, either, even for a little while. I just don't know what else to do."

Daylight didn't seem to be in any hurry to fade away. Molly looked Isaac's way but couldn't read his undecipherable expression. She did hear the tone in his voice as he said, "I'm your friend, Molly. I'll do what I can to help you out. You know that."

She extended her hand his way.

Isaac looked her in the eyes, seemed to momentarily hesitate, but then grabbed her hand and pulled her toward the growing crowd arriving around them. "Let's get this mess with Samuel Bawell settled, once and for all."

She liked the feel of his rough palm pressed against hers, the way his warm fingers intertwined around hers. A thrill shot through her, and she was surprised by the power of it. She glanced up at Isaac as they walked, tethered to him in a way that made her heart beat fast and wild. But all this wasn't real. He wasn't walking out with her, wasn't her true love. He was just a man who felt he owed her a favor and was paying her back in a kind way. Her joy died a silent death. Her smile faded. Once Samuel went back home, Isaac would step away.

Isn't that what she wanted? Her independence? Molly wasn't quite sure.

Isaac hobbled to a distant bench at the back of the baseball field and sat alone, his cane leaning against his leg. The volleyball game was going well, the *youngies'* enthusiasm growing as Molly launched the ball across the net again and again, winning points for her Amish teammates.

Memories came back to haunt him. Thomas had been playing the same game the day he died. They'd all yelled themselves hoarse encouraging their team. Thomas had twisted his ankle playing this game. It was the reason Isaac had been driving the old truck on the country road back to his Mennonite friend's farm.

A spasm of pain clutched his thigh, reminding him he hadn't died in the crash. So why did he feel so dead inside?

Two laughing Mennonite girls ran past and waved. Dressed less formally than Molly's pale blue dress and starched white *kapp*, they wore simple but bright colored dresses, with no *kapps*, their hair pulled back into long ponytails that streamed behind them. They ran barefoot across the soft grass.

He waved back at them, but didn't smile. He didn't feel like smiling. He felt like sobbing out his heart for Thomas right there on the bench.

Isaac looked up to see Molly's wild ball shoot over the net and win the game for her Amish team. The game ended suddenly, with a choir of shouts. She came running toward him, glowing with excitement.

"Did you see my last serve? I thought I'd completely missed the ball, but then it caught the edge of my fist and went soaring past them all." She plopped down next to him and grabbed him around the neck, her arms hugging him tight to his side. She smelled of fresh air and lilacs. He gently pulled her arms from his neck and shifted away an inch or two. "I'm proud of you. I really am."

Molly's laughter stopped. She scooted away, putting more distance between them. Isaac had a smile on his face, but it didn't reach his eyes. Her closeness had made him uncomfortable. "I'm sorry I got caught up in the moment. Forgive me for overstepping my boundaries."

"Don't be silly. We're supposed to be pretending to be courting. No harm done." A breeze picked up. He pulled his straw hat down, his green eyes avoiding hers. Then why did he look so uncomfortable? "It's getting dark. The singing should begin in a moment. You coming?"

"*Ya*, sure. I don't want to miss all the fun." This time he held out his hand to her.

She placed her hand in his and did her best to ignore the electricity that ran through her fingers as they walked across the field, him limping and her slowing her pace to match his steps.

"Most people sit in the bleachers, but we can use the quilt and sit on the ground if you'd prefer."

"*Nee*, the bleachers are fine," Isaac said, taking the lead, their hands still clasped, weaving them in and out of people until he found a spot big enough for the two of them on the first row.

Wedged in on both sides, Molly had never sat so close to Isaac before, but he didn't seem concerned about their proximity now. He grinned down at her and then gave all his attention to the singers who clustered together and began an old worship song Molly remembered from her younger years. The song was fast and lively, causing her to tap her foot as she'd done as a child.

Movement from the corner of her eye caught her attention. Samuel walked past, his eyes flicking over Isaac and then her. Unsmiling, he tipped his dark hat her way and then proceeded on.

"Was that Samuel?" Isaac inquired.

"*Ya*," she responded and witnessed the instant change in Isaac's expression, felt the tension in his hand she still held. It took every ounce of willpower she possessed to remain still and calm. The expression Samuel threw her way spoke volumes. Samuel would tell her *mamm* that she and Isaac were setting close, holding hands.

There was the lie to tell her *mamm* about her and Isaac's courtship and then the questions she'd be asked. Her *mamm* would be disappointed in her, make a fuss. How would her mother treat Isaac once she had heard? Would she ask him to leave their home?

The tempo of the music became soft, the words to the old Amish song tugging at her heart. The words said *Gott* would sustain them, keep them strong in the Lord. Had she angered *Gott* with her plan? Would her lie distance her from Him, from His salvation?

She watched as Isaac rubbed at his leg, his brow creasing into deep furrows. "Is your leg troubling you?"

He looked down, pale, his mouth a fixed line. "Some."

"We can go now if you want."

"*Nee*, you said you wanted to hear the singing. I'll be fine."

Molly rose and tugged at his arm. "Come on. The singing will go on until ten. Let's go home."

He stood and had to brace himself against his cane for the first time that day.

They moved toward the parking lot, their steps slow, Isaac holding on to his cane for support.

"I'm sorry, Isaac. I didn't think of the long walk to the bleachers. I should have suggested we go somewhere less strenuous because of your leg," Molly said as they reached the golf cart.

He slid into the passenger seat. "I'm fine. The doctor said I should be venturing out more now, putting more weight on my leg."

Molly started the engine and turned on the cart's lights. "I think we should talk about this courtship, Isaac. I hadn't thought about how my *mamm* might act toward you once we began the ruse." She reached out and touched his arm. "It could get ugly. She might even ask you to leave the house."

"You let me worry about your *mamm*. Your job is to look happy and smile a lot."

She drove away from the church, the little golf cart sputtering in protest as she gunned it. "I had a good time tonight," she said, glancing at him. She saw him grasp the edge of the cart and hold on. Molly knew she did many things well, but driving wasn't one of them.

"So did I. We'll have to do something else later this week if you're free. I heard there's a pie-eating contest coming up soon, and a public auction I'd like to go to if you're interested."

Molly sped down the well-lit street, her thoughts a jumbled mess. The words to the old hymn came back to haunt her. *Gott will take care of you.* She longed to have this charade over, but knew she'd miss Isaac more than she wanted to admit when he walked away.

Chapter Seven

Dressed in dark trousers and a fresh white shirt and matching vest, his cane polished to a honey glow, Isaac gave the Old Order Amish church a glance and favored his healing but still throbbing leg as he slowly rode past the brick building on his bicycle. A row of traditionally dressed Amish men stood at the side doors of the building, their line ending on the grassy lawn.

He leaned toward the more modern Anabaptist church philosophy, not that he ignored Ordnung rules or bylaws of the church. One of the many reasons he'd decided to come to Pinecraft was to get away from his disappointed, angry, Old Order Amish father. The man ran his home with harsh rules that felt more man-made than *Gott*-given since Thomas's death.

Isaac rode on. When he'd arrived in Pinecraft, he'd been surprised to hear the community had built churches, their houses too small to accommodate local church services during peak seasons.

With the turn of his bike handles, he pulled into the driveway of the smaller New Order Amish church a few streets over and headed to the back parking lot.

A line of six young, unmarried men stood behind a stretch of older men with long beards blowing in the wind. Some nodded in his direction as he parked his bike and hobbled up. Several were stone-faced as his father had always been on Sundays before church, but most smiled a greeting.

Isaac glanced around, saw a few familiar faces, but Molly was nowhere in sight. They hadn't agreed to meet at church when they'd gone their separate ways the night before. She'd gone to her room without a glance back, and he'd avoided the kitchen when he'd left early that morning in hopes of avoiding Ulla.

Several of the elders filed into the church through the building's side door. Isaac recognized Mose, and his father, Bishop Otto Fischer.

A line of married men went into the church. He entered with the single men. He was pleasantly surprised to see the church had been well cared for and freshly painted.

He took his seat and positioned his leg for comfort. He knew the three-hour service was going to be taxing, but he'd made a promise to *Gott* about being an active member of this new church, and he was going to keep that promise.

Opening prayers were said. Mose Fischer sang a hymn, his voice a rich baritone. He led the congregation in several songs, some Isaac knew from his home church services and some new to him. Peace calmed his troubled soul. He sang with all his heart, his love for *Gott* deepening as he took in the words of salvation. *Gott*'s promise of hope and forgiveness reached him, the needed words preached by a zealous pastor whose youthful voice still broke at times.

Gott spoke to Isaac's heart, revealed His promise of forgiveness for all who would ask. The pain of his bottled-up grief and guilt eased some. Perhaps his Father's love for him had remained strong, even though Thomas was dead.

A child began to cry, drawing Isaac's attention to the women's side of the church. Molly sat beside a red-haired woman who held a small *bobbel* in her arms.

He caught Molly's eye and nodded. She nodded back, a quick smile playing on her lips, but then she turned back toward the singer standing at the front of the church.

Three hours later his leg hurt like stinging ants and his stomach rumbled, reminding him he'd missed breakfast. He needed to move around, get the blood flowing back in his leg. He also needed to eat. Living off two meals a day was hard on a man, especially one with his big appetite.

When he had entered the church, he had noticed signs for the church-wide meal Molly had mentioned the night before. The food would be served on the grounds at Pinecraft Park directly after the service. The thought of good homemade Amish food had his mouth watering as he headed out the door into the bright Florida sunshine. Maybe he'd get a chance to talk to Molly if he hurried.

Two containers of hot food fit in Molly's bike basket, with just enough room for condiments and dessert. She pedaled as fast as she could, but a combination of cars and bikes whizzed past, forcing her onto the graveled verge for the last mile. Hopping off the bike and pushing it through the grass, she looked around for her mother and found Samuel Bawell waiting for her at the end of a row of long plastic tables. Women with hungry husbands bustled around, quickly covering the tables with white tablecloths.

Samuel frowned into the sun as she approached, his rich brown eyes looking her up and down. He wore a blue shirt of fine cotton fabric, his dark suspenders holding up well pressed and creased dark trousers.

A gust of wind blew off his straw hat, exposing his mussed mahogany-colored hair cut bowl-shaped around his ears.

"Here, let me help you," he offered, and began to unload her basket, wanting to make points with her no doubt and squelch any possible rumors of her and Isaac's budding courtship.

She avoided giving him a side hug of thanks, as was the custom for non-courting couples that were looking for mates—not that she would want Samuel as a future husband, or any other man for that matter. Samuel was her mother's idea of the perfect Amish man. Not hers. His controlling nature and self-importance irritated Molly beyond words.

Every time she saw him, he pushed for a commitment from her. Just because she was twenty-one years old and a spinster didn't mean she had to throw herself at the first man who asked her to marry him.

Samuel grabbed her hands, held her gaze. His dimpled smile should have set her heart to racing, but it didn't.

She sighed, hearing her mother's rasping voice in her head. *You need to make a good marriage so I can end my days in comfort, Molly.*

Everyone knew the Bawell family had big money—a

lot more than most Amish families who came to Pine-craft for the winter. Their large farm prospered, the rich Ohio soil yielding big crops that added to their wealth yearly.

Samuel made sure everyone heard about their success each winter. He was proud of the farm and how successful the family had become after leaving the dry dirt of Lancaster County. Molly wasn't impressed and prayed *Gott* would speak to him about sharing more with his community and talking less about his prosperity.

His thumb rubbed her hand as he spoke. "I missed you."

"You just saw me last night at the singing." Molly pulled her hands away. She took a plastic container of whoopie pies from her basket and placed them on the table. Samuel groaned, a hopeful smile playing on his lips as he recognized the container of mouth-watering desserts. "Did you make red velvet this time?"

With a nod Molly continued to unpack. The first wave of men lined up at the head table. She had to hurry.

Busy watching Molly, Samuel almost spilled a covered plate of fried chicken. He performed an impressive balancing act, recovering cleverly. He bowed at the waist, impressed with himself. "Have I told you how sweet you look today?"

"*Nee.* I've told you repeatedly that compliments embarrass me. I'm not a vain person, Samuel. I don't need to be told when my hair shines or my eyes sparkle." Knowing she was being harsh, she put her head down as she took the pickle relish out of her bike basket and then grabbed for a large pickle jar full of hot celery soup that needed to be poured into her mother's old tureen.

"*Ya*, sure. I'll try to remember. No more compliments." Samuel rushed around the table and poured the soup for her, smiling, trying to be helpful.

Molly shrugged, her stomach roiling. She had to explain to him about her and Isaac and finalize the lie about their courting. Her words would confirm Samuel's suspicions and make him furious, but they would hold back his advances and send him home to Ohio single.

Maybe one day she'd be ready for marriage, but never to Samuel.

"I saw you with that cripple last night," Samuel said, handing her a container of chocolate-chip cookies for the children.

"That's cruel, even from you, Samuel." She turned her back on him.

Several servers showed up, stopping Molly and Samuel's conversation, but she knew he'd have more to say. He always did.

"I'll find us a spot under our tree." Samuel walked past her and began filling his plate with most of the crispy fried chicken she'd brought and a huge mound of hot potato salad. He headed for the shaded area where the *youngies* gathered during outdoor meals. Molly watched him walk away, his stride long and confident. He was handsome, but his good looks hid a dark side she wanted to avoid at all costs.

Molly welcomed her mother and several friends as they approached the tables.

"Where's Samuel?" Ulla asked, setting down a huge platter of potato pancakes covered in waxed paper. The older woman wiped sweat from her face with the hem of her apron.

"Somewhere with the singles, I guess." Molly moved

the pancakes over, removed the covering and added a fork for serving.

"You should go join him, take him a plate of food."

"*Ach*, he's got plenty to eat. He's a real *wutz*."

"So the man likes his food. That doesn't make him a pig. Did you talk to him, serve him yourself?"

"*Ya*. We talked for a few moments." A strong gust of wind ruffled her hair, pulling strands from her bun and tickling her neck. "He seemed in a hurry to eat and rushed off."

"Join him. Let him know you're interested in being beside him. You'll never catch a husband like this, Molly." Her mother leaned in close. "Remember what I told you. We're getting fewer and fewer renters each year. Soon we'll be alone in that big house, just you and me…with little money coming in and a burden on our community. A good marriage would end all that." Ulla's eyes narrowed as she hissed, "Go on. Show him what a catch you are."

This seemed the perfect time to tell her mother she meant it when she said she had no interest in Samuel, but people mingled around them, gathering food, making small talk.

Molly filled a plate for herself and walked away, leaving her mother to believe she was being an obedient daughter. But she had no intention of finding Samuel. A solitary meal near the river appealed to her more. She'd worked hard all week at the café and delivered two babies, both late at night, the births cutting deep into her sleep. Tired in body and spirit, she longed for a place to contemplate all the wonderful nature around her and leave her stress behind.

* * *

Isaac's boots dug into the soft sandy dirt as he gathered a plate of food and made his way across the small park, leaving the swarm of chattering people behind. He was in no mood for idle chitchat. The sermon had stirred his heart, put a grain of hope in his heart for the future. He had a lot to think about. It didn't matter where he ate, as long as it was quiet and peaceful. Over the course of the past few months, he'd grown used to eating alone.

Clusters of young orange trees grew all around the park. An old picnic table called to him, and he headed toward it.

Setting his plate on the warped wood, he took a seat, glad to be off his aching leg. True to the doctor's words, his bones were mending, his leg hurting less and less, but the way he was forced to walk hadn't changed. He'd live with the noticeable limp in his stride forever. He knew he deserved nothing more.

He prayed silently over his food, grateful for the chance to eat and not worry how he'd pay for his next meal. His savings spent, *Gott*'s mercy and love surrounded him as he whispered his appreciation for this bounty provided today and the fresh, growing peace in his heart.

Isaac lifted his head and began to eat, shoveling in food as fast as he could chew. For days his lunches had consisted of nothing more than crackers and peanut butter. Ulla had warned him she'd start charging extra for evening meals. This free Amish food tasted like manna from heaven.

"You miss breakfast?" Molly meandered up the slight grassy incline, her plate in hand. A cool breeze tilted her white *kapp*, leaving it at comical angle.

"*Ya*, I did. *Willkumm*. Share my table." Isaac motioned for her to join him. He brushed leaves off the table and watched her hesitate only a moment before sitting on the other side of the wooden bench.

Her presence was a breath of fresh air, a joy to his senses. He longed to share his newfound appreciation and love for *Gott*, but sharing meant explaining why he'd run away from Missouri, why his life was broken into pieces. Perhaps he'd tell her about Thomas's death one day, but he wasn't prepared to share the raw pain today. Not even for Molly.

"Danke," Molly murmured, and began to nibble at her food.

"I'm surprised you're not with your friends." Isaac stuffed a round whoopie pie into his mouth. He struggled to politely chew the enormous mouthful. The red velvet cake was as light as a feather and moist, better than any he'd ever eaten. He grinned at her and stuffed in another small pie. "I'm going to marry whoever made these," he teased, and reached for the last pie on his plate.

"You'll be marrying me for real then," Molly said, giggling like a young girl.

He set down the last of the round cake. "I had no idea…" Isaac coughed.

For the moment Molly seemed to be enjoying his discomfort. Her smile was wide and easygoing. "Oh, now he tries to *rutsch* his way out of a fine proposal," she said to the wind, her smile growing as his embarrassment increased.

"Nee, I didn't mean to suggest…"

Molly forked a tiny red potato and held it near her mouth. "What? Suggest we really court, get wed this Christmas season?"

"I was just saying how delicious this whoopie pie tasted. My remark was meant only as a joke. Something to laugh at." He felt his face grow warm. He prayed he wasn't blushing like a foolish *youngie*.

"It wonders me. Are you saying you *don't* want to marry me for real, Isaac Graber? That I'm not good enough for you?" Molly's expression had been playful and relaxed, but now she looked serious, her brow furrowed, her mouth a firm, angry line.

At first he'd enjoyed the idea of pretending to be Molly's future husband, but now her teasing conversation awakened new thoughts in his mind. What if she had taken his comments seriously? He hadn't meant to make her believe he was truly interested in her, in a real courtship.

They had no future together.

Pain pierced his knee. He'd never forgive himself for what he'd done to Thomas, even if *Gott* forgave him. His newfound joy evaporated. He cleared his throat and spoke without humor. "What I meant to say was, you're a wonderful cook."

Cleanup was always the worst part of church picnics, especially if the person cleaning up was in a bad mood of her own making.

Molly pulled a big plastic trash can over to the table and began disposing of leftover food, banging plastic containers against the soft side of the plastic-lined trash container. Deep in thought, she ignored the shadow falling across her face and kept working.

"I thought we were going to eat together," Samuel said, his brow arched in an angry scowl. "I looked everywhere for you. Where'd you disappear to?"

Molly stilled, the pot she'd been scraping forgotten. Samuel stood in front of her, his hands planted on his hips, a frown on his sunburned face. Behind him the sinking sun created spikes of pale reds and yellows behind wispy gray clouds.

This is not the time to push me, Samuel Bawell.

Her attention wandered back to the pot in her hand. "I never told you I was joining you." A stubborn glop of burned cheese refused to budge. Her temper flared. She exchanged her spoon for a dull knife and scraped as if her life depended on removing the gluey food.

"You didn't answer my question. Where did you go? To find that cripple, Isaac Graber?"

"That's my business, Samuel. Not yours." Her eyes cut in his direction, narrowed, angry. Words were about to be unleashed, and he wouldn't like them.

"This is no way for a courting woman to act, Molly. I know you're inexperienced, but…" He took a step around the table and reached for her hand.

Molly inhaled a deep, cleansing breath and forced it out again. It was time he understood where they stood. "We are *not* courting. I keep telling you over and over again, but you don't like what you hear so you refuse to listen. We are just friends. We have gone to a few volleyball games and attended church singings. Nothing more. I am *not* your girl."

"But your *mamm* said you were interested, that we could be wed in the church by the end of this year."

A tide of fury washed over her. "I'm sorry. My *mamm* was wrong to tell you I was ready for marriage. I'm not interested in you that way, Samuel. You're not my type."

"But Isaac Graber is?"

"My mother doesn't own me, nor can she decide

who I marry. This talk of courtship and marriage has to end now."

Somewhere close by, a seagull shrieked a warning and Molly glanced up, watching Samuel.

He flushed red. His gaze dropped. "You'll be sorry you turned me down someday. You'll see. But I won't bother you again, Molly." No dimples appeared on his cheeks as he turned on his heel and walked away, his broad shoulders squared, his gait fast.

Her thoughts scrambled. The idea of hurting anyone wounded her soul, but it had to be done. She had to have a serious conversation with her *mamm*. These embarrassing situations had to stop. Why wouldn't she let her live her own life, make her own choices? Everyone in Pinecraft seemed to know all her business, think it was their job to give her advice, and she was tired of it. She would have to go through with the farce she'd planned with Isaac if she was to find peace. She had no other choice.

She scrubbed with renewed vigor until the pot's bottom was spotless. Something drew her eye, and she watched as Isaac hobbled across the grass toward the walkway, his dark hat pulled low on his head. He spoke to no one as people passed.

She grabbed a pan and began to fight the dried-on food, thinking back to Isaac's expression when he'd told her what a wonderful cook she was, but in the same breath proclaimed his lack of real interest in her.

A refreshing wind blew, ruffling the loose hairs on her sweaty neck and cooling her. She silently prayed as she finished emptying the last of the dishes and pans, asking forgiveness from *Gott* for her show of temper.

People passed, spoke and strolled away. Men assigned to help the ladies fold away tables and carry dishes finally showed up full of conversation about the awesome domino gamed they'd played.

"*Ya*, I would have won if I hadn't used that double ten when I did." Chicken John Schwarts, one of Pinecraft's favorite pranksters, cackled like one of the hens he raised on his farm just outside Sarasota. The thin, frail man had gained her mother's interest the past few weeks, and they had begun to court. But with their growing money problems, and Molly's refusal to marry, she knew her mother was probably leading the wealthy man on in hopes of a profitable marriage. If he didn't propose soon, her *mamm* would drop him, leave him with a broken heart and look for another man with money. Not that their financial problems were so dire. If her *mamm* would stop spending foolishly, they could make ends meet, pay all the bills beginning to pile up.

Chicken John lifted a box filled with plastic food containers that belonged to the church and the bottom fell out. Dirty containers scattered in the ankle-high grass. Everyone laughed, enjoying the scene of the little man on his knees, scurrying around picking up lids and containers. But Molly remained somber, her heart heavy. She carried two lightweight boxes to the golf carts lined up as transport back to the church. There'd be dishes to wash and put away. She looked forward to the hard work. Her mind would be too busy to think about what she'd said to Samuel and what he'd said back to her.

Would she regret turning him down? She glanced at her built-up shoe. Isaac was temporarily disabled, and it was evident he didn't want her as a *frau*. He needed someone strong to help build his bike shop into the success he dreamed of. There were plenty of young girls looking for someone to court and wed. Someone would catch his eye one day soon.

She threw her leg over her bike and began to pedal. So what if she'd have to live her life single and alone? It was better than marrying without love. The image of Isaac walking alone across the park came back to haunt her. Did he feel lonely, too?

Chapter Eight

Isaac woke from a restless night, his breathing labored and his hair damp with sweat. The recurring nightmare that disturbed his sleep still tormented him.

He had been driving. Headlights sped toward him. He fought to swerve, his fingers gripped the truck's steering wheel until his knuckles turned white. But the crash still came. The sound of metal tearing metal cut through his brain. Pain was everywhere. Thomas lay on the ground. Isaac stifled a shout and pulled himself out of the black fog.

With the back of his hand, he wiped sweat off his brow and threw back the covers, the ache in his leg forcing him to slowly maneuver out of the bed. He limped to the window.

Somewhere in the house Molly sang a familiar worship song, her voice sweet and low.

He had wanted to get out of the house early this morning, before she woke and started her day. He needed time to think about their pretend courtship. He owed her a big favor, but it wasn't like him to break form and lie. He didn't think it was Molly's way, either.

What if they fell in love after spending time together? Stranger things had happened. They could never have a future together. Not after the choices he had made. When she found out about the accident, Thomas's death…she wouldn't want him. He had to face that there may never be a real courting or marriage for him. He didn't deserve the joy of being a husband and father.

He ran his hands though his hair, his frustration growing. He knew so little about *Englischer* laws. Would he go to prison if the *Englischer* police found out he'd been driving Thomas's truck that night?

The Amish had their own laws and ways of handling legal situations. The power of his community, the rules his bishop laid down, was all Isaac knew. When his *daed* directed him to speak up to the bishop and elders, he'd confessed his sin to them. They'd prayed for his forgiveness from *Gott*. Wasn't that how he'd always done things? Hold firm to his Amish ways? So why was he still feeling so guilty? Would he ever feel forgiven, be able to live a normal life?

He had no money, no home. There was only his business, and it might never be a moneymaker. He lived hand-to-mouth and wasn't about to ask any woman to live that way, too.

Especially Molly.

He quickly showered, dressed and sneaked out the kitchen door, his hair still wet, his cane in hand. The pavement was damp from an early-morning rain shower. He wiped down the seat of his golf cart and backed out of the driveway, not looking back.

Molly's hand smoothed out the crumpled quilt and then punched her pillows into fluffy mounds. She'd

slept poorly, her eyes stinging with grit from too little
sleep after spending two hours of her night with a first-
time mother's false alarm. Outside her window Isaac's
new golf cart started up. She turned from her bed, her
attention pulled toward the noise of the cart engine.
She pulled back her bedroom curtain and watched as
he drove down the drive and onto the street, headed
toward town.

"Ach!" She'd wanted to talk to him while her *mamm*
wasn't around. They had to come to a clear understanding before she spoke to her mother.

Glad for a day off from the café, she began to ready
the rooms for guests coming the next day. The kitchen
always took the longest to clean and required the most
work. She started by cleaning the oven and then wiped
down all the wooden cabinets with linseed oil and a
soft cloth.

"You look busy," Ulla said, coming through the back
door a few moments later. She flung a thrift-store bag
in the middle of the kitchen table.

"Was tut Sie bier?" Molly asked, glancing at the
store bag and then her *mamm*. She flashed her a scowl.
The table had been freshly scrubbed a moment before,
and now it would need to be cleaned again.

Ulla pulled out a pair of cutoff jeans and a large
man's T-shirt from one of the bags and held the trousers up against her body, muttering unintelligible words
that clearly had something to do with them possibly not
fitting her ample hips. Ulla glanced up. "I live here,
bensel. Where else would I be?"

"I thought you were spending the day fishing with
Chicken John." Molly smirked as her *mamm* winced

at the man's community nickname. Ulla flushed rosy pink, something Molly hadn't seen her do in a long time.

"I've told you before. Stop calling him that, especially to his face. There's nothing wrong with him owning a chicken farm. It's a respectable occupation, and you like eating the eggs his chickens lay well enough." Ulla reached for a glass from the overhead cabinet next to the sink and turned on the tap.

Molly couldn't help but notice her *mamm*'s flush had crept all the way down to her neck when she turned around to scold her.

"Are you stringing Chicken John along for his money?"

"What a thing to say to your *mamm*. Of course I'm not. I truly like him. He's good to me, and kind spirited." Ulla took a sip of water and then added, "I know you'll probably find this hard to believe, but he seems to like me, too."

"Is there an announcement coming soon?" Molly almost laughed out loud when her *mamm* swallowed down the wrong pipe and sputtered. "You've gotten very rude since you began working at that café. Perhaps it's time I pay a visit and speak to your boss about manners."

A mental image of her mother and Willa Mae going toe-to-toe in front of a café full of gossipy customers put a grin back on her face. "That's a good idea. Maybe you could bring Chicken John with you and then have a meal on me."

"*Ya*, a real smart-mouth, just as I said, and in *mei haus*. I've known John for years. He's been like a *bruder* to me. There's nothing more to say." Ulla snatched her bags off the table and stomped past, her bedroom door slamming with a resounding *bang* a few seconds later.

Molly smiled as she hurried to answer the front doorbell.

His bowl-cut gray hair shoved under a navy blue baseball cap, Chicken John stood on the doorstep, his small body swallowed up by a checked, long-sleeved fishing shirt. Pale, skinny legs protruded from his baggy work pants rolled all the way to his knobby knees.

Molly held back a titter of laughter. "Looks like you're ready for a sunny day of fishing."

"*Ya.* Seems your *mamm* has no intentions of coming home until we catch our dinner." He grinned and then glanced around Molly. "Your *mamm*'s not ready yet?"

"She's dressing now. Would you like to come in?"

"*Nee*, not like this." He looked down at his worn fishing boots covered in sand and shrugged. "I smell of fish bait and the old boat. Maybe next time."

Dressed in a plain dress, with jeans that covered her legs, Ulla rushed past Molly, her tennis shoes squeaking on the hardwood floors as she headed toward the door. "It makes me to wonder why you've become so foolhardy of late, Molly. Perhaps there's more for us to talk about when I get home."

Molly shut the door and leaned against it.

Had Samuel told her *mamm* about her commitment to Isaac?

Isaac rang up the inexpensive tire valve and forced a smile on his face as he handed back the change from his customer's dollar bill. "*Danke.* Come back to see us," he said, and watched the burly teenager walk out the door. The boy had come in for two new bike tires, but he didn't have the right size in stock for one. Another sale lost.

He looked down at the dollar bill in his hand. Should he add it to the two quarters, two dimes, a nickel and four pennies in the money drawer? Not even enough to buy his lunch. He folded the money and dropped it in his pocket and then wrote the sale down in his book under the correct date. At this rate he wouldn't be able to pay for new supplies at the end of the month, much less his rent to Ulla, even if she let him stay after she heard the news of his courting her daughter. Where would he go to live?

Silence ate at him. He could hear the low hum of a dryer going around and around at the Laundromat next door. He'd had no business for hours, yet there was always a line out its door, Amish and *Englischer* snowbirds waiting for fresh clothes during peak season. Maybe he'd gone into the wrong business. Maybe he should go back to Missouri, face his family's disappointment and the police with the truth.

Isaac sat on the red couch and watched traffic go by. He perked up in his seat and stretched to watch as Molly flew past his window, pedaling her bike like time was against her. Her medical bag bounced in the wire basket behind her seat. Another baby to be birthed by the ever-busy woman. Her profession and work ethic warmed him. He'd never liked lazy people. There was nothing lazy about Molly Ziegler.

His stomach growled, but he ignored the call for food. He'd eat an apple in a bit and then wait for another inexpensive but delicious meal at home. *Home.* When had he started to think of Molly's house as his own? He'd lived there almost a month now. Even Ulla had warmed to him and treated him almost human at times. But would she treat him so well after she learned of them courting?

Isaac picked up a fashion magazine an *Englischer*

had leafed through while waiting for a handlebar adjustment on her bike.

A thin *Englischer* woman in bright clothes that barely covered her body stared back at him. For a fleeting second he wondered what Molly would look like in a modest *Englischer* dress instead of the plain Amish clothes she wore.

An appealing image of her flashed through his mind. He sighed and started to toss the magazine in the trash, but caught a glimpse of an advertisement about bettering your business profits. He looked up the article's page number, turned to it and began to read. The writer was big on start-up loans for small businesses.

He thought about what he needed on the shelves, how a couple of extra rental carts could double, maybe triple his profit margin. He laid the magazine on the couch cushion next to him and leaned back, his eyes closed. Was he just being stubborn? Why not borrow a small loan from the church, just enough to get regular customers coming in?

Mose Fischer could help him make a decision. He was an elder in the modern Amish church they attended. Maybe he would be knowledgeable about loans and such. Isaac stood and stretched, his leg hurting, but not as much as it had in the past. The limp would remain, forever his companion.

Turning the Open sign over to Closed, he locked the main door and strolled toward the back exit. Excitement coursed through him. This loan idea could be the chance he needed to make his business thrive.

Tired but exhilarated after her patient's quick and easy birth of a healthy seven-pound boy, Molly returned home. She headed straight for Isaac's private room, a stack of fresh linens over one arm, her basket of cleaning supplies over the other.

She knocked on his door to make sure he hadn't come home early, then went in. Entering his room when he wasn't there felt strange. Her arm pimpled with goose bumps. She was being ridiculous. She'd cleaned his room a dozen times before.

She had a job to do and got busy working, a hum coming from the depth of her soul, calming her.

His bed was tidy but not properly made. *Typical male.* His curtains were closed so tightly not a beam of sunlight filtered in. Using both arms, she threw his drapes back and opened the two windows, allowing fresh air to blow into the small room. Rooms needed to breathe, her *mamm* had taught her as a small child. The scent of oak trees and sea breezes blew in, ruffling the curtains and flushing out the stale air.

She tore at his sheets and light quilt, and made a messy pile on the floor with the dirty linens. Leaving the mattress to air, she cleaned the windows with ammonia water and rubbed a shine into the glass windowpanes. A swipe of lemon water and baking soda cleaned the window ledges and doorknob. She grabbed a container of beeswax and went to work polishing the bed's headboard.

Moving over to his dresser, she lifted his Bible and couldn't resist the temptation to sniff the old leather-bound book. It reminded her of her *grossmammi's* Bible from so long ago. As a child, she'd spent many hours in the Word, enjoying the pictures of the animals and people separating the pages of God's infinite words. Molly gave the old book a swipe of beeswax and then cleared the top of the dresser. She smeared a wax film all over the surface, hitting the sides and drawers for good measure. When she was finished, the old dresser had a golden shine that would have impressed her *gross-mammi* if she'd still been alive.

Prepared to remake the bed, Molly flipped out the clean bottom sheet, tucked in the corners and smoothed out any wrinkles left on the top sheet. She reached for the quilt on the chair and saw something white on the floor by the closet door. Almost ready to dust mop the room's wooden floors, she walked over and picked up an envelope, this one smaller than the ones she'd seen in his room before. It smelled of roses.

As the envelope was roughly opened, the name of the sender was partially torn. But Molly could make out the first name and the address clear enough. The name Rose, written in a small, feminine print, drew her attention. She turned the envelope over. Near the seal was a small X and the words *See you soon.*

She read the name Rose again and tapped the envelope against her hand as she pondered. Who was this Rose? His *mamm*? A sister? Maybe a cousin. She sniffed the envelope again. No *mamm* she knew would douse a letter to her son with sweet water. Perhaps he had a girlfriend back home?

Could he already be courting someone? Maybe he'd agreed to her deception because he felt sorry for Molly?

Her face flamed. She often regretted her impulsive decision to ask him to fake a courtship. Maybe he did, too. Could she be causing him problems? She looked around for more letters on the floor, but only found dust bunnies under the bed.

Molly put the letter on the dresser and went back to

making the bed, her thoughts lingering on the name Rose as she flipped the fresh quilt across the bed and punched air into Isaac's feather pillows. Whoever this Rose was, she lived in the same town Isaac had come from. Jamesport, Missouri.

She grabbed for the dust mop and began pushing it across the floor.

"I see you're still handy with the mop."

Molly flushed, remembering the bump she'd put on Isaac's head that first day. She glanced at the letter she'd just placed on the dresser and then leaned on the mop handle and sheepishly grinned his way. "*Ya*, the mop and I have become good friends." She tugged one of her *kapp*'s ribbons away from her face. "You're home early. No business?"

"Not much, but that could all change soon." He flashed a smile and then rested against the doorframe, his arms across his chest in a relaxed manner. He seemed content to stand there and watch her finish the last of the cleaning. "I read an article in an *Englischer* magazine this afternoon."

"*Ya*, and what kind of advice did this magazine article suggest that puts such a big smile on your face?" Isaac seldom smiled like he meant it, and here he was smiling like the proverbial Cheshire cat over something *Englisch*. "I find hard work and perseverance usually pay off for me."

Isaac pulled off his straw hat and tapped it against his leg, his expression serious again. "*Ya*, well. I'm working hard at getting the business going, but if I don't have bikes to rent or parts to sell, it's tough meeting my customers' needs."

"You make a good point, but all businesses take time to get going."

"That's just it. I don't have the cash flow to wait for business to pick up. I need income now, and this article reminded me of something."

"And what is that?" Molly walked to the door, her mop and supplies in hand. She looked up into his green eyes and saw a fresh flash of fire smoldering there.

"I'm going to meet with Mose and see if I can get a loan from the church. I just came home to clean up a bit before I go." He tugged at his shirt, revealing golden dots of some kind of oil on his light blue shirt. A smear of bike-shop goo on his left cheek could have been anything from mud to motor fluids.

"I'll leave you to it," Molly said, and turned to go, only to glance back. "I put fresh towels in your bathroom and there's plenty of hot water. I'll be praying *Gott's* will for your life."

His hand on the doorknob, Isaac said, "*Danke*, Molly. I need those prayers."

"You can pray, too, you know. Where two or more are praying, He's in the midst of them."

Isaac's head dropped. "Sometimes I think *Gott* doesn't listen to my prayers anymore."

Molly paused. Isaac stood inches from her, prepared to shut his bedroom door behind her. She really didn't know anything about his life, his family, what he believed, but she did know he was hardworking and kind. Since showing up at their door, the road-weary expression he wore on his face convinced her there were things undone in his spiritual life. Threads that had unraveled, leaving him feeling alone and lost. She knew what that loneliness felt like.

When her sister, Greta, had died suddenly in childbirth, it had taken Molly a long time to trust God again, to believe He knew what was best for her life. Maybe Isaac was going through loss, too. She smiled her encouragement. "You'll see. Just pray for *Gott*'s will and wait for the good to happen."

Chapter Nine

There was no hesitation in Isaac's steps. He strolled up to Mose's furniture store as if he didn't have a care in the world. He wanted to exude confidence. His pain level down, his limp was less noticeable and not as apt to hold him back.

He remembered Molly's words about prayer and whispered, *Gott, let this meeting go well. Give me the right words. Have Your will in my life.*

He opened the main door. A bell announced his arrival. He stepped into the furniture showroom and wiped his feet on the rough, fibrous floor mat underfoot. The barnlike building, full of beautiful handmade furniture, amazed him. There was no lack of stock here. Mose Fischer was obviously an intelligent and talented man with a thriving business.

A man dressed Amish, but one Isaac didn't recognize, waved from the back of the store. "*Willkumm*, I'll be right with you." Tall, well-built and obviously energetic, his movements were quick and fluid as he finished wrapping the desk next to him, coating it in plastic wrap to protect the finish for shipping.

"How are you this fine morning?" The man approached. He extended his hand and grasped Isaac's in a powerful handshake that told Isaac the man had lifted heavy furniture for years.

One of the man's fingers flicked his name badge. "Name's Fredrik, but people 'round here often call me Fred." He grinned, keeping the conversation friendly.

"*Gut* to meet you, Fred." Isaac put his hand behind his back and flexed blood back into his fingers. He had to work on his upper body strength, not just his legs. Since the wreck he'd lost considerable weight and muscle tone. Too much time lying in a hospital bed.

"What is it you're looking for? A bed, or perhaps a table for your new *haus*?" The man moved from side to side, flicking his dust rag from his pocket and polishing the tables nearby as he spoke.

Isaac liked the man's work ethic. He'd need this kind of employee one day if he could ever get the business off the ground and start making enough profit to hire someone ambitious. "No, I'm not a customer today. I was hoping to talk to Mose Fischer for a moment if he's in."

"*Ach*, and me running my mouth about furniture." The man grinned from ear to ear, as only the young and eager did. He pointed to a room just off to the side of the building. "That would be his office. Just give a knock. He'll call you in if he's not on the phone with business. It's good to meet you, Herr…"

"Graber, Isaac Graber." He suffered through another crushing handshake.

"*Gut* to meet you, Herr Graber. You come see us before your wedding day. We can fill your home with beautiful furniture."

"I'm not getting married anytime soon." Isaac thought

of his pretend courting with Molly, but they had no future together. Their ruse meant absolutely nothing.

Turning to head back to his work, Fredrik murmured, "Oh, you will be. And soon. *Ya*, all the signs are there."

"Signs?" Isaac asked the man, staring at his broad back.

The man stopped and turned toward Isaac. "*Ya*, signs. You're young and single. That's all it takes to get tangled up with one of the smart Amish women here in Pinecraft. Lots are looking for husbands." He laughed like he knew all the secrets of the world and headed to the back of the store, whistling the same song Molly had been singing that morning.

The hair on his arms stood up as he walked across the shiny tile floor to Mose's office. He knocked, glancing back at Mose's busy employee while he waited.

Mose Fischer opened the door, the man's blond hair a messy nest of curls covered in sawdust. "Good to see you again, Isaac. Hope the shop's doing well."

The men shook hands and Isaac flinched.

"I see you've meet Fredrik," Mose commented. "He has quite a handshake, doesn't he?"

Isaac laughed, trying to hide his embarrassment. "I thought he'd squeeze my hand off. I'd better start lifting weights before I come back to buy furniture."

Mose motioned for Isaac to sit in a comfortable-looking chair. He moved behind an old, scratched desk and dropped into a squeaky computer chair. "I'd never considered myself a weakling until I hired Fredrik a couple of years ago. He had me pumping iron just to endure his morning greetings," Mose added with a smile. "So what can I do for you? A new desk and computer chair for your office?" Bright blue eyes gazed at him expectantly.

Isaac breathed deeply. "I came to talk to you about the church. Well, not exactly the church, but the chance of a church loan. I could pay it back in say…five years, give or take a year."

"A loan for business or personal?" Mose pulled at his long beard, his forehead creased.

"Business."

"How much do you need?"

Isaac slumped in his chair. He had no idea how much money he needed. He hadn't thought that far ahead, convinced he'd be laughed out of the man's office as soon as he opened his mouth about borrowing church money.

He straightened, looked Mose in the eyes and sputtered. "I…well, I was thinking of a couple new golf carts and several really nice new bikes to sell, not rent. Having stock would help pick up profits and maybe fill the shelves with parts. *Ya*, parts, lots of them because I'm sick of turning away customers because I don't have what they need." Isaac stopped talking because Mose was smiling broadly, as if he was ready to burst into laughter, just as Isaac feared.

"You remind me of myself all those years ago," Mose said. "I was young and fresh as a corn cob that had fallen off the back of my *daed*'s truck. I had no idea what I'd need to get this furniture business off the ground, but it was my heart's desire and I was willing to do whatever it took. Even fight for it if I had to, and I did. My *daed* wanted me to be a farmer, like him. He made my life miserable for years. I went to *Gott* with my problem and He set the path, just like He set yours when you came in here today, ready to do battle for your dream."

Isaac swallowed a lump in his throat. Mose had seen

his vision, felt his earnest desire to make his business grow. *Danke, Gott.* "I was afraid you'd laugh at me."

"Laugh? *Nee*, not laugh. But I will speak as your representative to my father, Otto Fischer. He's the community bishop and calls the financial committee together for requests such as this. I usually head those committees, so rest easy. You'll get a fair hearing. You should know our answer in a few days, a week at most. Hold on to your faith. If this is *Gott*'s will, all will go well. And relax. You look wound tighter than a kettledrum."

Isaac considered telling Mose about his past, but shame held him back. "*Danke*, Mose. You've been so helpful. I can't thank you enough for—"

Mose cut him off. "There's no need for thanks, Isaac. Just remember. The community of Pinecraft is here for you. You seem to have made a good impression on Molly, and I trust her judgment."

Isaac's gaze veered away. "Molly's a kind woman, full of promise. Someday she'll make a wonderful, spirited wife."

"That she will, but I don't want her hurt by anyone."

Isaac laughed a little. Mose didn't have to worry about him. He had no interest in falling in love with anyone, especially Molly. "She's a good friend. You don't have to worry about me. I'm no threat to Molly's happiness. For now, my mind is set on work, and nothing more."

"But hearts grow close at the least expected time. I know from experience. Don't pull Molly into your life if you have no real intentions toward her. Let her get on with her search to find someone she can love if you feel so strongly about using your time and energy to build your business. All I had to offer my Sarah was a prom-

ise of a future. Little more than hard work and my rambunctious *kinner* to care for. She jumped at the chance.
Molly might, too, if you show the least bit of interest."

Isaac rose and extended his sore hand. "*Danke*, Mose
for your help with the loan…and the good advice. *Gott*
has a plan for my life, and I don't want to be out of His
will ever again."

The sun woke Molly an hour early the next morning. In a hurry to get out the door, she dressed quickly
and rushed to eat a bowl of cereal, only to get waylaid
by her mother at the kitchen table and caught up in an
argument.

"I don't want to talk about Samuel again. You know
I don't love him, *Mamm*." She spoke over her empty
cereal bowl. "He's not my type and I'm…" Her voice
trailed off, weary of the fight. She was tired of being
treated like a child because she wasn't married. She'd
said all this before, but each chapter and verse of her
argument was being ignored.

"You have little option, Molly. This foolishness about
Isaac has to stop. He's not the man for you. He's as poor
as a church mouse and has no future to offer you," Ulla
said from across the table.

Molly rose and faced her mother. "I don't want to
marry without love, and I don't love Samuel." Her
mother's expression reflected grim determination. She
shoved her coffee cup into the hot water glistening with
suds, silently praying her mother would be reasonable
just this once.

Dressed in a freshly ironed dress of navy blue, her
apron heavily starched, Ulla wiped her mouth on a linen
napkin and then pushed away from the breakfast table.

She slammed her plate against the kitchen counter. "I said forget about Isaac. After church this Sunday, I want you to tell Samuel that you *do* love him. Explain that you were just testing the waters, do you hear?" She moved away, rammed her chair back under the table and headed for the door, her steps quick and angry. "You have to marry the man. We need his money to keep the boarding *haus* open. Too many of our seasonal renters have passed on to be with the Lord. New hotels are opening all around us. Each winter we are left with the crumbs; the leftovers no one else wants to rent to. If we are to survive—"

"You mean if *you* are to survive, *Mamm*. Money was never an issue when *Daed* was alive and running this home. You insist on buying what we don't need, spending money on things you want. Your knickknacks and whatnots clutter this house." Molly lifted a wooden chicken off the counter and held it up for her mother to see. "I won't sacrifice my life to pay for your expensive trinkets. If Samuel is such a good catch, you marry him. I'm not—"

Ulla walked over to Molly and grabbed her arm with steely fingers. Anger pressed her mother's features into a harsh scowl. "I have sacrificed all my life for you. It is time you sacrificed for me."

Molly jerked out of her mother's grasp and stood her ground. "*Nee*, not anymore. I have done all I am going to do. A loveless marriage is where I draw the line."

Her eyes narrow slits, Ulla leaned close and poked Molly on the chest. "You are Amish and unmarried. You will do as you are told. I will not allow this behavior to go on in *mein haus*. When you see Samuel, make it clear you are prepared to court and marry."

Turning on her heel, her *mamm* slammed out of the house, leaving Molly slumped against the kitchen counter.

The time had come for drastic changes. She had to take a stand or be railroaded into something she didn't want. Her mother had gone too far.

She looked around the room. She'd grown up in this house. Most of her happy moments with Greta were experienced here. They'd laughed together in this kitchen as *kinner*. And cried together, as well. They'd shared the big double bed until the day her sister married Mose Fischer. Her sister's book of poems were hidden in Molly's clothes drawer, along with the *kapp* Greta had worn the day she'd died. There were no pictures of her to look at and remember. Just memories from the past.

Molly didn't wait for her thoughts to clear. She wasn't going to stay in this *haus* a moment longer. She'd bring her suitcases to work with her, work her shift and later go to Mose and Sarah's for wisdom.

They lived in Pinecraft, where church rules were often bent and twisted. She saw no reason why she shouldn't become more independent. She was twenty-one now, after all. An adult. She didn't have to live under her *mamm*'s thumb or be forced into a loveless marriage.

Sarah had gone through a lot back in Lancaster. She was a *gut* person to ask for wisdom, and Mose would keep her in line, help her not break Ordnung rules. She didn't want trouble with her church, or the Bishop. She loved Otto Fischer like a father and respected his position in the community.

Packed and ready to leave, Molly walked through the house, touching the chair her father had always sat in. His place at the table was still held in reserve out of respect. His death had come as a powerful blow to Molly and Greta. She'd tried hard to accept *Gott*'s will for her life but secretly resented *Gott* for taking her father so soon, and then Greta.

Walking into the great room for one last time, she grabbed a sheet of writing paper from the desk and wrote with heavy strokes of the pen.

Mamm,
I need to get away and think. Please don't look
for me.
Molly

She pushed her note away from the edge of the table and walked out the front door, her small zippered suitcases beating against her thighs as she hurried to the driveway.

With her legs pumping fast, she rode her bike to the café, parked in the back and pulled her bags from the basket. She rushed in through the employees' door, her two small suitcases in hand, pretending everything was fine. She felt gutted inside, her stomach heaving, but she had customers to feed, hard work to do when her shift began in a half hour. Work would keep her mind off things best not thought about. Like her *mamm*'s reaction to her moving out. She put on her apron, looked through the windows toward Isaac's shop and saw a Closed sign hanging on the door handle.

She turned and headed to the kitchen.

The grill spit and sputtered hamburger fat all over the thick cotton apron stretched across Willa Mae's generous figure. The older woman turned toward Molly, her spatula flipping meat patties with precision. She'd had years of practice. "Hey, you look like someone ran over your favorite cat. What's up, Sugar?"

"*Ach*, you don't want to know." All morning she'd been able to think of nothing but Isaac and her mother, but now that Willa Mae was standing in front of her, she questioned her decision. Maybe she'd acted too rashly when she'd packed her bags. Was moving out a good idea? Mose would probably advise her she should have waited and prayed for *Gott*'s direction, but she'd had enough of her *mamm*'s demands. She would not marry Samuel without love.

Willa Mae flipped a rare burger on the toasted bottom bun, slathered it with mayonnaise and then slapped on a tomato slice, lettuce leaves and two rings of red onion on the mustard-covered top bun. "Sure, I wanna know. Spill it. Tell your mean ole boss what's on your mind." She sandwiched the two halves together and leaned on the mountain of food, squeezing it down to a reasonable height before she slid it on a plate already lined with potato chips.

How could she tell her what was going on without sounding like a spoiled child? "It's my *mamm*."

"Ulla again? What did she do this time? Make you eat your greens?" Willa Mae put the plate through the food window and bellowed like a pig farmer, "Food's up." She jerked down the next slip of paper from the roundabout and read the food order, her lips moving. "I know she treats you like a nine-year-old and shows you no respect. So what's new?"

Molly picked up a pickle slice and popped it in her mouth. The sour flavor puckered her lips and made her cheeks hurt. "She's really crossed the line this time."

"You said that the last four times you came into this kitchen grumbling. You're gonna have to come up with something fresh if you're gonna keep my interest piqued." Her deep, throaty laugh, the result of too many packs of cigarettes twenty years ago, filled the small kitchen. She coughed and wheezed into the sleeve of her chef's uniform and then went back to work at the grill.

"She told Samuel he could court me and she didn't even ask how I felt about him. She had no right. I was so embarrassed, and now she says I have to marry him, like it or not."

Willa Mae broke an egg with one hand and then broke another. They sizzled on the hot grill. Two strips of bacon joined the eggs and instantly shriveled. "Isn't he that rich Amish kid, the big-time farmer from Ohio?" Two slices of light wheat toast popped up, perfectly brown and ready for a brush of melted butter.

"*Ya*, his family's got money, but—"

Willa Mae cut Molly off. "Look, child. He's got money. Your mama likes spending money. Makes perfect sense to me. If I was young enough, I'd marry him myself. Anything to get away from this hot stove." The piping hot plate of food was shoved through the food window, followed by two tiny containers overflowing with pickles. "Food's up."

Molly caught Willa Mae's gaze and saw confusion in her honey-brown eyes. "I'm a twenty-one-year-old spinster. I live with my domineering mother, work two jobs. I've never courted seriously, and I'm supposed to marry Samuel for his money. Does that help you understand?" Tears welled up in her eyes, making everything go blurry around her.

Willa Mae moved in closer, her arm slipping around

Molly's trembling shoulders. "Oh, don't be starting no tears up in here. I'm sorry you're sad, honey. I really am. I thought this was just one of your usual rants. I didn't know you were really upset, or I wouldn't have teased you."

Molly cried like a child all over her boss's shoulder. "I've been pretending to court Isaac, but I think he may have a girlfriend back home."

"Wait up a minute. Who has a girlfriend? I thought we were talking about your mama forcing Samuel on you. Keep it simple for me, honey. I'm old as dirt and I can't keep up with your rambling."

Molly's bottom lip trembled. She sniffed, taking the dish towel her boss thrust at her. It smelled of bacon grease and tomatoes. She wiped her eyes, but the tears kept flowing. "This man I've been seeing, Isaac... I think he might have a girlfriend. He got a letter from somebody named Rose, and we're supposed to be courting, or pretending to be courting. If she comes here for a visit and is truly his girlfriend, how will we keep up our ruse?" Molly groaned. "Oh, I don't know. I'm just so emotional lately."

Willa Mae nodded, her dark ringlets, covered by a hairnet, dancing on her head. "Let me see if I've got this right." She splayed out her fingers and started counting off offenses. "Your mom upset you by trying to sell you to the highest bidder?"

Molly nodded. *"Ya."*

"And you and some guy named Isaac are mixed up in some kind of ruse, and now his girlfriend might come to Pinecraft and spoil all your plans?" Willa Mae's brow arched. "How am I doing so far?"

Molly pulled on her prayer *kapp* ribbons. "You forgot the part where I packed my bags and moved out and have no place to live."

"Oh, girl. You've gone and done it this time. Your mama's gonna run wild through the streets looking for you by this time tomorrow, and this café is the first place she's likely to come. What do you want me to tell her?" Willa Mae frowned as she flicked another order off the roundabout, threw a small steak on the grill and then dunked a basket of fries into hot, bubbling oil.

Molly dropped into the chair near the back window and put her head in her hands. "I don't know. I haven't thought any of this through. I've made a real mess of my life, and no one's to blame but myself."

Molly wanted to scream in frustration. What had she gotten herself into?

Chapter Ten

Damp and miserable, Molly dodged rain puddles as she hurried through the streets of Pinecraft, the sky darkening with the promise of more rain. Mose and Sarah's home was only a couple of blocks away from the café, but Molly was tired from a long day at work. The short distance felt like miles.

The Lapps' baby had taken hours to deliver, hours with nothing to do but wait, think and panic. In her mind her problems had become insurmountable, more than she could deal with without good counsel. She'd called Mose in desperation, asked if she could come to the house as soon as she was free. Now she wished she hadn't. Talking would just add to her stress. But Mose might have a solution, something she could do that didn't include tucking her tail between her legs and going back home.

Someone had left the porch light on, a beacon of hope in the shimmery drizzle soaking her hair and dress. She ran up to the door, knocked and heard the high-pitched squeal of children. Sarah opened the door, her smile welcoming, a circle of blond-haired children clustered around her skirt.

"Come in, Molly," she said, speaking over small voices demanding they get to their aunt first. "Beatrice, take your aunt's bag and then run and get a towel from the bathroom. She looks wet and tired."

"Why do I have to get it? You never ask Mercy to do anything." Beatrice's fake tears gathered in her eyes.

"Go," Sarah insisted. "You don't want your aunt Molly to think you're not my biggest helper, do you?"

"Nee," the little girl groaned, her small bare feet slapping against the polished tile floor as she ran toward the back of the house.

Mercy climbed like a monkey, her small arms wrapping tightly around Molly's neck. She offered up a huge, toothy grin. "I free now," she said, and held up four tiny fingers. Molly pretended to bite at her fingers. The little girl giggled and snuggled her head into Molly's neck.

Mose walked into the room and relieved Molly of her wiggling bundle. "Let's give your aunt a drink and a slice of your mom's strudel before you overwhelm her with hugs and kisses." He smiled at Molly. "You look like you've had a difficult day."

Molly patted her blond-haired nephew's head. Levi had grown since she'd last seen him. He was tall for almost two and strikingly beautiful for a boy. He grinned up at her, his arms clamped on to her leg like a vise. She returned his smile and told Mose, *"Ya,* I did. Just as I was leaving my shift I got the call. My patient wasn't due for another week, but babies decide when it's time to come, convenient or not. The mom's fine and her son's a gorgeous *bobbel.* I'm sure she'll be showing him off at church next week."

Sarah rubbed her own protruding stomach, smiling. "Why don't you come in, instead of standing at the door?" She took Molly's arm, and they strolled toward the kitchen. "Let me grab you some strudel, hot from the oven. We can sit and talk."

Beatrice ran in, a white hand towel clutched to her chest. "Here, Molly."

"Thank you, *liebling*. You're such a good girl." Molly took the towel and patted her face and neck dry before bending to give the child a tender kiss on the cheek. Beatrice glowed, her love for her aunt reflected in her deep blue eyes. "I went to visit *Grossmammi* today. She said—"

"We don't want to hear what Ulla said, Beatrice. She should not speak of adult things around you. It would be best if you learn not to repeat what she tells you," Mose instructed. "Find your little sister and brother and take them into the playroom, and mind that you are kind to them. No angry words. Do you hear?" His hand propelled the sulking child toward the back of the house. "Sometimes I wish… Never mind what I wish. Let's forget about Beatrice being so like Ulla and eat our strudel." A growing smile wiped the frown from his face.

The kitchen was warm and inviting, the fragrance of freshly baked pastry hanging heavy in the air. Molly eased herself into a chair and forced a smile. "Thank you for allowing me to come."

Sarah, busy plating slices of hot pastry, returned Molly's smile. "You are always welcome here. You know that."

A tear trailed down Molly's cheek, then another.

"Oh, what's wrong?" Sarah said, and hurried over, putting her arms around Molly's shoulders.

"I've made such a mess of things," Molly groaned.

Mose pulled out a chair and sat, a look of concern creasing his face. "What's happened?" He pressed a napkin into her hand.

Molly dried her eyes, her chin wobbling, new tears threatening. "I moved out."

Sarah spoke to Mose under her breath. "I suspected this would happen."

Dabbing at her eyes, Molly released a deep sigh. "It's Samuel Bawell."

"Ah… I'd wondered." Mose rubbed at his beard. "For a while there's been talk that a courtship has begun between the two of you."

"I know, but it's not true. I don't love him, or his money." She lifted her head and looked Mose in the eyes. "I promise you I didn't lead him on. It's *Mamm*. She keeps pushing me, insisting I encourage Samuel's attention. Telling him to pursue me. I'm not interested in courting and marriage right now. Well, not with Samuel anyway." She thought of Isaac, his dark hair shining in the sun across the picnic table, just before he told her he wasn't interested in courting her. She took in a shuddering breath.

Patting Molly's hand, Sarah asked, "And you've told Ulla this, made yourself clear?"

"*Ya*, I've done everything but stand on my head and shout my words at her. She just won't listen. All she speaks of is the man's connections, his big farm. The money he has."

"Where are you staying?" Sarah asked, squeezing Molly's hand.

"I don't know yet," Molly said in a raspy voice laden with tears.

"Moving out wasn't the best course to take, Molly," Mose said, his tone that of a big brother. "It's not proper for a young woman to live alone. This world is a dangerous place. Especially for a young, innocent girl like you. You need to think hard about this. Your mother could have you banned from the church, and my father's hands would be tied. Otto will not break Ordnung rules for anyone, not even you, *liebling*."

Molly blinked. "*Mamm*'s already threatened to talk to your *daed*, but I'm not going back." Molly's eyes grew bright with determination. "I won't!"

A restless night of tossing and turning at Mose and Sarah's *haus* brought no relief to Molly's troubled mind. She wiped the sweat off her brow with a napkin and washed her hands for the millionth time. The café had been busy all day, and a half hour past closing time the stragglers were still asking for another cup of coffee or piece of pie.

She wanted to tell everyone to go home, walk out the door, but she put on her happy face and kept cleaning tables and booths, running for food when Willa Mae called out.

"How many customers we got now?"

Molly grabbed a hot plate of fries and dropped an empty ketchup bottle into the trash. "Two couples and a strange little man who's having a great time talking to himself."

"He's not dangerous, is he?" Willa Mae scraped at the cooling grill, removing a day's layer of fat and bits of egg white.

"*Nee*, not dangerous. He seems harmless enough." Molly wiped down the food window while she talked, glancing over her shoulder every few seconds to keep an eye on the front of the café.

"I called my landlady a minute ago. She's got a place near me, but it's an efficiency in her motel, 'bout the size of a closet."

Molly could feel her face morphing from happy smile to worried frown. "Exactly how big is it?"

"She said maybe fourteen by fourteen feet, but it's furnished and even has kitchen supplies." Willa Mae's smile was warm and bright, her teeth flashing white in the fluorescent lighting as if she'd just told Molly she'd just won the lottery. "She said you can rent it for as long as you need to. Two days, a month. It doesn't matter to her, and it's better than what you've got now. Nothing."

The ugly truth hit Molly. Willa Mae was right. A small room was better than a park bench, and that was her plan B. "You think the room comes with sheets, too?"

"What you want for two hundred dollars a week? A swimming pool and spa?" Willa Mae pulled off her apron and reached for her walking shoes. "We closing this place down in five minutes, girl. Don't let nobody in and don't take no more orders. The grill's clean and the coffeepots washed. No fill-ups."

Molly walked to the front and locked the main door, trying to imagine a living room, bedroom and kitchen in one room. She gave up. It couldn't be done. Molly's head began to thump. Her feet already hurt, and she was tired of smelling French fries and fried beef patties. All she wanted was a hot shower and some sleep.

She made her way to the kitchen and watched as her boss washed her arms up to her elbows. "If I take the place, can I move in tonight?" She didn't know what she'd do if the answer was no. Willa Mae had offered her a bed, but she had three half-grown kids and a grumpy husband. Her boss was being the kindhearted woman Pinecraft knew her to be, but Molly didn't want to put her out, even for a night, and she'd bothered Sarah and Mose enough. Sarah was pregnant. She didn't need the extra work.

"I'll ring her and see what she says. She's probably still up. She watches lots of TV, like us old folk do. You'll probably be able to hear it in your apartment. She's that close."

Molly grimaced as she reached up to straighten her *kapp.*

"We all got to learn to be grateful for what we get in life, girl." Willa Mae continued, "God don't like no whiny kid crying to Him 'bout hardship."

Molly smiled her apology. She was ashamed of her own childishness. "Thank you for calling your friend about the apartment. I'm sorry. I was being silly. I'm just scared."

She could see her own reflection in Willa Mae's dark eyes.

"None of us is perfect, child." Her smile grew. "She might give you a discount. She likes to rent to you Amish folk. Says you pay on time and never run out on her."

"I know you're right about the apartment. I just had dreams." Molly brushed down her white apron, ashamed of herself.

Willa Mae put her arm across Molly's shoulders and squeezed. "We all have dreams. I wanted to be a famous movie star and make lots of money, but God said, 'You be the best cook you can be.' I didn't go to Hollywood, but I did get this place and my kids. That's enough. Sometimes enough has to be enough, Molly." She laughed, her belly jiggling. "You're young, but smart. One day you gonna meet some nice Amish man like that Isaac fella and get married. Children become your dream and a clean house your job. You'll see if I'm not right."

Molly thought of Isaac and a tiny boy with dark hair like his *daed*. She smiled, but then remembered she and Isaac were just pretending to court. He wouldn't be her children's father, but *Gott* would send someone someday, and he'd be a perfect match for her when she was ready. She believed that with all her heart.

Asked to come along as moral support an hour later, Isaac held the door as Molly and Lalalu, the motel manager, stepped into the apartment. The word *tiny* instantly came to Molly's mind. She looked at Isaac, and he shrugged, silently telling her he had no opinion.

The room looked clean and didn't smell.

Molly put on a brave face and handed over two crisp hundred-dollar bills. Lalalu looked both bills over carefully and then handed her a single key. Molly smiled her appreciation, grateful to have a place to lay her head for the next week.

Short, bony and her hair wild as if a tornado had styled it, Lalalu grinned and exposed gaps in her upper teeth. "Willa Mae said you're dependable and a hard worker. That's good enough for me." A remarkable underbite left the woman's jaw jutting like a bulldog's. The colorful caftan she wore dragged on the floor as she pointed out a miniature bathroom off the back of the room.

Molly stuck her head through the open door. Most of the bathroom's floor space was taken up by a walk-in shower with a plastic flamingo shower curtain that spilled out against a bowl-sized sink. The toilet was shoved into a corner of the room and low to the ground. The white fixtures sparkled clean and bright under a bare light bulb hanging from the ceiling.

Isaac stuck his head in the confining space and rubbed his clean-shaven jaw. "Big enough for one," he remarked, and backed out into the living quarters.

"I won't charge you a deposit, honey. I know you'll be straight up with me. My Amish tenants are always tidy and quiet and pay on time."

"*Danke*, I promise you I won't be a bother." Molly followed as her new landlady walked to the side of the bedroom.

"This here's your kitchen area."

Molly glanced at the wall across from the bathroom door. A short butcher-block counter had a mini-sink and backsplash, as well as two regular-sized electric burners. Wooden shelves lined with apple-trimmed paper held a plate, glass, two cups and a stack of saucepans. Molly glanced around, looking for a table to eat at and realized there was none. Not even a small one.

"I don't supply TVs, but you can bring one in if you want."

Molly blinked at her and blinked again. She'd read *Alice in Wonderland* as a child and felt just like Alice must have felt falling down the rabbit hole.

"I don't watch television." She straightened her *kapp* and tugged both ribbons to pull it down tighter on her head.

Isaac put his hand on the small of her back and then

stepped aside as Molly moved to the bed. "Do you supply sheets, or will I need my own?" The bed looked made up, but perhaps there was just a bedspread on it for show.

Lalalu threw back the flowered spread and exposed white sheets neatly tucked in the foot of the bed. "We got you covered, Molly. I washed those sheets this afternoon and line dried them the way you Amish like." She grinned as she glided back toward the apartment door. "I probably don't need to tell you, but I'm gonna do it anyway." Her bony finger pointed toward Molly. "You're my renter. Not him." She frowned at Isaac, her forehead crinkling into a road map of lines. "There's to be no overnight guests." Her eyes cut to Molly and then back to Isaac. "No loud music and no lounging in the yard in a bathing suit," she advised in a carefree way.

"*Ya*, sure. That sounds fine. I'll obey the rules."

"I know you will," the older woman said, then glanced Isaac's way again. "But what about you?"

Molly cringed as Isaac looked up, flushed red and then nodded. "*Ya*. That all sounds fine to me."

"Good. Now you let me know if you need anything, Molly," Lalalu murmured, then went out the door and shut it softly behind her.

The room was silent.

Molly could hear Isaac breathing.

She latched the dead bolt and wiggled the doorknob, making sure it locked and smiled at him nervously. "The deed is done."

"*Ya*," he said, watching her. "No going back now." His eyes darkened. Was he concerned for her? Tonight would be the first time in her life she was completely alone.

She wandered around the room with Isaac trailing behind her at an easy pace. She checked out the apartment-sized refrigerator under the kitchen cabinet. The freezer compartment held an empty tray for ice, which left little room for anything else. The inside of the fridge was clean and smelled fresh.

She sniffed the new white dish towel hanging on a nail and smiled, the feeling of ownership finally sinking in. She had her own place, somewhere to come to after long days at the café.

"I'd better go before Lalalu comes back and kicks me out," Isaac said, edging for the door.

"*Danke* for coming with me tonight."

"You have to know I'm not sure about all this, Molly." Isaac took another step toward the door.

"*Ya*, well. Mose thinks I'm making a mistake, too, but I had to take a stand."

His hand on the doorknob, Isaac cleared his throat. "Make sure you lock this latch behind me."

"I will."

"Call me if you have any problems or...well, you know. Get scared or something."

"I'm not a *kinner*, Isaac. I should be fine." She fingered the key to her newfound freedom and slipped it into her apron pocket.

"*Ya*, I'll see you tomorrow."

She tugged at her prayer *kapp* ribbons. "Tomorrow."

The door shut behind him, and Molly locked the dead bolt. She saw the door handle wiggle. Isaac had checked to make sure she'd remembered that lock, too.

Alone at last she dropped to the edge of the bed and then jumped to her feet as the sound of a blaring television invaded the silence of the tiny room. *Lalalu must be watching television.*

She unpacked, putting her starched and ironed *kapps* and what few things she owned on a shelf in the make-shift closet by the bed. She hung her church dress, two aprons and several everyday work dresses side by side and swished the tablecloth, hung from a string and two nails, closed.

Tired beyond words, she crawled into the surprisingly comfortable bed and lay on her back, listening to the muffled voices and Lalalu's laughter. She drifted off to sleep, her last conscious thought a prayer for Isaac. *Gott, keep him safe and don't let* Mamm *kick him out of the house before he finds a new place to stay.*

Chapter Eleven

Not wanting a confrontation with Ulla before he found a permanent place to live, Isaac showered, dressed and slipped out of his rental room before seeing the older woman.

He opened the bike shop and greeted two waiting customers. Molly's situation hovered at the back of his mind as he rented his last two big-seated bikes to two round-faced Amish women with heart-shaped *kapps* signifying connections to an Old Order community up north. Their crisp money would look nice in the drawer.

His cell phone rang, and he answered the call with a good-humored smile in his voice, even though he still wasn't used to the Pinecraft custom of using a phone for his business needs. "The Bike Pit, Isaac speaking." He dropped into his computer chair, pride of ownership giving him a sense of peace as he waited for his caller to speak.

"Otto Fischer here. You got a minute to meet at the café?"

Isaac's smile vanished. This meeting had to be about the church loan. He rubbed his aching leg and propped it on a box of bike tubes. "*Ya*, I do have time. I can see you in five minutes, if that works for you."

"*Ya*, I got all day and nothing to do. I'll see you soon."

What if he didn't get the loan? Would a bank consider him a good risk? He doubted it. He had no credit history, no experience as a salesman or repairman. He shoved the cell phone in his pants pocket. *I need Gott's will for my life more than ever.*

His empty stomach growled, reminding him he hadn't eaten since supper, and that had been a pack of peanut butter crackers. Maybe he'd eat a plate of pumpkin pancakes while he waited for the bishop. He took several fives out of the drawer, wrote the money draw in the book and locked up the shop.

Inside the busy café, an empty booth offered him a chance to sit down. Hurrying over, Isaac crossed paths with several customers. He slid across the booth's red-leather seat before anyone else could snatch up the spot, and stretched out his aching leg. He didn't bother checking the menu. He already knew what he wanted. A stack of steaming pancakes with lots of syrup and a couple of sausages, but he had to wait for Otto. The fragrant aroma of the hot café was killing him.

"Hello." Molly came up behind Isaac and greeted him with a shy smile.

"You slept well last night?" he asked, eyeing the dark circles under Molly's eyes.

"*Nee*, I didn't get much sleep. You?"

"Like you, I tossed and turned. I'm meeting with Bishop Fischer today, and it's important."

Molly wiped down the table and placed a fresh cup of coffee in front of him. "Has *Mamm* said anything to you?" She leaned in close, pretending to wipe down the saltshaker. "She could make your life difficult."

"I left early and avoided her, but that can't go on forever, Molly. We need to talk, get our stories straight."

"*Ya*, I don't like what all this deception is doing to you. Perhaps my plan was a mistake. Maybe I just need to stand up to her and Samuel, speak more firmly."

Isaac took a sip of the black coffee she poured. "Standing up to him hasn't worked so far."

Molly's shoulders drooped. "*Nee*, he is a stubborn man, used to getting his way, but I can be stubborn, too, when pushed into a corner."

"We need to talk tomorrow and work out what's to be done."

Isaac glanced up and saw Otto Fischer walk into the café. The old man glanced around, then hurried over. "*Guder mariye*, Molly. And you are well today?" He sat and tossed his hat on the table.

"*Ya*, I'm *gut*. And you?" Molly asked.

Isaac watched their exchange of words and tried to get a feel of the man's mood, but Otto Fischer gave no secrets away, his expression calm, as always. He was a quiet man, one who spoke only when he had something to say.

"*Gott* is good, and I have no complaints worthy of hearing." The old man grinned.

"I'll send your waitress over quick as I can." Molly poured Otto a steaming cup of coffee. "You two enjoy your breakfast," she said, and hurried back to the kitchen.

Otto faced Isaac "Have you ordered yet?"

"*Nee*, I waited for you."

"Let's get our food ordered and then we talk." He

motioned for the blonde-haired waitress at the back of the café and tossed aside the menu as she walked their way. "*Hallich geburtsdaag,* Heidi. Your special day is *gut, ya?*"

"*Danke,* Grossdaddi! But I had to work on my birthday. One of the girls called in sick. I couldn't tell Willa Mae no, but later there is a party in my honor. You and *Grossmammi* will come?"

"I wouldn't miss the chance to call you an old maid now that you've turned eighteen."

"Grossdaddi, you are terrible." Laughing, the blonde-haired, blue-eyed teen gave her grandfather a fleeting kiss on the cheek.

"So your *grossmammi* keeps telling me." His expression glowed with love for the blonde-haired girl. "She's made a special treat for you, like when you were a *kinner* and she spoiled you with too much attention. You'll be surprised."

"Is it strudel, with lots of apples?" The girl's smile brightened.

"Time will tell all things, *liebling.* Patience is a gift from *Gott.*"

Heidi gave her grandfather a hug, and turned his coffee cup over. "Coffee?"

"*Ya, kaffi* sounds *gut* and a stack of Willa Mae's special peanut butter pancakes for your favorite *grossdaddi.*"

Still grinning as she poured from a steaming carafe of coffee, Heidi filled his cup, her gaze turning to Isaac. She poured coffee into his waiting cup when he nodded. "And you, sir. Pancakes, too?"

Isaac grinned. "Pumpkin pancakes for me, with sausage, *bitte,* and ask for my syrup to be warmed."

"*Ya*, I will." She hurried off, her skirt swirling.

"I didn't know you had grown grandchildren, Bishop."

"Heidi is *mei* oldest son Ruben's child. She is a good girl, and we are proud of her, but we did not gather here to speak of my family. It is the loan you are interested in talking about."

Isaac took a sip of coffee and nodded. "It is. I wouldn't ask for help if I had another choice. It's time to swallow my pride."

"Pride is a sin, Isaac. At your age you should already know this. We strive to be like *Gott* and accept His guidance and instruction. You play an important part of our community now. We often help new businesses flourish." He smiled at Isaac. "I have talked with the elders, and I think we've found a plan that will work well for all of us."

Heidi carried over two white plates topped with stacks of perfectly browned pancakes, breakfast sausages and two jugs of warm syrup. "This should keep you two going for a while." She topped up their coffees and smiled. "Just wave if you need anything."

There was silence at the table as both men prayed silently and then dug in to their food. Isaac laid down his fork when his belly was full and watched Otto Fischer take his last bite of pancake. "This plan you speak of. How will it work to both our advantages?"

"The church will become partners with you for a time. We will buy a share of your business, and you can use the cash to add stock, increase your business, whatever you need. If you work hard, you'll make a go of the bike shop. We will continue to back you financially until you are steady on your feet, and in the black for a time. Then you can buy us out, and we will help another new business."

"*Ya*, this plan is a good one," Isaac said and watched as his bishop nodded his agreement.

"The elders would be happier if you were a married *mann* with a family, or at least courting. Is there a girl?"

Molly walked out of the kitchen, her blue dress covered in a work apron splattered with food. Sunlight danced off her dark hair as she walked past the café window. She glanced toward their booth and her gaze locked with Isaac's for seconds. She hurried back into the kitchen, but her sudden shy smile told him she was glad to have seen him.

"There's one I'm considering, but I'm not sure the time will ever be right."

The next morning loud conversation woke Molly with a start. She shoved her covers off her shoulders and then froze, listening. The forceful voice had the unmistakable high-pitched superiority her mother used when trying to make her point.

"*Mamm*," she whispered, falling back among her pillows and pulling the covers over her head. She knew she'd find her. People talked in Pinecraft, but she had hoped for more than a day to prepare for the onslaught.

Just as stubborn as her mother, Molly kicked back the covers and rose. She flung open the door, pulled her mother off the doorstep and into her room, ending her mother's public display of bad behavior. She smiled at her angry landlord. "I'm sorry."

"I tried to send her away, but this woman is determined," Lalalu said, hands on her bony hips.

"I know. *Danke* for your efforts." Molly waved a gentle goodbye, closed the door and then faced her mother. "What are you doing here?"

Ulla paced around the tiny room, agitation in her steps, her mouth slashed in an angry line. She spun toward her daughter. "*Ya*, just as I suspected. You've lost your sense of reason. You chose this room and that horrible *Englischer* woman over your wonderful bedroom at home…and me?"

Molly held her *mamm*'s gaze. "*Ya*, I did, *Mamm*. I chose this place, and Lalalu happens to be a very giving person. She's made me feel welcome here. This room is *my* home now. While I lived in your home, I showed you respect. Now I require as much from you."

Molly stood her ground, shoulders back, her mind screaming, *Help me, Gott.* Determined to ignore her *mamm*'s barbs, she pulled her robe over her nightgown and began to boil water for a mug of tea. She needed something to do while waiting for her mother's fury to end.

"It makes me wonder. Why have you shown this disrespect to me now? Since your *daed* passed, I have tried my best to be a *gut mamm* to you, but no. You would not let me be kind and loving."

"Don't bring *Daed* into this conversation. This is about you and me and the demands you make in my life. Leave *Daed* at peace in his grave." Her voice broke, tears swimming in her eyes. Her *daed* had been too gentle a person to hold her *mamm* in check. They'd all suffered the consequences of her mother's harsh tongue.

"Your *daed* would be ashamed and disappointed in you." Ulla threw the hurtful words at Molly, her eyes dark with anger. "You choose to be…like this. You are Amish. It is time you behave like a young Amish girl and not abandon your moral and spiritual values." Ulla kicked at the ugly tile floor underfoot. "I blame that boss of yours at the café. She has been an evil influence in your life, that *Englischer* woman with her fancy ways."

Molly turned away from her mother, toward the screeching teakettle. She wiped tears from her face with the back of her hand before she poured boiling water over the tea bag. "Now you blame Willa Mae? Perhaps you're right, *Mamm*. Maybe she did help me grow up, become an independent woman. If what you say is true, then I must remember to tell her *danke*."

Ulla waved at the door. "You come home with me now, or I will report your irresponsible behavior." Ulla's eyes grew large, threatening. "Bishop Fischer will bring the *bann* down on you at my request. You need your job as community midwife to support yourself and this—" she threw her arms up in the air "—room you call a home. You'll have no place to stay on your miserable café tips and wages. This room will disappear, and so will your rebellion." Her *mamm* smiled, but there was no joy in the smile. Only anger.

"Do what you must. I have no intention of going back with you today."

"You want independence, a home of your own so badly? *Gut*, all this can be resolved by a quick marriage to Samuel. I've worked hard trying to find a suitable husband for you, someone who will put up with these willful ways of yours."

"*Ya*, you had me on the selling block, along with your jars of peaches and jams. You'd sell me to the highest bidder. Why can't you understand? I'm not ready for marriage. Why would I want to wed? I'd be replacing you with a bossy husband telling me when to eat, how to dress. What do I need with a husband? I have you to bully me."

Ulla walked toward her daughter, her fists clenched. "Thank *Gott* your sister was different. Greta never gave me a moment's trouble. She followed rules, showed respect to me and your *daed*. You were always jealous of Greta's successful marriage, weren't you? It was Mose you wanted all along, but you waited too long. Now he has Sarah. You must look elsewhere."

Molly forced back the wave of tears that threatened to overwhelm her. "You're wrong, *Mamm*. I was never jealous of Greta's joy. Besides, Mose is like a big *bruder* to me. He was my dead sister's husband. It was your plan that I should marry him when Greta died, not mine. I would have never gone along with that. I loved my sister. You know I did. She was a kind and gentle person, like *Daed*. Greta never had to push for her rights. You gave them to her, allowed her to grow up and gave her so much more than me, things I never got. Like love."

Color high in her cheeks, Ulla slammed her fist on the counter and rattled Molly's tea mug. "I don't know what you're talking about. I treated both of you with the same love and respect." Her eyes grew red and watered. "Greta was easier to raise, less difficult."

"She was the pretty one, the one who pleased you. I always knew I was second best, the one to cook and clean, but never good enough to cherish."

"You are a foolish girl, full of yourself and pride. *Gott* will punish you for this rebellious spirit."

"I want you to leave now." Molly pointed to the door, her face set in angry lines.

Ulla walked to the door, held the knob in hand as she

threw her words over her shoulder. "I'm serious, Molly. I *will* speak to Otto and the elders. He will follow the laws of the Ordnung. You will be unchurched." Ulla's eyes narrowed, her face pinched. "Is your freedom that important to you?"

Molly glared at her, her heart breaking. She fought to hold back the flood of tears she felt coming.

Ulla's arm raised as if to strike Molly, and then it fell to her side. "This decision is yours."

"Go!" Molly said in a firm, but quiet voice and then cringed when her mother slammed the door behind her. What had she done?

She punched Isaac's number into her cell phone and trembled as she waited for him to pick up.

Molly grimaced as she spoke. "There's big trouble. *Mamm* just left, and she's angrier than I've ever seen her. I think I might have made a mistake moving out. She's threatening to have me shunned." Her voice wobbled as she spoke the words.

"Do you think she'd do it?"

"*Ya*, sure she would." Molly wiped a tear from her cheek. She heard Isaac take in a deep breath. She shouldn't be bothering him with is, but she didn't know who else to reach out to who would understand.

"Do you think Mose and Sarah would let you move in with them for a while?"

"*Ya*, I hate to burden Sarah, but she could use my help when the baby comes. Still, that won't stop *Mamm*. She's relentless when it comes to getting her way."

"We'll see about that."

Chapter Twelve

Molly stirred in bed, then rose up on one elbow, her eyes blinking, not fully awake. Had someone called her name? She glanced around the pink bedroom. Where was she? Why was she in a child's room full of books and fluffy pink teddy bears and not in her tiny apartment? Then she remembered—Isaac lived in the tiny apartment now, and this was Beatrice and Mercy's room. The children had been shifted elsewhere in the house when she'd moved into Mose and Sarah's home the night before.

Guilt roiled her stomach. She'd managed to pull Isaac into her drama again, fool that she was. She should have refused his offer to take over her apartment and taken responsibility for her own actions. But no. She'd allowed herself to be rescued again. The poor man. What must he think of her?

"Are you awake, Aunt Molly?"

She looked in the direction of the small voice. Mercy stood at the foot of the bed, dressed in a long white nightgown, egg yolk smeared across one cheek, her blond hair a riot of untamed curls. Molly smiled at her younger niece. "*Ya,* I'm awake, *liebling. Gut mariye.*"

Hopping on one leg, Mercy grinned shyly and said, "*Mamm* said wake up, or no pancakes for you." Picking up the hem of her long gown, the little girl ran out of the room, slamming the door behind her.

Molly threw back the covers and placed her bare feet on the cool wooden floor. She stifled an enormous yawn with her hand as she rose. She didn't want to do anything but hide her head under the covers and go back to sleep, but years of self-control had her tidying the tossed bedsheets and quilt moments later. She'd had a restless night of disturbing dreams, but faced a busy day at the café, with no letup until seven, if she was lucky. She needed the distraction of a busy day to keep her from thinking about her life, her recent mistakes.

Beatrice met her coming down the hall, her faceless doll tucked under her arm. "*Mamm*'s waiting on you."

"*Ya*, Mercy told me," Molly said, picking up the girl and laughing at her squeals of delight as she marched her into the kitchen. "I have a captive. Anyone want her?"

Sarah smiled. "*Gut mariye.* Did you sleep well?"

Molly shrugged. "Well enough." She patted Beatrice on the back and slid her down to the floor and then greeted Levi with a hug and kiss. "What a lovely boy. He's grown so tall. You must be so proud of him."

Two steaming pancakes were lifted off the grill and onto a plate for Molly. Sarah nodded and smiled. "We are proud of him, even when he dumps bugs on the floor and can't understand why he has to take them back outside."

"*Danke,*" Molly said, taking the pancakes. She pulled out a chair at the huge wooden table and sat, reaching for the warm maple syrup just out of reach. "I'd imagine the girls find a brother interesting to have around."

"You have no idea, but you will now that you're staying here," Sarah said with a laugh as she sat across from her. "Beatrice has had her fill of him already. She says he's a gross little boy with no manners and refuses to play with him, but Mercy has no problem with the bug-filled dump trucks he pushes around."

Molly took a bite of her pancakes and groaned with pleasure. "You really should open up a restaurant. These pancakes are wonderful."

"And when would I have time for this wonderful dream? Between diaper changes and dirty hands?" She grinned and then added, "But right now we need to talk about you, not me." She took Molly's hand and squeezed. "Tell me what's going on."

Closing the shop an hour early two days later, Isaac enjoyed the breeze blowing leaves at his feet and ruffling his hair. His leg hurt less, allowing him to leave the cane behind. He strolled by Molly's side, glad she'd accepted his invitation to go to the park and enjoy the warmth of the late-afternoon sun.

The twang of fiddles from Willie Burgess's Bluegrass Band could be heard all the way down to Gilbert Avenue. They crossed Pinecraft Park and finally drew close to the crowd of Amish, Mennonite and *Englischers* already seated in Birky Square on quilts, blankets and fold-out chairs.

Isaac's eyes searched for a patch of ground for him and Molly to settle on, the homemade quilt folded across his arm, along with a wicker basket of food Molly had put together at the café. The outing was supposed to be a way to keep the rumors of their courtship going, but they had decisions to make. The situation was getting out of hand.

Molly tugged at Isaac's shirtsleeve and got his attention. She motioned toward a bare spot under a huge tree draped with strands of Spanish moss and grinned as he nodded in agreement.

He hesitated and then grabbed her warm hand, pushing her through a swarm of *Englischers* toe-tapping to the lively music all around them. Laughing at Molly's pleased expression, Isaac flipped out the colorful log cabin quilt and placed the basket of food in the middle of the colorful squares.

"This spot is perfect. We can see the stage from here," Molly shouted over the music.

"Don't break your arm patting yourself on the back," Isaac shouted back.

"You're terrible," she said without malice, and smiled. She held his gaze for a heartbeat and then began to glance around. "I didn't expect so many people to show up with this blast of cool air blowing in from the north."

He watched her settle on the quilt and was surprised to see her pat the spot next to her. "Come join me." Her expression was calm and inviting, no doubt an act to convince those around them that they were a courting couple. She was playing the part of a woman in love.

He favored his leg as he lowered himself, but made sure he was close enough to her to be convincing. "This is nice," he said, and wished he hadn't. They weren't really courting, after all. Only pretending.

He had been instructed by her to be attentive when people were around, but he was finding it hard to follow the plan, pretend to love her only when it was necessary. The more time he spent with her, the more he realized he had begun to have real feelings for her. He longed to leave his past behind him and make this courtship real, but his common sense told him not to be foolish. His baggage from the past had to be dealt with. Until then he had nothing to offer her but his own brand of misery and hardship. He couldn't press for a real relationship with her, even if by some chance she might come to care about him in the future.

Molly laughed out loud as a Mennonite couple strolled past, pushing a small boy in a red wagon with wooden slates. "He looks like he's having a good time," she said, glancing at Isaac. Her foot tapped out the beat of the song being played, her cheeks glowing pink from the brisk, cool air.

"Maybe you should have brought a jacket," Isaac mentioned, seeing her rub her hands together from the cold. "This cold front has a sharper bite than forecasted."

She began to dig into the basket, withdrawing plastic containers full of his favorite food and placing them on the quilt within reach. "*Nee*, I'm good. If I get cold, we can always snuggle," she said and leaned against him for seconds, her words casual, her smile innocent and teasing. "You hungry yet?"

"That's a silly question." Isaac grabbed the paper plate she held out. He added two golden-brown chicken legs to a pile of German potato salad and dropped a sour pickle in the middle of the feast. "This food looks wonderful. Did you cook it?"

Molly took a generous bite of her corn on the cob. "*Nee*, Willa Mae cooked it special, just for you."

"That was nice of her," Isaac said around a forkful of creamy potato salad.

"She's one of the nicest women I know."

"She knows about our ruse?" Isaac wondered out loud.

"*Ya*, and she's all right with it, but she says you're too nice for your own good. That's why she fried the chicken and made potato salad for you. She knows it's something you order at the café and wanted to make the meal special for you. It's her way of saying thanks for helping out."

"That was nice of her, but not necessary." He expressed his gratitude by biting into a crunchy chicken leg.

"I know, but you're a kind and loyal friend. You deserve special treats."

Isaac looked down at his plate and moved his food around, his appetite suddenly gone. Molly's comment made him sound more like a faithful family dog than a suitor.

The musicians took a break, and people began to mill around, chatting in groups. Mothers cleared up their picnic spots, called to children playing close by. Isaac took the whoopie pie Molly handed him and placed it on his plate of half-eaten food.

"Something wrong?" Molly asked, her gaze searching his face.

Isaac shook his head. "I guess I'm not as hungry as I thought." He'd been pretending about a lot of things lately. The idea of a fake courtship didn't set well with him anymore. They were spending a lot of time together, and he realized he longed for her attention to be real, not pretend. Not a day went by that someone didn't ask him, "When's the wedding?" He found himself wanting to answer, "Christmas," but couldn't. Conviction ate at him. He knew the truth was always more profitable than a lie, but he couldn't let Molly down. Not when she needed him most.

Twilight brought a new round of people to the park and seemed to scatter the family folk with young children. Young *Englischers* walked the paths with their fingers intertwined, stopping to hug or steal a kiss. Molly watched Isaac talking with a couple of men from the church a few feet away. He looked handsome in his new blue shirt and black suspenders. She'd made the shirt herself, with Sarah's help. She'd even sewed snaps down the front, something she'd never been able to do before. He'd been so surprised when she'd presented her gift to him. She got the impression he hadn't received many presents in his life. She had no idea what his childhood had been like, if he had a good family, or if he had a good relationship with them. He never spoke of family back home. Someone named Rose was connected to him in some way, but Molly didn't let herself dwell on the woman. It was none of her business.

Echoes of her fight with her mother came back, stealing her joy. She'd only seen her *mamm* once since she'd asked her to leave her home. The day before, Ulla had been with Samuel Bawell at the café, their heads close together, as if plotting some new scheme to pull Molly back into their world. She fought down her anger and busied herself with clearing up the leftover food, determined not to let her mother's controlling behavior spoil her time with Isaac.

The band left for the night, and a few choir members sang gospel songs. The crunch of freshly fallen leaves made her glance to her side. Samuel Bawell stood there looking down at her, his feet just off the quilt, his smile bright.

"I didn't see you at choir practice. How have you been?"

"I'm *gut*. Just busy. And you?" Molly said, trying to be friendly without giving him false hope. There was no telling what her mother had told him about his chances with her.

"Oh, I've been fine, just fine." He tugged at his collar and snapped it closed. "I went wind sailing yesterday with some friends. It was quite the experience." He grinned, flashing sparkling white teeth. "I wish you had been there. I left a message for you at your job. I miss our time together."

"I was busy with work. I really didn't have time for answering messages or playing sports." Molly straightened her *kapp*.

"You'd have time for lots of things if you stopped resisting and married me."

His words hang in the air.

"Your *mamm* told me you've moved out. The bishop can't be happy with your actions. He's bound to call you in for counsel. Your reputation could easily be sullied."

"It's none of your business where I live or what I do, Samuel. We've had this conversation before. You know I don't love—" Molly began, only to have her words cut off by Samuel.

"*Ya*, I know you say you don't love me, but I'm not giving up, Molly. I love you. Have for years. You know that. I want to provide you with all the things you deserve. You could have a wonderful life with me. A big home, our children would want for nothing. Your *mamm*'s already said she's prepared to leave Pinecraft and come with us to Ohio if you're worried about being lonely."

Molly shook her head, exasperated.

"What could possibly stand in our way?"

"I could," Isaac said as he wandered over and placed a protective hand on Molly's shoulder. "Molly's not interested in you or your money. She doesn't need you."

Molly watched Samuel's gaze become intense. "And what can you offer her, Isaac Graber? Financial struggles for the rest of her life? Your children starving on your store's meager income? Is that really how you want her to live? Hand-to-mouth, wondering where the next meal is coming from? I can offer her so much more, and I have her mother's blessing. Why don't you step aside for Molly's sake? Do the right thing."

Molly rose from the quilt and stood next to Isaac, her arm going around his slim waist. "I think it's time you went your way, Samuel. Isaac and I are courting now, making plans for a Christmas wedding. I'm an adult. I don't need my mother's blessing to be wed." She took a deep breath and continued speaking as she walked up to Samuel. "And how Isaac and I manage financially is none of your business. Money isn't everything. Love is. You can tell that bit of news to my interfering *mamm*."

"I understand you're infatuated with him, Molly, but if you change your mind—"

"I won't change my mind. Isaac is a good man, who's loyal and honest. I love him. I once thought you were a nice man, too, but you're not. You're spoiled. You think only of yourself, the better things in life. And you're a bully, Samuel Bawell. Now go! Get out of here before I report *you* to Bishop Fischer. I think he'd be interested in knowing the way you've tried to intimidate me and push your way into my life." Molly motioned toward the path and repeated, "Go!"

Molly watched Samuel walk away. She didn't start to tremble until seconds later when she realized what she'd done. She'd placed Isaac in a very difficult position. Their pretend courtship could have easily been explained away when Samuel left Pinecraft if she'd only kept her mouth shut about love and a wedding date.

She and Isaac could have stopped seeing each other, told their friends the courtship didn't work out and that would have been the end of the farce. But her words of love for Isaac and comments on an upcoming Christmas wedding had firmly cemented them into a real relationship.

If Samuel repeated her declaration of their upcoming marriage to anyone, especially her *mamm*, her lie would have far-reaching repercussions and would be more difficult to explain away.

Molly dropped her head to her chest. Isaac hadn't bargained on anything more than a pretend courtship that might last a few weeks at best. Her lie was a sin, and she'd caused Isaac to sin by the act of omission.

Isaac deserved better than this. He'd become a good friend and tried to help. Now she'd paid him back for his generosity with lies. Lies that only she could set straight. Now they would have to go to the bishop and explain. She'd have to confess and ask for forgiveness, and hope that Isaac would be able to forgive her, too.

Chapter Thirteen

Ten minutes of waiting in Otto Fischer's office the next day had Isaac's stomach churning. His heart racing. What would happen now? He thought about the shop, and Mose's inexperienced nephew who was filling in for him.

He leaned forward and glanced at Molly. She sat straight and prim in a wooden chair next to her brother-in-law, Mose. Her pale blue dress accentuated the color of her fair skin and hair, making her lovelier than he had ever seen her.

Isaac smiled, trying to reassure her, but her brown eyes quickly darted away and focused on her hands. Her fingers continued to tear at the tissue he'd given her moments before.

The door opened and the bishop walked in, bringing with him the fragrant aroma of chicken pot pie, no doubt his noontime meal. He looked around the room, his sharp blue eyes taking in first Molly and Isaac, and then his son, Mose. Pulling out a chair, he made himself comfortable behind his desk. "I hear I have a bit

of bother to concern myself with instead of eating rhu-
barb compote and sponge cake under my shade trees."

Mose cleared his throat, as if to speak, but Molly
jumped up and spoke first. "I have sinned and drawn
Isaac Graber into my foolishness, Bishop Fischer."

Isaac watched her every move. He noticed her hands
trembling at her sides. His heart went out to her. He
stood, not willing to let her take all the blame. He'd
been at fault, too. He could have stopped seeing Molly,
ended the game. Instead, he'd pretended their courtship
was real. He wouldn't let her face this situation alone.
Not while he had breath in his body. "We both have
sinned," he stated.

Molly turned toward him, her face creased in frustration. "Isaac, please sit down! You've already done
enough. I won't have you taking my blame as your own.
We both know—"

Otto banged his empty coffee mug like a gavel. "Perhaps you both could sit down and give me a chance to
ask a few questions. I'll decide who's at fault here and
who's not."

Isaac felt like a reprimanded child. He dropped into
his chair and rubbed the side of his bad leg.

Molly slowly took her seat and tucked her feet under
her chair. She glared at Isaac and then glanced back at
Otto, who waited patiently behind his desk.

Mose stood. "I don't think this will take long, *Daed*.
Molly and Isaac have a problem regarding Ulla. They
spoke to me today, and I suggested they come to you
for counsel. We're hoping you can unravel this situation with as little repercussion as possible."

Otto stroked his beard, his forehead creasing. "Ulla,
huh. What has she done this time?" He turned toward

Molly, his lips curved into a sympathetic smile. "Speak up, child."

"Ah…you see. Oh, there is no way to make this story short, Bishop." Molly let her chin fall to her chest and used what was left of her tissue to dab at her eyes.

"I'm here, Molly. Let me help. My job is to lead and direct the good people of this community. Judgment comes from the Lord, not from me."

She lifted her chin. "My *mamm* and I have a difference of opinion. She wants me to marry Samuel Bawell. I told her I wouldn't under any circumstances. I'm twenty-one, not some *youngie* who doesn't know her own mind. She has no right to tell me who I can and cannot marry." She sucked in air and went on. "We quarreled and I got angry." She lowered her chin. "I moved out of my *mamm*'s home."

"I know your *mamm* can be—" Otto cleared his throat and seemed to choose his words carefully "—difficult when riled, but moving out on your own was not a prudent choice, Molly." He looked at her with an arched brow. "How long have you been living on your own?"

"Just a few days, *Daed*. Molly is staying with Sarah and me for now." Mose smiled as he informed his father of the news.

"*Gut, gut.* Go on, Molly."

"At Birky Square last night, Isaac and I were listening to music and Samuel Bawell…he, ah, he came over and asked me to marry him again. I turned him down, as I usually do. You see, my *mamm* gave him permission to marry me without my consent." She turned to Mose. "I don't want to marry Samuel. I never have. I don't love him, and I've told him so over and over. I got angry and spoke before I thought."

She shifted her gaze back to the bishop, her eyes glistening. "I told a lie, pure and simple." She sniffed and wiped at her nose. "I told Samuel that Isaac and I were courting, which wasn't true. We were only pretending to walk out together to keep *Mamm* out of my business." She dropped her head again. "Then I told Samuel that Isaac and I would be married by Christmas."

She shrugged. "I just wanted Samuel to go away and leave me alone, once and for all. Now I need *Gott*'s forgiveness and your help to get out of the mess I've created."

Molly drew in another deep breath and glanced at Isaac. "All Isaac did was go along with the pretense in order to help me. He didn't mean to sin. It was me," she said, her voice rough and high. "He's not at fault. I was the one—"

"*Ya*, so you said, Molly, but I still see Isaac as complicit in this matter." Otto turned toward Isaac. "He could have spoken up, corrected you."

Isaac nodded. "*Ya*, I could have, but I didn't."

Turning back toward Molly, Otto said, "I assume the news is out and Ulla knows about the impending wedding?" He rubbed his chin, pulling at his full beard as he waited for her response.

"I think so. I feel sure Samuel has told her and anyone else who'd listen. He was very angry when he left the park." Molly mopped the tears from her eyes.

Otto shifted his gaze back to Isaac. "You were there when Molly told this lie, and yet you kept silent. Why is that?"

Isaac nodded. "I didn't just keep silent. I added to the lie." Isaac felt his face heat with emotion. "The man's ego is as large as his bankbook. I lost my temper.

I didn't care if I became a part of the lie. I just wanted him to leave Molly alone."

Leaning forward in his chair, Otto tapped his fingers on the surface of his desk and pondered the situation for long moments. "Obviously you two are fond of each other, even protective." He glanced at both of them and flashed a quick smile. "It wonders me. Perhaps the way to correct this lie is by making the lie become truth. There's nothing wrong with an arranged marriage once in a while, even though it's not as popular among *youngies* as it once was. Sometimes arranged marriages are for the best."

Otto's smile reappeared, but broader now. "My parents picked my bride, and I've been a happy man for many years. Theda has proven to be my right arm, a real blessing in my life. I would hate to live without her wisdom and help. Your union can be the same, if you work at it. You said the wedding is to be in December?"

Molly nodded. "But—"

"Christmas weddings are the loveliest, though my schedule is already full. We'll work something out for you and Isaac," Otto remarked and then added, "Ulla will come 'round. You'll see. She'll want to be part of the planning and probably take over the arrangements." He laughed out loud, amusing himself.

Molly jumped up, her eyes large and round. She took a deep breath. "Bishop, you don't understand. We didn't mean for it to go this far. Isaac has no interest in marriage to anyone, especially to me, and I—"

Isaac stood with her, directed his gaze at Otto. He had to do something and fast. "You know better than most that the bike shop is struggling financially. If we married, I'd have nothing to offer Molly in the way of comfort or security." He struggled for breath, not sure what to say. If he didn't have his past to deal with, he would gladly agree to marry Molly under any circumstances, but not like this, with Otto forcing her hand. "I can't expect Molly to venture into a marriage without some security."

"This marriage solution is far better than her being unchurched, and that's how it will end if her *mamm* has anything to say about it, and you know she will. She'll stir the community into a frenzy, force my hand and ruin your name."

He looked at Molly, and she dropped her head again. "I'm sure you two will figure it all out, just like Theda and I did. We lived on cabbage and salt pork and received help from the community for the first two years of our marriage."

His gaze shifted to Isaac. "Theda never complained, and I'm sure Molly won't, either. We have a happy marriage and lots of rosy-cheeked grandchildren. You both can have this, too. Sometimes it's these impromptu moments in life that are the most fun. You'll see."

Molly sliced a desperate look Isaac's way and then turned back to Otto. "If only you'd—"

"There's no need to thank me, child. I'll announce the banns this coming Sunday morning. That should bring you peace with *Gott* and keep Ulla out of your hair for a while." Otto rose. "Now, it's time for my snack under the trees. Mose, show these two lovebirds out."

As they walked away from Otto Fischer's home a small rock in the road caused Molly to stumble. Isaac grabbed for her arm and steadied her.

"Danke," she said, not looking at him. She was too

embarrassed. What had just transpired was all her fault, and she'd firmly wedged Isaac in the middle of her mess.

She put one foot in front of the other, praying. Isaac was very quiet. Too quiet. She could only imagine what he was thinking, how he felt about being put in this kind of situation. He had no interest in marriage. He'd said as much in the meeting they'd just left. She glanced up at him. His face was hidden under the shadow of his black wool hat. *What is he thinking?* Was he concentrating on ways to get himself out of this predicament?

Isaac eased closer and asked, "Do you have a shift at the café today?"

"*Nee.* Willa Mae gave me the morning off. Why?"

"*Gut.* I thought we could…" He held down his hat as a brisk wind blew. "Perhaps you'd like to go to the park. Talk about things in private. There are things I need to tell you."

Molly pulled at the ribbon dancing against her neck. "*Ya*, okay."

Isaac took her arm as they waited for a cluster of bike riders to pass, then crossed the road leading to Pinecraft Park.

Fall leaves crunched underfoot as they made their way across the sun-drenched park, to the old picnic table positioned by a slow-moving creek. Several tourists and an Amish family of six, with homemade fishing poles poked under their arms, strolled past, offered greetings and warm smiles.

Molly did her best to respond to their friendly gestures, but her heart wasn't in it. She'd created a monstrous situation, turned Isaac's life upside down. He'd been threatened with being shunned, his reputation ruined. He had to be furious with her. She didn't look forward to the talk they were about to have, not that she didn't deserve every ounce of his anger.

Birds scattered as the couple trudged toward the worn picnic table and settled themselves across from each other. Molly was out of breath from their fast march, her slightly shorter leg causing her hip to hurt. She ignored her discomfort and searched for a clean handkerchief from her dress pocket. Her nose was stuffed from crying in frustration. Her lie, spoken impulsively and meant to ward off problems, had done nothing but seriously complicate her life and now Isaac's.

Her fingers rummaged around and found the white square of soft cotton. She shook it out and then blew her nose hard. She sniffed. She had to look a mess, her eyes puffy and her nose red.

Isaac said nothing. He seemed to be waiting for her to compose herself.

"I hope you know how sorry I am for all this. I should have never asked for your help. Please forgive me," Molly muttered, shifting uncomfortably on the wooden bench. She glanced up, studied the frown on his face.

"You owe me no apology, Molly. Let's talk calmly and rationally for a minute," Isaac suggested. "Let's just wait a few days, let things settle. I might be able to persuade Bishop Fischer to change his mind about a December wedding."

Molly stood, her frustration palpable. "I want that, too, but how do we manage to convince him? You heard what he said."

"Please. Let me finish," he urged, and motioned for her to sit.

Molly had no idea what his plan was, but she sat, arranging her skirt around her legs.

"We're both in this situation. You stretched the truth. I stretched it, too."

"Yes, but you didn't mean—"

"It doesn't matter what either of us meant now. I don't know about you, but I'm not okay with being unchurched, and if the bishop won't listen, then marriage is the only way out of this." He frowned as he spoke. "We've already asked for *Gott*'s forgiveness, so let's keep pretending we're all for this coming marriage and then maybe, if you want, we can back out at the last moment. I'll do something terrible that will give you an out. No one will even suspect, except maybe Mose and Bishop Fischer."

Molly wiped a tear from her eye. "Give me an out? You must be joking, Isaac. We didn't just buy a car that won't run and want to return it. Our bishop has just arranged our marriage. The rest of our lives kind of marriage."

She grabbed his hand. "I believe marriage is a sacred commitment, something a person doesn't enter into lightly. How can we just *not* get married if the bishop announces our banns and insists we go through with the wedding?" She gazed into his eyes, trying to read his mood.

"*Ya,* I know marriage is serious business," he finally said.

She dabbed at her nose. "In the meeting you said your business is just starting out, not bringing in enough money to support a family." Her brows rose in question. "Not once did you mention anything about feeling love or commitment to me. If you meant to fool the bishop that you really do love me, you failed miserably." Her face flamed hot. She looked down and murmured, "I know you don't love me, but the bishop doesn't. Shouldn't he think you do?"

Isaac leaned forward at the mentioned of the word love. He reached for Molly's hand, but she pulled away, determined to end the conversation.

Molly's mind raced. She needed to get away from Isaac, to think calmly without his searching eyes watching her so intently. He wore a pained expression. "I think I need to go home now."

"If you'll just let me speak, I can explain my hesitation," Isaac said, reaching for her again.

"No. You and I have both said enough. I need to think. This is not the way I envisioned speaking to my future husband about our coming marriage. No woman wants to be trapped in a loveless marriage, and we both know that could happen if your plan doesn't work. All my life I dreamed of a hero who would snatch me up into his arms and carry me off because he loved me, not because Otto Fischer says he must. *Gott* has a man in mind for me, and you're not that man."

Chapter Fourteen

Days passed without contact from Isaac. Christmas was fast approaching.

Theda skirted past Molly on her way to the refrigerator in Sarah's kitchen. "Why not use the electric mixer, *schatzi*?" The older woman smiled, her eyes fixed on the bowl of limp egg whites Molly was endlessly whisking.

Molly paused, moving her arm back and forth, ready to give up. She'd been working on the egg whites for a good five minutes, but wasn't getting anywhere with them.

"We're going to need that meringue in a few minutes. The pie crusts are almost brown and it won't take long for them to cool."

"*Ya*, my mind was on other things." Her mind had been a million miles away, thinking about Isaac, how fast time was flying, and not about the pie contest and auction on the church grounds later that day. She'd have to face Isaac again this afternoon, and she wasn't looking forward to it. Not after their talk in the park. Molly reached under the counter, grabbed the hand mixer and plugged it in.

"I can imagine your mind is on other things," Sarah said, giving her a wink.

The past few days Sarah had been hinting that she knew about the December wedding fiasco. She'd even made celery soup last night and commented at the dinner table how hard it was to find good celery for weddings this time of year.

Molly slowly added sprinkles of sugar to the frothy egg mixture until she saw the beginnings of peaks and was able to rev up the mixer's motor and drown out her own thoughts.

After church service tomorrow, there would be no turning back. Everyone would know about her and Isaac's courtship.

They would be officially engaged.

The men would start teasing Isaac about the quickly arranged wedding. The woman at the Anabaptist church she and Isaac attended loved planning winter weddings. They'd organize the event, with or without her help, making sure her color choice was used on the tables. They'd be asking her questions she didn't have answers to, talking about things she didn't want to deal with.

She turned off the mixer. The egg whites had peaked to perfection, despite her neglect. With a push of her finger, the frothy beaters dropped into the tub of sudsy hot water in the sink. She wiped down the mixer with a clean cloth and mindlessly unplugged it.

Molly had always thought her wedding day would be the happiest time of her life, but she didn't feel happy. She felt trapped into another loveless marriage. And, if their lie did come out, everyone would think she was an old maid who'd had to trick a man into marriage.

"Why so glum? You've always loved pie contests." Theda put her arms around Molly's shoulders and hugged her.

Tears began to swim in Molly's eyes. All she did was cry lately. She looked at Theda and saw compassion and understanding on the older woman's face. Molly broke down, tears flowing, holding on to Theda like a drowning child.

"That's right, *liebling*. You cry it out. Tell us how we can help," Theda said, patting her back.

"No one can help," Molly sobbed.

Sarah tore off a piece of paper towel and pressed it into Molly's hand. "Don't cry about the wedding. Everything will work out. You'll see."

Molly looked at Sarah. "You already know about the lie?"

Sarah nodded. "*Ya*, I know. We both do. Our husbands can't keep secrets from us." She grinned. "You'll see. Isaac will find it hard to keep secrets from you, too."

Theda led Molly to a kitchen chair and pulled one out for herself. "This wedding isn't the end of the world, *liebling*. Both Sarah and I started out our marriages on rocky ground, but look at us now. We're happy, our men content. So what if you told a lie to an unwanted suitor?" She put her hands on Molly's shoulders. "I might have done the same in your shoes. You've been forgiven by *Gott*, haven't you? He understands you and Isaac meant no real harm. *Gott*'s not punishing you. You're punishing yourself by thinking this arranged marriage is wrong and that *Gott* is not in it."

"But Isaac—" Molly moaned.

"Forget about Isaac. He's a man. He doesn't know what he wants. Time will bring him around," Theda assured her, patting Molly on the arm.

"He did nothing but help me, and it got him into this

mess. He didn't once mention he loved me when we talked," Molly sobbed, tears rolling down her cheeks.

"I wouldn't be so sure of that. I've seen how he looks at you when he thinks no one is watching," Sarah said. "Come on. Dry your tears, tidy yourself. Let's go to the church and help the ladies set up for the contest. Forget all of this for now. You have to trust in *Gott*'s will for your life."

Pedaling as fast as he could with a sore leg, Isaac rode through the empty streets of Pinecraft, his thoughts on what was facing him. Otto's wife had asked him to be one of the pie contest judges, but Molly would be there. They hadn't talked since she'd hurried away from the park days before, leaving him alone with his confused thoughts. He had no idea how she felt about their situation now that she'd had time to think.

At the side of the church, Isaac parked his bike, then dusted off the bottom of his black trousers before walking to the back lawn of the church.

Men were busy setting up tables, the women arranging chairs. Mose motioned for Isaac to join him. He ambled over, glancing around to see if he could find Molly. She was nowhere in sight, but he spotted Sarah and the children close by. Throwing his jacket across the back of a chair, Isaac lifted the other end of the table Mose was moving.

"*Gott* has given us a beautiful day, *ya*?" Mose said, walking backward toward several rows of tables close by.

"*Ya*," Isaac responded, pulling out a set of metal legs and helping to turn the table over.

"*Mamm* tells me she bullied you into being a judge."

Lifting another table, Isaac grinned at Mose. "She did. She's quite formidable for someone so small and fragile. She said it was my civic duty as a Pinecraft shop owner."

Mose laughed. "She used the same argument on me. Next year I'm not going to fall for her fresh apple pie and 'let's have a little talk.'"

"At least you got pie. I got an earful of 'loyalty to Pinecraft.' She even sent her grandson to the shop to fill in for me so I'd be free to judge." Isaac pulled out another set of legs at his end of the next table, and together the two men finished the last setup.

"Come on. Let's get something to drink before one of the women comes up with another job for us," Mose said, a twinkle in his eyes.

In a pink dress that made her cheeks look rosy, Molly stood behind the drinks table, wispy strands of hair blowing around her *kapp*, a bright smile on her face. She looked his way. Her smiled died a sudden death.

"Sweet tea or lemonade?" she asked Mose.

"Tea with extra ice," he said. "You look very nice today. Is that a new dress?"

"*Ya, danke.* I made it, with Sarah's help." She busied herself, adding more ice to his glass.

"You did a great job. Someday your husband will be proud of your money-saving talents," Mose said with a smile and stepped aside.

"Tea or lemonade?" Molly asked Isaac, her lips curved, but her eyes were not smiling.

"Lemonade, *bitte.*" Isaac took the glass she handed him and leaned in close. "Could we eat together later, after the pie contest?"

"I've got lots to do, Isaac. I'm not sure I'll have time for a meal."

"But we really need to talk," he murmured softly.

"*Ya*, we do, maybe later," Molly returned, ignoring him as she waited on the next person in line.

Mose put his arm around Isaac's shoulders and spoke to him like an older brother as they strode away. "Don't be discouraged. Women are strange but delightful creatures. They either love you or find you unbearably distasteful, and that can be in a single day." He laughed ruefully and downed the last of his tea in one long gulp.

Isaac watched Molly laugh out loud at something a beardless Amish man said. Jealousy ate at him. He wanted her to be that relaxed around him, show him the better side of her like she used to do, before the lie. He turned his head toward Mose. "*Ya*, I'm constantly in and out of hot water with Molly, and most of the time I have no idea why."

"My *daed* gave me some good advice years ago. He said, 'treat your wife with dignity and respect. Show your love in actions, not words.' I find it doesn't hurt if you make sure you come home while the food's still hot on the table, too. Use *Daed*'s bit of advice, and I can guarantee you'll always have a happy wife and kids."

"Kids?" Isaac hadn't thought about having *kinner*. If he and Molly did marry, children would be the natural result of their union. Was he ready to be a father? What if he became an angry, bitter old man like his own father? But then, he knew he didn't have to worry about children. Once Molly heard about his past, she'd break the engagement, finish with him for good. No one would blame her.

"Don't look so scared. *Kinner* are wonderful blessings from *Gott*. I can't wait for our next one to get here."

"But the responsibilities and money it takes to run a family… How do you handle the stress?"

Mose sat on a bench and made room for Isaac. "It's easy. I take each day as it comes and give all my concerns to *Gott*. He does the rest. He will for you, too."

"Molly doesn't love me." Isaac bowed his head, ashamed to be saying the hard, cruel facts out loud.

"Oh, I think she does. I know Molly. She wouldn't be letting *Daed* or her *mamm* put her in this situation if she didn't want to get married. The Molly I know is smart and resourceful. If she wanted out of this marriage arrangement, you'd be the first to know. Believe me. Deep down Molly has to know *Daed* wouldn't unchurch her over a lie, even if it is a big one." Mose looked at him and laughed. "*Nee*, not his Molly. She's like his own child."

"But why has she allowed Ulla to bully her into this rash decision?"

"Because deep down, Molly wants to marry you, *bensel*. Think about it."

Isaac sighed. He didn't know what to think. All he knew for sure was that his feelings for Molly had suddenly grown into something more powerful than his guilt about the past, or concern about his poverty. He was prepared to tell her about Thomas. He had to set the record straight, and today was as good a day as any. "*Ya*, you may be right. Maybe she does have feelings for me."

"Have you told her how you feel?"

"*Nee*. Not yet." Isaac rubbed his hands down his thighs, his stomach in a twist. "But I will."

All her chores done and too tired to care who won the pie contest, Molly gathered her belongings and crossed the church lawn, stopping only to bend and pat the old church cat who lived under the tool shed.

"Hello, kitty. You like your neck scratched? *Ya,* it's *gut.*" Silky soft, the adult cat began to purr and lean its body into her fingers.

"So you sneak away like a thief in the night."

Molly didn't have to turn. She knew who was speaking loud enough for everyone to hear. She stood and turned, facing her mother, not prepared to do battle in front of the whole church, but not in the mood to be mocked, either. "*Nee, Mamm.* Not sneaking away. Just going home. It's been a long day. I'm tired."

Dressed in a pale shade of blue, Ulla looked like she'd made an effort with her appearance today, something she seldom did. Her *kapp* was perfectly positioned, her dress starched and crisply pressed. "I see Isaac has already abandoned you. Too bad you didn't listen to your *mamm* about Samuel. He would never have left you to walk home alone."

She looked directly into her mother's eyes and spoke softly. "*Ya,* I know. Samuel is perfect. I've heard it a thousand times. I just don't happen to love Samuel. Doesn't that matter to you at all?"

"Is it a sin for a mother to want what is best for her younger daughter? *Nee,* I think not." Ulla tugged at Molly's arm, almost shaking her off balance.

Molly sighed. "What's best for me is—"

"You are too young to know what is best for you. You've proven that with your foolish choices. What has Isaac Graber got that Samuel didn't have? Samuel has money, a strong position in the community. Isaac has a run-down shop and no future here in Pinecraft. I've made a good match for you, but you whine about the foolishness of love. It's your financial future you should be most concerned about."

"Didn't you love *Daed* when you married him?" Molly jerked her arm away.

"Your father." Ulla laughed, her words grating. *"Nee,* I didn't love him. Not for one moment. He was weak and dull, even as a young man. I wed to get out of my parents' *haus,* to have freedom, but all I got was hard work and children."

"But *Daed* loved you," Molly declared, her voice rising slightly. "He worked until the day he died providing for us."

"Ya, well, that he did, but it wasn't enough. He and I struggled our whole life, and when he died he left me penniless, and I continued to struggle to support you and your sister. Do you know how it will feel to have to rely on the community for food?" Ulla leaned in, her voice lowered. "That's why I've been courting John. I'm going to marry him. There will be no more leaning on people who whisper behind my back and gossip."

Ulla lifted her hands, as if to shove Molly away. "But go your own path. Find this foolish love that brings you so much happiness. As for me, I will do as I always do. Take care of myself." Ulla turned and walked through the cluster of muttering onlookers, her back straight and proud.

Molly felt strong arms slip around her shoulders and turned to find Isaac, his face etched in anger as he watched her mother stride away.

Chapter Fifteen

Isaac lowered himself, sitting on the same deck step as Molly. He watched as she dug her toes into the green grass underfoot, her flip-flops tossed to one side. Today was the first time he'd seen her tiny feet bare. She always wore black dress shoes with thin stockings. He suspected the pale pink nail polish on the tips of her toes had something to do with her niece Beatrice.

Molly turned toward him, her face still blotchy from all the crying she'd done as they walked back to Mose and Sarah's house together after the pie contest.

"I'm always saying *danke* to you, Isaac," she murmured, her voice low, the wind catching her words of apology and carrying them away.

"What are you thanking me for now?"

She surprised him when she rested her head on his shoulder for a few moments and then whispered, "For putting up with all the drama. For being there when I need you most." She took a deep breath, gave him a watery grin and then looked away. "I'm sorry you had to deal with my wailing. All I seem to do lately is cry like a fool. You must have been embarrassed with all those people walking past, gawking at me."

"I have to admit it's not every day I walk down the street with a sobbing woman on my arm, but for you, anything." He grinned at her, but her chin was down again, her shoulders slumped.

"We have to have a serious talk." Molly sat upright, her voice hoarse from crying. She shielded her eyes from the sun shining through the tree's canopy overhead. "We can't allow the banns to be announced tomorrow." Scooting closer, her expression turned hopeful. "Perhaps you should try and talk to Bishop Fischer again, convince him you have no interest in marriage, especially to me. I would completely understand if you told him I was an unfit woman, not the kind you want to tie yourself to. He'd probably have something to say, but isn't getting lectured better than a marriage you don't want?"

"I could try to talk to him, but I've grown kind of fond of the idea of marrying you." He shoved back the bill of his black wool hat and pretended to write in the air. "Mrs. Isaac Graber. It has a nice ring… Don't you think?"

Molly twisted, her knees bumping his legs. "You can't be serious." Her dark eyes grew round with surprise.

"I am," Isaac proclaimed. "I'm very serious. I've been doing a lot of thinking. It's time I marry. I need a wife. Someone to do my laundry and cook my meals. I need to be practical." He smiled at her as he said the last sentence, but his stomach was in a ball of knots. He was stalling. He had to say the right words, how he really felt about her, about what he'd done to Thomas.

"Yes, but what about love and commitment? Are you willing to marry without love?"

"You seemed fond enough of me just a moment ago."

His brow went up in a suggestive manner. "You just had your head on my shoulder, and that's an outrageous act for a woman who insists she's not courting me and says she feels no affection."

"We aren't courting," she declared and then amended her statement with a shake of her head. "Well, not really courting. It's all an act. You know it. I know it. You only agreed to help stave off Samuel's unwanted advances. Otherwise I would never have asked—"

"What? Asked me to court you?" He pushed his thumbs under his suspenders and snapped them. "I think I'm a pretty fair catch, considering the considerable lack of local young men to pick from."

"Has anyone ever told you that you're conceited, Isaac Graber?"

"Nope. You'd be the first." Isaac shrugged. "Why don't we just go along with the ruse, let the banns be read, continue to court each other and see what happens. You never know. We might end up—"

The back door flew open and Beatrice ran out onto the deck, shouting, "Aunt Molly, come quick! *Mamm*'s having the baby."

Working on autopilot, Isaac managed to cook a bubbling pan of franks and beans and not burn the simple meal. He peeled three bananas and sliced them, chopped in a couple of apples and added a few walnuts chunks to the fruit salad.

A green grape tossed high in the air landed in his mouth. He chewed as he topped off the healthy dessert with the handful of the juicy green grapes.

"How long has it been now?"

Isaac placed three small plastic plates on the table

and then answered Mose. "Five hours, but who's counting?"

Mose tied a handmade bib of terry cloth around Levi's chubby neck and kissed the little boy on his rosy cheek. "He wants his *mamm*. He's been crying for hours. Sarah would have a fit if she knew I was feeding the *kinner* this late in the evening, but—"

"You've been a bit busy, Mose. Don't be so hard on yourself. The *kinner* are strong. They won't die from eating cookies once in a while instead of a hot meal."

"Shh. Not so loud. Sarah might hear and come out of that bed. I know her. She's a stickler for routine and homemade meals." Mose smiled, but there was no joy in his grimace. Just worry.

"*Mamm* said our sister will be here soon," Beatrice declared, her excitement visible in her shining eyes and the toothy grin that exposed her first missing tooth.

"Did you sneak into that room again?" Mose demanded, his tone harsher than usual.

Beatrice shrugged. "Yes, but Mercy told me to do it. She wanted to see *Mamm*." She pointed at her younger sister and almost fell out of her chair trying to avoid her finger being bitten by her younger sister.

"You both went in?" Mose's brows rose.

"No, I only went in. Molly pushed me out the door."

"*Gut*, I'm glad she did. You must not bother your *mamm* right now. She and Molly are very busy, and they don't need *kinner* around." He turned toward his younger daughter and frowned. "Mercy, don't bite your sister. We've talked about this many times. You must be a *gut* girl."

Mercy's face puckered, preparing for a boisterous wail. Mose dropped into the chair next to Levi and spooned food into the baby's mouth as he thundered, "Enough, both of you." He wiped Levi's face with a napkin and lowered his voice. "Eat your meal."

Isaac stuck a forkful of beans in his mouth and chewed. *So, this is what it's like to be a* daed. No wonder his own father often walked the back acres of their farm. Probably to get away from his own *kinner*.

He grinned as Beatrice glanced over at him, her mouth bulging with fresh fruit, a twinkle of mischief in her eyes. Her father's tirade hadn't affected her one bit. She was getting a new sibling, and nothing was going to spoil her mood. She insisted the child was going to be a girl, and Isaac secretly hoped she was wrong. Every man needed sons, but a better son than Isaac had been to his own father. He had pushed his *daed* away because of the man's strict rules. Rules that had probably kept him safe and grounded throughout his life until Thomas's death.

Levi began to raise a fuss, squirming, his short legs trying to push out of his chair. Mose wiped at the tot's mouth, stood the tiny boy on the floor. The child toddled toward the toy box a few feet away. "That's right. You play while we eat, son. *Mamm*'s busy right now, but she'll be wanting you soon enough."

He looked over at Isaac after wiping down the girls' faces and hands and excusing them from the table. "What could be taking so long? Sarah had Levi so quickly. I was hoping…" His words trailed off. He tugged at his beard as he glanced toward the hallway, then jumped out of his chair as the doorbell chimed. "That'll be *Mamm*. She's come to help Molly deliver the *bobbel*."

Isaac gathered up the dishes, scraping leftovers into the bin. He'd had this job at home as a young boy, his mother believing her sons should know how to fend for themselves in the kitchen as well as her daughters.

Theda hurried into the kitchen, her skirt swinging as she made the sharp turn into the hallway and quickly greeted him. "Hello, Isaac. Forgive me, but I must hurry."

Isaac watched as Otto Fischer patted his son on the back. Mose spoke, his words only for his father's ears. Otto hugged his son, holding on to his hand as he said, "*Ya*, well. This is true, but you should not fret. Sarah will be fine. Greta's death was unfortunate, but not something that happens every day. You know *Gott* is with your *frau*. Soon the *bobbel* will be born. *Gott*'s will be done."

Needing to keep himself busy, Isaac put a kettle of water on to boil and lined up mugs for coffee. It might be a long night, and something hot to drink would soothe the nerves.

"Ah, I thought I heard someone fiddling around in here." Otto stood just inside the kitchen archway, his hat in hand, the gray hair on his head standing to attention from fingers the older man kept running through his disheveled mop. "You're here with Molly?"

"*Ya*, I came to talk to her about the wedding," Isaac said.

"This is a *gut* thing you do, Isaac Graber." He walked closer and patted him on the back. "Keep your heart open. All this nonsense about lies and Ulla's persistence will pass, and you'll have a fine wife to go home to each night. You mark my words. Molly is a loving woman, but a bit spirited like her *mamm*," he interjected with an amused shrug. "All her life Molly's been a jewel to this community. She can be counted on in a pinch. She'll not disappoint you."

Isaac added a scoop of instant coffee to each cup and stirred, listening to Otto Fischer's words and agreeing with him. He wanted to confess he already had strong feelings for Molly, but didn't say a word. The time wasn't right. Not until she'd heard his story and accepted his past. Until then he would keep words of love to himself.

Drenched in sweat, Sarah writhed on the bed, her body doubled-up in pain. Molly glanced over at the bedside clock. It had been less than two minutes since the birth of the rosy-cheeked baby boy with hair the color of corn. But Sarah still suffered pains as regular as hard labor. Molly had witnessed this situation only once, but felt sure she knew what was happening.

"I feel the need to push again," Sarah cried out, her eyes wild, pleading for help.

Molly and Theda worked as a silent team. The older woman slipped a sliver of ice into Sarah's mouth as Molly pulled back the sheet to do a quick physical examination, and then gasped as a baby shot to the foot of the bed, its tiny body blue and covered in mucus and blood.

Reaching for the soft cloth shoved into the waistband of her apron, Molly gently wiped at the baby girl's mouth and nose, feverishly remembering procedures for underweight babies, facts she'd been taught by her mother. Not bothering to cut the cord yet, she siphoned out what she could from the baby's mouth and then lifted the baby and blew quick, gentle puffs of air into her lungs. Using her finger, Molly cleared the baby's small air passage, blew again and then used her hand to form a funnel for the air to flow through. Molly's heart beat loud in her ears. *Gott, help me. Breathe life into this baby's body.*

"My *bobbel*," Sarah wailed, struggling to sit up. "Is it alive? Please, *Gott*. Let it be alive."

"Don't fret, Sarah. Molly has everything under control. Your *bobbel* will be just fine," Theda promised, her gaze shifting between Sarah and Molly's quick movements.

The blond-haired baby twitched and then moved stronger in Molly's hands, its heart-shaped mouth opening like a tiny bird's as it took in gasps of air and released a whimpering cry. Right before Molly's eyes, the baby's body began to grow pink with life, her cries growing stronger, more robust. "She's alive, Sarah. Your baby girl is alive," Molly sobbed, the stress of the moment taking a toll. "But she's very tiny, maybe four pounds. We should get her to the hospital to be examined by a pediatrician."

Theda rushed to the foot of the bed, assisting as best she could.

Pale and damp with sweat, Sarah's mouth formed a wobbling smile. "Oh, *danke*, *Gott*, *danke*." She fell back against the pillows, weeping softly.

Molly wiped away a tear and waited while Theda tied off the cord in two places, her fingers working nimbly. The surgical knife quickly sliced through the cord, and then Theda swaddled the baby into a soft receiving blanket and placed it into Sarah's waiting arms. "She's a tiny little thing, but her coloring is good," Theda reassured the happy mother. "Keep her against your chest.

She needs to stay warm. Molly will call for an ambulance to take you and the *bobbels* to the hospital."

Molly nodded as she wiped off her hands and rushed to the greatroom, her legs flying.

Mose and Isaac looked up as she entered, their excited expressions turning to shock as she babbled, "We'll need an ambulance right away. Sarah's had another baby—a girl—but she's small and needs to be checked out by a doctor."

"But..." Mose stammered, grabbing for his work phone and punching in 911. He glanced over at Isaac and then to his son, cradled in his *daed*'s arms. "Twins? How could she have been pregnant with two and none of us know?"

"Sometimes the smaller baby is behind its larger sibling and its heartbeat isn't heard. The doctor will explain it all soon. I need to get back to Sarah. Hurry, Mose. She and the babies should get to the hospital as soon as possible."

Mose rushed toward the bedroom with Molly as he spoke into the phone, barking the emergency circumstances and his address in Pinecraft.

Isaac stood, his feet rooted to the floor. Molly gave him a grin and patted his cheek before rushing off toward the bedroom.

Locking up the shop, Isaac waved good-night to his new part-time salesman, then turned toward the café, his stomach rumbling. Twinkling Christmas lights beckoned to him from across the dark street.

He dashed between two slow-moving cars and paused at the café door, admiring the beautifully painted nativity scene on the big glass window. Baby

Jesus lay in a straw-filled manger, a contented smile on His face…contentment Isaac now shared. He knew life was precious, and Molly saving Mose and Sarah's baby daughter tonight made life seem even more precious. Isaac was proud of her abilities as a midwife, and found himself still smiling as he walked through the café door and searched for an empty spot among noisy *Englisch* and Amish customers.

He glanced around as he shimmied into an empty bench seat, recognizing several familiar families from church. Tomorrow everyone there would know about his engagement to Molly. He sighed, wishing Molly shared the excitement building in him. They were to be married soon, but he knew she still wasn't okay with the plans Otto had laid out for them. He placed his black hat on the café table and ran his hand through his hair.

"What can I get you, Isaac?" Willa Mae appeared next to him, her hands pressed in just above her apron, where her waistline used to be.

He smiled his greeting. "I've never known you to take table orders. Short-staffed tonight?"

Pen poised above a square tablet, Willa Mae grinned a surly smile, showing off her gold-capped front tooth. "Been short-staffed all day. Nothing new in Pinecraft. Employees drop out of sight and don't bother to call in sick. It's the sea. Something strange happens to people when they live close to it. You'll see. Being a shop owner so close to the beach is a hardship." Willa Mae laughed, the sound reverberating through the room, reminding Isaac of the red-suited *Englischer* Santa. "What can I get you?"

"A bowl of your delicious beef stew, if you have any

left," Isaac muttered, adding, "with a corn muffin and lots of butter."

"Good choice. The stew's been simmering all day." She scribbled, and her dark eyes glanced at him. "Anything to drink?"

"*Kaffi*, black and strong."

"Kinda late for coffee. You have a bad day?"

He grinned. "Not bad, really, just different. Molly delivered twins, and I was around to see her in action. She's a take-charge kind of woman when it comes to delivering babies."

"That girl's strong-willed and bullheaded, just like her mama."

Isaac frowned, his brow arched in disbelief. "I'm surprised you'd say she's like her *mamm*. I thought you liked Molly."

Willa Mae squeezed into the empty bench seat across from him, her smile gone as she held his gaze. "Look, I've got no use for Ulla, and never have had, but she's not all bad. Sure she has a mind of her own, but so does Molly." Willa Mae's hands went palms up. "For as long as I've known that little girl, she's been kind and loving, but she has an independent streak as wide as they come. Molly won't admit it—" a smile lit up her face as she spoke Molly's name "—but she's got all her mama's good traits and a few of her bad ones, too. The strong-spirited part she got from Ulla. It's got her in and out of trouble all her life."

Isaac scratched the heavy grizzle on his chin. "She is headstrong, but she's not mean-spirited. Not like Ulla."

She touched him on the arm, her tone quiet. "My old mama taught me not to go judging people. We don't know what motivates that streak of mean in Ulla. Could be she's miserable on the inside, like some old dog with fleas. Misery does strange things to a body. You just be glad Molly doesn't have that mean-spirited part of Ulla's personality." Willa Mae laughed again. "Listen to me spouting off the mouth, taking that old woman's side when she wouldn't give me the time of day. I'll get that stew." Willa Mae cackled as she rose and moved toward the back of the café, greeting her customers and wishing them Merry Christmas as she went.

Thoughts of his run-ins with Molly ran through Isaac's mind. She was headstrong like her *mamm* and determined to stay single. He didn't exactly know what motivated her hesitancy, but perhaps he'd have to re-think his approach toward their upcoming marriage, or lose the independent woman he'd grown to care about. She wouldn't be pushed and might run when she found out about his past.

Racing to get out of the sudden downpour, Molly scrambled through the café's employee entrance, patting rain off her face with the hem of her dress.

Willa Mae poked her head out of the kitchen and laughed at Molly's disheveled appearance. "I told you it was going to rain. My ole joints are never wrong."

"Wish your joints would have told you the rain was coming with high winds and hail the size of olives. I would have gotten a ride home." Her *kapp* slipping to the side, Molly pulled out several pins and repositioned it as she laughed at the silly face Willa Mae pulled.

"Your mama's not right about much, but she's right about one thing. You do have a smart mouth, child."

"I'm sorry. I was just teasing," Molly said with a smile. She prowled the hall wall, searching for the next week's shift list and found it scribbled on the back of a white envelope haphazardly stuck to the wall with a red thumbtack next to several Christmas cards from longtime customers.

Gut, she had Sunday off, but she didn't look forward to church. Otto would be announcing her and Isaac's engagement. She drew in a deep breath, wishing she could be happy about the occasion. She had strong feelings for Isaac, but the idea of trapping him into a marriage he didn't want brought her no joy.

"You have a busy day off?" Willa Mae asked, wiping her damp hands on a dish towel.

"Not really busy, but definitely exciting."

"Here, too." Willa Mae snapped her hairnet back over her ears and washed her hands. "That new girl I hired never showed up for her shift. I been waiting tables like I've got good legs, and you know that's not the case." Willa Mae leaned back and twisted, her spine cracking.

Molly grabbed a clean apron and threw it over her wrinkled dress. "I'll finish her shift and help you clean up at closing."

"You sure? You look beat."

Molly washed her hands next to her boss, her thoughts on what had transpired during the day. "I'm fine, just a little tired from delivering the Fischer babies today."

"Yeah, I heard the good news from Isaac." Willa Mae flipped two sizzling hamburger patties and placed a slice of cheese on both.

"The multiple birth came as a real surprise to us all, but everyone's doing fine now."

"That Fischer woman's gonna have her hands full."

"I know, but she's up to it." Molly quickly rinsed her hands and grabbed a handful of paper towels. "What can I help you with first?"

Willa Mae poked her head out the service window, looked around and then pulled it back in. "Table three needs menus and looks like table five's ready for their second slice of my mama's red velvet cake."

Molly took a quick glance, as well, then pulled back in surprise. Isaac sat in the corner booth, a warm smile lighting up his face as a young girl dressed in a simple pink blouse and jeans leaned across the table and grabbed for an extra napkin. Molly's jaw went slack. "How long has Isaac been talking to her?" Molly whispered, her voice low.

"Not long. Why?"

Molly licked her dry lips. Could this be the girl who had been writing to Isaac? He hadn't said much about his family back in Missouri, but the girl had the same hair coloring and piercing green eyes as Isaac. She could easily be his sister or cousin they looked so much alike.

"He seems to know her pretty good," Willa Mae said, her brow lifting.

"Ya," Molly responded. The young girl spoke, leaning in close. Isaac laughed.

Eyes narrowed, Molly watched as the young brunette brushed back long strands of hair falling across one shoulder. Her youthful giggle floated on the air toward the kitchen.

"Got any idea who she is?" Willa Mae shifted over so Molly could get a better view of what was going on.

"I think so." It was time to find out if this was Rose.

Molly hurried out of the kitchen. She grabbed the coffeepot and headed toward the occupied tables. Two feet from Isaac's booth, she paused and took a deep breath, then casually walked past, her attention on a middle-aged *Englischer* woman with an empty mug.

Three empty mugs later, she headed back toward Isaac and caught him watching her.

"I thought you were off all day," he said in greeting.

She set the coffeepot on an empty table and strolled close. "I was, but Willa Mae needed a hand closing." She looked at the girl across from Isaac and smiled. "Hello, my name's Molly."

"I thought as much. You look just like Isaac described you."

"Molly, this is my little *schweschders*, Rose. She started her *rumspringa* last week and decided to come down on the bus for a quick visit to Pinecraft."

"It's good to meet you," Molly said with a smile, and tugged on her prayer *kapp*. "Seems like you're enjoying your momentary freedom."

"*Ya. Daed* isn't so happy with me traveling alone all this way, but I like to put his teeth on edge. *Mamm* understands my decision to take some time away, so I can decide what I want to do with the rest of my life."

Molly smiled, thinking of her own *rumspringa* and her *daed*'s reaction to her not wearing her prayer *kapp*. "*Daeds* are that way. Always protective of their *kinner* from the *Englischer* world."

Her green eyes sparkling bright, Rose grabbed Molly's hand. "Isaac tells me your banns will be read tomorrow. I'm so happy he's found someone like you after what he went through after Thomas's death."

Molly cut her eyes toward Isaac. Who was Thomas?

Chapter Sixteen

Frazzled after organizing breakfast and dressing Sarah and Mose's three lively, uncooperative children, Molly answered the door.

Theda stood on the porch in the bright sunshine, her reddish hair a riot of uncontrollable curls under her *kapp*. "You look worse for wear, *mein liebling*." She set a plate of iced cupcakes covered in plastic wrap on the small table near the door and put out her arms.

Molly gratefully turned a crying Levi over to his doting *grossmammi*, then picked up the plate of cupcakes. The women headed toward the kitchen.

"*Ya*, I am tired," Molly assured her and then added, "Thank you for bringing these. They'll be a great distraction for Beatrice and Mercy. They keep asking for their *mamm* and new siblings."

Both girls ran to meet their *grossmammi*, accepting kisses and pats on the head with bright smiles.

"I'm sorry to leave you with such a mess in the kitchen," Molly said, the hair around her face and neck damp with sweat. She'd felt so confident when Mose left early that morning for a church meeting. She'd been in charge of the *kinner* before, but today they were uncontrollable. "There just wasn't time to clean up and get the *kinner* dressed, too. I don't know how Sarah manages."

The older woman promptly grabbed a tissue from her pocket, gave Levi's runny nose a swipe, making the *bobbel* fuss even more. She held him on her shoulder and began a soothing back rub. "It's a process, *liebling*." She raised her voice to be heard over Levi's protests. "Organization is something a mother acquires as she goes along, building her family, one by one. You'll get the hang of it. I promise you."

The image of a tiny boy with Isaac's green eyes and her hair flashed through her mind. She dismissed the thought as foolish. She'd never have children with Isaac. Pretending to be courting the dark-haired man had left her addle-brained and wishing for things she couldn't have. "I hope you're right. I'm sorry to leave you on your own, but I have to hurry." She slipped her shoes on. "I'll be back in a few hours. Are you sure you'll be able to manage these three alone?"

Theda smiled at the two little girls at her feet. "Oh, yes. Beatrice and I have an understanding, don't we, sweet one?" She patted Beatrice on the face. "As long as she behaves, I reward her for good behavior."

Beatrice nodded and smiled at her *grossmammi* and then turned toward the plate of cupcakes on the kitchen table. "I'll be *gut*, but Mercy might be naughty."

They both laughed at Beatrice's statement, but Molly remembered the time and hurried off to change her dress.

Ten minutes later she scurried out of the house, her pink dress flapping behind her as she ran the few blocks to the church. She would be late now, and she'd wanted to be early. She needed to talk with Isaac before services began. They hadn't been able to talk privately the night before with his sister there, but she knew one of them had to talk sense into Otto Fischer soon or their banns would be announced and serious damage done.

Overwarm and out of breath a few minutes later, Molly stood at the end of the line of young women entering the church's side door.

"You're about to lose your *kapp*," Rachel Lapp, an old school friend and bride-to-be, whispered in Molly's ear. Molly had always envied Rachel. The girl had a sweet, encouraging *mamm*, emotions she had always longed for from Ulla.

Rachel and Ralf Yoder had been an item for years. No one was surprised when they'd announced their wedding plans just before singing practice last October.

Molly scrambled to pull out pins and reposition her prayer *kapp*, her fingers trembling, making the process difficult.

Rachel smiled back at her. "Rumor has it you and Isaac will be announcing your intentions today."

Before she could think, she blurted out, "Who told you?"

With a wink, Rachel smiled. "No one. I just was guessing."

Molly's shoulders fell. She had leaked out her own secret. "*Ya*, well." What could she say to dispel the lie? Nothing, because the lie was fast becoming the truth whether she liked it or not.

Rachel pushed a pin into Molly's *kapp* for her and fussed with her hair for a moment. "We can't have Isaac seeing you look a mess."

"Danke." She ran her trembling fingers down her prayer *kapp*'s ribbons.

"You seem really nervous, Molly. Maybe you haven't taken enough time to think this engagement through. You've only known Isaac a little while, and courting is such a huge step." Dimples appeared in the girl's cheeks. "Ralf and I dated for two years, but now we can hardly wait to be wed. We've bought a house and started looking at furniture."

Ready to choke on the knot forming in her throat, Molly smiled, hoping her face expressed joy and not the horror she was feeling. "Oh, we're sure. We've done nothing *but* talk about this courtship." Announcing a wedding date, making promises to wed in front of her church family was an important step, and she and Isaac were making a mockery of it. This promise to *Gott* that was meant to be sacred. She had to stop all this somehow.

Isaac glanced around and searched for Molly in the line of worshippers entering the church. He got a fleeting glimpse of Chicken John and Ulla seated several chairs down from him. What were they doing in the engaged-couples row? Molly had mentioned her mother would be getting married, but he'd assumed it was just one of Ulla's stories, something said to upset Molly, who had been close to her father.

Where was Molly? She should have been there by now. He forced himself to sit still and then relaxed as he noticed her standing in a pool of early-morning sunlight just inside the church's side door. She stepped into the building with several other somber-faced young women, a line of school-aged girls following close behind.

Mose waited a few feet away and made a move in Molly's direction. Isaac watched him take her elbow and speak quietly in her ear. She said something to her brother-in-law, her brown eyes animated and sparking fire. She shook her head emphatically. She glanced in Isaac's direction. Her expression told him what he needed to know. She didn't want to join him in the engaged-couples row. Whatever Mose was saying, she was having none of it.

His stomach knotted. Bile threatened another stomachache. Isaac rose but then saw Molly's shoulders droop in surrender. She nodded as Mose spoke again and followed him over to where Isaac stood, her gaze downcast.

Mose greeted Isaac with a firm handshake and a pat on the back. "I see someone told you where to sit."

"*Ya*, one of the elders." Isaac tried to read Molly's expression as he spoke, but got nothing but a glassy stare from her. She sat on the bench where he'd been sitting. Her back ramrod straight, her hands piously folded in her lap, she looked straight ahead.

"How are Sarah and the *bobbels*?" Isaac asked.

Mose's face lit up at the mention of his wife and babies. His smile was generous. "Oh, they're fine. Just fine. Our little girl is small, but doing fine. The doctor said we owe her life to Molly's expert care. We're so grateful she is a skilled midwife and knew exactly what to do with our surprise *bobbel*." He grinned at Molly, who softened visibly.

Movement at the front of the church had Mose dismissing himself and moving away. He took his place in the line of preachers and deacons who would preach that day.

Molly scooted away, leaving more room than Isaac needed. He tried to catch her gaze as coming church activities were announced at the front of the church, but she stayed focused on the speaker. With a casual twist of her wrist, she dropped her plain white handkerchief to the floor.

Isaac bent to pick up the square white fabric and turned in surprise as Molly bent, too, their heads almost colliding.

"This farce has got to be stopped, Isaac Graber," she whispered, facing him.

"It's too late. Now is not the time—"

"And when *is* the time? After we are tied together with invisible ropes that can't be broken?" Her brown eyes snapped with anger. She straightened, the handkerchief clenched in her fist.

The first song of the morning began. Isaac wanted to sing, but couldn't remember the beautiful song's words, his mind too busy thinking of Molly. She was angry, and he couldn't blame her.

But what could be done about it now?

Two hours later, well-wishers clogged the door of the church. Molly pasted on a smile and pretended to be joyously happy.

"When's the wedding?" an old school friend Molly hadn't seen all winter asked.

"Two weeks, maybe less." She accepted a hug from the animated girl. Molly wanted to be anywhere but here in her home church, telling the good people of Pinecraft she was to marry when she knew every word she spoke was a lie.

A small voice of guilt murmured in her mind. *One*

lie upon another. The situation had snowballed out of control, and she had no one to blame but herself.

She accepted another warm embrace from Belinda, a shy girl she'd met and befriended years ago. They'd joined the singing group together, and now both were to be wed. She listened to her friend's words about the food they'd be serving at her wedding, what her special dress was made of.

Molly smiled, but wanted desperately to cry. She had no special dress being made, no house to live with Isaac and no date to announce. Their courtship was nothing but a sham. It took every ounce of strength she had to hold her tongue and not blurt out the truth.

The crowd was thinning, and Molly saw her *mamm* and Chicken John making their way toward them. Her mother grabbed her wrist just as Molly turned away.

"No! Wait, please, Molly," Ulla urged.

Isaac stepped in front of Molly, shielding her. "This is not the time or place for another argument, Ulla. I know you're Molly's *mamm*, but I am to be her husband. I'll have no—"

"Ulla and I have no wish to create chaos, Isaac," Chicken John reassured him. As the bald little man spoke, he kept a white-knuckled grip on his black Sunday hat. "We merely want to wish you both congratulations and a happy life together."

Ulla sniffed, her eyes glistening with tears. She released Molly's wrist and cleared her throat before she spoke, her voice hoarse. "Please give me a moment with *meine dochder*, Isaac. I have things I must say before she weds."

Molly stiffened, ready for the condemnation she

knew was coming. Her mother always had an agenda, and this time would be no different.

Isaac glanced at Molly. She gave a curt nod, her stomach heaving. "*Ya*, I will speak with her, but only for a moment." She moved a few feet away. Ulla followed. The two men stood back, waiting.

Her mother's body trembled as she spoke. "*Gott* has been dealing with me harshly for days. I must make my confession known to you." Ulla's chin dropped. "I've been hard on you." The older woman glanced at her husband-to-be. Chicken John smiled his encouragement, his expression hopeful. She looked back to Molly. "John has helped me to see the error of my ways. I have been harsh and often cruel." Her voice broke several times as she continued, "I took my grief out on…you when your *daed* died…and then your sister so soon after."

Ulla took a deep breath and held Molly's gaze, tears sparkling in her eyes. "When Greta died, I died, too. I thought only of myself, of my pain." She began to sob in earnest, her face pinched. "I became bitter and cruel." She took in a shuddering breath. "I am ashamed of my behavior. I gave no regard for your feelings, what you were going through. You were always such a good *kinner*. Kind and respectful."

Ulla grasped Molly's arm again, her fingers cutting into her flesh, her gaze intense, almost desperate. "You've grown into a godly woman, a *dochder* I should be proud of." Ulla swallowed hard. "I need your forgiveness, Molly. Please. Before I go mad with regret."

Molly sidestepped away from her mother, her face warm with threatening tears. Her stomach quivered with nerves. *Could* Mamm *be saying all this to make*

Chicken John think she's changed? She desperately wanted to believe her mother had changed for the better.

"Please forgive me, Molly," Ulla urged, taking her hands in hers. Her *mamm*'s chin wobbled as she seemed to search for the right words. "I've been so cruel and demanding. I have no excuse for my selfishness, except that I had a broken heart. I handled things badly and made your life miserable when I should have been comforting you. You lost Greta, too. I'm sorry for all my sins. Please say you forgive me." Tears ran freely down the older woman's wrinkled face as she waited for Molly's response.

Isaac walked forward and slid his arm around Molly's waist. He gave her a gentle squeeze. She glanced up at him, thankful for his bolster of strength.

Trembling, her eyes brimmed with tears. She turned back to face her mother and then slipped her arms around her shoulders. "I forgive you, *Mamm*. No more talk of the past. I have no right to judge." Molly smiled, but her lies ate at her soul. "Today we begin anew as *mamm* and *dochder*."

Chicken John joined them. "*Ya*, this is *gut*, but it makes me to wonder if it's not time to follow the crowd out to the communal meal." He laughed and took Ulla's arm, leading the way to the back of the church.

Isaac tried to take Molly's arm, but she pulled away from him, making her gesture all about straightening her *kapp*. "*Nee*, it's time to stop the pretense. I'm sick of all the lies."

Chapter Seventeen

Molly stabbed her fork into a tender piece of roast beef and then chewed mechanically. Her thoughts were on the wedding banns Otto Fischer had just declared between herself and Isaac in front of *Gott* and her church family. She'd always thought the banns were sacred, yet here she was squirming in her chair at her own engagement dinner, thinking up ways to get out of the mess she was in.

She glanced over at Isaac, who was sitting next to Chicken John. Both men were eating, wore a smile like everything in the world was perfect. She looked across the table at her *mamm*. Ulla was concentrating on getting the last of her peas on her fork. Her face showed no signs of hidden anger or agenda. Perhaps her *mamm* had meant all she had said. Maybe she was truly sorry for her behavior. For as long as Molly could remember, her mother had never used the word *sorry* in a sentence.

"You're very quiet," Isaac murmured into her ear.

Molly slapped him away like a pesky mosquito. She wanted to talk to him, but not here, not now. "I'm enjoying my meal."

"Then why are you taking such tiny bites?"

She heard a deep rumble of laughter in his chest. How could he enjoy this meal when she was so miserable? "I'm savoring every moment," she muttered back, keeping her eyes on her plate.

Isaac leaned in close to her as he reached for his glass of water. "You're being sarcastic, and it doesn't become you. I need to talk to you. There's so much to explain."

She accepted a slice of pineapple upside-down cake from Helen, Otto's nine-year-old granddaughter, and smiled her thanks. She turned back to Isaac and whispered, "You owe me no explanation. Banns read or not, we are not engaged."

Isaac lifted the chair under him and shoved it over until their chairs touched. "The banns sounded official to me."

To anyone watching they must have looked like two people very much in love, exchanging sweet words as they ate. "This is not the time to debate the issue, Isaac."

Isaac used his fork to take a bite of her cake, the appreciative sounds he made telling her he liked the cake she'd baked. He had no idea he was eating her secret gift to him, and she wanted it to stay that way, even though it pleased her that he liked the special treat. "We have to talk. You need to know—"

"I'll meet you in the kitchen." She rose and then groaned inwardly as he pushed back his chair, prepared to follow her. "No, not now," she whispered close to his ear. "In a few moments."

Molly scurried across the lawn and into the church kitchen, making her way past women clearing away dishes. When she saw Isaac come in, she motioned him into a quiet corner of the room, away from prying eyes.

He grabbed her arm and pulled her into the broom closet and shut the door behind them. Light bled into the square chamber, casting shadows across Isaac's face. "I haven't had five minutes alone with you for days," he said.

"I know."

They stood toe-to-toe, his height making her feel shorter than her five foot nothing. "I've been busy and so have you." She frowned in frustration and couldn't control her tongue. "Perhaps if you hadn't been avoiding me…"

"I haven't been avoiding you," Isaac shot back. "You didn't seem to want me anywhere near you." Still holding her hand, his thumb brushed back and forth across her fingers. "I didn't know Rose was coming for sure until the day she arrived, or I would have mentioned it sooner."

"I knew she was coming. I saw her letter."

Isaac peered down at her, the dark room making it hard for her to see the expression on his face. "What? How?" he asked.

Conversation could be heard outside the door. She lowered her voice while trying to avoid hitting a row of mop handles with her elbow. "In your room while I was cleaning one day."

His deep, gravely laugh annoyed her. "I never took you for a snoop." He ran his hand up her arm, and she tried to brush it away.

Her face flushed with heat. "I'm not a snoop. I just happened to find the letter on the floor and read the name Rose. I assumed it was from a family member."

"Not a girlfriend? You're so trusting."

"*Ya*, well. But I'm no fool, Isaac Graber. I know most

men have their secrets and can lie at the drop of a hat and be convincing."

"If you'd just listen for a moment, you'd understand so much." Isaac's voice sounded sincere.

"*Ya*, I'll listen, but not here, and only because it will get me away from you and out of this suffocating broom closet."

A half hour later Isaac's feet pushed down hard on the tandem bike's pedals, almost standing in his seat to propel them faster down the road. He tried to adjust for the tipping motion Molly was causing on the second seat. He'd never ridden a two-seater bike before and had no idea it would prove to be so difficult. A strong gust of northerly wind blew across them, and he fought to keep them upright.

"How much farther?"

Molly's words shot past him on the wind. He turned his head slightly, hoping she would be able to hear. "Another block."

"Where exactly did you say we were going?" Molly's voice sounded high-pitched with nerves.

"I didn't say," Isaac told her as he turned into the corner driveway on Lapp Lane. The plain white house looked smaller than he remembered.

The night before he'd come to see the outside of the house with Otto Fischer and been impressed, but in the bright light of day he realized the house was in desperate need of a repair. The peeling exterior was disappointing to say the least. Molly was sure to be dissatisfied and had every right to be, but a home like this was what he could afford for now.

He came to a wobbly stop, his arms and legs braced

against the wind. He glanced back to make sure Molly was all right.

"Whose *haus* is this?" Molly asked, her feet slipping from the bike pedals to stand on the stained driveway.

Isaac threw his leg over the bike. "Come inside with me. I have to check some things. It won't take a minute." He waited for her to free her skirt from the bike pedal. With the kick of his boot, he slid the bike stand in place.

"But I thought you said we were going to the park to meet your sister later." Molly straightened her apron and held her *kapp* down with her hand. Strands of hair escaped her bun and danced around her face with another gust of wind.

"*Ya*. We are meeting her, but I have to get this done first. Please come in. I don't want to leave you out on the lawn."

Molly glanced around, her gaze wandering to the peeling front porch swing swaying in the breeze. "Who lives here?"

Isaac took the crook of her arm and led her toward the house. "No one, right now."

She hesitated, pulling back. "Then why are we here?"

"Otto sent me on a mission. I have to check out the work needing to be done on the inside."

"Oh."

At the door he patted his pants pockets until he found the key ring and then dug it out, along with a piece of chewing gum and three dimes. The lock fought the key. He turned it upside down and the key slid in, the door creaking as it opened.

Isaac used his hand to push the door open all the way and then flip up the light switch. Nothing. No electricity. He stepped inside. Molly trailed silently behind him.

Bright sunlight flooded the small entry hall. The inside of the house appeared dingy, the walls needing a wipe down and thick coat of paint. They moved into the greatroom. All the blinds and curtains were drawn, leaving the space in gloom. Dust particles floated on the midday sun streaming in through the opened door behind them.

"It needs some work," Isaac commented.

Molly nodded in agreement. "*Ya.* A lot of work."

"Let's get some light in here."

Molly went with Isaac to the windows. She pushed against the drab olive-green drapes at the double window and shoved them open.

Isaac jerked on the cord behind the folds of curtain fabric and stepped back to avoid the avalanche of dust swirling around them.

Silently, both turned back to the room.

A huge peace sign had been spray-painted in black on the white back wall, just behind a mud-colored couch that had seen better days.

"Not good."

"*Nee.*" Isaac's heart sank as he watched Molly inspect the room, her head shaking in distaste.

She pinched off a dust cover with two fingers and revealed a sturdy tan recliner that rocked gently back and forth. Molly smiled at her discovery. "At least the chair looks usable," she murmured, and headed for the open kitchen off the big room. "*Ya*, well. Come look at this, Isaac."

He ambled over, noticing missing light fixtures, and several holes in the wall the size of a fist. The ceramic tile underfoot appeared dingy, but none seemed cracked. He rounded the corner and entered the kitchen.

His breath caught as he took in missing drawers and a hole in the counter where the sink had been. "At least they left the faucet." He tried to sound positive, but heard disappointment laced in his words.

"Ya." She pulled open the oven door and gasped. "What kind of people lived here?" Years of cooking had left the inside of the range the color of rust. She shut the door and moved away. The odor of burned-on food followed them across the room.

"Let's check out the bedrooms and then get out of here." Isaac led her down a dim hallway. He peeked into the decent-sized bathroom and promptly shut the door. "Lots of work to do in there." He knew the room would need gutting, the black-ringed, moldy tub scarred and unsalvageable.

The back bedrooms proved less depressing. They needed a coat of paint and the closet doors needed to be rehung, but nothing too drastic.

"This must be the master bedroom," Molly said, ambling over to the bare window. "The view from here is lovely. Look at those rosebushes against the fence. All they need is a good pruning. The lawn can be reseeded and watered. There could be red roses blooming and grass to mow by spring."

Isaac walked up behind her and put his hand on the windowsill. "What do you think of the *haus*, Molly? Does it have promise?"

"Promise?" Molly turned to him, something in her gaze giving him hope. "*Ya*, it has promise. All it needs is a few repairs and lots of paint and love. The bones are sound. I like the view from this window a lot. If it were my house…" She stopped speaking and looked up at him, a spark in her eyes telling him she was on to him. "Why did you bring me here, Isaac? This isn't a project for Otto, is it?"

"*Ya*, it is Otto's *haus*. He bought it as a rental a few days ago, but it could be our home once it's fixed up, if you'd let it be."

"What do you mean, *our* home? I thought—"

Isaac took her arm and pulled her close. "I feel different now. I'm all for us getting married, starting a family here in Pinecraft…if that's something you could live with."

He tried to hold her gaze, but she looked away, hiding her true feelings from him. "You lied to back me up, to protect me from my *mamm*'s plans for a loveless marriage. You had no interest in a wife. I remember you saying you couldn't afford one because the shop wasn't doing that well." She looked up at him, her gaze somber and searching.

"*Ya*, I did say that, but only at first. Before I…" Isaac knew now was the time to declare his love, but the tender words scrambled in his mind and wouldn't come off his tongue. How did a man tell a woman that she meant more to him than the very breath he drew and then confess himself to be a murderer?

"Before what? You can't be talking about love."

He drew air into his lungs and began to speak, praying his words were the right ones to convince her how much she meant to him. "I wanted to tell you for weeks that my feelings have changed, but there was so little time. There's so much you don't know about me, about my past."

Molly's brown eyes blinked back glistening tears, her chin trembling. "But you never said the words *I love you*."

Isaac's shoulders slumped, the weight of his own stupidity oppressing him. He looked down at the dirty floor underfoot. *What must she think, listening to my ramblings?* "I do love you and would have told you sooner, but I thought if I told you the truth about my past, you wouldn't want me in your life. I behaved like the coward I am."

"You're no coward, Isaac. You're the man I love. Please tell me about your past. All of it."

Isaac's lips brushed hers in a gentle kiss and then his words came fast, his deep voice quivering with emotions he'd held back for too long. "Like here in Pinecraft, the teens from Amish and Mennonite churches back home get together and play volleyball on Saturday afternoons in the summertime. A few months ago my friend Thomas twisted his ankle while playing, and since we lived close to each other, I offered to drive him the two miles to his *daed's* farm."

With a trembling hand, Isaac rubbed away a tear rolling down his cheek. "I'd driven his old truck before, but never on the country roads." His gaze caught hers, and he almost smiled. "You know how farm boys behave. We'd take turns driving around the freshly plowed fields like young fools."

Molly nodded, her eyes searching his.

"It had gotten dark, and Thomas was lying in the back of the truck so he wouldn't hurt his ankle." Pools of tears filled Isaac's eyes, making them red. "We were almost to his home when the accident happened." Big tears rolled down his cheeks, one after another.

He took Molly's hands and squeezed hard. "I tried to get out of the way of the other vehicle. I fought the wheel, but the lights kept coming straight at us."

He stopped talking, as if his mind were exploding with memories. A sob escaped his lips. "I must have been knocked out. When I came to, Thomas lay on the ground near me, but I couldn't go to him." He slapped his thigh. "My leg was a mess, but I called out to him. Begged him to be all right." He gulped in air, his breathing fast and hard. "It only took a few minutes for the *Englischer* police officer to show up, but it seemed forever. I must have passed out again because when I woke up I saw Thomas's body being placed on a stretcher."

Isaac stared into his memories, his eyes glassy. "I knew he was dead. He wasn't moving, and there was blood all over." He took in a deep breath. "Later at the hospital, the police told me the accident wasn't my fault. That the drunk driver of the other vehicle was to blame, but I knew better. I killed Thomas that day. I was driving the truck. It was my lack of experience that killed him. My *daed* wouldn't let me confess to the police. He said we Amish care for our own, but I wanted to tell the truth, take the blame for what I had done, no matter what the *Englischer* police would do to me." Deeps sobs escaped Isaac as she gathered him in her arms and cried with him in pain and regret.

Chapter Eighteen

The next day Liesel Troyer, Molly's friend, yelled from the sidelines of the shuffleboard court. "Knock her out of there!"

Molly bent, estimated wind and distance, eyed the round yellow disk and then propelled her puck down the court. It hit Rose's disk with a loud whack, sending it flying to the side.

Too competitive for her own good, Molly held her breath as she continued to watch the trajectory of the disk. It slowed to a crawl and then came to a stop exactly where she'd planned. *I've won!*

Rose sprang off the bench and good-naturedly hugged Molly's neck, her loose, *Englischer* styled hair blowing in the wind as they congratulated each other on the entertaining game of shuffleboard.

"I'm so glad you came to Pinecraft," Molly said with a grin, taking in Rose's sweet smile, the sparkle in her dark green eyes. At first she'd dreaded meeting Rose, but she'd been wrong to worry. The dark-haired girl, who looked so much like Isaac, turned out to be a charmer, high-spirited, with a winning personality everyone seemed to love. Molly felt sure Rose would grow into a sister and not an enemy as she feared.

"Me, too," Rose shouted over the noise of the shuffleboard players, her smile as genuine as a child's.

Molly searched for Isaac in the sea of faces around them and found him nodding, deep in conversation with Otto and Mose Fischer, at a domino table. She grinned, his words of love the day before still ringing in her ears, warming her heart. She was still reeling from his painful story of Thomas's death. No wonder Isaac had seemed so miserable when he'd first arrived in Pinecraft. His guilt had been eating at him, destroying his sanity. She smiled again as he looked up and caught her watching him. Her love for him grew stronger with each passing hour.

"You think we should disturb them?" Molly asked, sliding her arm through Rose's as they pushed their way through the crowd of Amish and Mennonite vacationers.

"Absolutely. I'm starving," Rose said, and took the lead. "Excuse me. Pardon," she muttered as she buffeted people, her smile never fading.

Otto rose and motioned them over, his disapproving gaze flicking over Rose's jeans and frilly blouse of bright red fabric. "So this is your sister, Rose," he said to Isaac.

Rose put out her hand, her smile widening, displaying perfect white teeth.

Otto took the hand she offered and returned her smile. "Hello, Rose," he said and turned to Mose. "This is my son, Mose. He's our local furniture builder and church elder."

Mose shook the young woman's hand, his expression

friendly, "*Willkumm* to Pinecraft. Isaac tells me you've just started your *rumspringa*."

Rose laughed. "*Ya*. I thought I'd visit my brother before going back home and coming to terms with my faith."

"If we can give you any assistance in making your decision, come and see me and Sarah. Isaac knows our address," Mose offered.

"We thought we'd go get something to eat. I'm starving." Rose pulled on Isaac's arm, urging him out of his chair.

"Rose is always hungry. She has my appetite." Isaac smiled at his sister, who grimaced at him but didn't deny his accusation.

Mose rose. "Why don't all of you come back to the house with Molly? Marta and Kurt, my brother and sister-in-law, are in town, helping out with the babies now that Sarah's finally home. Marta made a huge pot of chicken and dumplings this morning and chocolate whoopie pies were cooling on racks when I left. I'm sure there's more than enough for everyone. Besides, Sarah will want the chance to show off the *bobbels*."

Molly watched Theda Fischer's shoulders sway as she comforted her whimpering *grossdochder* with a gentle back rub, her blue-eyed gaze on the sleeping twin who lay tightly swaddled in a blue blanket a few feet away in his tiny cot. She tucked in the little girl's pink arm and adjusted the baby's blanket before she turned to her son, Mose, who sat next to her. "It makes me to wonder if the New Year will be rung in long before these *bobbels* get a name."

Sarah and Mose exchanged a knowing glance across

the table. "We have named them, but only this morning," Sarah admitted. "They are to be Wilhelm and Rebecca, or Willie and Becka, as Beatrice called them before she left for Ulla's *haus*." Sarah grinned at Theda's joyous expression. "Beatrice says *Gott* spoke to her in a dream about the names, but I think this time she just wanted to honor her *great-grossmammi* and *great-grossdaadi*, as Mose did when he named Beatrice after Ulla's mother."

Theda grinned. "My *mamm* and *daed* would have been so pleased. They were good people, full of *Gott*'s love. To name the *bobbels* after them is such a special blessing. *Danke*, both of you."

"It is our pleasure, *Mamm*. Sarah loves you as much as I do and was happy to honor your parents. You are the *mamm* Sarah never had and for that I am grateful."

Molly ate the last bite of her chicken and dumplings, contentment putting a perpetual smile on her face. She had a future with Isaac and had accepted his love. Nothing, not even the death of Thomas, could spoil her joy.

Her gaze drifted across the table to where Isaac sat in a chair next to Rose. He reached over and patted his sister's hand as he said, "It's been such a pleasure eating with this wonderful family. I've missed these kind of meals, where love is shared in abundance."

Rose turned to Isaac and added, "Like our meals at home. I've missed *Mamm* and *Daed*. It's been a week since I've seen them."

Otto laid down his napkin and cleared his voice with the authority of a judge. "Perhaps it is time to consider your options, Rose. Is the *Englischer* life for you, or will you be baptized and become a part of your community?"

Rose grinned and said, "You'll be glad to know I've decided to go home and join the church."

An hour later Sarah was feeding tiny Rebecca. "This child is never full." Sarah laughed, her finger trailing down her newest daughter's rosy cheek. The child turned toward its mother's finger and tried to suckle.

"Her hair is darker than Levi's, almost a honey color," Rose commented, her arms filled with baby Wilhelm, who was twice the size of his diminutive sister.

Molly sat in a chair by the window, enjoying the evening breeze and the close family interaction, but her mind soon wandered to Christmas next year. Would she be the one holding a *bobbel*, a child with her brown eyes and Isaac's good looks and dark hair?

"You're very far away, Molly. Something bothering you, or is it the wedding coming up in a matter of days?" Sarah bent to change Rebecca's mini-sized diaper.

Twisting, Molly faced her mentor and friend. "*Nee*. I wasn't thinking about the wedding, although I must, and soon. Time is flying."

Sarah placed her freshly diapered daughter into Theda's eager arms and strolled over to her bedroom closet, motioning with her finger for Molly to follow her. "Come with me. I have something to show you." She smiled, revealing a mischievous side to Sarah that Molly hadn't seen before. The mother of five turned on the light in a deep closet big enough to be a bedroom and went directly to a large plastic bag hanging among simple Amish dresses in every shade of the rainbow.

Sarah pulled off the protective plastic bag. A shimmery *kapp*, delicately fashioned out of the finest woven linen and lined with satin threads hung from a padded hanger. Behind it another hanger held a pale pink dress of polished cotton, the cut simple but beautifully stitched.

"Oh, Sarah. What a beautiful dress. Is this what you're wearing for Christmas?" Molly fingered the soft fabric of the skirt, touched the tiny flowers embroidered along the neckline.

Sarah tucked her arm around Molly's waist and smiled down at her, the dress held high off the floor. "*Nee*, silly goose. This dress is for your wedding day."

"*Mein* dress?" Overwhelmed with joy, Molly took the garment and pressed it to her chest. "Oh, look. It's the correct length. How did you guess so perfectly?"

Sarah laughed. "I didn't guess. I snuck one of your dresses out of your closet and took measurements for the ladies in the sewing circle who made the dress in just two days. It should fit perfectly."

"*Ya*, it should." Molly grinned at herself in the mirror, her surprise showing in her expression. "But how did you know for sure Isaac and I would marry? I wasn't sure myself."

"I had a feeling," Sarah said, smiling.

Molly smiled back. "*Gott* must approve of this marriage. He has been so faithful and made a way for all this to happen."

Sarah nodded. "Mose told me Otto has found a *haus* for you two. That should relieve your mind some."

"It did. We'll be renting the fixer-upper. *Gott* bless Otto Fischer. He's always there for me when I need him, just like Mose. The house will become a wonderful home once the work is completed." Molly worried her *kapp* ribbons, her mind revisiting the abandoned house, the long list of repairs that needed doing. Would it be ready in time?

"I heard the men talking around the table earlier this morning. Seems Isaac hired a man to work a full week at the bike shop, so he's free to gut the bathroom and kitchen. Mose and Otto will be putting in all new fixtures, a new sink and counters in the kitchen. Several men from the church will be painting once the dust settles. I don't think you have anything to worry about. I can't wait to see the house so I can make drapes for you and maybe a quilt for the new bed."

Theda slipped into the clothes-filled room, Rebecca asleep in her arms. "Oh, Sarah. You and the ladies have outdone yourselves. That dress came out beautiful!"

Rose quickly followed Theda in and caught her breath as she viewed the dress and *kapp* up close. "Molly, what a lucky girl you are. I am *so* impressed. You'll make such a beautiful bride. My brother will fall over his own big feet when he sees you in this."

Molly erupted into giggles, picturing Isaac saying his vows from the floor at her feet. "He may be a bit of a klutz, but he's a wonderful klutz and I love him more than I can say."

Chapter Nineteen

The Florida sun blazed outside, the December day perfect for a wedding.

Sarah's large bedroom was full of women, some ready to assist Molly as she dressed, while others seemed content to sit around, laughing aloud at the silly things Rose was sharing about Isaac as a boy.

"I kid you not, Molly. Isaac was impossible to live with between the ages of ten and fourteen. He was constantly in trouble with *Daed*, either for stealing the buggy and taking all his friends on joyrides, or coming home late and missing his ten o'clock curfew."

Molly smiled at the picture Rose painted. She would have loved to have known the rambunctious, mischievous Isaac, the man he'd been before Thomas's tragic death. *Gott* willing, he'd return to that same happy man with time and healing.

She was glad to see Rose had changed out of the jeans and a comical kitten T-shirt she'd worn at breakfast, into a plain dress in pale yellow, fit for an Amish wedding. She still wore no *kapp*. Her shiny dark hair curled around her shoulders, free from the traditional constraints of the bun most Amish women wore.

Otto would throw a fit when he saw her, but Molly knew nothing would be said in public. The wise old man understood *rumspringa* sometimes sent *youngies* into a spin, their decision to join the church, or not, often stymied their decision making for months, sometimes years. Rose was settling down, and once she was back in Missouri Molly felt sure Rose would join the church and find her way her way back to her Amish roots.

Her heart beat fast in her ears as Sarah breezed out of the closet and brought out the wedding dress. A hush fell over the room and then a united clap of hands broke out as the beautifully made dress was lifted over Molly's head and slid into place.

Two hours later, Molly stepped over the threshold of her and Isaac's new home. She laughed when she saw the banner over the fireplace that read ISAAC AND MOLLY GRABER.

"Did you know about this?" she asked her new husband, her gaze flitting around the perfect room. A traditional vase of flowering celery stalks decorated the beautiful dining room table in the alcove.

"I had no idea, but you know my sister was probably the ringleader of all this hoopla," Isaac said with a grin.

"Your sister does have a flair for the dramatic," Molly said with a laugh, sitting on the plush tan couch, another piece of furniture she'd never seen before. "Where did all this furniture come from? I thought we'd be sitting on crates and saving every penny we could spare for furniture."

"*Nee.* Otto wouldn't hear of you doing without. He

and Theda made it happen. So many people from the community donated to our cause and kept it a secret. Even Willa Mae."

"Willa Mae kept a secret? I'm shocked. She's usually the first to spill the beans. She never said a word all week. Wait till I see her." Molly laughed good-naturedly and hugged Isaac close. She took in all the changes to the kitchen behind them. "You've been busy in there. Look at this place. It's much too fancy for us. Granite countertops?"

Minutes later, hand in hand, Isaac trailed behind Molly as she made her way to the back of the house. "Oh, look. We do have a bathroom, and a wonderful one at that." The new white sink, toilet and tub sparkled in the filtered sunlight shining in through an oblong window over the tub.

Setting on the counter, a bowl of homemade soap balls filled the room with the fragrance of roses. "I see Rose was in here, too," Molly remarked with a grin, and touched a fluffy hanging towel in a pale shade of blue.

"Can you tell blue is Rose's favorite color?" Isaac asked, and smiled at Molly's reflection in the mirror.

Molly had experienced joy many times in her life, but no emotion had prepared her for the feeling of contentment she felt rushing through her. She grabbed Isaac's hand and hurried him down the hall, her excitement almost more than she could contain. "I can't wait to see our bedroom."

She opened the door slowly and gasped with surprise. The room looked like a picture from a fancy *Englischer* magazine, the bed neatly made and covered in the most beautiful wedding-ring-patterned quilt she'd ever seen. Sarah's work, no doubt. Two dark wooden nightstands flanked the bed, with matching lamps placed on each. Across the room a tallboy dresser, with six big drawers, graced the wall. "This is all too much," Molly whispered and sat on the bed, tears blurring her vision. "I thought—"

"I know." Isaac sat beside her, slid his arm around her shoulders. "You thought you were coming home to a fixer-upper and a list of must-haves a mile long."

"*Ya*—" her chin wobbled "—I did, but just look at all this." She spread her hands wide-open and then wiped away a tear.

Isaac laughed out loud, his voice deep and rumbling. "You make me so happy, Molly."

She leaned in close and pressed her head to his chest, listening to the steady beat of his heart. "And you, my love, are my joy. My everything."

His hands were gentle as he pulled her close. He lowered his lips to hers, and just before they touched, he whispered, "And you are mine."

* * * * *

PLAIN TRUTH

Debby Giusti

This book is dedicated to my wonderful grandchildren, Anna, Robert, John Anthony and William. You fill my heart with joy!

People were bringing children to Jesus that He might touch them, but the disciples rebuked them. When Jesus saw this He became indignant and said to them, "Let the children come to me; do not prevent them, for the kingdom of God belongs to such as these. Amen, I say to you, whoever does not accept the kingdom of God like a child will not enter it." Then He embraced them and blessed them, placing His hands on them.
—*Mark* 10:13–16

Chapter One

Dr. Ella Jacobsen startled with fright as a crash of thunder shook her rural medical clinic. Dropping the invitation she'd been reading for the upcoming medical symposium onto her desk, she glanced out the window as another bolt of lightning lit the night sky. Anticipating the power outage that would surely follow, Ella pulled the Maglite from the bottom drawer of her file cabinet and sighed with frustration as the lights flicked off, leaving her in darkness and fumbling with the switch on the flashlight.

If someone had warned her about how often she'd lose electricity, she might have chosen another location for the pediatric clinic. As it was, after five months, she was committed to the rural farm community near Freemont, Georgia, and to her patients, two of whom had just received IV fluids in her treatment room.

Relieved when the Maglite finally switched on, she followed the arc of light through her clinic to the hallway and peered into the room where the five-year-old twins rested comfortably. Their worry-worn mother, Mary

Kate Powers, slept on the chair next to the girls, oblivious to the pummeling rain and howling wind outside.

Ella wouldn't disturb the young mother's sleep. Instead, she slipped into her slicker and left her clinic
through the side door, heading for the generator that
provided a backup power source.

Quin would have called her generator inadequate,
but her deceased husband had been prone to point out
any number of her shortcomings. Surely eight months
after his death was time enough to cease worrying about
what Quin thought.

Ella grimaced as the storm exploded around her.
Lightning bolted overhead, followed almost instantly
by ear-shattering thunder. Rain fell in torrents, stinging her face and drenching her hair. Too late, she pulled
the hood of her coat over her head and bent into the
wind as she picked her way through the sodden grass
to the generator.

Tonight, the tin overhang that usually provided protection from the elements did little to stem the battering
rain and buffeting wind. She grabbed the gas can out
of the nearby shed and filled the generator's tank before she flipped the fuel valve to On and pulled out the
choke. After pressing the control switch, she grabbed
the pull cord and yanked once, then twice.

The engine failed to engage.

She tugged on the cord again and again, then sighed.

A sound caused her to turn. Through the downpour,
she watched the headlights of a car race along the two-
lane road in front of her property. For half a heartbeat,
she wanted to flag down the driver and beg for help.
Then she steeled her shoulders and shoved out her chin
with resolve. She'd come this far alone, and she wouldn't

waver in her determination to succeed. Although, in spite of her attempt to be self-reliant, a sinking feeling settled in the pit of her stomach as the car disappeared from sight.

Another bolt of lightning flashed across the sky. In the yard, the sign for the Children's Care Clinic snapped in the wind. She was alone, other than for an exhausted mother and her two daughters in the building. Like it or not, Ella needed to solve her own problems.

Opening the oil cap, she checked the level, making certain it was adequate. Then, after adjusting the choke, she pulled on the cord again...and again...and again.

Her hand cramped with the effort. Stopping to catch her breath, she stretched her fingers and listened to a sound that floated over the storm.

Turning her gaze toward the clinic, she tilted her head as the sound came again.

Was it a cry? No, a scream!

Her heart lurched.

Grabbing the Maglite, she hurried across the slippery, rain-wet grass. Her shoes sank into a patch of Georgia red clay that grabbed like quicksand. Pulling free, she raced to the side door, shook the rain from her hair and stepped inside. Before she was halfway across the office, she stopped short. Someone else was in the room. She narrowed her gaze and raised her flashlight.

A figure bathed in shadow stood over her desk. He raised an even more powerful light that blinded her in its glare. Momentarily frozen in place, she failed to react as he raced toward her and grabbed her shoulder. The crushing strength of his hold made her legs buckle. She dropped to the floor, losing her Maglite in the fall, and crawled on hands and knees to escape his hold.

He kicked her side. She collapsed. He kicked again. Air whooshed from her lungs.

She rolled over, and caught his foot before he could strike a third blow. Twisting his leg, she forced him off balance.

He cursed.

She grabbed his thigh above his knee and dug her nails into the tender flesh. He raised his right hand. She scooted sideways to avoid the strike, but her reflexes weren't fast enough. His fist made contact with her neck, below her ear. Her body arched with pain.

His shadowed bulk loomed above her. He drew a weapon from his pocket, aimed and squeezed the trigger.

She screamed, expecting to be killed.

The bullet failed to discharge. Again he tried. And again.

Lightning slashed outside, but all she saw was the glare of his flashlight and the gun that refused to fire.

He growled like an animal, a monster who wanted her dead. Raising his hand, he hurled the weapon against her skull. She screamed in pain, then slipped into darkness, surrounded by a cushion of oblivion.

Thoughts of her patients dragged her back to reality. She blinked her eyes open and listened to his footsteps moving away from her. A door slammed, then another wave of oblivion overtook her. When she came to, panic grabbed at her throat. Worried about Mary Kate and the girls, she knew she had to get help.

Ella inched toward the desk, where she'd left her cell phone. Her head and neck ached. Nausea washed over her. She raised herself far enough off the floor to grab her cell, tapped in 911 and turned to glance over her shoulder, using the light from her phone to scan the darkness.

A body.

No. Please, God, no.

Mary Kate lay in a pool of blood.

"Nine one one." The operator's raspy voice sounded in the stillness. "State your emergency."

"Children's Care Clinic on Amish Road." Ella gripped the phone with her trembling hand and forced the words from her mouth. "An...an intruder attacked two women. Send an ambulance."

"Ma'am, could you—"

Scooting closer, she gasped at the gush of blood from the young woman's side. Grabbing a towel from the nearby supply cabinet, Ella wadded it into a ball and pressed the thick terry cloth against the wound. With her right hand, she found the carotid artery, grateful to feel a pulse.

"Tell the ambulance to hurry," she told the operator. "I've got a patient who's bleeding to death."

"Stay on the line, ma'am. The police and ambulance are on the way."

Ella wasn't sure they would arrive in time.

Criminal Investigation Division Special Agent Zach Swain stood at the side entrance of the rural clinic that led into the doctor's office and blinked back the memory of another medical facility long ago. A patient lay sprawled on the floor, and a doctor knelt over her, forcing air into her lungs. Fear clenched his gut as he was once again the eight-year-old boy screaming for the doctor to save his mother's life.

Swallowing down the vision from his past, Zach focused on the swirl of activity before him and the information Officer Van Taylor, a young Freemont cop who had checked Zach's identification, was continuing to provide.

"Her name's Ella Jacobsen." Taylor, tall and lean and midtwenties, pointed to the woman sitting on a straight-backed chair.

"She runs the clinic?" Zach asked.

The cop nodded. "She bought the three-bedroom ranch and attached a clinic to the side of the residence. Local families and some of the Amish who've settled in this area appreciate having a doc close at hand."

An older police sergeant, probably fifty-five, with a receding hairline and bushy brows, stood near the woman. Zach read his name tag: Abrams. The sergeant held an open notebook in his hand.

Zach couldn't hear their conversation, but he recognized the ashen paleness of the doctor's face and the bloodstains that covered her blouse and the slicker that lay next to her on the floor.

"She's a northerner," the younger officer explained. "Moved here from Pennsylvania and opened this clinic for kids five months ago."

All of which sounded admirable. "So what happened tonight?" Zach asked.

"The power went out, only it wasn't the storm that caused the failure."

Zach raised his brow. "Someone tampered with the line coming to the clinic?"

"Seems that's what happened. He also fiddled with the spark plug on the generator the doc couldn't get to start. One of our men got it working until the repairman from the power company restored the main feed."

"I call that good customer service this far from Freemont."

Taylor leaned closer and lowered his voice. "The guy on call from the power company is married to Sergeant Abrams's daughter, so he rushed here to help."

"Keep it in the family, right?"

The young cop smiled. "In case you're interested, we took the doc's prints and collected samples from under her nails."

Which meant she had tried to defend herself.

Taylor pointed to his supervisor. "Looks like the sergeant is ready to wrap up his questioning, sir, if you want to talk to Dr. Jacobsen."

Zach nodded in appreciation.

Abrams closed his notebook, said something to the woman and then headed across the room. As he approached, Zach extended his hand and stated his name. "I'm with the Criminal Investigation Division at Fort Rickman, Sergeant Abrams. One of your men notified our office that active duty military personnel were involved in the case."

The sergeant returned the handshake. "Good to see you, Special Agent Swain. What we know so far is that an intruder attacked Mary Kate Powers, whose twin girls were being treated by the doctor. The woman's a military spouse. She suffered a gunshot wound to her side and is being transported by ambulance to the hospital at Fort Rickman. Doc Jacobsen tended to her injuries before the EMTs arrived. Saved the woman's life, according to our emergency personnel."

Zach glanced again at the doc's scraped face and disheveled hair. "Looks like the assailant took out his anger on the doctor, as well."

"She claims to be all right, although she can't remember much. Probably due to shock."

"Do you have a motive?"

The sergeant shrugged. "Could be drugs. The doc doesn't keep much on hand in her clinic, but dopers don't make good choices."

"Was the assailant able to access the meds?"

"Negative. Still, that seems the most logical explanation at this point."

Logical or convenient? Zach wasn't as easily convinced as the sergeant. "Mind if I talk to her?"

"Be my guest. Corporal Hugh Powers, the wounded woman's husband, is in one of the treatment rooms. You're welcome to question him, as well."

Zach appreciated the cop's openness to having a military presence in the investigation. As the sergeant and Taylor stepped outside, Zach grabbed a chair and placed it next to the doctor.

She glanced up. Blue eyes rimmed with dark lashes stared at him. Her brow furrowed, and her full lips drooped into a pronounced frown. She scooted back in her chair warily.

Zach introduced himself. "I'm from Fort Rickman. If you don't mind, I'd like to ask you a few questions."

"I don't understand." Her hand went protectively to her throat. "Why would Fort Rickman be interested in what happened at my clinic?"

Zach eyed the dark mark under her ear and the hair on the side of her head that was matted with blood. "The Criminal Investigations Division is called in when military personnel are injured or involved in a crime."

"You're referring to Mary Kate?"

"That's right. Mary Kate Powers. You were treating her daughters?"

The doc nodded. "They were suffering from a gastrointestinal problem and became dehydrated. I administered IV fluids to rehydrate the girls."

"Were they in the clinic at the time of the attack?"

"They were asleep, as was their mother." Ella pointed to the hallway. "The girls were in the first treatment room, on the left. Their stepfather got here before the ambulance. He wanted to check on his wife, since she and the girls had been gone quite a while. He was distraught when he saw her, of course, and called the grandparents. They arrived not long ago and took the children home."

"Am I correct in assuming the girls weren't injured?"

"Thankfully, they slept through their mother's attack."

"Could you start at the beginning, ma'am?"

She glanced down at her scraped hands. Dried blood stained her fingers. Rust-colored spatters streaked across her shirt. "I've been treating the girls for a debilitating disease, called CED, or childhood enzyme deficiency, for the last few months. They've improved, but when the gastrointestinal problems started, their mother was concerned. She called and asked if I could see them tonight."

"Was this a normal occurrence, Doctor?"

She narrowed her gaze as if she didn't understand the question. "If you mean do I see patients at night, then no, it's not the norm. But the girls are five years old, Mr. Swain. Their physical and fine motor abilities had been compromised by the disease. Less than two months ago, I was worried about their failure to thrive."

"You didn't expect them to live?"

She nodded. "They were becoming increasingly compromised."

"But you recognized the symptoms and started them on the proper medication?" Zach asked.

"More or less."

Now he was the one to pause and raise an eyebrow. "Meaning what?"

"Meaning my husband led the team that first identified the condition. I called the research center where he had worked to ensure the protocol he established almost a year ago was still the treatment of choice."

"And was it?"

"Yes, so after talking to the head of the Harrisburg center, I made changes in the girls' diets, prescribed the enzyme needed to overcome their deficiency and checked on their progress repeatedly."

"The girls improved?"

The doc nodded. "Improved and indeed began to thrive."

"Yet they got sick with the stomach ailment."

"Which had nothing to do with the genetic disease. As you can imagine, their mother was anxious. I assured her the girls would be fine with fluids and time. Antinausea drugs helped. I'll check on them again in the morning, but I feel sure they'll make a full recovery."

The doctor glanced at an area near her desk where blood stained the tile floor. "I wish I was equally as convinced of their mother's prognosis."

"You don't think she'll survive?" Zach asked.

"Mary Kate lost a lot of blood. A whole host of complications could develop. The next twenty-four to forty-eight hours will be key."

"Why would someone harm Mrs. Powers?"

The doc shook her head, a bit too quickly.

Zach leaned closer. "Is there someone who might have reason to attack the girls' mother?"

"You'd have to ask Mary Kate, although I doubt you'll be able to question her for the next day or two." Dr. Jacobsen glanced again at the floor. "Even then, I'm not sure…"

"I'll contact the hospital," Zach volunteered.

She glanced up at him, her eyes wide with hopeful optimism. "Would you let me know her condition?"

"Of course."

She almost smiled.

Zach let out a breath, checked the notes he'd made and tried to get back to his questioning. "Could you tell me about your husband, ma'am?"

"My husband?"

Any positive steps he had made took a backward dive as her frown returned.

"You mentioned that he had worked at a research center in Pennsylvania," Zach prompted. "Where is your husband currently working?"

"My husband…" She pulled in a ragged breath. "Quin died eight months ago."

Not what Zach had expected. "I'm sorry, ma'am."

"Thank you. So am I."

"You lived with him in Pennsylvania?"

"I did. That's correct."

"And after he passed away…" Zach let the statement hang.

"After his death, I moved to Georgia and opened this clinic."

"Georgia must not be home, ma'am. I don't notice a Southern accent."

She tilted her head. "I'm originally from Ohio. I met and married my husband in Columbus when I was attending medical school at Ohio State. He was doing research for a private company."

"What brought you South after his death?"

She touched the ring finger of her left hand as if searching for the wedding band she no longer wore.

"I came to Freemont because of the Amish who live in the area. Some of the families migrated here from Pennsylvania, a few from Ohio and Alabama. Seems everyone—even the 'English,' as they call us—wants a bit of the simple lifestyle. Land up north is hard to find, which forces young Amish farmers to settle new areas, away from the urban sprawl that has become a problem."

"So you were looking for an Amish community?"

"I'm a pediatrician." She sounded tired. Perhaps from too many questions. "I wanted to open a care clinic for Amish children."

"But the Powers twins aren't Amish."

"Mary Kate grew up around here. As you probably know, her husband—the girls' stepfather—is military and was deployed to the Middle East. Mary Kate and the girls moved home to be with her parents. My clinic is closer than going to town for medical treatment."

Zach studied the notes he had taken. Something didn't add up. "Your husband worked with the Amish in Pennsylvania?"

"Amish children. He specialized in newly emerging, genetically acquired diseases, as well as established conditions that impact the Amish."

"What specifically?"

"Metabolic disorders such as pyruvate kinase deficiency, Crigler-Najjar syndrome, maple syrup urine disease."

Zach held up his hand. "Evidently there are a number of conditions that attack Amish children."

"Too many. As I mentioned, Quin worked to identify new diseases and researched treatment protocols."

"Then you moved here after his death to carry on his legacy?"

"No." Confusion washed over her face. "I came because I wanted to make a contribution."

From the noticeable way she braced her shoulders and raised her head, Zach wondered if there was more to her statement than she cared to admit. Had the doctor been living in her husband's shadow?

"What was the cause of your husband's death, ma'am?"

She bristled. "I don't see how that has bearing on what happened here tonight."

"Yes, ma'am, but it's my job to put the pieces together. Your husband's death could play a role in the investigation."

"I find that hard to believe."

Zach raised his brow and waited. Dr. Jacobsen had to realize that police questions needed to be answered.

"My husband's cause of death is still under investigation," she finally admitted.

"Could you provide a few more details?"

"Quin attended a medical research conference in Memphis, Tennessee. He left the hotel Saturday afternoon before the end of the event. His luggage was in the rental car found on the edge of a bridge that spans the Mississippi River."

Her face twisted as if the story was hard to tell.

"Fishermen found his body washed up on the banks of the river some days later."

"Was foul play suspected?"

She swallowed. "The police ruled his death self-inflicted."

Suicide, but she failed to use the term. "Did you question their finding?" Zach asked.

"Of course. Anything could have happened. He could have fallen or been pushed."

"You suspected foul play?"

She shook her head. "I don't know what I suspected. Quin was a perfectionist. He held himself to a high standard. Succumbing to the sense of unworthiness that predisposes someone to take their own life hardly seemed in keeping with Quin's nature."

"Did you explain your concerns to the police?"

"They weren't interested in my opinions."

A negative undercurrent was evident from her tone of voice. Zach doubted the good doctor had much regard for law enforcement, present company included, he felt sure.

"What about tonight's assailant. Did you see anything that might identify the intruder?"

She raked her hand through her curly hair and shook her head. "I don't remember."

When Zach failed to comment, she leaned closer. "I passed out. Not long. A matter of seconds at the most, yet my recall is foggy at best."

Opening her hands, she shrugged. "The truth is I can't remember anything that happened shortly before or after I blacked out."

"What's the last thing you *do* remember, ma'am?"

"I was outside, trying to make the generator work. A scream came from the clinic. I hurried inside to make sure Mary Kate and the girls were all right."

"What did you find?"

Her eyes narrowed. "A man shadowed in darkness stood over my desk."

"Go on," Zach encouraged her.

She shook her head. "That's all I can recall."

The side door opened and Sergeant Abrams and Officer Taylor stepped back into the clinic. After saying something to the younger cop, Abrams approached the doctor. "Ma'am, the EMTs mentioned your need to be checked at the hospital. I can have one of my men drive you there in the next twenty to thirty minutes."

"That's not necessary. All I really need are a couple of ibuprofen and a few hours of sleep."

"If the Freemont police are tied up, I'd be happy to drive you to the hospital," Zach volunteered. "You've been through a lot and are probably running on adrenaline right now."

"Really, I'm fine," she insisted.

The sergeant leaned closer. "Ma'am, you owe it to your patients to be checked out. The sooner you get feeling better, the sooner you'll be able to see to their needs."

The man seemed to have struck the right chord.

"Perhaps you're right." She glanced at Zach. "You wouldn't mind driving me?"

"Not a problem, ma'am."

She looked down at her soiled hands and blouse. "If you don't mind, I'd like to wash my hands and change into clean clothes."

"Of course."

Abrams motioned a female cop forward. "Officer Grant will accompany you into your private residence, ma'am."

"But it adjoins my clinic," the doc objected. "I just need to go down the hall. The door connects to the kitchen."

"Yes, ma'am." The sergeant nodded. "But having someone with you is a safety precaution until you've been checked out at the hospital."

As if too tired to argue, Dr. Jacobsen rose and followed the female officer into the hallway.

Once the women had left the room, Zach turned to the sergeant. "Tell me if I'm wrong, but I get the feeling you don't trust the doc."

Abrams offered him a tired smile. "I'm being cautious. Dr. Jacobsen seems to be a woman of merit, but I've seen too many criminals over the years who look like Miss America and apple pie. I don't want to be hoodwinked by a physician in a rural clinic who's up to no good."

Zach hadn't suspected the doctor of wrongdoing. Quite the opposite. He wouldn't admit his feelings to the sergeant, but something about her tugged at his heart. Maybe it was the confusion he read in her gaze, or her vulnerability. Whatever the reason, he needed to focus on the case at hand. He also needed to remind himself of what he'd learned long ago.

Ever since his mother's traumatic death, Zach didn't trust doctors. He never had and never would.

Chapter Two

Ella stepped into the hallway and paused. Her head ached, and the muscles in her back and legs were strained. Although she'd survived the attack, her insides were still trembling. After Quin's death, she had moved to Georgia, looking for a better life. Now an intruder had robbed her of her peace and sense of security.

She doubted that the special agent could understand the way she felt. He was big and bulky, and impeccably dressed in a navy sports coat and khaki slacks, with a patterned tie that brought out his rugged complexion and dark eyes. Some might call him handsome. She found him intense.

Glancing into the small treatment room, she saw Hugh Powers, head in his hands, sitting in the chair where his wife had slept not that long ago.

Ella tapped on the door frame. "Corporal Powers?"

He glanced up.

"I'm sorry about Mary Kate."

"The EMTs said she would have bled out if you hadn't helped." He looked weary and confused.

A sound caused her to turn. The special agent had

entered the hallway and stood staring at her. "I thought you were going to your residence." His voice was low and clipped.

"I was talking to Corporal Powers." She glanced back at the soldier. "I know this isn't the homecoming from the Middle East that you expected, with sick children and an injured wife. If it's any consolation, the girls are getting stronger, and I'm sure the doctors at Fort Rickman are doing everything they can for Mary Kate."

"When can I leave here?" he asked. "I need to go to the hospital to be with my wife, but the sergeant said he might have more questions."

"Maybe Special Agent Swain can help you."

Zach stepped forward, getting much too close to Ella. All she'd been able to smell since the storm was Georgia clay and dried blood. Now she inhaled the clean scent of sandalwood and a hint of lime.

She looked up, taking in his bulk, and then glanced down at her tattered blouse and soiled hands, realizing once again that she couldn't let appearance define her.

Ella wasn't who Quin had wanted her to be—that became evident over the course of their short marriage. The problem was, she wasn't sure who she was or what she wanted anymore. Quin had that effect on her. Or maybe it had started with her father, who was never satisfied with anything she did. How had she married a man who reminded her of her dad? A psychologist might say she was trying to prove her worth to both men, but she was tired of having to prove herself to anyone, even the special agent.

He touched her arm. She glanced down at a hand that would dwarf her own.

"Are you okay?" he asked, his voice brimming with concern.

Evidently, she had been lost in thought longer than she realized. "I'm fine. Thank you."

Turning abruptly on her heel, she followed the female police officer into her private residence and sighed as she closed the door behind her. Of course she wasn't fine. She had been beaten up by an assailant who'd tried to shoot her.

The gun. Why hadn't she remembered the gun?

Ella hurried back into the hallway and stopped short in front of the treatment room. Zach moved to the door.

"Is something wrong?" he asked.

"The man...the assailant...he drew a weapon. The gun jammed. He kept trying to pull the trigger, over and over again."

The reality of her own brush with death overtook her. Tears burned her eyes. Her body trembled. Shock. She knew the signs, but couldn't help herself. She felt weak and sick and all alone.

Powerless to stop herself, she stepped toward the special agent with the wide shoulders and broad chest.

He opened his arms and pulled her into his embrace. "You're safe now."

Which was exactly how she felt. Then, all too quickly, she realized her mistake and pulled out of his hold.

"I'm sorry," she mumbled, embarrassed by her moment of weakness. Her cheeks burned as she retraced her steps and escaped into the kitchen.

Ella had hoped to find peace in Freemont, Georgia, but she'd found something else. She'd found a brutal attacker, a man who had tried to kill her. Why had he come into her clinic and what had he wanted to find?

* * *

Why had he opened his arms and pulled her into his embrace? Zach let out a stiff breath and mentally chastised himself for his emotional response to the doc. What was wrong with him tonight?

He stood staring after her as she closed the door at the end of the hallway, and willed himself to act like an investigator instead a guy taken in by a pretty face and big blue eyes. Inwardly, he shifted back to CID mode before he stepped into the treatment room where Corporal Powers waited.

After introducing himself, Zach inquired about the corporal's unit and why he had followed his wife and daughters to the clinic.

"I didn't follow them," the man insisted. "Mary Kate and the twins left the house when I was sleeping. The girls had been sick, and my wife mentioned calling the doctor."

"Dr. Jacobsen?"

The soldier nodded. "I figured they were here."

"So you came to find them."

"That's right."

"Tell me what happened when you arrived?"

"I already told the Freemont cop."

"But you need to tell me." Zach pulled out a notebook and held a pen over the tablet. He glanced at the young father and waited.

The sergeant clenched his hands. A muscle in his thick neck twitched.

Zach voiced his concern. "Does it make you angry to talk about what you saw, Corporal Powers?"

"I found my wife on the floor of this clinic. If it

hadn't been for the doc, Mary Kate would have bled out. How would that make you feel?"

"Worried about my wife's condition."

"I was also worried about my girls. I thought they'd been killed. I was frantic."

"And angry?" Zach added. "Perhaps at your wife for leaving you and taking the children?"

The corporal shook his head. "I was angry that my wife was hurt, and fearful for my daughters. When I found them unharmed and sound asleep, I... I lost it." Hugh pulled in a ragged breath and rubbed his neck.

"You and your wife married when?"

"Five years ago. Soon after the girls were born. Mary Kate was living in the Savannah area. I was stationed at Fort Stewart."

"She was pregnant when you met?"

"That's correct."

"Did you adopt the girls?" Zach asked.

"I'm their father." Anger flashed in his eyes. "Yes, I adopted them."

Other questions came to mind, like who was the biological father, but at that moment, Officer Abrams entered the room and nodded to Zach.

He posed one final question. "You're staying with your in-laws?"

"I am." The corporal nodded. "But right now, I want to go to the hospital and be with my wife."

"Looks like the Freemont police need to ask you some more questions." Zach handed the soldier his card. "Contact me if you remember anything else."

He handed a second card to Abrams. "I'll be in touch."

"You're taking the doc to the Freemont Hospital?"

"Roger that."

Zach returned to the office and studied the blood-stains on the floor. From the position of the blood spatter, he guessed Mary Kate had probably awakened, heard a noise and stumbled into the room, where the intruder had attacked her physically and then shot her with his weapon. Yet the doctor hadn't mentioned hearing gunfire.

He walked to where Taylor was lifting prints off the doctor's desk. "I was at Fort Rickman when the storm hit tonight. We had a lot of lightning and thunder. Was it the same around here?"

The young cop nodded. "Sounded like explosive blasts, one after another. Don't know when I've heard such deafening claps of thunder."

"Loud enough to muffle a gunshot?" Zach asked.

Taylor hesitated for a moment and then nodded. "As loud as Mother Nature was tonight, anything could have been masked by the storm."

"Yet the doctor heard a scream."

"Which could have come between the lightning strikes. I don't think that's a problem, if you're wondering about what the doc remembers. Sergeant Abrams said she's got a bit of amnesia on top of shock. Her memory might return with time."

Zach peered down at the top of the desk. "Have you found any good prints?"

"A few partials. Whether we'll be able to identify anyone from them is the question. They're probably Dr. Jacobsen's or the nurse who works for her. I told you that we took the doc's prints earlier. We'll get the nurse's tomorrow. Won't take long before we know if we've got a match. I'm sure Sergeant Abrams will keep you informed."

"He's got my number."

An engraved invitation embossed with a caduceus logo and printed on heavy ecru card stock caught Zach's attention. He leaned closer, not wanting to touch anything on the desk until Taylor had finished his work.

"Cordially invited… Medical Symposium… Atlanta…" The event was scheduled for the upcoming Friday.

Zach rubbed his jaw. Somehow he couldn't see the rural doc fitting in at what appeared, from the fancy invitation, to be a rather highbrow event. Although maybe there was more to Ella Jacobsen than he realized.

The sound of footsteps caused him to look up as she entered the office. She was wearing gray slacks and a matching rust-colored sweater set. From the damp hair that curled around her face, he guessed she had taken time to shower.

As she stepped closer, he inhaled a fresh floral scent that contrasted sharply with the stale air in the clinic. A roomful of law enforcement types working extended shifts late into the night didn't do much for air quality.

"I appreciate you driving me to the hospital." Her apologetic smile looked more like a grimace. "I doubt there's anything wrong with me other than some scrapes and bruises, yet I always encourage my patients to be examined after any significant injury. I wouldn't be much of a doctor if I didn't practice what I preached."

"Going to the hospital is a good decision."

She glanced at Officer Taylor. "I usually don't leave my desk in such disarray." She tugged a strand of hair behind her ear. "I saw the man standing over it. Maybe he went through my papers."

Taylor pointed to an open cabinet. "Looks like he was going through your patient files, too, ma'am."

"I can't imagine why."

"Have you treated anyone recently that might not want their diagnosis revealed?" Zach asked. "Most folks don't want their medical information to end up in the wrong hands."

"I deal mainly with Amish children. I can't think of anything significant that my patients or their families would want to keep secret."

"What about the twins' condition? Is there any reason for that not to get out?"

Dr. Jacobsen shook her head. "Not that I know of."

"Maybe we'll find a match with one of the prints," Taylor said.

"Are you going to talk to my nurse in the morning?" she asked.

"Yes, ma'am. I'll get her prints then."

Zach pointed to the door. "If you're ready?"

She took a step forward and then hesitated. "I need to tell someone to turn off the lights and lock up when they leave."

The concern for her clinic was understandable. "I'll talk to Sergeant Abrams," Zach said. "Wait here and I'll be back in a minute."

He hurried to the treatment room where Corporal Powers stood with his back to the wall and his arms crossed over his chest. Antagonism was clearly written on his face. Abrams saw Zach and stepped into the hallway.

"I'm taking the doctor to the ER in town," Zach explained. "She's worried about her clinic and asked that the lights be turned off and the doors locked when you leave."

Abrams nodded. "We'll be here until the crime scene folks are finished. Could take most of the night, but tell her I'll make sure we leave the place secure."

"Hopefully, we'll be back before then, but knowing how slow emergency rooms can be, it might be hours before she's seen."

Abrams smiled knowingly. "Our local hospital isn't known for speed, so you're probably right. I'll contact you if we learn anything."

Pointing toward the treatment room, he added, "Corporal Powers is anxious about his wife. He plans to stay at the hospital on post. I imagine someone from your office will question him more thoroughly."

"I'll contact the CID," Zach assured the cop. "One of our people will visit Powers at the hospital. We'll contact his unit and ensure he's getting some support from their end. I'll check on his daughters and in-laws after the doc is treated. He's not a flight risk, and we know where to find him."

"I'll tell him to expect someone at the hospital."

Zach returned to the office, where the doc stood, her eyes wide as she looked around her, no doubt, once-tidy space. What had the assailant wanted? Two women were injured, one seriously, and medical files had been accessed.

In spite of what Abrams had suggested, the guy hadn't broken in looking for drugs. He wanted information or else to do harm. Maybe both. If only the Freemont police would uncover evidence they could use to track down the assailant. Until then the doctor needed to be careful and on guard, lest the guy return to do more damage.

Zach would keep watch, too. He didn't want anything else to happen to the doc.

Chapter Three

If she made her patients wait this long she wouldn't have any. Ella sat in the exam room and hugged her arms around her chest, grateful that Zach hadn't deserted her. His frustration with medical personnel was evident by his frequent sighs and the pointed questions he asked the nurse concerning the lab results and CT scan. Yet he'd tried to buoy Ella's spirits and never complained about his own discomfort.

Of course, the nurse didn't have any way to speed up the lab technologists handling her specimens nor the CT techs, who had probably already given the results to the doctor. But Ella was beginning to feel as frustrated as Zach. Considering the number of patients in the waiting room when they'd arrived at the hospital hours ago, and the number of people who passed by in the hallway, if she received her test and lab results by lunchtime she would consider herself fortunate.

Not the way to run a hospital. Quin would have been equally as annoyed as the special agent, although her husband wouldn't have hung around while she was being treated. He would have mumbled some excuse about needing to get to his research, and left her to find her own transportation home.

Ella shook her head at the memory of what their life together had been like, and then let out a lungful of air, mentally refusing to dwell on the past.

A tap sounded at the door.

She sat up straighter and raked her hand through her hair, not sure who to expect. "Come in."

The door opened, and Zach stepped into the exam room, carrying a white paper bag. "Two coffees from the cafeteria, one with cream and sugar, and two breakfast sandwiches. Egg and sausage sound okay?"

"Sounds delicious. How did you know I needed food?"

"Just a hunch." He glanced at the clock on the wall and then handed her a coffee and sandwich. "Patients could starve to death while they're waiting in the ER."

"I'll remember that in case I'm ever a hospital administrator." She accepted the food he offered.

"You'd be a good one, for sure."

She was taken aback by his comment. He was probably just being nice and making idle chitchat, but she was so accustomed to Quin's negativity that she hadn't expected anything as affirming and supportive. For some reason, she suddenly wanted to cry.

She blinked back the tears that stung her eyes, feeling totally foolish as she removed the plastic lid and took a sip of the hot brew. "Coffee was just what I needed."

Hopefully, he hadn't realized the emotional turmoil that had taken her by surprise. She blamed it on fatigue and her recent brush with death. If only her memory would return, so she could grasp exactly what had happened.

"I thought you'd stepped outside to make a phone call," she said as she unwrapped the sandwich.

"Actually, a number of calls. The first was to CID headquarters and the second to Corporal Powers's unit to ensure they knew what had happened."

"And did they?"

"He called them on his way to the hospital."

"Did you learn anything about Mary Kate's condition?"

"That was my third and final call. She remains critical and in ICU, but her husband is there, and so is her father."

"Maybe they'll offer each other support."

Ella and Zach ate the sandwiches, and by the time they'd finished their coffees, another tap sounded at the door.

"I'll wait in the hallway." Zach left the room as the doctor entered.

"Did I scare him off?" the physician asked.

Ella appreciated Zach's thoughtfulness in leaving so she could talk to the clinician, who seemed oblivious to the importance of patient privacy.

"I'm sure my labs were in normal range," she said, to get the doctor back on track. "But what about the CT scan?"

"You have a slight concussion, so I want you to take it easy for the next twenty-four to forty-eight hours. Continue to ice that lump on your head. You might have headaches for a day or so. Expect muscle soreness, especially where you were kicked. Ibuprofen will help or I can prescribe something stronger."

She held up her hand. "That won't be necessary."

"I don't know if you're a churchgoing woman, but I believe in God's benevolence. He was watching over you last night."

His comment took her aback. She'd never had much of a relationship with God in her youth and had stopped asking for His help when her marriage had fallen apart.

"You were fortunate not to have broken ribs," the ER doc continued. "Or something worse. If anything changes, don't hesitate to come back. I doubt you'll have to wait as long next time."

"I'm hoping there won't be a next time."

"We're short staffed right now, Dr. Jacobsen." He tapped her file. "If you are looking for some weekend or evening work, I'm sure the personnel office would be happy to accept your application for employment."

She smiled at the job offer. "Thanks, but my patients keep me busy."

"I'm sure. We don't see many Amish at the hospital. Every once in a while we'll set a broken bone or tend to some farm injury. As you probably know, the plain folk usually tend to their own medical needs. I know they probably appreciate having you in their area."

"Some do. Some don't."

He nodded. "That's always the way. I wish you the best with your clinic. Let us know if we can be of help."

Ella appreciated his comments almost as much as she was grateful for the clean bill of health. She found Zach in the hallway, and after receiving her treatment notes from the nurse, hurried with him to his car.

He opened the door to the passenger side and held her arm as she settled in the seat. She wasn't used to such attention, but wouldn't do anything to dampen his enthusiasm or good manners.

"I'm glad you're okay," he said.

"Just a little tired, which I'm sure you are, as well. Thank you again."

"No problem." He was silent until they turned onto the main road leading to the Amish community. "I need to know a bit more about Mary Kate, if you feel up to talking."

"I don't know much about her family. She mentioned an older brother in Atlanta."

"Any family history of violence?" Zach asked.

Ella looked down at her hands folded in her lap and weighed what she should tell the special agent. She needed to be truthful, but she also worried about the young family, who seemed to have so many problems.

"Her husband was recently diagnosed with PTSD."

Zach kept his eyes on the road, but pursed his lips before he asked, "Do you know if he's had any volatile incidents?"

"She mentioned a few problems, but nothing about any outbursts on his part. Still, she might have glossed over the severity of their situation."

"One of the CID agents from post plans to question him later today."

"Is he a suspect?"

Zach shook his head. "Not at this point."

"You're sure? Because if you do suspect him, then I'd be worried about the twins' safety."

"After I drop you off, Doc, I plan to pay the grandparents a visit."

"We'll go together. Their house is on the way."

"Didn't the ER doctor prescribe rest?"

"A house call won't tax me unduly. Plus it will ease my mind to know the girls are all right."

"We'll make a short visit. Then you're going straight home."

"Aye aye, sir."

He laughed. "You're mixing branches of the service."

"Whatever works." She smiled. "But do me a favor. My first name's Ella."

"And I'm Zach."

She pointed to the upcoming intersection. "Turn right. Then make another right at the four-way."

She stole a glance at his sturdy shoulders and strong hands. Quin had been a small man. Zach was the exact opposite. He was all brawn and muscle, with deep-set eyes that continued to glance at her.

The strange ripple of interest she felt surprised her. Her marriage had been a failure. She wouldn't try again with any man. Her clinic and her work provided everything she needed. And more.

"There's the house. On the left." She pointed to the two-story colonial with a circular driveway.

"I don't want you to overdo it," Zach cautioned again.

"I'm okay. Really. Ensuring the twins' condition has improved will be better than any meds the doctor at the hospital could have prescribed."

After Zach parked, Ella stepped from the car. Together, they walked to the front door, and he rang the bell.

Lucy Landers, the twins' grandmother, cracked open the door. Her hair was pulled into a bun, and she wore a white apron over a calico dress. "Yes?"

"Mrs. Landers, I'm Dr. Jacobsen from the Children's

Care Clinic. I've been treating the twins and wanted to ensure they were feeling better."

"Oh, forgive me, Dr. Jacobsen. I didn't recognize you." She opened the door wide. "Come in, please."

Ella introduced Zach. "Special Agent Swain is from Fort Rickman. He's investigating what happened at my clinic."

The older woman's eyes filled with tears. "My husband has been at the hospital all night. The doctors told him the next twenty-four hours are so important."

Ella reached for her hand. "The medical personnel know what they're doing."

Mrs. Landers sniffed. "I hope you're right."

Ella glanced around the living room with its simple furnishings, and peered into the hallway. "What about the girls?"

"They're still sleeping."

"Did either child run a temperature in the night?" she asked.

The woman shook her head. "I checked them often. They stayed cool."

"May I see them, Mrs. Landers?"

"Of course." She motioned for Ella and Zach to follow her, and stopped at the threshold of a small bedroom where the twins lay sleeping.

Ella quietly approached the double bed and touched each child's forehead, relieved that both girls felt cool and afebrile. One of the twins blinked her eyes open.

"Hi, Stacey." Ella smiled down at her. "How are you feeling?"

"Fine."

"Does your tummy hurt anymore?"

The little girl shook her head. "I'm hungry."

Ella glanced at the grandmother. "Seems Stacey is ready for breakfast."

"I'm so glad." The woman held out her hand. "Come on, sugar. Let's go into the kitchen. I'll fix you a soft-boiled egg on toast. Won't that taste good?"

The child looked at her sister. "What about Shelly?"

"She'll wake up soon, sugar. When she does, I'll make her an egg, too."

Ella checked the second twin, who stirred and then snuggled down even deeper into the bedding.

"Thanks for bringing me here," Ella whispered to Zach as they left the room. "I'm relieved knowing the girls are better."

"Can I fix something for you folks?" Lucy asked from the kitchen. "How 'bout some coffee?"

"I need to get back to the clinic," Ella said. "If anything changes, call me there."

The front door opened and the twins' grandfather entered the house. Heavyset and in his late fifties, Mr. Landers wore a plaid shirt and dark slacks.

"Are the girls sick again?" he asked in lieu of a greeting.

"No, sir." Ella shook her head. "Both of them seem better. Stacey's in the kitchen waiting for your wife to fix her something to eat. Shelly's sleeping, but her fever has broken. I expect both girls to be back to normal by tomorrow morning."

She introduced Zach.

"You're from the fort?" the older man asked.

"That's right, sir. I'm with the Criminal Investigation Division. We're looking into your daughter's attack. Mrs. Landers said you were with her at the hospital on post. How's her condition?"

"The doctor said she's critical and wouldn't let me stay with her long."

"That's standard policy for patients in intensive care," Ella tried to explain.

He nodded. "Hugh and I took turns. He's having a hard time, and I'm worried about him."

"Grandpa!" Stacey ran from the kitchen and into his open arms.

"How's my Sassafras?"

"I'm not your Sassafras, Grandpa. I'm your Sweet Tea."

His eyes widened. "Then you're not Shelly?"

The little girl giggled. "Shelly's a sleepyhead. Grandma said she'd wake up soon."

"You're feeling better, honey?"

The child nodded. "And hungry. Grandma wants to know if you'll eat some eggs."

"Tell Grandma I'm hungry enough to eat a bear."

The girl laughed and raced back to the kitchen. "Grandpa wants bear with his eggs."

The older man's eyes clouded. "Don't know what we'd do without those girls."

"Sir, does anyone come to mind who might want to harm your daughter?" Zach asked.

He hesitated. "Hard to say."

"So there is someone?"

Mr. Landers nodded. "Levi Miller."

"Has he caused problems, sir?"

"Not problems, but he's passed by a number of times in the last couple months."

"I'm sure many Amish farmers and their families drive their buggies in front of your house," Ella said. "You live on one of the main roads in this area."

"But Levi is different."

"How so, sir?" Zach asked.

"He always had his eye on Mary Kate."

"Levi has a wife," Ella insisted. "They're expecting a child."

Landers snarled. "That doesn't make a bit of difference to some men. If I see him hanging around again, I'll give him a piece of my mind."

"Might be wise to notify the police, sir, if you have a grievance against Mr. Miller," Zach cautioned.

The older man bristled. "I can take care of my family and don't need the cops."

"Sir, your daughter is in ICU. Someone shot her. I beg to differ. You do need law enforcement." Zach handed the man his card. "If you see Levi around here, call me. I'll question him."

"I'm not sure you can help." Mr. Landers excused himself and headed for the kitchen. "You folks can let yourselves out."

When they'd stepped outside, Zach turned to Ella. "At some point, I'll need to talk to Levi Miller."

"Let me know when, and I'll go with you. Levi's wife is a patient of mine." Ella headed for the car and thanked Zach as he held the door for her, before he rounded the vehicle and slipped behind the wheel.

"Mr. Landers isn't a very welcoming man," he said as he turned the car onto the road.

"He's worried and not thinking rationally."

"I'm sure that's the case," Zach agreed, "although there might be some truth to what he told us."

Ella didn't want to see Levi pulled into the investigation. He was a good man and a helpful neighbor. Again, she thought of how life had changed since the attack.

Staring out the window, she took in the rolling hills and farmland that she loved. In the distance, she could see a number of Amish homes. Their way of life had attracted her after Quin's death, when she didn't know where to go or to whom to turn. She'd found comfort here and a sense of welcome from some of the families.

But all that had changed when the intruder broke in last night. Could he have been stalking Mary Kate? If so, Ella refused to believe that Levi was the assailant. He was a man of peace with a sweet wife and a baby on the way.

Zach parked in her driveway and walked her to the front door of the clinic. She pulled the key from her purse, stuck it in the lock and turned the knob.

Glancing into the waiting room, she gasped. Her heart skittered in her chest and the fear she had felt last night returned full force.

"What's wrong?" Zach asked, dropping his hand protectively on her shoulder.

"The attacker," she whispered, unable to control the tremble in her voice. "He returned. This time, he destroyed my clinic."

Chapter Four

Zach grabbed Ella's arm and stopped her from entering the clinic. "Wait in the car. You'll be safer there. I want to check inside to make sure no one's lying in wait."

Her eyes widened. "You think the attacker from last night came back?"

"He wanted something he didn't find. Any idea what that could be?"

She shook her head. "I don't know. I... I thought he was after Mary Kate."

"Which might be the case. What about the children's medical records? Could there be something in their charts that he doesn't want revealed?"

"Maybe."

Zach stared at Ella for a long moment and then pointed to the car. "Stay in my vehicle and keep the doors locked while I search the clinic."

Thankfully, she complied with his instructions and hurried there. She slipped into the passenger seat, hit the lock button and nodded to him when she was securely inside.

Zach pulled out his phone and called Sergeant Abrams.

"I'm at the Children's Care Clinic. Looks like the perpetrator from last night came back. I'm going in to do a search. The doc is outside in my car. I'd appreciate a couple of your people to process the scene. We might find a print that matches something from last night."

Disconnecting, he tugged back his jacket and slipped his SIG Sauer from its holster. He doubted the perp was still on-site, yet he didn't want to go in unprepared. The guy wanted something, or perhaps he'd left something behind and returned to retrieve whatever he'd lost.

Cautiously, Zach entered the clinic, his eyes scanning the room, left to right. He hugged the wall and stepped through the waiting area. The door to the office hung open. Zach stared through the doorway, searching for anything amiss.

The perp had been thorough. The drawers of the doctor's desk hung open, and the contents lay scattered on the floor. Manila folders from the file cabinet were strewn helter-skelter about the room.

Had he been hunting for a certain patient's records? If so, who and why?

Zach checked the closets, where someone could be hiding. The medication cabinet was locked. From all appearances, drugs hadn't been the reason for the break-in.

After moving into the hallway, Zach searched the two treatment rooms, then headed to the door that opened into Ella's residence.

He entered the kitchen, a warm and welcoming room with a round table positioned in front of a bay window. A yellow print tablecloth matched the valances that hung at the windows, and a bouquet of fall flowers adorned the middle of the table.

Zach remembered his home when his mother was still alive. She'd loved flowers and always had them in the house.

They bring God's beautiful nature indoors, he recalled her saying as she'd arranged a bouquet in a crystal vase that had been passed down from her mother. The memory made him pause and stare at the mums on the doc's table. His mother had been a woman of faith, but God didn't play favorites. Or so it seemed.

Shaking off those thoughts, he moved quickly through the living room, then checked the master bedroom with an attached bath and the guest room with its own bath. A third room served as an office. Unlike the clinic, this one had pictures of children on the wall. Zach stepped closer.

A few of the girls wore long dresses, and some boys had dark trousers and hats that covered their bobbed hair. Amish children. From what he knew of the sect, they didn't like photographs. Evidently the doc had gotten special permission to snap the shots.

Diplomas from a number of universities hung near the pictures, along with a picture of Ella and a slender man of medium height with deep-set eyes. He was frowning, as if the photographer had surprised him when he didn't want his photo taken.

Ella stood awkwardly at his side, her hand reaching for his. Had the stoic husband rejected his wife's attempt at closeness, or was that merely Zach's imagination adding a dramatic spin to the reality of what Ella's life had been?

He liked to think he could read people, but the doc was a closed book. Her husband appeared to be equally hard to read.

Turning from the photos, Zach backtracked through the clinic and hurried outside to where Ella waited in his car.

"Did you find anything?" She opened the door as he neared.

"Nothing except a lot of chaos in your office. The treatment area and your residence seem untouched, but the guy was looking for something. Patient records are scattered on the floor. Any ideas?"

"None at all. You tell me what someone might want."

"Information. He attacked Mary Kate. Perhaps he followed her to your clinic, then cut the electricity so he could enter in the dark. He attacks her, probably thought he had killed her, which may have been his goal."

Ella's hand rose to her throat. "I can't imagine anyone wanting to do her harm."

"What information could he be searching for in your patient files? Tell me about the girls' condition."

She shrugged. "Childhood enzyme deficiency is a newly emerging condition. There's a symposium this coming Friday in Atlanta that will focus on a number of conditions, including CED, followed by a charity dinner that will celebrate the research center's success. The proceeds raised will help Amish families with their medical bills and also fund the clinic to ensure the research continues."

"The research center is where your husband worked?"

"That's right. The Harrisburg Genetic Research Center." She pointed to her clinic. "Now if you don't mind, I need to go inside and assess the damage."

Zach held up his hand. "Not yet. The local authorities have to process the crime scene first. You wouldn't want to contaminate the evidence."

"Contamination is something found on a petri dish," she groused.

He tried not to smile, knowing she didn't think waiting on the porch was humorous. Nor did he, but her nose wiggled sometimes when she was upset, which he found amusing, if not charming.

"Does anyone else have a key to your office?"

"Just my nurse and nurse-receptionist, but I trust them completely. I'm more inclined to think someone didn't secure the doors last night. Who was the last one here?"

"We'll ask the officers when they arrive. Sergeant Abrams is on the way."

Ella rubbed her forehead. "Everything still seems so foggy about the attack. I lost consciousness briefly. Short-term memory loss sometimes follows, which seems to be the case."

"Have you remembered anything else?"

She shook her head. "Only my surprise in finding someone standing by my desk. He raised the light he was carrying, and I was caught in its glare. I couldn't see his face. Then…"

Zach saw the anguish in her eyes.

"I… I remember his kicks. The pain. I couldn't breathe."

"You fought back."

"Did I?"

Zach reached for her hand. "Look at your nails and the scratches on your skin."

She glanced down at her broken fingernails and scraped knuckles.

"Does that surprise you?" he asked.

"A little, but it makes me glad. Quin…" She hesitated before adding, "My husband claimed I never stood up for myself."

"Maybe you didn't need to assert yourself when he was around."

"You mean because Quin kept me safe?"

Zach nodded. "That sounds logical to me."

"From what I've seen of you, Special Agent Swain, you are a protector. My husband? Not so much."

Her comment about being a protector gave him pause. He hadn't been able to protect his mother, and while that was long ago and he'd been a young boy, the memory troubled him still.

"You're a doctor," he said, hoping to deflect the conversation away from himself. "You save lives. That's a big responsibility."

"I like children. Being a pediatrician seemed like a good fit, but you're giving me more credit than I deserve."

Before Zach could reply, a patrol car raced along Amish Road and turned into the clinic drive. Sergeant Abrams stepped from the car and nodded as he approached.

"Doctor." He glanced at Zach. "Long time no see, Special Agent Swain."

"Sorry to call you out again." Zach extended his hand. In short, clipped sentences he explained the chain of events that had them hanging out on the porch of her clinic.

"I'd like to go inside as soon as possible to assess any damage that may have occurred," Ella said.

"Yes, ma'am. Just as soon as we take some photos and make a sketch of what we find."

"We?" She glanced into his car, then raised her gaze as another police sedan approached the clinic and turned into the parking lot.

"Officer Taylor," Abrams said by way of an intro-duction as the driver came forward.

"Sir." The younger cop nodded respectfully before shaking Ella's and Zach's hands.

"We met last night," Zach said with a smile.

"You brought your camera?" the sergeant asked.

"Yes, sir. I'll take pictures inside. Shouldn't be too long."

"I don't see why I can't enter my own clinic," Ella com-plained.

"Let us get the photos first. Then I'll want to talk to you," Abrams explained.

"More questions?"

"Yes, ma'am."

The two officers entered the clinic. Ella turned to Zach. "You don't have to babysit me."

He didn't need to hear the frustration in her voice or see the firm set of her jaw to know the doc was upset. "This is all SOP—standard operating procedure—with law enforcement. It's not personal, Ella."

"Remind me to tell you the same thing when your office is trashed."

Perhaps he needed to be more considerate. Getting her mind on something other than her clinic might help.

Zach pointed to the small house on the property next door. "Tell me about your neighbor."

Ella followed his gaze. "Levi Miller and his wife, Sarah, are a nice young couple. They're expecting their first child. Sarah is a patient."

"You deliver babies, too?"

"I can. The Amish hesitate going to large medical facilities and prefer to have Amish midwives or other local medical personnel assist with their deliveries."

"You've been here five months, and it seems you have a good number of patients from the charts strewn about the office."

"I had trouble at first. After the first couple of families sought my help when their children were sick, word spread. Cash can be a problem for the Amish. Sometimes I'm paid in produce or baked goods, sometimes homemade sausage and milk and cheese."

"That hardly covers your mortgage."

"No, but I get by."

"What'd you do before this?" Zach asked.

"You mean in Pennsylvania?"

He nodded. "You talked about your husband, but you haven't mentioned what you did."

"Quin worked for a research clinic that was headquartered in Harrisburg, as I probably told you last night." She raked her hand through her hair. "I'm still fuzzy on a lot of things."

"I thought the Amish were in Lancaster County."

"That's the largest community, but Amish live near Carlisle, as well. Besides, a well-known clinic handles the area around the towns of Intercourse and Bird-in-Hand. Quin's group covered some of the other areas."

"And you?" Zach asked.

"I had a pediatric clinic in Carlisle."

"Where the Army War College is located."

"You've been there?" she asked.

"A few years back. Carlisle seemed like a nice place. Dickinson College is located there."

"That's right."

"What made you move South?" he asked.

She tilted her head and shrugged. "I needed a change. I would always be Quin Jacobsen's widow if I stayed there. I wanted to make my own way." She smiled weakly. "That sounds self-serving, but I don't mean it in that way. Quin was a larger-than-life type of guy, speaking academically. Sometimes I felt dwarfed by his presence."

From the short time Zach had known Ella, she seemed down-to-earth and committed to her patients. Thinking of the picture he'd seen of her in the office, he could understand what she was saying.

She rubbed her hands together and glanced at her clinic. "What's taking so long?"

"I'll check." Zach hurried inside and found Abrams. "The doc wants to assess the damage. Have you gotten all the photos you need?"

"Almost. Taylor needs to take a couple of her desk and then we'll be finished."

"What about fingerprints?"

"We lifted a few from the file cabinet and the folders strewn over the floor. Two or three look promising. I'll run them when I get back to headquarters."

"You'll let me know?"

"As soon as I hear anything."

As Taylor snapped shots of the desk, Zach stepped closer. He leaned over the engraved invitation he'd seen the night before.

Abrams glanced over his shoulder. "From the looks of that, the event appears to be a snazzy gathering. The doc seems more like a country girl."

"I'm sure she would fit in no matter the environment."

"You're probably right." The older officer looked around the clinic. "Looks like we've got what we need for now. Tell the doc she can come inside."

When Zach opened the door, he was surprised to see a young man standing on the porch with her.

Ella introduced him as he neared. "Special Agent Swain, this is my neighbor, Levi Miller."

The neighbor was dressed in the typical dark slacks held up with suspenders. A wide-brimmed hat sat atop his blond hair, and he wore a cotton shirt probably sewn by his wife.

"You live in the next house?" Zach pointed to the small one-story home.

"*Yah*. My wife and I live there."

"Did you hear anything last night, Mr. Miller?"

"I heard the storm."

"Did you hear sirens or see the police here?"

The man's face clouded. "My wife glanced from the window. She was worried about Dr. Jacobsen."

"But you didn't check on her last night," Zach pressed.

"That's why I came today." The Amish man turned to Ella. "You are all right?"

"Someone broke into the clinic. He shot Mary Kate Powers."

Levi's face blanched. "She was hurt?"

Ella touched the Amish man's arm. "Quite seriously, I'm afraid. She's at the hospital on post and is in critical condition."

"May *Gott's* will be done."

Zach didn't understand the comment. "You know Mary Kate?"

"Her parents have a home not far from here. We knew each other as children."

Zach wondered if that friendship had continued into adulthood.

"What about the twins?" Levi asked. The concern in his voice was clearly obvious.

"They're fine," Ella assured him. "Thankfully, they were asleep in the treatment room, and the attacker left through the front door after accosting their mother."

Levi let out a ragged breath. "I am relieved."

"You know the twins?" Zach asked.

The Amish man steeled his gaze. "Twins are easy to recognize, Special Agent Swain. They have been getting treatments at the Children's Care Clinic for some months now. I have a farm and work outside. Of course I have seen them."

"What would you call your relationship with their mother?" Zach remembered the grandfather's words about the Amish man who seemed much too attentive to his daughter.

"There is no relationship."

"You haven't tried to reconnect with Mary Kate?" Zach asked.

"A married man has eyes only for his wife." He looked at Ella. "If you need my help, let me know."

"Thank you, Levi."

With a nod, he turned and walked back to his property.

Zach watched him enter his house. "There's something Levi's not telling us."

Ella lowered her gaze, as if she, too, had something to hide.

Zach stared down at her. "Is there something about Levi that I need to know?"

"Of course not." After an abrupt about-face, Ella pushed open the door to her clinic and stepped inside.

Zach glanced back at the Miller farm. A cold wind

whipped across the expansive pasture area and along the road, picking up dust and blowing it in the air.

What was the truth about this Amish community and the doctor who had left her practice in Pennsylvania to move South? Was she being less than forthright? If so, why?

All her work had seemingly been for naught. Standing at the entrance to her clinic, Ella was overcome with despair. She had tried to create an environment where Amish children, used to the simple basics in their own homes, could be comfortable even when they were sick and upset. Surrounded by medical instrumentation and equipment, they could easily become wide-eyed and fearful, which only made their parents more on edge. The adults were often torn between their concern for their sick children and their own hesitation to trust the new doctor.

As she gazed at the disarray, Ella wondered what they would think if they saw the place in such a state of chaos. Her hard work up to this point and her dreams of what the clinic could be in the future had been all but dashed by the hand of a madman.

"Who would do this?" she asked, struggling to articulate even that brief question. Wrapping her arms around her chest, she glanced at the officers, who had stopped processing the crime scene and were staring at her.

Did they think she was becoming hysterical?

Zach entered the clinic behind her and touched her arm. Was he offering comfort or was he, too, afraid she might be ready for a breakdown?

"Who was the last person in here last night?" Ella demanded, feeling a swell of anger. She stared at Abrams. "Did you lock the door? Did you secure my clinic or did you leave the door open and vulnerable to the madman, who returned to find what he'd wanted the first time?"

They continued to look at her as if she were crazed, and perhaps she was—crazed with frustration at all that had happened.

Abrams stepped forward. "I asked one of my officers to make sure your clinic was secure. I trust he did as I directed."

Officer Taylor moved closer. "The assailant could have had a key. You know he cut your power, ma'am. It wasn't the storm that caused your outage. Someone tampered with your wiring. We got it working last night, and I checked your generator. The spark plug had been unscrewed. No wonder it wouldn't engage."

"So someone was prowling around here before the storm?" She shivered at the thought of the assailant stalking her and her clinic.

"Seems that way. Is there anyone who'd want to do you harm?"

"No, not that I know of." She glanced at Zach, hoping he would offer some other reason for the attack.

"The young mother, Mary Kate Powers, might have some bearing on the case," he volunteered. "Her husband recently returned from the Middle East. Her father is concerned about the Amish man who lives next door."

"You mean Levi Miller?" Abrams asked.

"Levi wouldn't have done anything to harm Mary Kate," Ella was quick to point out.

"Why do you say that, ma'am?" the sergeant asked.

"He and Mary Kate knew each other in their youth. I believe they were close friends."

The cop looked puzzled. "Amish and English, as they call us, make for an unusual friendship."

"They were young, Sergeant Abrams. That hardly seems strange to me."

"Yes, ma'am, but Mary Kate would have gone to Freemont High," the sergeant said. "Levi Miller would have received his instruction at the Amish schoolhouse."

"They could still be friends even if they didn't go to school together," she insisted. "The Landerses live in this area. Amish children roam the fields and think nothing of walking great distances. They don't have the fear that keeps some of the town children from wandering far from their homes."

Ella looked at Zach and then back to the Freemont officer. "As you probably know, the Amish children work hard, but when their chores are finished they're free spirits. I can see Mary Kate getting to know Levi as a youngster."

"Yet her father seems to harbor a grudge against Levi," Zach interjected.

"Landers holds a grudge against a number of people in the local community," Abrams volunteered. "He's known as a grumpy old man."

"Are you saying his animosity toward Levi should be ignored?" Zach asked.

"Hardly." The sergeant shook his head. "We'll take everything into consideration, but I'm not going to falsely accuse anyone based on what a crusty old codger has to say."

As Zach and he continued to discuss the case, Ella rubbed her neck. Her head pounded and her body ached from the attack last night. Ibuprofen would help, but she didn't want medication, she wanted to breathe in fresh air and feel the sunshine on her face. A more holistic approach to healing.

"If you'll excuse me for a minute, I've got a patio out back," she said. "I just need some air."

Rubbing her temple, she hurried into her kitchen and out the back door. She had expected warm sunshine, but was instantly chilled by a stiff wind that blew from the west. Wrapping her arms around herself, she stared into the wooded area behind her house, seeing the fall colors and the branches swaying in the breeze. Overhead, geese honked, flying in a V formation. If only she could fly away from the chaos like them and find a peaceful spot to land that would calm her troubled spirit.

Movement caught her eye and she glanced again at the woods. What had she seen? An animal foraging in the underbrush?

Or...

Ella narrowed her gaze and took a step back as if subconsciously recognizing danger. Her heart lurched. She turned and ran for the protection of her house. Tripping, she fell on the steps.

A sound exploded in the quiet of the day.

A ceramic flowerpot shattered at her feet.

Another shot was fired and then another.

She screamed, stumbled up the porch stairs and reached for the door.

Zach was there, pulling her inside to safety. He shoved her to the floor and slammed the door. "Stay down."

"A man," she gasped, her pulse racing, a roar filling her ears. "In the woods. He—he had a rifle..."

Zach lifted the curtain ever so slightly and stared through the window.

The two policemen raced into the kitchen. "Gunfire?"

Zach pointed. "The doc saw a man at the edge of the forest."

"A dirt road runs parallel to the tree line." Sergeant Abrams motioned to the younger officer. "We'll head there from opposite directions."

Abrams radioed for more squad cars. "There's a shooter in the woods behind the Children's Care Clinic. We need to search the area and set up roadblocks. Someone needs to check the wooden bridge that's along that road, as well."

Zach locked the doors when the two officers had left, racing away in their squad cars. The sound of sirens filled the air as more Freemont police responded to the call.

Ella huddled against the wall in the corner, while Zach kept watch at the windows. The tension that lined his face spoke volumes about the danger, but she didn't need to look at him to know that the situation had escalated.

What she realized made her tremble with fear. Last night, the police were looking for an assailant who had broken into her clinic and attacked two women.

Today that assailant had become a killer.

And the person he wanted to kill was her.

Chapter Five

"We found spent rifle casings at the edge of the tree line," Sergeant Abrams said, holding up the evidence bag to Ella, when he and Officer Taylor returned to the clinic.

Seeing the casings made her feel even less secure.

"Looks like thirty caliber." Zach stepped closer and studied the back of one of the rounds. "They're 30-30 to be exact."

Abrams nodded. "Someone was holed up for a period of time, judging from the way the underbrush was trampled down. Could have been the guy from last night. He hides in the woods and watches for the doc to return, only he can't see the parking lot in front of the clinic."

"So he didn't see squad cars parked there and didn't realize law enforcement was on-site," Zach mused.

"That's what I'm thinking." The sergeant scratched his chin. "If he didn't find what he wanted last night, he could have waited for the doctor to return."

"You're sure he was after me?" Ella rubbed her hands together, trying to dispel her nervousness.

"Seems that way, although we can't be sure," the cop

said. "Folks who commit crimes aren't always the smartest people. He might have another reason to be lying in wait. We'll process the prints we took earlier and see if any are on the shell casings. We might find new prints that match what we lifted last night. That would mean the attacker came back. If not, we could be dealing with two independent crimes, although that doesn't seem likely." He looked at Zach. "Anything come to mind?"

"Never say never."

Abrams nodded. "That's exactly the way I feel."

The two Freemont officers headed for the door. "We'll increase patrols in this area and keep our eyes open in case the shooter returns, but we're finished here for now," Abrams said. "We'll stop by Mr. Miller's farm and talk to him. Join us, Special Agent Swain, if you have time."

Zach nodded. "I appreciate the offer, but I'll talk to Levi a bit later. If he happens to reveal anything of value, I'd like to be notified."

"Will do." Abrams turned to Ella. "Might be a good idea to install dead bolts and even an alarm system, Dr. Jacobsen. A watchdog would be a deterrent to crime, as well. Keep your cell charged and near you at all times. You might want to move to town until this case is solved."

"I'm staying here, Sergeant Abrams. My patients need to know where to find me. I wouldn't be much good to them if I was holed up in a hotel in town. Besides, I refuse to run scared."

"I wouldn't call that running, ma'am. I'd call it being prudent and safe."

The cop shook Zach's hand and nodded to her. "I'll be in touch, Dr. Jacobsen. Don't hesitate to call us if you think of anything that might have a bearing on this case."

"I'll be sure to do that."

The officers left the house yet again. Ella stood at the window and watched as they climbed into their patrol cars. Then, letting out a deep sigh, she turned her gaze to the Miller home.

Levi's wife, Sarah, was a sweet young woman, though somewhat reserved. Ella hoped that everything that had happened wouldn't upset her unduly or cause her more worry. The baby was due in three months. Hopefully, the birth would be uneventful, but the last thing Ella wanted was for the young wife to be distressed.

Zach stepped to her side and followed her gaze. "You're worried about Levi?"

"I'm more concerned about Sarah and their baby. They've requested genetic testing, but the results won't come back for some time."

"Do you suspect a problem?"

"There's no way to tell until I hear from the lab."

"Could the Miller baby have the same condition as the twins?"

Ella nodded. "It's a possibility."

Zach started to say something, but her office phone rang. She reached for the receiver.

"Children's Care Clinic. This is Dr. Jacobsen."

"It's Nancy Vaughn, Ella."

The director of the research center where Quin had worked.

"Is something wrong, Dr. Vaughn?"

"Actually, I'm calling to make sure you're all right. A reporter from the *Atlanta Journal-Constitution* asked for a statement about the medical symposium this Friday. He wanted to know if Dr. Jacobsen's widow would be attending. I haven't heard from you and thought there might be a problem."

"You don't need me there, Dr. Vaughn."

"Quin's death hit us hard, as you know, Ella. We were in the midst of gathering data and coming up with our final determination. Now that the studies have been completed, we want to recognize Quin."

"I hardly think that's necessary."

"Don't keep us from honoring one of our own, Ella."

"No, of course I wouldn't do that."

"Then it's settled. You'll come to Atlanta and be with us this Friday. Freemont is only two hours from the city. There's no reason to stay away."

Ella picked up the embossed invitation. "Perhaps I'll come for the symposium..."

"And the dinner following," the director insisted. "I want you there. It's a black-tie event, so that's a good excuse to get a new dress. I'll look forward to seeing you."

"I'm not sure."

"I won't take no for an answer."

Nancy Vaughn was like that.

Before the director could hang up, Ella quickly added, "Did you review Quin's data on the Amish Project? I've looked through most of his notes, but I can't find any discrepancies."

"Discrepancies? Why are you questioning his work?"

"I'm not, but something bothered him, as I told you when we last talked. He was concerned about the response of twin patients who were given the treatment."

"There were no problems, as I already told you."

"But—"

"No buts. We'll see you Friday."

The director disconnected before Ella could say anything else.

She sighed as she hung up the phone, and then looked up to see Zach staring at her.

"Is something wrong?" he asked.

She shook her head. "No, nothing's wrong. My husband's research center is discussing their findings on CED."

"The disease the twins have?"

Ella nodded. "I called the director when Mary Kate first brought the girls to the clinic."

"It sounded as if you were concerned about something your husband found."

"Quin was intense, especially when he was working toward a breakthrough. He became more and more upset about some results that he couldn't understand. He kept saying the Amish twins held the answer."

"You're not talking about Shelly and Stacey."

"No, there were other cases. Three sets of twins that hadn't responded the way he had hoped."

"You mentioned his notes on the Amish Project?"

"That's what the CED study was called. The director, Dr. Nancy Vaughn, never wanted work taken home. There's always a worry that some other clinic will get access to the data and use it as their own."

"Stealing data for scientific gain or for financial compensation?" he asked.

"Probably both, although I don't think Quin ever worried about his work being stolen. He was more concerned about why the treatment he had developed wasn't effective."

"The director couldn't offer any answers?" Zach pressed.

"She has a lot on her mind and seemed surprised the last time we talked about Quin taking his notes home. I assured her he was careful to keep his files secure."

"You've gone through his notes?"

"And found nothing."

"Does that seem strange to you?"

Ella weighed her words. She didn't want the special agent to jump to the wrong conclusions. "Quin's entire focus was on his work, especially close to his death."

Zach stared at her. "Does that mean he turned his focus away from you?"

It wasn't a question she expected. "I didn't say that."

"But it's what you didn't say."

She shook her head, suddenly flustered. "You're reading more into my statement."

"Am I?"

She dropped the invitation onto her desk and bent to pick up some of the scattered papers.

"I'm sorry if I upset you, Ella."

"It's not you." She let out a deep breath. "It's everything that's happened."

"You'll feel better once the clinic is back in order. I'll help you."

"I don't need help," she insisted, although she did. But right now she was so confused and worried. Would her life ever get back to the way it had been?

"Perhaps you don't, but I'm not leaving you alone with so much to do," Zach insisted.

"You sound as strong-willed as my husband."

Instantly, she regretted her remark. Zach wasn't strong-willed, and he wasn't anything like her husband. When she looked at Zach, she saw compassion and understanding in his gaze.

At least she thought she did.

Or was she as wrong about Zach as she had been about Quin?

* * *

Zach encouraged Ella to sit and direct him as he cleaned up the clinic, but evidently, she didn't trust him to get it right, because she insisted on doing everything herself. At least she let him install the dead bolts she had bought some weeks earlier but hadn't taken out of the shopping bag.

She had a toolbox filled with the basics, one that might have belonged to her husband. Although if the tools had been his, then Quin Jacobsen hadn't been much of a handyman. Still, Zach found what he needed and soon had the dead bolts installed.

He checked her windows, relieved to find double-paned glass and substantial locks that would be hard to pry open.

"Sergeant Abrams mentioned a security alarm," Zach reminded Ella, after securing the doors and checking the windows. "Even the most basic, easy-to-install wireless system, would be an excellent safeguard."

She cocked her head and frowned. "And if the alarm goes off, who comes to my rescue?"

"The alarm service calls the Freemont police."

"How long would it take them to respond?" she asked.

"As long as it takes them to respond to a 911 call. The idea is for the alarm to warn you if an area of your house, namely a window or door, is breached. In the middle of the night, you could sleep through someone trying to get into your clinic. The alarm would alert you."

Ella stared at Zach for a moment and then nodded. "I see your point. The receptionist who works for me is married to an electrician. He might be able to install a system."

"The sooner the better," Zach added.

"What if the Amish decide I'm not someone they want treating their children?"

He didn't understand her logic. "Because they'll see the alarm system?"

"Yes, and because of the shots that were fired today. Am I being foolish?"

"Only if you don't think of your own safety. The Amish may not even hear about the break-in at your clinic or the shooter in the woods."

She sighed as she picked up a pile of files and returned them to the cabinet. "Obviously you haven't been around the Amish. Even without modern conveniences like telephones and social media, news travels."

A key turned in the door, surprising both of them. Zach stepped protectively in front of Ella.

The woman who pushed her way inside was dressed in light blue scrubs that covered her full figure. The embroidered emblem on her uniform read Children's Care Clinic. Evidently the newcomer—in her midforties, with rosy cheeks and pink lipstick—worked for the doc.

The nurse opened her arms and headed straight for Ella. Zach had to step aside to keep from being run over.

"I've been so worried," the woman gushed. "The police stopped at my house. They took my fingerprints and wanted to make sure I hadn't given the clinic key to anyone. Why didn't you call me?"

She wrapped Ella in a warm embrace.

"I'm fine, Wendy. You shouldn't have worried. I planned to call you, but somehow time got away from me."

"You were hurt and fought for your life? That's the story I heard."

"I wasn't injured, but Mary Kate Powers is in the hospital at Fort Rickman with a gunshot wound."

The woman pulled back, her eyes wide. "I had no idea. Tell me the twins weren't hurt."

"They're fine and staying with their grandparents."

Seemingly, the newcomer posed no threat. Zach stepped closer, and Ella introduced him to Nurse Wendy Kelsey.

"You're from post?" she asked, after hearing "CID" in the introduction.

"That's right." Zach nodded. "I'm working with the Freemont police. How did you learn about the attack?"

"The cop who took my prints said someone broke in and attacked Ella." Wendy patted her chest as she glanced at her employer. "I called your cell but couldn't get an answer. I decided to drive here and see if I could find out what happened."

"Someone ransacked the clinic this morning. Special Agent Swain is helping me tidy the clutter."

Wendy stuck her purse in one of the cabinets and hung up the sweater she was wearing. "Why don't you fix yourself a cup of tea and let me get to work."

Ella visibly relaxed. "That sounds perfect. Thank you, but I'll brew some coffee and be back with cups for everyone." She turned to Zach. "You take yours black?"

"Black and strong."

Ella headed to the hallway that led to her residence and returned ten minutes later with three steaming cups. The hot brew was exactly what Zach needed.

He and Wendy quickly cleaned up the remaining items, and the nurse had the place looking even better by the time he had finished his coffee.

"I'll call the patients who have appointments and

see if they can come another day," she said. "In fact, I suggest the clinic remain closed through the weekend and open again on Monday."

"Our Amish patients don't have phones, Wendy. How can you contact them?" Ella asked.

"The twins were the only children scheduled for today. I'll call their grandmother and cancel their visit and reschedule the other non-Amish patients. Thankfully, you don't have any appointments with Amish patients for the rest of the week."

"That's a good idea." Zach glanced at Ella. "The case may be solved by Monday. Plus it gives you more time to heal and gain your strength."

"You might be right." She stepped closer to the nurse. "I stopped by the Landerses' house this morning and checked on the twins. They're both doing well."

"You've made a difference in those girls' lives." Wendy turned to Zach. "If Ella hadn't diagnosed their condition, they wouldn't have survived. That assured many of the local folks, when they saw the twins improve."

The nurse continued to share stories about the positive impact Ella had made on the community until the doc waved off her praise. "I did what any physician would do. Fortunately, my husband's work provided the answers. Otherwise everything could have been very different."

She went to the window and pulled back the curtains. "The sun is shining. I want a little of that to brighten the clinic. You've both done so much to make it better. Thank you, Wendy."

Turning to Zach, Ella said, "I didn't expect a special agent in law enforcement to be so handy. The dead bolts will keep me secure and give me peace of mind."

Looking at her nurse, she asked, "Would you call

Beth and inquire if her husband can install a security alarm for me?"

Wendy nodded. "Good idea. I'm on it."

Glancing out the window, Zach noticed a red pickup racing along the road past the clinic. The tires squealed as it turned into the farm next door.

"Looks like Levi Miller has company," he said, heading for the door.

Ella peered out the window. "It's Mary Kate's husband. What's he up to?"

"I'll check it out."

"I'll go with you," Ella stated. "I want to find out about Mary Kate's condition."

"You should stay here," Zach insisted.

"Nonsense." She opened a cabinet and pulled out a black medical bag. "I need to check on Levi's wife, as well."

He glanced at the bag. "Doctors still make house calls?"

She nodded. "They do in rural Georgia."

"We'll take my car."

Ella was puzzled. "But the Millers live next door."

"And someone tried to shoot you in your backyard."

She nodded, realizing he was right. Her eyes fell on the weapon he carried under his jacket. She couldn't deny the sense of security that knowing Zach was armed gave her.

"You'll protect me." She said it as a statement.

"Of course I will."

The confidence and assurance of his answer warmed her heart. She'd be safe with the special agent. At least, that was her hope.

Chapter Six

Some folks might call the doc headstrong. Zach thought independent was more apropos. Had her need to prove herself gotten her in trouble? Or had the attack at the clinic been a result of a strong-willed doctor trying to push her way into someplace she wasn't wanted?

Last night, she'd been scared and needing reassurance when she'd stepped into his arms, after remembering the gun the attacker had brandished.

What had made Zach pull her into his embrace? He wasn't one to be swayed by a pretty face or silky hair and big eyes, yet he'd reacted without thinking.

Everything within him had wanted to comfort Ella and protect her. Not because she was a doctor. He didn't have much use for physicians, especially country docs, like the one who had made a tragic error that had led to his mother's death.

No, the woman he'd seen last night had been Ella Jacobsen, without the physician facade. Perhaps she hadn't realized the vulnerability she'd revealed to him at that moment. Something that was at the heart of who she was when she didn't try to be in charge.

Ella paused momentarily by the door to glance at her reflection in a wall mirror. Gingerly, she touched the puffy bruise on her cheek and frowned.

A number of bruises were all too evident in the sunlight steaming through the window. The sight of her injuries made Zach's gut tighten. No one should ever hurt a woman. Seeing the marks on her face and another bruise on her arm enhanced his desire to find the heinous individual who had caused Ella so much pain. Unless the attacker was found and apprehended, he'd be back again.

"I'm ready," she said. "Let's pay the Millers a visit."

"You haven't slept, Doc. Sure you wouldn't rather stay here?"

She straightened her shoulders. "You haven't slept, either, Special Agent Swain."

"Zach, remember?"

Some of her bravado faltered, and she smiled, causing a jolt of energy to take him by surprise. He'd thought Ella Jacobsen was pretty last night, but in the light of day, he realized how wrong he'd been. She was beautiful.

"We'll go together," Zach said. "But do me a favor and follow my lead."

"Of course."

Was she being sincere or condescending?

Clutching her doctor's bag, she opened the front door and stepped outside. Hurriedly, she descended the stairs and walked with determined steps to his vehicle. As much as it seemed like a waste of fuel to drive such a short distance, Zach needed to keep Ella safe.

After parking in the Millers' driveway, he stepped from the car and flicked his gaze to the wooded area behind the house and the pasture in the distance, looking for anything that might spell danger.

Before he could round the hood to open the passenger door, Ella had stepped out and, bag in hand, was racing toward the house.

The woman had stamina, Zach would give her that.

"Are you in a hurry?" he asked, falling into step beside her.

"Just focused on seeing if Sarah is okay. I've got a strange feeling that all of this hubbub has taken its toll on her. She's in her early twenties and has been racked with morning sickness for the last six months."

"I thought it eased up after the first three."

"That's usually the case, but some women continue to have problems into the second and even third trimester. Sarah has lost weight instead of gaining, and she's anxious about the health of her child. She and Levi lost a baby at seven months. That was before I arrived in the area. As you can imagine, she's worried this baby might have problems."

"I'm sure having a doctor next door has eased her worry."

"I wish that was the case. Instead, I've opened up other concerns."

"You mean the incidents of genetically acquired diseases that the Amish carry?"

"That's it exactly. Some of them would rather not know about the complications."

"Are any upset enough to break into your clinic?"

Ella turned to stare at him quizzically. "You must not understand the Amish or you wouldn't suspect them."

"I understand human nature and the fact that bad people can be found in any population. Even the Amish."

"They're a peaceful people who put their faith in God."

"Perhaps that's their mistake."

She narrowed her gaze. "You don't believe in God?"

"I believe there is a God, but I believe man is responsible for his own actions. I also know that some men and women live by another rule, other than the golden rule. Evil exists. I'm sure it exists even in the Amish community."

Nearing the house, Zach turned his focus to sounds that were floating from the side of the property. Sounds of an argument.

"Stay here, Doc."

He hurried ahead and made a wide arc around the house to better see the source of the raised voices. Hugh Powers and Levi Miller came into view. The corporal was waving his hands in the air, visibly upset. Levi kept his at his sides and was responding to Hugh in what sounded like a calm and steady voice. Zach moved closer to hear more of their conversation.

"Do you understand what I'm saying?" The muscular military guy jabbed his finger against Levi's chest. "You have no business hanging around Mary Kate."

"I would not hurt your wife," Levi replied, his voice even and his body relaxed.

Zach admired the young lad for keeping his cool.

Hugh raised a fist. "You know what happens to people who harm anyone I love?"

"Corporal Powers," Zach called, stepping closer.

Hugh's brow furrowed. "What are you doing here?"

"That's the question I wanted to ask you. This is Levi Miller's property. Did he invite you onto his land?"

"He invited my wife." Hugh's voice was laced with

anger. He steeled his jaw, turned his gaze back to the Amish man and pointed a finger at Levi's suspenders. "You may look peaceful with the funny clothes you and your friends wear, but you're hiding your true nature."

"I have nothing to hide."

"You need to pay for your transgressions." The soldier's eyes narrowed. "For your sins, Mr. Miller. My father-in-law told me what you did to my wife. Then you disappeared, hiding out in your closed community that claims to be holier than thou. But in reality you're a pervert who preys on an unsuspecting woman."

Zach moved closer. "We can discuss your suspicions, Corporal Powers, but in a less heated manner. Take a step back, and give Mr. Miller some space."

"He doesn't deserve space."

"Do you need to go to CID headquarters, where we can discuss this at length? That's not going to help Shelly or Stacey. Or your wife."

At the mention of his wife, the soldier's head drooped. He turned and walked away from both of them, his shoulders shaking.

Levi glanced at Zach but said nothing.

Zach gave the soldier a minute to pull himself together, then stepped to the man's side and touched his back. "You're upset, Hugh. I understand that you want to find the person who hurt your wife, but you need to work with law enforcement and not take things into your own hands. If you harm or even antagonize Mr. Miller, I'll be forced to haul you in. That's not what you want."

The big guy pursed his lips and then blew out a breath. "I can't stand seeing Mary Kate hurt like that. She's hooked up to tubes and looks like she's going to die." He stared at Zach. "I saw enough death when I was deployed. I didn't expect to come home to see my wife bloody and beaten. Do you understand why I want to fix her pain and make everything right?"

"Of course I understand, but you've got to let law enforcement handle the investigation." Zach passed his business card to the soldier. "I gave you my card last night, but here's another one. Keep this in your barracks or your truck, and call me whenever you think of anything that might have bearing on the investigation. Or call if you want to check on what we've uncovered. I won't hold back the truth from you, but you have to be forthright with me, as well."

The soldier nodded. "I told you everything I knew last night."

"Then why did you come here? What were you hoping to accomplish?"

"I… I wanted to warn Miller to stay away from my wife."

Zach glanced at Levi and then turned back to Corporal Powers. "What makes you think Levi was interested in Mary Kate?"

"My father-in-law saw them together more than once."

"Before you redeployed home?"

"That's right. He was worried about Mary Kate. Worried about her safety."

From what Zach knew about Mary Kate's father, the old man was prone to jumping to the wrong conclusion, yet there had to be some semblance of truth in what he'd told his son-in-law.

"Is everything okay?"

Ella's voice.

Zach turned to see her standing at the side of the house. She walked toward Levi. "How's Sarah?"

"She's sick again, and it troubles her. Her father says it's *Gott's* will, but she worries that it means something's wrong with the baby."

"I told you the nausea had nothing to do with the baby's condition. It's caused by the hormones Sarah's body is producing because she is pregnant."

"Her mother had no sickness, and she delivered healthy children."

"But Sarah is her own person. Every pregnancy is different."

Levi's gaze darkened. "Yet Sarah was sick the first time."

"Again, Levi, that's her body's response to the pregnancy and doesn't have anything to do with the well-being of this baby."

"I want to believe you, Dr. Jacobsen, but I still worry."

"I understand." Ella patted his arm. "You love your wife, but you can believe me, Levi."

"I believe in *Gott's* will. He may take this child like he took the first. Perhaps because of my mistake years ago."

Ella glanced at Zach and then back at Levi. "Your mistake?"

"I was young and headstrong. My father said a man needs to keep his eyes to himself. He told me *Gott* would find a righteous woman. Instead I looked elsewhere."

Hugh turned, his face flushed with anger, and pointed to Levi. "Are you blaming Mary Kate for what happened? It was your fault, Miller. You're a hypocrite.

You told her you loved her, that you'd never leave her and that you could have a life together, but those were all lies."

Sadness washed over Levi's face. "I did not lie."

"You didn't do anything to help her. You lousy—"

Zach grabbed the soldier's arm. "Let's all take a deep breath."

Hugh stopped and shook his head. "I'm not going to hurt him. I don't touch men who don't fight back and who don't protect the woman they say they love."

He glared at Levi. "You lied to Mary Kate. You told her you loved her and that you wanted to marry her. She was young, and she trusted you, Miller. That was her mistake. Your mistake was to get her pregnant."

Hugh jerked his arm from Zach's hold. "I'm going home to be with my daughters. The precious children you abandoned, Miller. I adopted them. They bear my name and they're my children. So stay away from them, and stay away from my wife."

The soldier walked purposefully back across the yard. Zach let him go. As the red pickup pulled out of the driveway, Zach phoned Sergeant Abrams and passed on what Hugh had just revealed.

"Might be a good idea to head to the grandparents' home and question both Mr. Landers and Hugh," he added. "Find out if either of them own a rifle. I'll stay here and talk to Levi Miller. Did you learn anything from him earlier?"

"He seems to be on the up-and-up."

"That's what I wanted to hear."

"I've got a patrol car in the vicinity of the grandparents' house. My guys will make sure Corporal Powers stays put until I have a chance to question him."

Relieved that the Freemont police would check on the Landers family, Zach disconnected and glanced over his shoulder at Ella, who stood next to Levi.

"I didn't hurt her," the Amish man insisted, as Zach moved back to them. "I would never hurt Mary Kate." Levi's voice was tight with emotion. "I loved her. It wasn't as her husband said."

"What about now, Mr. Miller?" Zach asked. "Do you still have feelings for Mary Kate?"

"Levi?" A frail voice sounded from the small, wood-frame house.

Zach glanced at the door, where a young woman—a very pregnant woman—stood staring at her husband.

"Are you all right, Levi?" she asked.

"*Yah*, Sarah. I am fine. Do not worry."

Her hands rubbed her belly, and her eyes filled with sadness as if she'd heard everything that had transpired.

The strain visible on Ella's face revealed that she, too, understood the gravity of the situation. Had she known all along that Levi was the girls' biological father?

The disease Ella had diagnosed was found most often among the Amish. Zach should have put two and two together last night, but he'd been so focused on the doctor that he'd failed to realize what seemed so obvious today.

Had Levi attacked Mary Kate out of anger because she'd come back to Freemont and disrupted his life, perhaps causing his wife untold anxiety? Or was he after the medical records that revealed the disease the twins had inherited? Information in their file could point to their Amish background and could even mention their biological father. If that were the case, then Ella had kept that information from Zach, as well.

He flicked his gaze to her, berating himself for being

so easily swayed. He didn't trust doctors, not even pretty ones with bruised cheeks and big eyes—eyes that stared at him now as if he was the one who had brought pain to this small Amish community.

Do no harm. Ella tried to practice medicine according to the Hippocratic Oath, but she had caused pain and suffering. Had coming to Georgia been a mistake?

She read distrust and questions in the special agent's eyes as he continued to stare at her. Did he blame her, even as she was blaming herself?

"Levi?" Once again, Sarah called to her husband.

"Everything is all right," he said, as if hoping to reassure her. One look at Sarah's face and it was evident his words had no effect on calming her unease.

The *clip-clop* of horse hooves caused them all to look toward the road. A bearded man sat holding the reins as an Amish buggy passed. He nodded to Levi.

Zach watched as the buggy continued on. Then, turning, he studied the wooded area behind the house and the pastures to one side. His expression of concern made Ella realize that standing outside in the open exposed all of them.

"We need to finish this discussion inside," Levi said, no doubt picking up on the special agent's worry. "Please, come into my house." He motioned them toward the door.

"Sarah can come to the clinic with me," Ella suggested. "If you men want to talk in private."

"No." Levi shook his head. "Sarah needs to hear what I will say." Again, he pointed to the door. "Please."

Ella hurried up the steps to where Sarah stood.

"You're not feeling well today?" She took the Amish woman's hand.

"Levi says I must place my trust in _Gott_, and I do, but I still worry about our baby."

"I brought my medical bag. Let's go to your bedroom. I'll check the baby's heartbeat."

"That will bring me comfort."

Seeing the worry in Sarah's drawn face, Ella rubbed the younger woman's shoulder, hoping to offer reassurance. "I told you everything looks good."

"I believe what you said with my head, but not with my heart. Do you understand?"

"I understand your desire for a child. What happened with your first pregnancy does not mean that it will happen again. This second child is gaining weight and growing. She or he will be healthy and will bring you and Levi joy for the rest of your lives."

"You bring me hope." A weak smile formed on Sarah's thin lips. "May I offer you a slice of apple pie?"

"That sounds wonderful." Ella glanced at Zach. "I'm sure the special agent would like some, as well. Let the men talk while I check the baby. Then we can enjoy your pie."

Entering the bedroom, Ella found her gaze drawn to the beautiful quilt that covered the bed. The workmanship was so detailed. The colors were muted, as was the Amish way, but the intricate pattern was like a work of art.

"Did you create this quilt?" Ella asked.

"Before Levi and I married. I did it as an act of love."

"You're an artist, Sarah."

"My sister taught me to stitch. She is a good teacher,

but the praise goes to *Gott*. He creates the beauty in my mind before I sew the pieces together."

"You're much too humble," Ella said, as she helped her stretch out on the bed. Sarah's hands clenched as Ella listened to the baby's heartbeat.

Once satisfied, she helped the pregnant woman to a sitting position and assured her that the beat was strong. Relief spread over Sarah's sweet face and a twinkle returned to her eyes. Together the two of them hurried back to the kitchen, where the men sat at the hand-crafted table.

Zach was bent over a notebook, scribbling something onto a page. "When did you first meet Hugh Powers?" he asked, then looked up, distracted, as the women entered the room.

Levi stared at Sarah as she passed the table and hurried to where the pie sat on the counter. Ella stood close by, ready to help serve.

"He's only recently come back from the Middle East," Levi said. "I never met him, but I was riding in my buggy near their house not long ago and saw him get out of his truck."

"Did he see you?"

"He glanced my way. Mary Kate was with him, but I did not see the girls."

"Have you had any connection with the twins?"

Levi shook his head. "Their mother asked that I stay out of their lives. She does not want to confuse them with two fathers."

Zach started to respond and then glanced at Sarah, who was pulling plates from the cabinet.

Levi must have read his thoughts. "It is all right that you continue to ask your questions, Special Agent

Swain. I told you, Sarah and I do not have secrets. I have confessed my sin. The bishop says *Gott* has forgiven my transgressions."

"Is there anyone who might be holding a grudge? Perhaps a family member of yours?" Again, Zach glanced at Sarah. "Or someone in your wife's family?"

"Her brother, Daniel, was not happy when we married. He did not think I would be a faithful husband."

"Is he still antagonistic?" Zach asked.

"He moved to Alabama, so I cannot speak for him," Levi said. "But the Amish do not hold grudges."

Sarah turned from cutting the pie. "Daniel was protective of me when we were children. It is hard for him to let go of that responsibility."

"Protective of you in what way, if you don't mind me asking?" Zach said.

"In the Amish home, the father is the disciplinarian, and he has total authority. That is usually not a problem when a man has love in his heart."

"You're saying that your father was a stern authoritarian?"

"My mother died three months after their last child was born. My father could never get over her loss."

"Where are you in the birthing order?"

Sarah's eyes turned serious. "I am the youngest."

"Your father took his grief and frustration out on you?" Zach voice was laced with understanding.

"He said I was a difficult child."

"Where does your father live now?"

"On a small farm not far from here."

Zach looked at Levi. "Would your father-in-law become violent and do Mary Kate harm?"

The Amish man pursed his lips. Finally, he said, "I cannot see anyone harming a woman."

"Do I detect a bit of hesitation on your part, Levi, in answering my question?"

"I do not want to falsely represent Sarah's father. He is a proud man, and he forbade her to marry me."

Ella's heart went out to the fragile woman with the soft voice who stood with her back to the counter.

"Sarah, you married Levi against your father's will?" Zach asked.

She stepped to the table and placed her hand on Levi's shoulder. "I love my husband. He is a *gut* man. In youth, we often make mistakes. Levi had not yet been baptized. He was on his *rumspringa*. It is a time for the youth to explore other ways. He returned to the Amish community and was baptized. *Gott* accepted him. So did I."

Sarah glanced at Ella as if to gain support. "Although a daughter is to obey her father, my *datt* was making bad decisions for my future," the Amish wife continued. "I went to the bishop. Thankfully, he listened. Levi told him of his love for me, and the bishop gave us his blessing. This is something I have never regretted."

"I know this is a difficult question, Sarah." Zach hesitated, as if to let the seriousness of what he was about to say settle in. "Do you think your father is capable of harming Mary Kate?"

The young woman gripped her husband's shoulder. Levi raised his hand and touched her fingers, offering encouragement.

"I do not doubt that my father could and would do physical harm to Mary Kate. As he ages, his mind becomes more twisted. He could think that getting rid of her would erase everything that happened, including having a daughter who disrespects his authority."

"Is that what he's said?" Zach asked.

"He has said this, yes." She wiped her hands on her apron, then stepped back to the counter and lifted a knife to cut the pie. "Perhaps you are hungry and would like something to eat?"

Ella looked at Zach and nodded almost imperceptibly. Thankfully, he picked up on her subtle cue.

"Thank you, Sarah. I would enjoy a piece of pie."

"*Gut*." The young woman's face broke into a strained smile. "We will eat."

"Could you give me directions to find Sarah's father?" Zach asked Levi as Sarah cut the pie.

He drew a map on Zach's tablet. "My father-in-law's farm is off Amish Road. The turn is hard to see when the leaves are on the trees. He likes to remain secluded. Be careful. He has a shotgun and will use it."

"I thought the Amish were pacifists," Zach stated.

"That does not stop my father-in-law from brandishing his hunting rifle."

A chill wrapped around Ella's heart as she saw the concern on Zach's face.

"Do you have a rifle?" he asked Levi.

"I do, but I only use it for hunting."

"Could you get it for me?"

Sarah turned abruptly to stare at her husband. Fear flashed in her eyes.

"Is something wrong?" Zach asked.

She shook her head. "Everything is fine."

Levi slowly rose from the table and went to the back of the house. He returned with the rifle and passed it to

Zach, who looked through the barrel. "When was the last time you cleaned your rifle?"

"After I went hunting," Levi said. "Probably two weeks ago."

"You haven't used it since then?"

"That is right. I have not used it since."

"Then there's a problem." Zach touched the chamber. A black, powdery smudge dirtied his finger. "This doesn't look like cleaning oil to me. It looks more like gunpowder residue."

He stared at the younger man. "The gun's been fired since you cleaned it, Levi. Either you're mistaken about your cleaning routine or you've fired the rifle in the last two weeks."

Levi stared back at him but didn't respond.

Sarah gripped the counter as if to regain her balance, then covered her mouth with her hand and ran from the room.

Ella glared at Zach for half a second, uncertain what had just happened. Surely he didn't believe that Levi had viciously attacked her or Mary Kate. Nor had Levi fired on Ella today. Then she remembered what Zach had told her earlier.

Evil could be found anywhere, even in the Amish community.

Chapter Seven

Ella followed Sarah into her room and found the young woman sitting on the bed, head in her hands. As she stepped closer, she heard the deep intake of air and then faint sobs as Sarah began to cry. Ella sat next to her on the thick quilt.

"Sarah…" She kept her voice low. "Nothing is worth your tears. Tell me what's wrong."

The young mother-to-be shook her head.

Ella hesitated a moment, giving her time to work through the swell of emotions that had obviously over-powered her.

"I'm your doctor, Sarah, but I'm also a neighbor and a friend. I won't share the information unless you give me permission. You can trust me."

"I… I know." Her voice was weak and fraught with feeling.

"Is this about Levi and the gun?"

She shook her head again. "Not Levi."

"But it concerns the rifle?"

Sarah nodded. She dug for the handkerchief tucked in her sleeve and wiped her cheeks. "Levi worries about me when I am alone. He has always been protective of me, but even more so now because of the baby. Sometimes I think he worries that someone will do me harm."

"He wants to keep you safe because he loves you," Ella said encouragingly. "That's not a bad thing."

"I know that is true, and I love him and always want to do what he asks of me."

"I'm sure you're a wonderful wife. Levi is blessed to have you."

Sarah continued to hang her head, as if ashamed of what she was about to reveal. "My father said I was a fool to marry a man who loved another."

Ella rubbed her hand over the woman's slender shoulders. "But you said that your father does not have a loving heart. He might not have approved of any man you chose to marry."

Sarah's brow furrowed for a moment and then she nodded. "Perhaps you are right. Although a child is to obey her parents, especially her father. I tried to be a dutiful daughter."

"You shouldn't worry about your father."

"He frightens me at times. Especially since his mind is failing him. His anger has increased."

Ella glanced down at the intricately pieced quilt and wished the pieces of information Sarah had provided would fit together half as well. "Did your father have something to do with Levi's gun?" she asked.

"No, but there was a man..."

The new detail made Ella's heart lurch with concern. Again, she patted the young woman's shoulders. "Tell me what happened, Sarah."

"Two days ago, Levi went to town. He wanted to find some work to do for extra money so we could bet-

ter prepare for the baby. He worries that there might
be a problem and the baby may need special help at
the hospital."

"I told you that I'd deliver the baby and wouldn't
charge you."

"That is right, and we are so grateful. But you also
mentioned that the baby could need special care, if..."
She dropped her head into her hands and started crying again.

"Sarah, you need to be strong. I told you the pregnancy is going well. The baby is growing and gaining
weight. The heartbeat is good."

With a decided sniff, Sarah wiped her eyes and raised
her head. "Levi says that I fret too much, but I know
he worries, too. He is worried about how to provide
for another mouth to feed." She looked around. "Our
house is small."

"Your Amish neighbors will help."

"Some will. Others, like my brother and father, will
not help. They cannot accept Levi."

"But your faith tells them to forgive."

"Some precepts are harder to accept, and some people think they are above the teachings and the truth that
we hold so dear."

"It's the same in all cultures, I'm afraid," Ella answered, thinking of the people in Carlisle who had become aloof after Quin died. Perhaps because he had
taken his own life; perhaps because they didn't understand his work, or the way he had grown more and
more distant.

"That is why I didn't tell Levi." Sarah spoke slowly,
her voice little more than a whisper.

Leaning closer, Ella asked, "Tell Levi what?"

"About the man I saw. Two days ago. The sun was setting, and darkness was settling over the land. I looked out the window and saw a man walking from the stand of trees."

"The trees behind our houses?" The same area that the shots had come from today.

"That is right. A dirt road runs along the property line. I thought he must have come from that road."

"Who was it?"

"His dress was *fancy*. He wore denim pants and a hooded fleece shirt. The hood covered his hair, but he also wore a hat with a wide bill—" She raised her hand to indicate how it would fit.

"A baseball cap," Ella suggested.

"Yes. It was low on his brow so I could not see his face. He hurried toward our house."

Ella tried to think where she had been at that time of day. "Was I at home?"

"I heard you leave earlier. Maybe you were in town?"

She nodded, remembering her schedule. "I didn't have patients and went to the grocery store in Freemont. I got home after dark, but I didn't see anyone hanging around."

"He was gone by then. I watched him walk around my property. He peered in one of the windows as if he wanted to see if anyone lived here."

"I'm sure you were frightened." Without a phone, Sarah couldn't call for help.

"Levi told me never to touch his gun. He worried I could hurt myself."

"But you were afraid," Ella volunteered.

"I was. The man tried the front door. I feared he would go to the back door and try to get inside. When he came around the house, I opened the door a bit and yelled at him to leave."

Ella was surprised the young woman had had the courage to do so.

"He took a step closer. I did not think he would go away, so I fired Levi's rifle." She looked at Ella. "Not at him, but at the ground. He ran to the woods. I watched for him to return, but he never did."

"You didn't tell Levi?"

"I planned to, but Levi was discouraged when he got home. He had found no jobs, and I could see the worry in his eyes. He said he'd had a strange feeling that something was wrong at home. He'd hurried back and wanted to arrive before dark, but a wheel on the buggy had a problem, and he had to fix it along the way."

The woman searched Ella's gaze as if for acceptance. "I could not tell him about the man or that I had used his rifle. I did not think he would find out. I thought the next time he went hunting he would not check his gun first, but I was wrong. Now I fear the special agent from Fort Rickman thinks Levi is the person who shot at you today."

"You need to tell both men what happened."

Sarah nodded. "I should not have kept the truth from my husband."

"Can you describe the man?"

"Only what he was wearing, as I told you."

"Was there anything about his face?"

Sarah shook her head. "His hat was so low that I could not see much. Plus I was frightened and shaking. When I think back, everything is blurred."

"Which is how I feel about last night. I can't recall what the attacker looked like. He had a flashlight that nearly blinded me with its brightness, but I should be able to remember more."

"We have both tried to block out evil that has tried to touch our lives." Sarah rubbed her hands over her arms as if she was cold. "I must tell Levi and Special Agent Swain."

"You don't have to worry about Zach. He's a good man, just like Levi."

"I can see it in his eyes. You have been friends for a long time?"

Ella was surprised by the question. "No, we just met last night. Why do you ask?"

"The way he looks at you. His gaze carries more with it, as if you share a special bond."

Ella stared at Sarah for a long moment and then stood, unable to make sense of the tangle of emotions tugging at her heart. "You probably noticed his inquisitive nature. He investigates crime and wants to get to the bottom of every situation. That's what you see in his gaze."

The girl shook her head. "No, there is more. But now I must tell my husband what I have kept from him and ask his forgiveness."

Ella opened the bedroom door and was the first to step into the kitchen. Zach raised his gaze and stared at her. A feeling stirred deep within her that made her breath catch in her throat.

She pulled her eyes away and turned as Sarah walked toward her husband.

"Levi, I must tell you something that I have kept from you."

His face was creased with concern. "Is it the baby?" He rose and went to her.

"The baby is fine." She glanced at Ella. "At least, that is what our nice neighbor keeps telling me. But there is something else. We will sit and have pie, and I will explain what happened."

"Why don't you begin," Ella suggested. "I'll serve the pie." As she cut slices, she watched Levi's face, which was so filled with love for his wife. He was concerned about her health, and hearing about the stranger who had tried their front door made him turn pale with fear for her safety.

Zach leaned across the table, taking in everything the young woman shared. Just as Ella had mentioned in the bedroom, he wanted a full description of the stranger and any other details Sarah could remember.

Levi was too distraught to eat and kept holding his wife's hand and apologizing for returning home late that night.

Zach asked a number of questions, obviously hoping to unlock Sarah's memory, but she could think of nothing more than what she had told Ella.

Ella picked at the pie. The apples were green, but Sarah had sweetened them with just the right amount of sugar. Still, Ella's stomach tightened, and she had no appetite. The few bites she ate were to comfort the young wife who wanted to please everyone.

Zach turned again to stare at Ella. As if reading his thoughts, she realized the stranger had been canvassing the area before he stopped by her clinic.

Was his visit in any way involved with Levi and Sarah? Or was it about Ella, the patient records she kept on hand or the treatment she provided to the local Amish community?

What was going on in this once-idyllic part of Georgia? Ella tried to read Zach's gaze, but all she saw were questions about who she was and what had happened to her peaceful life.

"You're quiet," Zach said from the driver's seat as they left the Millers' property. The map Levi had drawn to his father-in-law's farm lay between them.

"Just thinking back to everything that's happened," Ella said. "If I hadn't come to Freemont, Levi and Sarah wouldn't be in the middle of an investigation."

"It isn't your fault. Besides, Levi is merely a person of interest. So is Mary Kate's husband. After Abrams talks to her father, Mr. Landers might be, as well. Any investigation has a number of folks who need to be questioned. That doesn't mean they're guilty or involved in the crime."

"Then you don't suspect Levi?"

"I don't know what to think. He and his wife seem to have a loving marriage in spite of his earlier relationship with Mary Kate. She's moved on, as well."

"Was she the reason for the clinic break-in? Did the assailant want to do her harm?"

"Perhaps. Still, every angle needs to be followed. What's in the twins' medical record that might cause someone to want those files?"

"You know that's not something I can share. I'm sure you're well aware of the Privacy of Information Act. Information between a physician and her patients is privileged."

"I'm not asking about any psychological evaluations, Doc. I just need to know some general facts. I'm sure the file mentions the genetic condition you uncovered."

Ella refused to comment.

"What about the biological father? Was Levi's name in the files?"

She sighed but failed to respond.

"Ella, I'm not interested in their medical information, per se. I need to know if the father's name was listed." Zach stared at her, feeling mildly frustrated. "I can get a court order, if you won't help me out, but I don't think what I'm asking is anything we haven't discussed with both the adoptive and biological fathers."

"You're right. Both men have been open about their role in the children's lives." She rubbed her hands together and then sighed. "Corporal Hugh Powers is listed as the adoptive father."

"So you didn't include Levi's name in the records?"

"It wasn't necessary to include anything about him. Plus, I didn't know who the birth father was, nor did I ask Mary Kate."

"Yet the disease you diagnosed has been specifically associated with Amish children."

"Perhaps I should have pressed Mary Kate to reveal the biological father, but I was more concerned about restoring the girls to health. Now that they've improved, that detail may be something that would have bearing on future children, should Mary Kate get pregnant again. You're correct in saying that the disease occurs more frequently with Amish, but it could also appear randomly in nature."

"So it isn't just an Amish disease?"

"That's right, although the incidence is much higher in the Amish community due to the limited founding families."

Zach held up his hand. "Can you backtrack a bit?"

"A certain number of Amish fled to America because

of religious persecution. Those families remained close-knit and intermarried. Recessive genes that would dissipate in a larger population were enhanced within the small founding pool. My husband studied those families and the diseases they develop because of their intermarriages. If Quin were still alive, he would have traced the girls' lineage. That was his interest, but not mine."

"Still, it seems you would have wondered about the father."

"I knew Corporal Powers had adopted the girls. Mary Kate left the area before the twins were born and moved south of Savannah. She has an aunt who lives there. I'm sure the aunt provided lodging while she was pregnant. Some people think nothing of out-of-wedlock pregnancies. Other folks still don't want the information to be made public. I have a feeling Mary Kate's father was the latter."

"Has he ever mentioned knowing who the biological father was?"

"I haven't heard him talk about Levi, except what he said today. I'm sure he knew. That's probably why he is so antagonistic toward Levi."

"Mr. Landers insinuated that Mary Kate and Levi had met recently."

"I'm sure Levi wanted to find out information about his daughters. Plus he wanted to know how the condition affected the girls."

"Did he ask you about the disease?" Zach inquired.

"Only in general terms. I've drawn blood samples on both Levi and Sarah and am awaiting the test results, as I told you. With CED, both parents have to carry the gene in order for their offspring to be susceptible."

"Both parents provide a gene?" Zach pressed. "Does that mean it's recessive?"

Ella nodded. "That's right."

"So Mary Kate comes from Amish lineage?"

"I… I don't know. As I mentioned, the disease can appear in the general population, yet it's much more prevalent among the Amish."

"Did you ask Mary Kate about her background?"

"No, never." Ella let out a stiff breath and shoved her hair back from her face. "I never thought about it. My husband said I didn't have a mind for research. He must have been right. I shouldn't have missed the connection."

"You're a good doctor, Ella."

She looked embarrassed and somewhat surprised by his comment. "I appreciate the compliment, Zach, but I have a feeling you just want to lift my spirits. Besides, I don't seem to be tracking down all the information that should be important in a genetic study."

"Which sounds as tricky as a criminal investigation. Sometimes I'm too close," he admitted. "I need to step away for a moment to let my mind work without any hindrance."

He glanced at Ella and wondered if that was the problem with this investigation. Had he gotten too close to her and become blinded to the truth? Another thought stirred within him, even more disconcerting. Was he blinded by false testimony, an assortment of half lies or innuendos that didn't add up?

In military circles, he was considered a top-notch special agent, but this case was different. Had he changed? For the better? Or for the worse?

Chapter Eight

"There's the turn." Ella pointed to a narrow road almost hidden by undergrowth.

"I'm glad Levi provided directions." Zach steered his car onto the narrow lane. Deep potholes pocked the path.

"Why don't you stay in the vehicle while I meet with Mr. Fisher," Zach suggested.

"I'd feel safer with you than I would sitting alone on this desolate road."

The dirt track meandered through dense underbrush. Overhanging limbs batted at the car.

"I'd hate to travel this road in a buggy," Ella admitted.

"Perhaps there's another entrance that's less of a hazard."

"Then I suggest we take that route home."

Zach laughed. The sound filled the car and bolstered her flagging spirits. She hadn't laughed with Quin; at least, she couldn't remember laughter. Maybe in the beginning when she'd been in love with him—or in love with being in love. Had that been the reason she'd gotten married?

Zach pointed through a break in the trees. "Looks like there's some type of a structure on the ridge."

A one-story home came into view as they rounded the bend and pulled into the clearing. The house was similar to Levi and Sarah's, but the small wooden structure was anything but welcoming. The tin roof on the front porch listed as if held upright by a few rotten two-by-fours.

"If that house were in the city, it would be condemned," Ella said as she stared through the car window. "Maybe staying in the vehicle would be a safer option."

Zach pulled into the short driveway, then backed up and turned the car around so it was facing the road. "In case we need to make a fast getaway," he explained.

"Now you've got me worried."

He winked. "Law enforcement types try to be prepared for any situation, Doc."

"After all we've been through, I'd appreciate if you'd use my name instead of my title."

He pulled the keys from the ignition and turned to stare at her. "You got it, Ella. Remember to stick by me and follow my lead. We don't want to get separated, and if I say run, we run."

"Yes, sir."

He stepped from the car and studied the house, which looked more like an abandoned shack.

"See anything?" Ella asked when she joined him.

"There." Zach pointed to a dilapidated barn that listed as much as the porch. The door hung open. "I saw movement inside."

He reached under his jacket and touched the weapon he carried on his hip. "Hello," Zach called. "Mr. Fisher?"

The door of the house creaked open, and the barrel of a rifle poked through the opening. Zach flicked his gaze back and forth between the barn and the house.

"Get behind me, Ella," he said out of the side of his mouth.

She hesitated.

"Now."

Ella did as he asked, but peered around him when the door opened a bit wider. A man stepped onto the porch. He wore typical Amish clothing and had a gray beard that added volume to his gaunt cheeks.

"He doesn't look very friendly," she said under her breath.

"Nor is he interested in providing a warm welcome." Zach squared his shoulders and stared at the old man. "I thought the Amish had big hearts and a love of God and neighbor."

Ella stepped a bit closer. "I'm guessing Sarah's father is an exception to the rule."

"Mr. Fisher?" Zach called again.

"Get off my land."

"Sir, we come as friends. I'd like to talk to you. I'm an officer of the law and work with the Criminal Investigation Division at Fort Rickman. If you step onto your porch, I can show you my identification."

"I have nothing to do with the army."

"I've brought Dr. Jacobsen." Zach pointed over his shoulder. "She has a clinic not far from here and treats Amish families. Your daughter, Sarah, is one of her patients."

"Sarah disobeyed me."

"Sir, she and Levi are expecting a child," Ella interjected. "Your grandchild."

"She lost one child, which proved *Gott* was upset with her and didn't approve of the choices she made."

"I'd like to get a family history from you, sir. That would help assure a safe delivery for your grandchild."

"Did you have anything to do with the last baby? The baby who died?"

Ella shook her head as she peered around Zach. "No, sir. I lived in Pennsylvania at the time. I'm a widow, Mr. Fisher. Sarah said you lost your wife some years ago. I know how hard that can be. My husband worked with Amish families in Pennsylvania. You probably have kin from that state."

"*Yah*, that is right. But the English moved in and bought land, so we had no place to farm. I moved to Alabama with my wife, and to Georgia after she died. It is not good for a man to be alone."

"I'm sorry for your loss, sir, but I want to help Sarah and your grandchild. Please, put down your gun and talk to us."

The old man hesitated for a long moment.

"Mr. Fisher, I'm coming to you, sir." Zach took a step forward. "We can talk on the porch."

"Be careful," Ella whispered.

"He's thinking, and that's a good sign. I want him to know that we won't do him harm."

The old man sighed heavily, then lowered his gun and propped it against the wall. "I will talk to you, but not because of Sarah. For the baby, I will do this. The child deserves life."

"You've made a wise decision," Ella offered. She stepped around Zach and climbed the steps. The old man motioned for them to sit in the swing, while he settled into a rocker.

"Sir, you're not alone," Zach said. "Someone's in the barn. Is that a friend or family?"

"My son, Daniel. He came home to help me."

"He's been away?" Zach asked.

"*Yah*. In Alabama, where we lived when he was a baby. My daughter lives there, as well."

Ella smiled. "I'm sure your son was worried about you living alone here in the country. I know Sarah worries, too."

"Sarah should have stayed with me, then I would not be alone."

"It is right for a woman to marry, Mr. Fisher," Ella said. "I'm sure you would agree."

"To marry, *yah*. But not to marry someone her father does not approve of."

"Do you recall anyone in your family or your wife's family having children who were sickly or couldn't thrive?" Ella asked.

"You mean children who died?"

"Yes, sir, that's what I mean."

He thought for a moment. "*Mein bruder* was weak and could not eat. He became so thin and did not survive the winter."

"When was that, Mr. Fisher?"

"Years ago, when I was a boy."

"Were other family members affected?"

He shook his head. "I do not think so. What does this have to do with Sarah?"

"There are certain diseases that are seen more often among the Amish. I need to know if any of those illnesses run in your family."

"You think this baby will be born sick?"

"I hope not. But if that is the case, by knowing a family history, I can begin to treat the infant immediately."

"Another child, on my wife's side, was sickly. The child was born in the winter and did not live to spring."

"Did anyone mention the baby's cause of death?"

"The winter was cold. The father tried to cut wood to burn in the stove, but he hurt himself with his ax. He became sick, and the baby did, as well."

"I'm sorry about the loss of life."

"*Gott's* ways are not our ways."

Noticing the old man's shortness of breath, Ella glanced at Zach. He nodded, joining in her concern.

"Sir?" She patted the man's arm. "How long have you had trouble breathing?"

"I am fine." He waved her off.

Refusing to be deterred, she leaned in closer. "Your breathing is labored. As we age, our bodies sometimes need help. I'd like you to come to my clinic, Mr. Fisher. I could check your heart and your lungs."

"My heart is strong, and my breathing is fine. You can keep your medicine."

"There would be no charge. You could visit Sarah while you were there. I know she'd like to see you."

"I do not want to see my daughter or have my body examined by a woman."

"Sir," Zach interrupted. "Dr. Jacobsen is only thinking of your health."

"The Amish do not go to doctors."

"Some do," she corrected.

"Like my daughter, who does not follow the Amish ways."

"I think you'd find her very Amish, sir. She'd like to see you."

"Sir, someone broke into the doctor's clinic," Zach said. "I wondered if you'd heard of anyone who wanted to do harm to Dr. Jacobsen. Or anyone who didn't want her clinic to succeed."

"There are many who wonder why she came here."

"I came to work with the Amish, Mr. Fisher. As you may know, the nearest medical care is in Freemont. That's a long ride in a buggy."

"But we do not need doctors."

"Even the Amish get sick," she responded.

"Can you think of anyone in particular who might want to do the doctor harm?" Zach asked again.

"The Amish are peace loving people."

Who shun their family members, Ella wanted to mention. Even those who remained within the community could be excluded, such as Sarah, all because she went against her father's wishes. Mr. Fisher didn't see the hypocrisy of his statement.

Zach pointed to the rifle propped by the door. "Do you use your Winchester for hunting?"

"I do not hunt much." The old man touched his fingers to his eyes. "It is hard to see."

Ella scooted closer. "Have you had your eyes checked recently?"

"As I told you, I do not go to doctors."

"But you might need glasses," she said. "Cataracts form later in life. An eye specialist will be able to fit you for glasses. The cataracts can be removed, if your vision is compromised."

The old man ignored her and turned back to Zach. "Do you hunt?"

Evidently talk of hunting was more to his liking than any talk about his physical condition.

Zach nodded. "Although I don't have much time these days. When was the last time you shot your gun, sir? You might need to have it cleaned. I'd be happy to help you with that."

"My son helps me, as I already said. He hunts."

"Has he taken the gun recently to do some hunting?"

"*Yah*, earlier today."

Zach looked at Sarah. "Would you mind calling your son so I can talk to him?"

The old man slowly rose and walked to the edge of the porch. He put his hands up to his mouth and called, "Daniel, come."

The man Zach had noticed earlier peered from the barn.

"Come." The father motioned him forward. Turning to Zach, he added, "It is my son, Daniel."

The man walked slowly across the dirt drive and approached the house. He wore Amish trousers and a black hat pulled down on his head. He was clean shaven, which indicated he was single. But he also wore something that made Ella sit up and take note. Over his light blue shirt, he wore a navy blue hooded sweatshirt, which wasn't typical Amish clothing. Ella touched Zach's arm.

His eyes widened ever so slightly.

Ella stared at the man. Surely Sarah would recognize her brother if he had been snooping around outside her house. Had he also broken into Ella's clinic last night and then ransacked the office today and fired rounds from the woods?

She and Zach had come to the Fisher home hoping for information. But they may have found even more. They may have found the assailant.

Chapter Nine

Zach questioned Daniel while his father sat on the porch scowling. Ella had retrieved her medical bag from the car and tried to take the old man's pulse and blood pressure, but he refused to cooperate. Instead he stared at Zach and made a growling noise like an angry dog.

"Did you go near your sister's home anytime this week?" Zach asked the younger man.

"Neh."

"Did you look into Sarah's home and try the front door to see if it was locked?"

"I would not and did not."

"You went hunting today. Where were you, exactly?"

Daniel pointed to the woods. "I was in the forest. There is nothing for miles so no one stopped me, but I cannot tell you how far I went into the thicket."

"Did you shoot any game?"

"There is a bobcat. I have seen him. I fired a shot to scare him away."

"Did you wound him?"

"I did not. I shoot only that which I can eat. My father taught me well."

"Tell me about your sweatshirt," Zach said.

"I wear it when I work to keep my shirt clean."

"Is it normal for the Amish to wear fleece?"

Daniel blinked. "I am not a normal Amish man."

"Oh?" Zach hesitated before asking, "What does that mean?"

"I did not stay here, but moved back to Alabama."

"Was there a reason you left the area?"

"I needed space. Land is cheaper there."

"But you came back," Zach said.

"My father is getting older." Daniel glanced at the house. "As you can see with your own eyes, this place needs work. I came home to help him."

An altruistic cause, although Zach wondered if Daniel was telling the truth. "You are not married?"

He shook his head. "I am not."

"Isn't that unusual?"

"Are you married?" he asked Zach.

"No, I'm not."

"Do you think that's unusual?" Daniel asked.

"I'm not Amish." Zach stated the obvious.

The son sniffed. "And I'm not convinced I should remain Amish."

"You do not believe in the Amish way of life?" Zach asked.

"Living alone is difficult. If I could find a wife, I would appreciate the plain life more."

"The Freemont police will want to talk to you, Mr. Fisher."

He frowned. "I have done nothing wrong."

"Do you carry a grudge against your brother-in-law?"

"Why would I?"

"You tell me. Were you against your sister marrying Levi Miller?"

Daniel nodded. "I did not want her to marry a man who had been with a woman and conceived children out of wedlock."

"But Levi had asked for forgiveness."

"Sometimes forgiveness is difficult to give, even if the person is sorry for their wrongdoing."

Zach narrowed his gaze. "Were you ever in love?"

"I was never in love with an English woman."

From all appearances, Daniel seemed close to Levi's age. "Did you know Mary Kate when you lived here?"

"I knew who she was."

"You and Levi were friends?"

"The community was small." Daniel nodded. "I knew the other Amish children, so yes, I knew Levi."

"Did you tell him to stay away from Mary Kate?"

Daniel shrugged. "I told him she would not be good for him."

"Were you worried about Levi or worried about yourself, Daniel? Were you interested in Mary Kate?"

The man's face tightened. Zach knew he'd touched a chord. Could it be that Daniel Fisher had feelings for Mary Kate, the same girl who had fallen in love with Levi?

Vengeance wasn't the Amish way, but Mr. Fisher and his son didn't fit the mold. Daniel had prowled around the Miller home and had run away instead of identifying himself to his sister. Perhaps he'd wanted to have words with Levi, never expecting to find Sarah there without her husband.

Stepping off the porch and away from earshot, Zach

called the Freemont police and spoke with Abrams, who promised to send a patrol car to the Fisher home.

In hopes of winning Mr. Fisher over, Ella encouraged him to talk about his wife and their life together. His love for Sarah became evident when he shared some of her escapades as a small child, but his mood changed when the sound of a car engine announced he had additional visitors.

He became even more upset when two officers parked in front of his property. Daniel went willingly with them to police headquarters, claiming he had nothing to hide. With Mr. Fisher's permission, the police also took his rifle for ballistics testing.

Ella encouraged the Amish man to visit her clinic for a checkup, but he merely muttered under his breath and went back into his house.

She and Zach left the farm over a different road, equally as bumpy, that led to a wooden bridge.

"On the phone, Abrams suggested I try this way out," he told her. "It's a bit shorter, although the road looks to be as bad."

"I didn't know there was a river out here."

"It feeds into the one that runs through Freemont. The bridge was built years ago, but it's still functional."

Ella looked pensive and unsettled as they crossed the bridge. "I've been thinking about what you mentioned concerning the Powers twins," she finally said.

"You mean that a recessive gene had to come from each parent in order for both girls to have the genetic condition?"

Ella cocked her head and smiled. "For a special agent, you're pretty smart."

He laughed. "You must have a low opinion of law enforcement types."

"That's not true. It's just that I picked up on your obvious antagonism toward the medical profession."

He held up his hand. "Present company excluded."

"I'm not so sure," she teased.

"Cross my heart." He traced the sign on his chest, then glanced at her and winked. "Really. You're the exception to the rule, Doc."

She rolled her eyes. "And I thought you were so affirming."

He held back a smile, trying to be sincere in spite of the frivolity of the moment. "But I meant that as a compliment, Ella. Most doctors are self-absorbed and enthralled with their own abilities. You're humble and concerned about others."

She blushed. Her obvious embarrassment warmed his heart. "I mean it, Ella."

Just that fast, the intensity of her gaze melted a brokenness he'd carried for too long. Zach kept his emotions in check. It was the way he lived life. Ever since his mother died he'd built a wall around his heart as a protective measure, so he'd never feel that overwhelming pain of separation again. The fear of being hurt had forced him to be as reclusive as old man Fisher and had cut him off from experiencing life to the full.

His cell rang, pulling him back to the investigation. Sergeant Abrams's name appeared on the monitor.

"We just left Fisher's farm," Zach said in greeting. "Your men are hauling his son in for questioning."

"I got a call filling me in," the sergeant said. "Good work tracking down both of them. If what Sarah Miller told you about her brother is true, he could be our man."

"I'm not ready to call the case closed. Did you talk to Corporal Powers?"

"I did. He wasn't happy about being detained."

"What did you uncover?" Zach asked.

"Not much," the sergeant confessed. "He's distraught about his wife. His father-in-law mentioned Levi Miller hanging around Mary Kate. Powers suspected the worst."

"So the corporal doesn't trust his wife?"

"I didn't get that impression," Sergeant Abrams said. "But he certainly doesn't trust Levi."

"Is there anything you want the military police and CID to do?"

"No more than you already are. Corporal Powers is back at the hospital, keeping vigil over his wife. Might be good to ensure he stays on post."

"I can make that happen," Zach said. "What about Mr. Landers?"

"He's got a rifle, but it's not a 30-30 caliber. Besides, he was in the ICU with his daughter when the shots were fired today. A chaplain was visiting at the time and confirmed his alibi. Leave your cell on. I'll let you know about Daniel Fisher."

"Appreciate you keeping me in the loop."

"We're in this together," the sergeant assured him.

Ella stared at Zach when he disconnected. "Are we going to talk to Mr. and Mrs. Landers?"

"Sounds like a good idea to me, unless you're too tired."

"I'm okay, just a little surprised that you didn't tell Sergeant Abrams where we were headed."

"I was thinking of your patient privilege. I trust

the sergeant, but he doesn't need to know about Mary Kate's background unless it has bearing on the case."

"Thanks."

"Just doing my job."

She smiled. "You're good at what you do."

"Now I'm the one who feels a bit embarrassed. I'm not used to getting compliments from beautiful women."

Her smile faded and a look of confusion washed over her face.

He glanced at her. "You're not blushing because you don't believe what I just said."

"No one has ever called me beautiful." Her voice was low.

"Shame on everyone else then."

"You're not only affirming," she said, "but also prone to offering compliments. That's a winning combination."

"I aim to please, ma'am."

Being with Ella lifted Zach's spirits and made him feel good about himself. She was easy to talk to and affirming in her own way. It was hard to believe that no one had ever told her she was beautiful, because she was.

For a moment, as he drove through the Amish countryside, Zach forgot about the investigation. But when he turned into the Landerses' driveway, he knew he needed to keep his mind off the doctor and focus on the job at hand.

"I'd like to talk to you about the twins," Ella said when Mrs. Landers opened the door. "Special Agent Swain is with me."

"Did something happen to Mary Kate?" The older woman motioned them inside. Just as before, she wore a solid color housedress and an apron, and her hair was neatly tucked into a bun.

"As far as we know, there's been no change," Zach said. "Is you husband at the hospital?"

"Bob's in the other room with the girls. They like Grandpa to read a story to them before they take a nap."

"I'm sure that's a special time for Shelly and Stacey." Ella took a seat on the couch Mrs. Landers indicated.

"A special time for their grandfather, too." She sat next to Ella, while Zach settled in a nearby chair. "Would you folks like coffee?"

"No, thank you," Ella said. "We're only staying a short time. I'm sure Mary Kate told you about the genetic condition the girls have."

"Of course, but they're doing well. You identified the problem, and they've improved." Mrs. Landers's smile was sincere. "God brought you into their lives, Dr. Jacobsen. They were so sick, but you saved them. I'll always be grateful."

Ella thought of the circumstances that had brought her to the Freemont area. Had God been involved?

"The girls are back to their active selves," the woman continued. "As worried as Bob and I are about Mary Kate, it's a relief knowing Shelly and Stacey are getting stronger."

"It brings me comfort, as well, Mrs. Landers," Ella said. "Did your daughter mention that the girls' condition is usually seen in the Amish population?"

She nodded. "Mary Kate said the twins inherited the condition from their father."

Zach leaned into the conversation. "You're talking about their biological father?"

She nodded again. "Sergeant Abrams was here earlier. He probably told you about Levi Miller. The girls inherited the condition from him."

"Actually," Ella explained, "Levi provided one of the two genes necessary for the girls to have the condition. Your daughter provided a gene, as well."

The older woman's eyes widened. "I'm not sure what you're saying."

Ella explained that two recessive genes, one from each parent, were needed in order for the condition to be transmitted. "Is anyone in your family or your husband's family Amish?" she asked in conclusion.

Mrs. Landers drew in a deep breath. "Are you sure there's no other way for the girls to get the condition?"

"The disease could manifest randomly, but that's not as likely, Mrs. Landers."

Judging from her expression, Ella was certain the grandmother had something to share. To offer reassurance, she said, "Whatever is said here would be kept private." Ella looked at Zach for confirmation.

"Yes, ma'am," he quickly agreed. "I see no reason that any medical information would need to be made public. Unless, of course, it has bearing on the current investigation."

"Do you have Amish relatives?" Ella pressed.

Mrs. Landers rubbed her hands together. "I was raised Amish. My husband lived in the neighboring town. All the teenagers hung out at a nearby lake in the summer. That's where we met and fell in love."

"Did you leave the community to marry your husband?" Ella asked.

The woman dropped her gaze. "You might say that my daughter followed in my footsteps, although she doesn't know she was conceived before we married. My father forbade me to see Bob, so I ran away."

Ella rubbed her hand over the older woman's shoulder. "That must have been difficult for you."

Mrs. Landers nodded. "Leaving my mother was hard. When Mary Kate told us she was pregnant, I felt responsible. Bob insisted she stay with his sister, who lives in Savannah. I joined them there during Mary Kate's last trimester and for some months after the twins were born, to help care for the babies. Bob visited whenever he could get away from his company."

"Is that where your daughter met Corporal Powers?" Zach asked.

Mrs. Landers nodded. "He was stationed at Fort Stewart. They met at a fund-raiser for a wounded warrior who needed medical care. By that time, Mary Kate had a job. She had rented a house and was making it on her own, with just a little help from us. We're real proud of her."

Ella offered an encouraging smile. "You should be, Mrs. Landers."

"Mary Kate admitted that she and Levi had thought they were in love. After meeting Hugh, she knew her father's decision not to let her stay with Levi had been the right one."

"Do any of your relatives have children with similar symptoms as the twins?" Ella asked.

"I wouldn't know," Mrs. Landers admitted. "I have two sisters, but I've never gone back home. I hadn't been baptized, so I wasn't formally shunned, but my father wouldn't let anyone talk to me after I defied his authority."

Which sounded like Sarah Miller's father.

"Bob and I have a son, but he's not married. Now I'm worried about any future children Mary Kate might have," the grandmother continued.

"It's doubtful they would have the condition," Ella assured her. "Unless Corporal Powers carries the gene, and that seems highly unlikely. I could do DNA testing if they want to know for sure."

Tears welled up in Mrs. Landers's eyes. "At this point, I'm not sure Mary Kate will survive. Bob and I are praying so hard for her."

Turning at the sound of footsteps, Ella saw Mr. Landers standing in the hallway. His face was ashen.

"Did we lose Mary Kate?"

Ella shook her head and stood. "No, sir. I'm sorry if we frightened you."

Mrs. Landers hurried to her husband. "The twins got sick because of my Amish background, Bob."

"What are you saying, Lucy?"

She explained about the recessive genes. "Both Levi and Mary Kate had to give a gene in order for the girls to get sick. The condition is found in the Amish, so she inherited it from my side of the family."

"The good thing is that the girls were diagnosed early and have responded to treatment," Ella said, hoping to offer encouragement.

"I still blame Levi." Mr. Landers's voice was harsh.

"No one's to blame, Mr. Landers. I'm just glad the girls responded to the treatment."

His wife patted his hand. "We'll get through this, Bob. My father always said everything that happened was God's will, but I don't think this was His doing or what He wanted for Mary Kate. Knowing God the way I do, He's not going to let anything happen to our daughter."

"They say love conquers all," Zach said as he and Ella hurried to his car. "Mrs. Landers had to sacrifice a lot to marry her husband."

Ella nodded. "I thought about Sarah Miller, who even as a married woman is worried about her father. I doubt men realize the important role they play in their daughters' lives."

"Levi seems like a loving husband," Zach mused. "And it sounds like Corporal Powers loves the twins, although right now, he's worried about his wife and focused on her."

"I can't see Mr. Landers harming his daughter."

Zach agreed. "Some of his anger dissipated when he found out about the Amish tie-in with the girls' condition. Maybe he feels responsible, just as Mrs. Landers mentioned. If they hadn't moved to this area, their daughter never would have known Levi."

"I wish Mrs. Landers could contact her Amish relatives so they could be tested."

"Perhaps you could arrange to do that through the research center in Harrisburg," Zach suggested.

Ella nodded. "I could talk to the director. Dr. Vaughn wants me to attend the event this weekend."

"Do you think that's wise?"

"I'm not sure."

Zach didn't want Ella out of his sight. He needed to convince her to stay in the Freemont area until the investigation was over, although he knew the medical symposium was important because of her husband's role in the Amish Project.

His fear was that after seeing the people with whom her husband had worked, she might not want to return to her clinic and the simple life in the Amish community.

What was wrong with him? He was thinking of his own happiness. Ella's happiness was the important thing. That and keeping her safe.

Would she be safer in Freemont, where a killer was on the loose? Or in Atlanta, far from the assailant who wanted her dead?

Chapter Ten

Ella was beyond tired. Her head throbbed and every muscle in her body ached as they pulled into her driveway at the clinic.

"Are you okay?" Zach asked.

"No." She had to be truthful. "I'm tired and upset and worried about what we might find when we go inside."

"I'll check the clinic. You stay in the car."

She gave him the key and was relieved when he returned with a smile, opening the passenger door and offering her his hand.

"Everything looks just the same as when we left. Your nurse left a note. The receptionist's husband installed an alarm system. The details are on your desk."

Ella let out a grateful sigh. "That's good news."

Entering the clinic, she was overcome with relief. Not only were things back in place, but Wendy had vacuumed and mopped the floors. She'd even washed the windows, and the fresh scent of furniture polish and floor wax filled the air.

On Monday, Ella would see patients again; at least she hoped she would. No telling what the Amish families would decide after the attack. Knowing how skittish they could be, she wondered if the parents would trust their children to a doctor involved in a criminal investigation.

"Why don't you go on," she told Zach. "I need to take a nap, and there's no reason for you to stay here, especially since I have the security alarm."

"You can't get rid of me that easily." He pointed to the hallway. "Get some sleep. I'll check my email. I also need to make a few phone calls."

Although his voice was firm, she saw the concern and sincerity in his gaze.

"If you insist. But I'll set my alarm clock for an hour so I don't oversleep."

"Make that two hours, and I'll be happy."

"Can I get you something to drink before I disappear?"

"A cup of coffee would be good. Or water."

"One of each coming up."

She hurried into her kitchen and returned with coffee and a chilled bottle of water.

"The coffee's just what I need, and I'll chase it with the water. Thanks." Again, he pointed to the hallway. "Now go."

She gave him a mock salute. "Yes, sir."

He laughed, and the heaviness that had weighed her down lifted for a moment, until she entered her residence and saw a photo of Quin that sat on the hutch in her dining room. For some reason, his frown pulled her down again.

She hurried into her bedroom and locked the door—not because she was worried about Zach; she didn't fear him and believed him to be an honorable man. But she wanted to lock out the memories from her past. She had left Pennsylvania and started a new life for herself, yet no matter what she told Zach, she was vulnerable.

The security alarm would be a deterrent, but would it save her if the assailant returned? The police in Freemont were too far away to protect her. Anything could happen by the time they arrived. She wouldn't be able to summon Levi in the dead of night, since he didn't have a phone, and even if she called Zach, he lived at Fort Rickman, miles away from the Amish community.

She thought of the invitation to Atlanta. Perhaps that would offer her a reprieve, at least for a day or two. By the time she returned, the local police might have apprehended the assailant. A change of scenery could be just what she needed.

Zach would leave later today, and she'd be on her own again. He had become a comfortable—too comfortable—presence. They seemed to work well together, but he was a special agent who was merely investigating a case.

As she washed her hands and face, Ella looked into the mirror. She'd vowed never to make the mistake of getting involved with a man again. She'd done so in giving her heart to Quin, a mistake that had hurt her deeply as he became more and more reclusive and less and less interested in her.

So many times she had yearned for something more, for a family like the ones who brought their children to her Carlisle practice. She'd envied the love she'd seen reflected in the parents' eyes.

She'd had her chance and ruined it with the failure of her marriage. Again, the terrible guilt overwhelmed her.

Had Quin turned away from her because she wasn't lovable, wasn't the woman he had wanted her to be? She'd made mistakes—he'd said it more than once. But did the failure of their marriage rest on her shoulders alone?

Turning away from her reflection, she dried her hands and face and then stretched across her bed, not even pulling down the Amish quilt that reminded her of the good people who put God first.

Where had she put God? He wasn't even in her life. Was that why nothing seemed to go well for her?

She gripped the edge of the quilt and closed her eyes so that everything that had happened would disappear. So that she'd slip into oblivion, where she didn't have to worry about an evil man who had attacked her so violently he must have wanted her dead.

What was wrong with him?

Zach was sitting in Ella Jacobsen's clinic, a rural facility similar to the one where his mother had died and the very place he never wanted to be. He'd been taken in by the doctor. He needed to be a CID special agent and not the doctor's guardian, yet that's exactly what he wanted to do—protect Ella and make sure she was safe from the terrible predator.

He had never felt so committed, determined and focused on keeping someone safe, which was a good thing. But there was something else, a feeling deep in his heart that was about more than keeping a witness secure. A feeling that he couldn't explain and didn't completely understand, yet it made him stronger and tougher and more determined to do what was right.

He called Tyler Zimmerman at CID headquarters.

The special agent answered on the second ring. "What's up, Zach?"

"I'm at the Children's Care Clinic and wondered if I could ask a favor."

"Shoot."

"I need a burner phone. When you head home, would you mind stopping by the PX and buying one? If you could drop it off here, that would be perfect. Otherwise I can stop by your place once you get home."

"The doc doesn't have a cell phone?"

"Negative. It's her Amish neighbor. I'm hoping he'll agree to keep the phone so Dr. Jacobsen can contact him if she's threatened in the night."

"You trust him to protect the doctor?"

"Only if someone tries to break into her clinic again. He's the closest neighbor. The doc is taking care of his pregnant wife and will deliver their baby. That's got to have bearing on his desire to keep her safe. I'll hang out here as late as possible, but she'll eventually tell me to go home. Fort Rickman is more than a thirty-minute drive. I won't be able to respond quickly enough if someone tries to get in here."

"You know I live along Amish Road?"

"I knew you lived off post. Are you close by?"

"Just after the turnoff from town. Give her my number. In fact, I've got a spare bedroom. You're welcome to stay there."

"That sounds like a plan. How do I find your house?" Zach asked.

"You've seen the big antebellum home?"

"I have. Is that your place?"

"It belongs to Carrie York."

"Your fiancée?"

"That's right. I'm in the small ranch south of there. I'll get that phone and deliver it later today, along with a spare key to my house so you can come and go as you please."

"I appreciate the hospitality and your help. I've got a gym bag in my office and an extra set of clothing. Would you mind bringing them to me, as well?"

"Will do."

Zach felt a surge of relief. He had planned to hang out in the Amish area late into the night to make sure Ella didn't have any strange visitors. Staying at Tyler's house meant Zach could come to Ella's aid at a minute's notice.

"What about Corporal Hugh Powers?" he asked Zimmerman. "Has anything new surfaced on him?"

"I questioned him extensively, but he kept to his story. The guy's exhausted and worried to death about his wife. He seems to be the doting husband, although we both know that can be faked."

"Did he mention having PTSD?"

"Roger that. He was forthright about his condition, although he's so distraught that it's hard to say if it is caused by his deployment or by what happened to his wife."

"How's she doing?"

"Still on a ventilator and unable to talk. No one is offering any encouragement. Her kidneys started to shut down. They're watching her blood pressure and are concerned about infection."

"Have you seen her parents?"

"The dad visited early this morning. He's cranky and complains about everything that's being done. I'm giving him the benefit of the doubt and blaming it on his love for his daughter."

"Have you gotten a sense of how he and the husband get along?"

"Both men are emotional wrecks. The tension is high and one of the nurses said they've had words. I can't tell you if there's a true animosity or just the fatigue and worry that comes when a loved one is in critical condition."

Zach looked at his watch. "Let me know if anything new surfaces."

"Will do. I'll be in touch."

After disconnecting, Zach called Sergeant Abrams. "Any success with Daniel Fisher?"

"He's a strange one. I'm not sure if he's really Amish or just pretending to be in the fold to keep his father happy. We're running a ballistics on the rifle. Seems a coincidence that both he and Levi Miller own the same type of gun."

"Actually, it makes sense. The Model 94 is a good hunting rifle. Perfect for deer or wild boar, and it's a dependable weapon, yet fairly inexpensive. The Amish use their rifles to hunt for food. Seems the 94 would be a good choice."

"You might be right."

"Did you question Daniel about his past relationship with Mary Kate?"

"He says he knew who she was and that's it. Do you think he was jealous of Levi?"

"It's a possibility. Or he could be a protective older brother who's concerned about his sister's marriage. He comes back to Georgia on the pretense of helping his dad. Maybe he saw Levi and Mary Kate together. Her father said Levi had been hanging around. Of course, Levi's story is that he was inquiring about the twins. His wife is pregnant, and they're worried the condition the twins have could be passed to their own baby."

Abrams picked up on the direction Zach was headed. "So Daniel sees Levi with Mary Kate and suspects his brother-in-law might be involved with her again?"

"Stranger things have happened. Lots of folks jump to the wrong conclusion. Daniel seems to be a bit on the hotheaded side. I can see him getting aggravated and feeling that he needs to defend his sister's name."

"So he tries to kill Mary Kate?" Abrams asked.

"He could have followed her to the clinic. The storm works into his plans. He cuts the electricity, hoping the doc will think it's an area-wide power outage. She leaves the house to tend to the generator, and he confronts the twins' mother. Maybe he wanted to scare her or threaten her, and everything goes south. Emotions could have run wild. He fires without thinking through his actions."

The officer let out a stiff breath. "I see what you mean. We'll hold him for another hour or so and see if his story changes. Something needs to break soon."

"We've got bits of information. Somehow they have to fit together. Stay in touch."

After Zach disconnected, he called CID headquarters. Sergeant Raynard Otis answered.

"Hey, Ray, it's Special Agent Swain. I'm interested in talking to law enforcement in Alabama that would have jurisdiction over an Amish community. As I recall, it's located not far from the town of Harmony."

"Yes, sir. You've got that right. Special Agent Colby

Voss was involved in a case near there. Give me a minute and I'll access the information."

Zach stretched back in the chair and waited. His eyes wandered to the picture of Quin Jacobsen on a table behind Ella's desk. He needed to find more information about her husband's death.

Ray came back on the line. "I found it, sir." He provided the name and phone number of the lead officer. "Sheriff Lewis Stone should be able to help you."

"Thanks, Ray. I've got another request. A research physician died in Memphis about eight months ago. He was attending a medical conference and drove his rental car to one of the bridges that span the Mississippi River. Supposedly, he jumped, and his body washed up on shore some days later. I want to contact the law enforcement agency that handled the case."

"Do you have more information, sir?"

"Only the doctor's name. Quin—or Quinton—Jacobsen. He lived in Carlisle, Pennsylvania, and worked for a Harrisburg research center that studied genetic diseases affecting children, primarily Amish children." Zach hurried to Ella's desk and leaned over the invitation he'd seen the night before. "The name of the facility is the Harrisburg Genetic Research Center."

"I'll do some checking and get back to you."

After disconnecting, Zach called the Alabama sheriff. He introduced himself and stated the information he needed. "Do you know a Daniel Fisher? He supposedly has lived in an Amish community near you. Medium height. Kind of bulky build. Probably five-eleven and two hundred pounds. No distinguishing features or marks that I was able to see. His sister may live nearby, although I don't have a name for her."

"I know Fisher," the chief quickly replied. "He built a little house on the edge of the Amish community. Far as we could determine, he wasn't living the Amish life. He'd come into town at times and do some odd jobs to make money. At first, he seemed like a hard worker, but the longer he stayed on a job, the lazier he became. A number of times he argued over the pay he received, declaring that he'd been promised a higher wage. I've known some of the construction bosses who hired him. They're God-fearing men who are known for their honesty and the care they provide their workers. I trust them and their business practices. A couple of the firms fired Fisher after he put up a fuss."

"Were other Amish men working construction?"

"A few do at times, especially when money is tight. Farming is hard work. In the lean years, when crops don't do well, we see a number of Amish lads looking for employment to support their families. A couple guys work as volunteer firemen. They get paid when they go out on a call. The Amish ladies sell their produce and baked goods at our Saturday farmers' market. Some of them take in sewing and alterations."

"But Fisher didn't seem like part of the Amish community?"

"That was the way I saw it. He was standoffish and could be surly at times, which, as you probably know, doesn't fit the Amish mold."

"Did you ever suspect him of illegal activity?"

The chief hesitated a moment and then pulled in a deep breath. "Funny you should mention it. We had some petty thefts in the local area. Not big-ticket items, but small things that could be easily pawned in one of the neighboring towns. A few GPS systems were lifted from unlocked cars. A woman's purse was taken when she was in the gym. We later found her wallet and handbag in a city trash can. The credit cards hadn't been used, but two hundred dollars in cash was gone."

"Did you suspect Fisher?"

"He was seen in town that day. I didn't have any witnesses or evidence, but it made me wonder. I talked to him about where he'd been and listened as he provided a lame excuse about walking to town on a back road. Seemed suspicious to me, but I never found anything that tied him to the robberies."

"Did he mention his father or sister or an English woman named Mary Kate Powers, all of whom are from Freemont, Georgia?"

"Not that I recall, but he does have a sister in this area. Elizabeth Glick. She and her husband are good people. If only Daniel had taken after them."

Zach disconnected with a nervous feeling in his gut. Fisher didn't fit the Amish mold, yet would he have broken into the clinic and attacked two women in cold blood? Something didn't add up.

Resting his head back in the chair, Zach closed his eyes and let his thoughts wander. Sometimes when he was stuck on a case, if he gave his mind free rein the answer would come like a flash. Today, all he got was confusion.

His cell rang. He checked the monitor before he connected and greeted Sergeant Otis. "Hey, Ray. Thanks for getting back to me."

"I've got contact info for the Memphis agency that handled the death investigation for Quinton Jacobsen." The sergeant provided a name and the police department's phone number.

"Good work, Ray. I owe you."

"Negative, sir. Just doing my job."

Zach smiled as he clicked off. Ray was a good man and an asset to the CID.

After tapping in the phone number he had provided, Zach pulled out his notebook and made a notation of Officer George Davis's name and number.

A receptionist answered and redirected him to Davis's private line. Zach groaned when the call went to voice mail. He left an overview of the information he needed, along with the call-back details.

"I'd appreciate any help you could provide," Zach added before he clicked off.

He spent the next thirty minutes checking emails on his phone. Hearing a car turn into the clinic driveway, he peered through the window and then hurried outside to meet Tyler.

"Thanks, buddy." Zach took the clothing and burner phone. "You're fast and reliable."

"Turns out we had an extra phone in the office that we didn't use on a previous case. That meant I didn't have to stop at the PX." Tyler handed him a key. "This is to the front door of my place. I need to run a few errands in town. See you whenever."

Zach slipped the key into his pocket and placed the gym bag and extra clothing in his own car as Tyler headed back to Freemont.

Seeing Levi on his front porch, Zach hurried to talk to the Amish man about keeping the phone as security for Ella. Thankfully, he agreed, and after giving Levi a short course in cell phone usage, Zach returned to the clinic.

He downed the last of the water and settled onto the

couch with a sigh, realizing how tired he felt. He'd gone too many hours without any shut-eye.

After stretching out his legs and leaning his head back, Zach closed his eyes and drifted into a light sleep.

Visions swirled through his slumber. He saw Ella lying on the floor of her clinic, bleeding from a gunshot wound. Another doctor leaned over her, doing CPR. Zach rushed to her side, but hands held him back. He fought off their grasp and screamed for someone to save her. But when the doctor stepped away, Zach could see her face. It wasn't Ella, but his mother.

He jerked awake and sat up, unaware of where he was for half a second until he got his bearings.

His cell phone rang. Reaching for it, he connected to the call and listened as the Memphis cop identified himself.

"I pulled the file on the case to be sure my information was correct," the officer went on. "Mr. Jacobsen attended the seminar held at Saint Jude's Medical Center. He stayed at the Peabody Hotel downtown. When we traced his steps the night he disappeared, he had gone out to dinner with colleagues and had returned to the hotel, claiming he was tired."

Zach pulled out his notebook and pen and jotted down some of the facts.

"At approximately 8:00 p.m.," the cop continued, "Dr. Jacobsen changed his return ticket for a flight later that night and checked out of his hotel. Security cameras spotted his car heading on I-55 over the Memphis-Arkansas Memorial Bridge forty minutes later. He parked the rental on the far side of the river. Sometime that night, he must have hurled himself into the water."

"Who alerted you to his disappearance?"

"Dr. Ian Webb. He was Jacobsen's assistant. Webb tried to contact Jacobsen the next morning to verify the time they would drive to the airport together. When Jacobsen didn't answer, Webb became worried. He talked to the front desk and was even more concerned when he learned the researcher had checked out of the hotel the night prior. Webb called Jacobsen's wife. She hadn't heard from her husband. We found the abandoned rental car later that day. Search teams scoured the banks of the Mississippi, hoping to uncover some sign of the missing man. The following day, a couple of fishermen found him tangled in some debris along the shore. We notified the wife, but she was already en route to Memphis."

"Dr. Ella Jacobsen flew to Memphis?"

"No, sir. She drove."

Zach let out a stiff breath. "That's got to be a two-day trip. Probably more than nine hundred miles."

"She insisted her husband would never take his own life, but we hear that a lot. I'm sure you do, as well. Mrs. Jacobsen was adamant that he hadn't taken his life and became openly hostile at our attempts to help."

"Did she provide an explanation for her antagonism?"

"She kept saying her husband was working on a cure for a new disease and focused on helping children who suffered from the disability. She couldn't believe that he would have jumped from the bridge. He was afraid of water and didn't know how to swim. As I recall, she couldn't, either. She said he never would have chosen that type of death. Bottom line, she refused to accept our findings and became somewhat belligerent, so much so that we had to warn her to control her outbursts."

"How'd that go over?"

"Not well. She stormed out of my office and said she refused to accept suicide as the cause of death."

"Have you heard from her since?"

"Not after the body was released. She had him buried in Pennsylvania, then sold her house in Carlisle and moved South. We told her to keep in contact, but she failed to do so. Glad someone else is looking into the death. For some reason, I haven't been able to get the case off my mind." The cop sighed. "It might sound strange, but I keep wondering if she knew more than she was willing to reveal."

Before Zach could comment, the door from the hallway opened and Ella stepped into the waiting room, wearing a broad smile and a fresh outfit. Her hair was damp, indicating she had probably showered.

Zach hadn't figured her for being a suspect. Had he been too focused on her pretty face to think of her as anything but an innocent bystander?

"She's in the middle of it, I feel sure," the officer stated before he disconnected.

As much as Zach wanted to ignore the last phone call, he had to use caution. The Memphis police considered Ella a person of interest. What was wrong with him? He'd never been suspicious of her. Was he losing the investigative skills he needed to find the assailant before he struck again?

Levi Miller, Hugh Powers, Daniel Fisher and even Bob Landers could be involved in some way. What about Ella? Could she be involved, as well?

Chapter Eleven

Trouble. The look in Zach's eyes told Ella something was wrong. Terribly wrong.

"Did you get bad news?" she asked, almost afraid to learn what was causing his sour expression.

Earlier he had been concerned about her well-being and had insisted she rest. Now, his face was filled with questions and suspicion.

"Just tracking down some information."

"About Daniel Fisher?" she asked.

"The Freemont police are questioning him."

She glanced out the window to the Miller house. "I hope that doesn't cause Sarah more upset."

When Zach didn't answer, Ella took a step closer. "I'm fixing something to eat. You must be hungry."

"Anything would be appreciated." He got up and started to walk away.

She grabbed his arm. "Look, I don't know who you were talking to on the phone, but something's going on, and I have a feeling it involves me. Why don't you just come out with whatever is bothering you?"

He stared at her for a moment and then nodded.

"You're right. It involves you and your husband. I contacted the Memphis police who handled the investigation of his death. They said you drove there, and you were adamant that your husband couldn't have taken his life."

"And that bothers you because I stood up for my husband?"

"What do you know that you weren't willing to tell them?" Zach demanded.

"I know how my husband reacted to stress. He became more committed to finding answers. That was the type of person he was. I've never seen him morose or despondent."

"I thought you said he wasn't acting like himself."

"He was upset about the data that was collected on the children he had treated. There was something about three sets of twins. I told you that. They didn't respond like the other children. That's why I called the research center in Harrisburg when I first suspected that Shelly and Stacey had CED. I wanted to make sure the protocol hadn't changed and that the treatment was the same as Quin had determined more than a year ago."

"If your husband was upset about the findings, he may have blamed himself. Did the twins get worse? Did any children succumb to the disease?"

She shook her head. "No, it was nothing like that. No one died. All the children were treated and survived."

"Then what was the problem?"

"I don't know. I'm not sure he even knew. But something was amiss."

"And that something—whatever it was—could have been too much for him to handle. Sounds as if your husband was temperamental."

"Aren't all geniuses that way?"

"So he was a genius?"

"He was an intelligent man who had a love of science and research. He understood genetics and how recessive genes manifest in small, limited populations. It was his life's work."

"That led to his death."

"He didn't take his own life," Ella insisted.

"You think someone killed him."

She gasped. "I never said that."

"What else could it be? If he didn't jump of his own volition, then someone pushed him. That's a crime, Ella. It's called murder."

"He could have slipped and fallen," she suggested.

"Did you see the bridge? Is that likely?"

She shook her head, realizing Zach was right. Quin didn't lose his footing and slip off the bridge. Nor had he jumped. He was afraid of water and had never learned to swim. There were other ways that would have been less traumatic to end his life, but again, that wasn't Quin.

She looked at Zach and saw the questions in his eyes. What was he keeping from her?

"Did you drive to Memphis or were you already there?" he asked, his voice stern.

"What?"

"It's evident by your facial expression when you talk about your husband that something was amiss in your marriage. You wanted to fix everything, but you couldn't. Would it be better to have your husband die rather than face what was to come? Had he asked for a divorce? Was there insurance? You could have built an even larger clinic if he had a big policy, but that money wouldn't be paid if it was suicide. You didn't think about that, did you, Ella?"

Tears filled her eyes, and she fought to keep them in check. "I can't believe you would suspect me." She pointed to the door. "I'd appreciate you leaving now."

His face changed again. "I'm not leaving. You need protection. I had to find out if there could be any hint of truth to what the Memphis officer shared."

"You were testing me?" Her anger increased. Today of all days, she didn't need more hassle. "I thought you were on my side."

"I had to be sure which side you were on, Ella."

"Right now, I'm frustrated and angry. Stay in the waiting room, if you want, but I'm going back to my residence."

"I had to make sure, Ella, that you were innocent of any wrongdoing."

"And when will you need to make sure again, Zach? I can't handle someone who doesn't believe in me and changes in a heartbeat. I thought I could trust you. Now I realize I can't."

She turned and hurried from the room overcome with emotion, from upset and heartache to a feeling of being abandoned and wrongly accused. Shame on Zach for playing tricks on her. Shame on her for believing he was something other than an investigator focused on the case. She had learned her lesson, and she wouldn't make the same mistake again.

Zach wished he could take back the callous comments he'd made. Too many investigations and too many cross-examinations had made him aggressive. He walked down the hallway and knocked on the closed kitchen door. Would Ella hear him, and if she did hear his knock, would she want to talk to him? He doubted he would be welcome, but he needed to tell her what had happened.

Again, he rapped on the door.

Footsteps sounded, and it cracked open. She stood on the threshold with one hand on the door and the other on her hip. Her gaze was guarded.

"I'm sorry," he said. "I was acting like an overzealous investigator. You don't understand, I'm sure, but law enforcers need to be careful and get to the bottom of every situation."

"You believed the Memphis police officer instead of believing me."

"I was wrong, Ella. I'm sorry if my questions upset you."

"It wasn't your questions as much as the hostility I heard in your voice. You suspected me. You probably still do."

He couldn't say anything to change her mind, he felt sure. Maybe with time she'd start to trust him again.

"I need to bring you up-to-date." He took a step closer. "Then I'll leave."

Did he detect surprise in her expression? Had she thought he'd stand guard through the night, when she had been so insistent about wanting him to leave?

"Special Agent Tyler Zimmerman stopped by the clinic with a cell phone. I gave it to Levi Miller. Here's the number." Zach handed her a small card. "Program it into your phone. Levi will be next door and will respond immediately if you feel threatened or hear anything or anyone outside."

"Are you sure Levi doesn't mind?"

"He's more than happy to help out."

"Then you think he's trustworthy?" Her question held more than a touch of irony.

"Tyler lives along Amish Road. You've probably seen the antebellum home."

"He lives there?"

Zach smiled. "He's engaged to the woman who inherited the big house from her father. Tyler lives in the brick ranch south of it."

"I know the Amish neighbors on the other side of the old home. Isaac and Ruth Lapp have brought their young son, Joseph, to the clinic," Ella murmured.

"Tyler invited me to stay at his place for the next couple of days. I won't be far. Call me if you have a problem."

"But you live on post."

"I do, in the bachelor officers' quarters, but the drive takes a bit of time. I wanted to be closer to you."

She leaned against the doorjamb. "Thank you, Zach."

"Cops have to worse-case every situation, Ella. It's not personal. It's the way we roll. I don't disbelieve you. I just needed to make sure. Your reaction proved to me that you've been truthful and sincere."

"Evidently I don't understand law enforcement."

He almost smiled. "And I don't understand medicine. Doctors have never been on my list of most favorite people."

"Is it personal?"

He pursed his lips. "I'm not sure what you mean."

"Personal, as in a female doc broke your heart so you won't like any of us."

"No girlfriend. No fiancée. No ex-wife."

"Then I'm wrong."

"It stems from my childhood, but I'll leave it at that."

"And did that play in to your verbal attack against me?" she asked.

"It wasn't an attack, Ella. I had questions that needed to be answered."

"Which seemed more like an interrogation."

He nodded. "I understand how you could misinterpret my intentions."

She looked into the kitchen. "I've got a pot of chili cooking, if you're hungry."

"Are you sure you want company?"

"Of course. I'm sorry if I came off as antagonistic."

Zach smiled. "Isn't that what you accused me of being?"

"And you were exactly that, but I'm tired and not as forgiving as I should be."

He raised his eyebrow. "Did I ask for forgiveness?"

She stared at him for a long moment. "If you didn't, you should have. I'm trying to play nice."

"You're succeeding."

"Does that mean you'll accept my invitation to dinner?"

"Most assuredly. As they say in the South, 'My mama didn't raise no fools.' I'd enjoy sharing a meal with you, but only if you let me take you out sometime."

He hadn't expected Ella's surprised expression.

"Are you asking me out on a date?" she asked.

"No." He raised his hand as if to block anything she had been thinking along those lines. "A friendly dinner to pay you back for your hospitality."

She blushed. "Now I'm feeling embarrassed. I wasn't fishing for a date. You took me by surprise, especially after I kicked you out."

"You made chili."

"I'm reheating chili that was already made," she corrected.

"That makes no difference. Food is food, and I'm hungry."

Ella smiled. "The way I figure it, you've got to be down a couple meals."

"It's par for the course for a special agent. We work 24/7 when needed. I can live on coffee for longer than you would like to know."

"Has your doctor mentioned the damage that could do to your stomach and esophagus? You're opening yourself up to acid reflux and even more serious complications."

Again, he held up his hand. "I'm doing okay, and I don't have a primary care doc. If I get sick—and it's rare that I do—I go on sick call. Although I can't remember the last time I needed to be treated."

"Hardy stock, eh?"

"Maybe it's the coffee." Zach couldn't help but smile.

Ella laughed. The tension that he'd felt earlier evaporated. She stepped away from the door and motioned him into the kitchen.

"We'll eat in here, if you don't mind."

He glanced at the vase of flowers by the window. "The least I can do is set the table."

She pointed to a cabinet near the sink. "You'll find silverware in the top drawer. We'll need soup spoons, as well as knives and forks."

Ella shoved a cast-iron skillet into the oven. "Do you like corn bread?"

"I do. That's good Georgia food."

"It'll be done by the time the chili is hot. There's butter in the refrigerator, if you want to put it on the table while I make a salad."

She also made a pitcher of sweet tea.

Seeing the sugar she dumped into the warm liquid, Zach had to laugh. "You're from up north, yet you make tea like a Southerner?"

"Does that seem strange?" She smiled. "Adding sugar when the tea is warm ensures it will dissolve, which is a lot more economical than putting it in individual glasses. Plus I like the taste."

"No wonder the locals enjoy having you around."

"Only some of them," she said as she dropped ice into the pitcher.

"You've had problems before?"

"Not really. It's just that some folks, especially the older Amish, don't want me interfering in their lives."

"Is that what they've said?"

She nodded. "A few, mainly men. The woman are relieved to have a doctor nearby in case their children get sick."

Zach glanced out the window. "Do you ever get lonely out here, all by yourself?"

She hesitated for a moment before she pulled two glasses from the cabinet. "The weekends can be long, although I usually have something that needs attention around the clinic."

She filled the glasses before glancing up at him. "What about you? Don't you ever get lonely?"

"I wouldn't call it lonely. Usually I stay busy. If I have some downtime, I head to the gym or go for a jog outside."

"You can't jog all day long."

He laughed. "You're right. After jogging, I shower

and leave my BOQ, seeking food. Like a hunter of old, only I don't have to stalk my prey. It's usually served at one of the local restaurants. Which," he said with a smile, "brings us back to my earlier question. Would you like to join me for a meal sometime?" He shrugged. "We can call it a business dinner if we talk about the investigation. If we stick to more general topics, it can be a chance for two people who know each other to connect. Or—" he smiled "—if you'd feel better, we could call it a date."

Ella laughed. Her face softened, her eyes sparkled in spite of being tired, and she took on a new light-hearted appearance that he found enchanting. A date would be fun.

"Is this your normal modus operandi?" she asked.

"You speak Latin?"

She nodded. "Most doctors have a good understanding of the language."

"I took it in high school," he admitted.

"Really?" She seemed surprised.

"My mother loved biblical Roman times. She died when I was young. Reading the books she treasured and learning the language she had studied allowed me to feel closer to her."

"I'm sorry."

Zach shrugged. "We all carry baggage, the hurts and struggles from the past."

Ella nodded knowingly. "Would I be correct in assuming that your mother's death has something to do with your dislike of the medical profession?"

Not only did the doctor like to talk, she was also perceptive.

"I thought we were discussing dinner together."

She nodded again and turned to ladle the chili into soup bowls. "That's exactly what we were talking about. Mind if I ask one more question."

No telling where she was headed. "Shoot."

"Do you invite all the witnesses in your investigations to dine with you?"

Ella stood at the stove with her back to him, so he couldn't read her expression. Was she still being frivolous and lighthearted, or had the mention of his mother's death turned her more pensive?

Zach regretted the direction their conversation had gone. "Perhaps dinner should wait until the investigation is over."

Which made a whole lot more sense than going out when the case was still active. Either way, she was right to have asked the question. Zach didn't usually socialize with witnesses. Make that never. He had never before gone out with a witness.

So what made Ella different?

Turning with a hot soup bowl in hand, she stared at him for half a second before placing the dish on the table.

Her pretty face and blue eyes looked as perplexed as he felt. Talk about a flood of emotion. Zach prided himself on being a man of action, on not letting his personal life get in the way of anything to do with his job. Yet he'd done exactly that, no matter how much he wanted to think being with Ella wasn't personal.

He glanced at the chili she'd set before him and inhaled the rich aroma. "This smells and looks delicious. For me, chili usually comes out of a can. This has homemade written all over it."

She smiled and turned back to the stove for her own

bowl. "You asked what I do on weekends. Often I cook and then freeze what I fix in smaller containers. That way if I'm busy with patients late into the day, I can eat a nourishing dinner without having to spend time getting everything made."

"Smart lady."

She turned back and smiled. "You're an affirming person."

He rounded the table and helped her with her chair. "And you're perceptive," he said.

"Which a doctor needs to be."

Settling into his seat, Zach thought about what she'd said. "My father was a positive man. Perhaps I learned affirmation from him."

She nodded. "He was probably worried about you after your mother died. Sounds like he was a good man who wanted to build up his young son."

"He *was* a good man. I lost him last year. Too young."

"Do you have other family?" Ella asked.

Zach shook his head. "What about you?"

"An only child. My father's still alive, but we don't have much of a relationship. I call him at Christmas. He sends a check for my birthday."

She glanced down. "The chili's getting cold."

Zach nodded and reached for his spoon, then noticed that she had bowed her head as if offering a blessing.

When she glanced up, he smiled sheepishly. "I haven't paused to give thanks before eating since I was a kid. My mother always led us in saying grace before meals. You've taken me back."

Ella's expression lightened again and the sparkle returned to her eyes. "The Amish are rubbing off on me. I'm not religious, and I haven't had much to do with

God for years, but their trust in the Lord and the comments they mention about doing His will have made me think about the importance of faith. For your information, research has proved that people of faith have a better chance of surviving a significant illness, such as cancer, than unbelievers."

He raised the soup spoon. "So you're experimenting on yourself?"

"I hadn't thought about it in that way. If faith has a positive influence on quality of life, then shouldn't I attempt to integrate it into my own?"

She sounded clinical.

"Doc, you're talking with your head instead of your heart." Zach tasted the chili. "My compliments to the chef."

"Thanks. My mother worked. I took over the kitchen at a younger age than most of my peers. Cooking was something I could do right."

He glanced at her as he enjoyed another spoonful of her chili. He might not be as perceptive as the doc, but he sensed she came with some baggage, too.

Zach thought of his own past and the pain he still carried. Pain and guilt. Not that he had to go there, especially not tonight. He needed to turn the discussion to mundane matters of little consequence, instead of faith and lonely children who couldn't find their way.

The conversation changed to lighthearted chatter that Zach enjoyed. How long had it been since he'd relaxed with a woman? Most of the ones he associated with were army types who talked about military topics, like the guys.

The doc wasn't one of the guys, at least not tonight. Maybe in medical circles, when she was spouting facts about the pediatric needs of children, she might seem more focused on her career. Right now, sitting in her warm and welcoming kitchen, eating the hearty chili she had made, took him away from the investigation that had brought them together.

After coffee and a slice of apple pie that Levi's wife had sent home with them, Zach looked at his watch and scooted back from the table.

"I don't want to overstay my welcome." He carried his soup bowl and silverware to the sink. "Let me do the dishes while you put the leftover chili away."

"You know how to get on a woman's good side." Ella smiled as she placed her own bowl in the sink. "Just rinse the dishes, and I'll get to them later."

"No, ma'am. I'm not leaving you with dishes to wash." He ran water in the sink and added soap. "I'll have these done in a flash."

"You could use the dishwasher."

He nodded. "I could, but you'll think more of me if I wash them by hand, then dry them and put them away. You're exhausted and need a full night's sleep, instead of spending time tidying up the kitchen."

"I won't argue with your logic, Mr. Swain." She pulled a container from an overhead cabinet, transferred the rest of the chili and placed it in the refrigerator. "There's enough left over for lunch, if you're in the neighborhood."

The invitation warmed his heart. Zach quickly washed and rinsed the dishes and then dried them and handed them to Ella, who put them in the proper places on the shelves.

Once that was done he wiped his hands on a dish

towel. "Thanks for the chili and for the opportunity to relax a bit."

"I enjoyed it, too."

"You've got the number to my cell?"

She nodded. "It's programmed into my phone. I've also got the number to contact Levi. Hopefully, I won't need to call either of you."

"I'll go out through the clinic."

He held the hallway door open, and she walked ahead of him. Returning to the scene of the attack brought them back to the reality of what had happened, and the levity Zach had felt in her kitchen came to an abrupt end.

Ella hesitated when they reached the waiting room. "I haven't adequately thanked you, Zach, for taking me to the hospital. You stayed throughout the night. That meant a lot to me, and I know hospitals aren't your favorite places to be."

"That's your perceptive nature. I hope I didn't embarrass you when I quizzed the nurse about why the lab and X-ray results were taking so long."

"I appreciated having a champion." She placed her hand on his arm. Her touch was light, yet it had an effect on him. He stepped closer, seeing the openness of her gaze, the fullness of her lips. She leaned closer and for a moment he longed to touch his lips to hers.

Intellectually, he knew how foolish his reactions seemed, yet he couldn't find the wherewithal to step away. Some unknown yet attractive force pulled him to her.

"You're a good man, Zach." Her voice was low and rich with resonance, as if she meant to say much more than the words themselves.

His chest swelled, and he felt taller and stronger and ready to slay giants or dragons or anything untoward that might come against her. For a moment, he was her champion, a man who would protect her from harm, who would give her his allegiance and—did he dare acknowledge an even deeper feeling?—give her his heart.

The office phone rang.

Ella blinked, as if some imaginary thread held them together and she wasn't ready to cut free from its hold.

"I need to go," Zach said, coming to his senses much too quickly. The world seemed to spin around him as he turned and headed for the door.

The phone continued to ring, but when he looked back, she remained in the middle of her office, staring in his direction, oblivious to the phone or anything else except him.

Chapter Twelve

Ella couldn't move. Her heart thumped hard and a knot had formed in her throat. Not from tears. She'd cried too many times after Quin had died, and she didn't know how to rebuild her life.

The lump in her throat tonight was pure emotion that made her want to wrap her arms around the handsome special agent's shoulders and have him pull her into his embrace, as he'd done yesterday in the hallway when she'd remembered the gun.

The gun?

All too clearly, she saw the glaring light that had almost blinded her and the assailant's hand holding the revolver.

Earlier, as she sat in the kitchen with Zach, Ella had pushed everything that had happened the night before out of her mind. Now it flooded over her. Mary Kate's scream, the pounding rain, her own attempt to come to the young mother's rescue, only to find a man, bathed in shadow, standing at her desk.

She turned, seeing the desk again.

And heard the phone.

How long had it been ringing?

Tripping over herself, she raced to her desk and lifted the handset to her ear.

A dial tone sounded.

She tapped in star 69 to recapture the caller's number. A number she recognized. Nancy Vaughn, director of the Harrisburg Genetic Research Center.

Pulling in a deep breath to calm her pounding heart, Ella tugged on the curtain and watched through the window as Zach drove out onto the main road. She stared after him as his taillights disappeared into the night.

A sense of sadness washed over her, bringing with it a nervous anxiety that made her scurry to the front door of her clinic. She checked the lock and engaged the dead bolt, refusing to dwell on what could happen if the locks didn't hold. Stepping back into her office, she checked the side door to her clinic, then the kitchen and main doors to her house.

Satisfied with the extra protection the dead bolts provided, Ella returned to her office and called the director.

"I thought something might have happened when you didn't answer," the woman said, sounding breathless. "I was worried about you."

Ella tried to laugh off her concern. "I was in the other room."

"You were going through Quin's things?"

"No, why would you think that?" she asked.

"One of the times we talked, you mentioned that you still had boxes from his office to unpack."

"You're right, but that wasn't what I was doing." Ella rubbed her free hand over her face. The spot where she'd been struck was tender to the touch. "I'm returning your call, Dr. Vaughn. Was there something you needed?"

"It's time to stop with the formality. I'm Nancy, and I called to let you know that I reserved a room for you at the hotel. Even if you can't make the afternoon symposium, be sure to join us at the benefit that evening. It's what Quin would want."

Quin had never been a black-tie type of guy. In fact, Ella had had to convince him to wear a suit to their wedding.

"I appreciate the offer, Nancy, but I just don't think—"

"Let's talk in the morning. Sometimes things look brighter in the light of day."

But this had nothing to do with daylight or sunshine.

"Have you heard from Ross Underwood recently?" the director asked. "He was extremely distraught when Quin died. I know the two men were close."

"Ross called soon after I opened the Children's Care Clinic and asked if there was anything I needed. I appreciated his thoughtfulness."

"He was worried about you, Ella. We all were. As I mentioned at Quin's funeral, I would have liked you to join the team."

"Research isn't my interest, Nancy, but I was grateful for the offer. Quin's work was the main focus of his life. He felt strongly about the good that was being done, especially with the Amish Project."

"We share those feelings, of course. I won't keep you tonight, but I'm counting on you to join us on Friday. I'll be in touch."

Ella stared at the invitation after she disconnected, feeling even more confused. Over the last twenty-four hours, she had experienced a gamut of emotions. Everything from grief for Quin to a surprising attraction for another man.

She flipped off the light and returned to the kitchen, locking the door to the hallway behind her. Peering out of the side window, she was relieved to see a faint glow coming from the Miller home.

Sarah and Levi were probably sitting in their kitchen, the room lit by a gaslight.

Her cell rang.

Surprised, she smiled when she saw Zach's name on the monitor. "I hope nothing is wrong," she said in greeting.

"I'm at Special Agent Zimmerman's house. Just wanted to let you know that I'm not far away. Don't hesitate to call me."

A warmth filled her chest. "You're being cautious, which I appreciate. The assailant was probably after meds. Nonmedical folks think that doctors stockpile drugs. That's why he came back today."

"Let's hope that's what he was looking for. Did you set your security alarm?"

"Not yet, but I will."

"Don't hesitate to call me," Zach repeated.

She disconnected, armed the security alarm and walked into her bedroom. Knowing he was close by was reassuring. The assailant wouldn't come back. At least not tonight. She'd sleep soundly and wake refreshed in the morning.

Peering out the rear window into the darkness, she felt a ripple of anxiety stir within her.

At least she hoped she would be able to sleep.

Zach hadn't planned to call. He had said goodbye to Ella less than five minutes earlier, yet as he'd pulled into Tyler's driveway, he was tapping the call prompt and raising the phone to his ear.

Was it important for Ella to know he wasn't far away, or was it important for him to hear her voice again? Either way, the call hadn't been necessary, although he had heard concern in her voice when she asked if anything was wrong. Nothing was wrong on his end, and in a way, everything seemed right. Except that was glossing over a very real problem about an attack against two women and an assailant still on the loose.

Zach stepped from his car and grabbed his gym bag and extra clothing. The spare outfits would get him to the weekend. Perhaps the investigation would be solved by then.

Tyler opened the front door before Zach could pull the house key from his pocket. "Welcome to rural life." He motioned Zach inside. "I picked up pizza on the way home, by the way. I wasn't sure when you'd get here."

"Thanks, buddy, but I ate at Ella's."

Tyler smirked with surprise. "Since when did Dr. Jacobsen become Ella?"

"You know her?"

"I know of her, and it's all good. She's treated my neighbors' son, and they give her high praise."

"We spent a number of hours together at the ER last night," Zach explained, "while waiting for her test results."

"I've heard some recent complaints about the local hospital."

"If what we experienced is any indication of their competence…" Zach shrugged. "But then, I've never been a fan of anything medical. In all fairness, the nurse and the doctor said they were short staffed."

Tyler pointed to the hallway. "Guest room is on the left. The bathroom is to the right. The coffeepot is programmed for 6:00 a.m., if that works for you."

"Sounds good."

"Colas are in the fridge, or I can brew a pot of decaf."

Zach held up his hand. "Thanks, but I need to hit the sack."

"I'm right behind you," Tyler said. "Tomorrow afternoon, the chief is headed to Fort Belvoir. He assigned me to go with him. It's last minute, but that's typical."

"Have a safe trip."

"Will do, but I'll see you in the morning."

Once in the bedroom, Zach placed his cell on the nightstand and checked the volume. If Ella phoned, he wanted to be sure to hear the call.

If only he had met her before the assailant broke into her clinic. Then he could have invited her out to dinner and they could have called it a date.

He would have liked that.

His eyelids grew heavy. The last things he thought about were Ella's blue eyes and the way her laughter touched a lonely portion of his heart.

Chapter Thirteen

The night had never seemed so dark, nor had Ella been so aware of sounds. She heard the throaty croak of bullfrogs and the incessant chirp of cicadas, but other noises—a tree branch brushing against the house, a groan as the hardwood floors settled, the heat turning on and the freezer emptying a tray of ice cubes into the holding container—seemed especially annoying tonight. Even the *ticktock* of her alarm clock grated on her nerves.

She draped one arm over her eyes in an attempt to blot out the world, but tired as she was, she couldn't sleep. With a frustrated sign, she flipped onto her side, buried her head in the pillow and, at some point, drifted off.

In the middle of the night, her eyes blinked open. She glanced at the clock on her nightstand: 2:00 a.m.

What had awakened her?

Ella raised up and listened, unable to decipher a sound that came from the side of the house.

A scratching. Surely not a rodent?

She stepped from her bed and grabbed her robe off the nearby chair. Slipping into the thick flannel, she toed on her slippers and pulled back the curtain ever so slightly. Peering outside, she couldn't identify anything, yet the sound continued. She grabbed her cell off the nightstand and stepped into the living area, where she stopped again and listened.

The noise sounded like a chisel, biting into wood.

Her kitchen door!

Before she could hit the prompt to call Levi, the back door opened. Fear swept over her. Seconds later, the security alarm blared a warning.

The sound filled the house.

Heart pounding, Ella ran back to her bedroom and hesitated. The assailant would expect to find her there, so she scurried across the hall to the guest room, closed and locked the door and entered the attached bath, grateful for the night light that illuminated the room ever so slightly. She shut the bathroom door and turned the lock, but felt little sense of protection.

With trembling hands, she tapped Levi's number. Voice mail.

What had happened? He knew she was alone.

A swell of panic filled her chest. Had Levi ignored her call for help because he was in her house? Footsteps sounded. She backed up against the bathroom door.

Not Levi. It couldn't be Levi.

She fumbled with her phone. It slipped through her fingers. She caught it in midair, her heart in her throat.

Hitting speed dial, she called Zach.

The phone rang in her ear. Why didn't he pick up?

The assailant broke through the locked guest room door.

Oh, God, she silently prayed.

"Ella?" Zach's voice.

The security alarm continued to scream. She pushed the phone closer to her ear. "He's in the bedroom."

"I'm on the way. Gouge out his eyes, jam your hand up under his chin, knee him where it hurts."

Inwardly, she screamed for Zach to hurry. She didn't have time for lessons on self-defense.

Heavy footsteps crossed the bedroom.

She glanced down as the doorknob jiggled.

"I know you're in there." A gruff voice, muffled as if he was speaking through a handkerchief. Did he have an accent?

If she recognized the voice, she could warn Zach. Then, even if—

She couldn't go there.

"The police are on the way," she shouted, trying to sound assertive and in control. "They'll apprehend you. You won't get away with this."

The doorknob stopped moving. Had she scared him off? *Please, Lord.*

She pressed her ear against the door, trying to make out the sound. A faint swish, barely audible over the peal of the security alarm, as if—

Even before her mind processed the sound, she leaped into the bathtub and screamed as round after round of gunfire splintered the door. Fragments of wood flew through the air, stinging her back and peppering her hands, which she'd wrapped protectively around her neck.

Ella trembled with fear. In a matter of seconds, he would push through the shattered doorway and turn his weapon on her where she huddled like a terrified child, hiding in the protective steel tub.

A siren mixed with the shrill of the alarm. Was her mind playing tricks on her?

Footsteps. Running toward her or away?

"Ella." Another voice.

Her heart lurched. "Zach!"

He was there, reaching for her, pulling her up and into his arms. "Are you hurt?"

She shook her head, struggled to speak and then fell against his chest and gasped for air, realizing she hadn't breathed since the door exploded.

"He...he tried to...kill me."

With his arm protectively around her, Zach guided her into her living room. She disarmed the security alarm. Silence filled the house.

"Did you see him?" Zach asked.

She shook her head. "No, but I heard his voice. It was muffled, but with an accent."

"French? German?"

"I'm not sure. Maybe one of the islands."

"Hawaii?"

"The Caribbean." She rubbed her neck. "How did the police—"

"Tyler called them as I left his house. A patrol car must have been in the area. Plus your security alarm sent a signal to the dispatcher."

Zach pulled out his cell phone and called police dispatch. "I'm at the Children's Care Clinic. A shooter tried to kill Dr. Jacobsen. He's on the run. Notify all units. Set up roadblocks. Comb the woods. He can't get away."

Disconnecting, Zach stared again into Ella's face. "You're sure you're okay?"

She nodded.

"Why didn't you call Levi?"

Tears welled in her eyes. "Oh, Zach, I did, but he was already in the house."

"You think Levi was the assailant?"

"I don't know, but why didn't he answer the phone?"

* * *

Zach wouldn't let Ella out of his sight again. He couldn't risk losing her. He kept thinking *What if?* What if his car hadn't started? What if there had been an accident on the road that delayed him? What if he hadn't gotten to her in time?

As it was, he'd floored the accelerator and fishtailed out of Tyler's drive. If anything had been in the road—a buggy, or a herd of cows that had broken out of their pasture—he would have arrived too late.

He fought the lump that filled his throat, thinking the unthinkable, and shoved his way back to the present.

The first officers to arrive on-site searched the woods behind the house. Tyler had alerted post. The military police joined with local law enforcement in setting up roadblocks.

They were dealing with more than a punk kid looking for the next high. The guy hadn't been searching for drugs. He'd been searching for Ella. To kill her.

Police interrogated Levi. They'd found him groggy with sleep in his house. Sarah, frightened and shaking, had confirmed that he'd been next to her in bed all night, and because of the distance between the two houses, they hadn't heard Ella's security alarm.

The cell phone that should have alerted him to Ella's distress had been inadvertently turned off. At least that was the alibi Levi used. He didn't know technology and had adjusted the volume of the ring so as not to disturb his wife. In reality, he had turned the cell off.

So much for Zach's good intentions, which had almost cost Ella her life.

As distraught as the pregnant Amish wife had been earlier in the day, Zach wondered if she might have tampered with the phone in order to ensure her husband could sleep through the night. Zach wasn't sure that Sarah had been forthright about her relationship with her brother. The two siblings could be working together, which meant Daniel Fisher could be the assailant.

Zach raked his hand through his hair and approached Sergeant Abrams, who had interrogated Levi. "What's your assessment?" he asked.

"Levi seems sincere and is openly contrite about the phone."

"What about Sarah?"

The cop sniffed. "She's harder to read. I can't decide if she's sincere or playing us for fools. I've got two of my guys heading to her father's house to question the old man and haul his son in for interrogation. I'm holding Daniel for at least twenty-four hours this time."

Zach rubbed his chin. "All this could have started with his desire to destroy the twins' medical records, if he thought Levi was identified as the father. A breaking and entering escalates, and he turns his hatred for Levi against the doc."

Abrams nodded. "I've heard of stranger things happening. The guy's not wired tight, we know that. Add an overzealousness to defend his sister and anything could happen."

The cop glanced into the living room, where Ella sat, head in her hands. "How's she doing?"

"She's ready to collapse, but if you ask her, she'll say she's fine."

"Any need to take her back to the ER?"

Zach shook his head. "Not that I can determine. Something to calm her nerves might be beneficial, but

I doubt she'd take anything more than ibuprofen. She's strong as a mule."

A corner of the cop's mouth twitched. "My suggestion, don't let her hear you make that comparison. The ladies I know wouldn't cotton to being compared to a domestic work animal."

Zach had to smile. "You're a wise man, Sergeant."

Abrams patted Zach's shoulder. "I'm not blind. Something's going on with you two. I'm not pointing a finger, but getting personally involved in a case makes for mistakes, if you get my drift."

Zach didn't know if he was being chastised or counseled. "I'm law enforcement first."

The cop slapped his shoulder. "I know you are. I'm just telling you what I see that maybe you don't. Freemont PD can handle the investigation. We'll keep you in the loop, but let us take the lead. You hover over the doc and be a first line of protection, while we track this guy down and apprehend him."

"You might be reading more into this?"

The sergeant stared at him. His eyes were filled with understanding and not the condemnation Zach had thought he might find. "I fell in love with my wife when I was working a case. It wasn't as big as this one, but I can read the signs."

Zach blew out a stiff breath.

Love?

Abrams had it all wrong. Yes, Zach felt a bit of attraction, but nothing more.

Ella glanced up, and their gazes met.

A warmth flooded over him, a feeling that was a bit disconcerting and took him by surprise. Maybe there was some truth to what the cop had said, after all.

* * *

"I'm going to Atlanta." Ella held the invitation to the symposium in her hand and waved it at Zach. "You're worried about my safety, but I'll be safer in Atlanta than around here."

She glanced at the policemen who were still combing through her house, looking for clues. "A man almost killed me. He broke into my clinic last night and he came after me again tonight. There's something he wants, and I'm afraid it's that he wants me dead."

Zach stood staring at her as if he wanted to talk her out of making the trip to the city.

"I won't tell anyone where I'm going," she rationalized. "The clinic is closed until Monday. I'll keep my cell on, and I'll call you when I arrive."

"I'm going with you."

"What?" She hadn't expected him to acquiesce so easily, which only proved he was as worried about her safety as she was.

"So you agree that I'll be safer in Atlanta?"

"I hope so. It doesn't seem to be working out so well around here."

The calmness in his voice and his dark gaze made her even more afraid. She had to face the truth that someone wanted to do her harm.

"I'll be all right, Zach. You don't need to go with me." Although as the words came out, she knew their folly. She did need Zach. She needed his arms to support her and his strong shoulders to lean on when the darkness became too intense.

He had come to her rescue once again, in the nick of time. If he hadn't…

She shivered, thinking of what could have happened, what had almost happened.

"I'm going with you," he repeated. "That's non-negotiable. I'll call the hotel and get a room across from yours. Tell the director that someone will accompany you. You can't go into the city alone, even if it seems a safer place than Freemont."

She knew he was right. "The invitation includes a guest, but I don't want anyone to know why you're with me."

"Tell them I'm interested in learning more about the research. Helping the local Amish has been a priority for the commanding general at Fort Rickman. I'll brief General Cameron when I return, so you'll be telling the truth."

"Your boss will let you off work?"

"I'll get a pass. That won't be a problem. I'll let Sergeant Abrams know, but I'll ask him to keep the information to himself."

"You suspect someone in law enforcement?"

"Not at this point, but the fewer individuals who know your whereabouts, the better."

"What about Sarah Miller, in case she needs medical care?"

"She could be involved, Ella."

"That's ridiculous. Do you suspect Levi, as well?"

"I'm more prone to question his wife's motives because of her brother."

Ella turned away and hung her head. Zach's words cut into her heart. What had she done by coming to Freemont? She was destroying a young couple who had done nothing wrong.

Letting out a deep sigh, she turned back to Zach.

"I'll call the director and let her know. We can leave tomorrow morning."

"You can't stay here tonight."

"Maybe I can stay with Wendy or my receptionist."

Tyler stepped into the room. He had evidently heard the last portion of their conversation. "You need a place to stay?" he asked.

"I do."

"My fiancée has room at her house." Tyler moved closer. "I'm sure Carrie won't mind. Zach and I can keep watch throughout the night."

"Sounds good," Zach said. "I'll head to my BOQ first thing in the morning and pack a bag for Atlanta. I also want to stop at CID headquarters and brief the chief before he heads to the airport."

Tyler pulled out his phone. "I'll call Carrie and confirm the plans with her. There shouldn't be a problem."

Once he had left the room, Zach took Ella's hand.

"This won't last forever," he said, as if he could sense her unease. "The local police will track down the attacker. Or he'll make a mistake, and they'll catch him before—"

She stared at Zach, knowing what he was thinking but couldn't say out loud.

There would be a next time. She wasn't safe anywhere, and if the police didn't put the pieces together fast enough, the next time could be fatal.

Then a thought caught at her heart. What if the danger that confronted her turned on Zach? What if something happened to him when he was trying to protect her?

The assailant had to be stopped. Before he hurt Ella, and even more important, before he harmed Zach.

Chapter Fourteen

"You've been too gracious," Ella said as she hugged Carrie goodbye the next morning, and then handed her bag to Zach.

"Anytime you need a place to stay," Tyler's fiancée said, "don't hesitate to call me."

Ella nodded and then hugged Tyler. "You and Zach did a good job keeping the ladies safe last night, but I don't think either of you slept."

He smiled and shrugged. "Zach and I are used to running on no sleep. Plus we spelled each other for an hour or two."

As Zach placed Ella's luggage in his car, Tyler added, "I needed to force him to grab a few z's. I don't think Zach's slept in days. Keep talking as you drive to Atlanta to keep him awake."

She laughed. "I'll be a chatterbox. He'll ask me to shut up."

"I doubt that." Tyler looked at her knowingly, as if he realized something special had developed between them. Was it that obvious?

After saying their goodbyes, Ella slid into the passenger seat, nodding her thanks to Zach before he closed the door and hurried to the driver's side.

They both waved, and as they drove away, Ella turned to watch Tyler and Carrie fade from view. "They're a great couple, and they had high praise for you, Zach."

He smiled and turned onto the road that would take them into Freemont and then to the interstate. "They're good people. I thought they'd be married by now, but they're both taking their time and getting to know each other, which is probably smart."

"Carrie said it wouldn't be long."

"Tyler insisted I get some shut-eye last night. You probably coerced him into taking care of me."

Ella held up her hands and laughed. "I plead innocent. He recognized the fatigue lining your eyes. He's a smart guy who wanted to help out. Friends like that are hard to find."

"You're right."

She patted his hand. "I'm relieved you got some rest. I must admit that I slept, as well. Probably for the first time since the attack."

She glanced out the window and then asked, "Have you learned anything new about Mary Kate's condition?"

"She's responding to treatment, so evidently there's improvement."

"Which is what we want. Did you contact Corporal Powers's unit?"

"They're keeping him under watch, although he's allowed to visit his wife at the hospital. The main concern is that he might do something rash and hurt himself. They don't seem to think that he'll hurt anyone else."

"That's a tough way to come home from a war zone."

"The counselors and medical personnel working with our PTSD soldiers are top of the line. I'm satisfied that he's getting the best care possible."

"What about Mary Kate?" Ella asked.

"The military hospital at Fort Freemont is staffed with highly competent physicians and other medical personnel. Mary Kate will pull through."

Ella shook her head. "I don't want to think of what could happen.

"They're doing everything possible to ensure she improves."

"I'm sure they are." Ella glanced at Zach. "Before you, I had never known anyone who was career army."

"What's your assessment now that you know me?"

She hesitated, weighing her words. "You're a great guy, Zach, with a big heart. Even though you try to put up a tough front, down deep you're a softy."

"Is that right?" He laughed, causing her heart to flutter. "That's somewhat like the way I see you." He flicked a quick glance at her before he turned his eyes back to the road. "You're ever the medical expert, spouting information and speaking in long sentences."

"Really?" Her cheeks burned.

"Maybe you feel the need to prove yourself. But…" He hesitated a moment. "I don't see a medical professional when I look at you. I see a very interesting lady with a big heart who must love children and wants to make the world a better place. Your husband was the intellectual. You were the heart."

Moved by Zach's comment, Ella glanced out the window.

He touched her hand. "Am I right?"

She turned back to face him, seeing the openness

of his gaze. "You said I was perceptive, Zach, but you seem to be, as well."

"An investigator puts the pieces together. You've mentioned your husband a number of times. All I did was make the connections."

"Just as you said, Quin was all head. I like to think that I am more heart. Unfortunately, we couldn't seem to find a midpoint that worked for both of us."

"I'm sorry." Again, Zach reached for her hand, only this time he didn't let go.

The highway stretched before them, taking them to Atlanta for a symposium that would highlight her husband's work.

Zach was right; for all her attempts to appear strong, she was apprehensive about what the day would bring. She appreciated the warmth of his touch and was grateful for his friendship and support.

But wasn't it more than friendship? Something much more? The special agent with the understanding gaze had wormed his way into her heart.

Confronting the medical research team who had worked with Quin would be a challenge. Thankfully, Zach was with her. No matter how strong she tried to be, she couldn't have faced them alone.

Navigating Atlanta traffic made Zach realize he was a country boy at heart. Even early in the day, the connector that led into the heart of the city was sixteen lanes of bumper-to-bumper traffic.

At least the front desk personnel at the hotel were accommodating. He had requested a room across from Ella's when he'd made his reservation, but he'd ended up on the twelfth floor, while she was on the seventh.

Thankfully, the staff was able to make the change, which placed Zach three rooms away from her.

"You're worried about my safety," she said as they rode up in the elevator.

"I can't turn off being a special agent," he answered, although there was far more to it than that. Someone was out to do Ella harm. Even though she had left Freemont, and hopefully, the danger remained there, Zach wouldn't let down his guard.

"Let's stick together, okay?" he said with a smile. "Then I won't have to worry quite so much."

"Did you want to check my room to make sure no one's hiding in there?" Her comment was offhand, but Zach realized she understood the importance of being cautious.

"Now you're thinking like someone in law enforcement." He took the key from her, swiped it against the sensory pad on the door and stepped into the room. Quickly, he checked the closet and bathroom and under the bed, before motioning her inside.

"Everything looks fine," he assured her. "I'll be three doors down on the opposite side of the hallway. Room 712. What time do we need to head to the symposium?"

"Let me check the welcome packet." The large manila envelope had been waiting at the front desk for Ella. She pulled out a number of papers and searched through them.

"I found the information," she said. "The symposium's being held in Decatur. Due to a lack of parking, they ask everyone to use MARTA, the city's mass transit system. The station's not far from here."

"What time should we leave?"

She glanced at another paper and pointed to a paragraph halfway down the printout. "Nancy's scheduled to speak about CED at 1:00 p.m., immediately after the lunch break. Why don't we leave here at eleven fifteen? We'll arrive at the symposium ahead of schedule and grab lunch there before the talk."

Zach checked his watch. "I'll knock on your door in an hour. Don't forget to engage both locks, and don't open the door to anyone. I'm going to scout out the hotel. You can reach me on my cell." He pointed to the printout with the schedule of events. "Mind if I take a look at where we'll be later today?"

She handed him the information. "You take it. The dinner and program will be held in the Magnolia Ballroom, here in this hotel."

"I'll find it." Stepping into the hallway, he waited outside her door until she had engaged the security bolt.

His own room was a mirror image of Ella's. He left his luggage inside and then followed the hallway to the stairwell and went down to the third floor, where the ballrooms were located.

Once he knew the layout for the evening event, and the various elevators and stairways, he returned to his room and called Sergeant Abrams.

"Anything new on Daniel Fisher?" Zach asked.

"Nothing from Alabama, but we've got something on him from Florida. Guess he headed to the Sarasota area last year. Daniel rented a room and left without paying his bill. I'm still digging, but at least that gives me a reason to hold him. I'm counting on him coming clean about the attack on the doc. He's got an angry edge and a sense of entitlement. The world owes him. Why, I'm not sure."

"Let me know if you do have to release him."

"How's Atlanta?" Abrams asked.

"Crowded with people and overflowing with traffic. They suggest we take MARTA to the medical talk, which is probably a good idea."

"I'm glad you're with the doc. She's probably safer in Atlanta than she would be at her clinic, but you never know. She needs someone watching her back."

"I'll call you when we return tomorrow."

"Stay safe, Zach."

"Right." He disconnected. The most important thing was to keep Ella safe.

Why was she on edge?

Ella hadn't expected the anxiety that welled up within her as she and Zach left the hotel. She glanced at her watch. They had plenty of time to get to the symposium and grab a sandwich or salad before the presentation.

Zach took her arm and guided her along the sidewalk. "There's the MARTA station." He pointed to an entrance just ahead.

They hurried down the stairs to the platform, which was awash with a mix of people, from men and women in business suits, to college students and blue-collar workers, to street folks, all of whom relied on MARTA for transportation within the city.

Ella pointed to a train that was loading. "Is that the one we need to take?"

Zach shook his head. "We've got about ten minutes before the Decatur train arrives."

Ella weaved her way through the crowd and stopped not far from the edge of the platform. She peered over the drop-off and stared down, approximately four feet, to the tracks below.

"Better not get too close," Zach warned, wrapping his hand protectively around her elbow.

"Just trying to see how the cars are powered. I went to school in Columbus, Ohio, but I still consider myself a country girl. I've never been around mass transit systems."

Zach pointed to an outside rail covered partially with a metal sheath. "That's the conductor rail, also known as the third rail. The trains have what's called a 'shoe' that slides over it and transfers power to the engine's electric motor."

"Remind me not to walk on any MARTA tracks."

"Folks have died who haven't realized the danger, or who…" He looked at her as if he'd said the wrong thing.

…*who wanted to end their lives*. Mentally, she completed his thought.

Quin hadn't taken his own life, no matter what the Memphis cops had told Zach. Frustrated, Ella pulled out of his hold and wrapped her arms around her waist.

Zach pointed to a train schedule posted on the wall. "We want the blue line heading east."

His phone trilled. He checked the caller ID on his cell and shrugged. "No name, just a number."

He raised the phone to his ear. "Special Agent Zach Swain." His brow furrowed, and he turned his head to the side. "Could you repeat that?" He glanced at Ella and pointed to a corner alcove away from the crowd.

She nodded, knowing he'd be able to hear more clearly away from the people who packed the platform.

Ella again glanced down at the tracks. A group of kids holding skateboards shoved past her.

"Watch out," she warned, for their safety as well as hers.

A swell of new arrivals hurried down the steps and filled the platform, forcing her dangerously close to the edge. Someone pushed against her. She struggled to keep her balance.

"Stop," she cried, feeling propelled forward. Her heart lurched. Her arms flailed as another shove sent her over the lip.

She screamed and fell to the tracks below, her shoulder and hip taking the brunt of the fall. Gasping, she struggled to sit up, her hand coming close to the live rail.

"Someone's on the track!" a bystander shrieked.

Ella looked up, dazed, realizing people were pointing at her.

A roar filled her ears. The ground rumbled.

She peered down the track and saw nothing, then, glancing over her shoulder, discovered a huge train barreling down upon her.

Her heart pounded at breakneck speed. She tried to move, but her body failed to respond. Knowing she'd be crushed by the giant rail car, she opened her mouth to scream again. The sound caught in her throat. She couldn't breathe, and all she could hear was the roar of the train.

"Ella!"

Zach jumped from the platform. He grabbed her shoulders and rolled her away from the rail and into a narrow recessed area under the platform. Nestled in his arms, she heard the terrible rumble, louder than a bomb exploding around them. She closed her eyes and buried her face in his chest, too afraid to cry, too panicked to think or move or do anything but cling to Zach, who had pulled her from danger.

Just that quickly, the train passed.

"Are you hurt?" he asked, his voice husky with emotion. He pulled back ever so slightly to look into her eyes.

She shook her head, unable to speak and unwilling to leave the security of his arms.

"Hurry." He helped her out of the protective area. "We have to get to safety before the next train arrives."

People on the platform stood back, as if unable to believe they had survived.

"I need some help," Zach demanded.

Hands reached down and pulled her to safety. Zach climbed up behind her. Trembling, Ella clung to him, unwilling to let go of the man who had saved her once again.

"What happened?" he asked.

She shook her head, unable to come to terms with what had just occurred. "Someone...someone shoved against me," she finally said.

Her eyes scanned the crowd. Was the person still on the platform?

"Were you pushed?" Zach asked.

"I—I'm not sure. Pushed, or maybe it was the number of people. With the crowd moving forward, I was caught in the swell..."

He turned to study the crowd, just as she had done.

"It was an accident," a man standing near them told his friend.

But Ella had felt the pressure on her back. Someone had wanted her to fall. Someone had known the train was approaching, and he'd shoved her off the platform.

Chapter Fifteen

Zach should have known the Atlanta police wouldn't be convinced that someone had tried to kill Ella. At least the officer took down the information and seemed relieved that she had survived.

"You're fortunate, ma'am," he said, as if Ella didn't realize death had been a breath away.

He turned to Zach. "Sir, you did the right thing. That space under the platform is an emergency area in case someone falls onto the tracks. Glad it offered the protection you needed. You know about the third rail?"

Zach nodded, thinking of how close Ella had been to the live power source. His heart pounded as he recalled hearing the shouts of the onlookers and realizing, almost too late, what had happened.

Seeing the approaching train, and Ella lying paralyzed on the track, he didn't have time to think; all he could do was react.

As the memory flashed through his mind again, Zach put his arm around her and let out a stiff breath.

The cop stared at him for a moment. "You okay, sir?"

"It was a close call."

"Yes, sir. You got that right." He turned to Ella. "Regrettably, the security camera in this area of the platform is broken. Unless you can identify the person who shoved you, ma'am, there's nothing the Atlanta PD can do at this point. I encourage you to be vigilant and on guard."

He handed both of them his card. "Don't hesitate to contact me if you think of anything else that might have a bearing on what happened, or if you feel threatened in any way."

"Thanks, Officer."

"Where are you folks headed?"

Ella told him the location of the symposium.

"I'm going that way. I'd be happy to drive you there. After what you just experienced, I have a feeling the last place you want to be is on a MARTA train."

Zach appreciated the officer's thoughtfulness and thanked him profusely when he dropped them at their destination.

"Let me know anytime you're in south Georgia," Zach said as he shook the man's hand. "I'll show you around Fort Rickman. We've got a nice museum, lovely Amish community and a friendly town, called Freemont. The fishing's good in the river that runs through the area, as well as a lake that's not far from post." He gave the officer his card.

"I'll take you up on the fishing," the cop said with a smile. "You folks stay safe."

As he drove away, Zach glanced at his watch. "It's twelve forty-five," he told Ella. "I doubt we have time to grab some lunch."

"Not if we want to hear Nancy speak. We can wait until afterward to eat, but I'd like to clean up a bit in the ladies' room."

She patted her purse. "And I'm still grateful for the Good Samaritan who retrieved and returned my handbag."

They hurried into the building. Ten minutes later, Zach ushered a freshly cleaned-up Ella into the presentation room and toward two seats on the far aisle, where he would have a clear view of both the crowd and the door.

The director was tall and slender and wore a wide smile as she hurried to give Ella what appeared to be a sincere hug of greeting.

"It's wonderful to see you," the woman said, her gaze warm and welcoming. "I know you probably think I twisted your arm, but I wanted to have Quin represented with the rest of the team. He did so much on this project."

"Thank you." Ella introduced Zach.

"Nice to meet you, ma'am."

"You're a friend of Ella's?" Nancy Vaughn's eyebrows rose ever so slightly.

"We met recently, and Dr. Jacobsen thought I might be interested in learning more about your Amish Project. I'll be sharing the information with the commanding general when I return to Fort Rickman. He's committed to improving relations between the military and civilian communities, especially our Amish neighbors. If there's anything we can do to help you folks while you're in Georgia, please don't hesitate to ask."

"Thank you so much, Special Agent Swain. I'm having a gathering in my hotel suite before dinner this evening," the director said. "It's listed on the program Ella received. I hope you'll join us."

He smiled. "If Dr. Jacobsen is there, I will be, as well."

"Wonderful. Now I'd better get to the podium. Why don't you move closer to the front?"

Zach smiled again. "You're so thoughtful, but we'll be more than comfortable right here."

Nancy waved to a man who had just entered the room. "Ella, be sure to say hello to Ross. He, probably more than anyone, has felt the loss of Quin's passing, as you can imagine."

Tilting her head toward Zach, the director added, "Quin and Dr. Underwood worked together. They were a good team. Losing Quin was like losing a friend and a brother, as well as a fellow researcher."

The man approached. He was six-two, well built and handsome, and for half a second Zach was jealous when he put his arms around Ella and kissed her cheek.

"It's been too long," the researcher said.

"Pennsylvania is far from Georgia, Ross. I'm glad you decided to release your findings closer to my new home."

"With the Centers for Disease Control and Prevention in Atlanta, we knew many of their scientists would be interested. The medical symposium was already scheduled, so we piggybacked on their event. Of course, they were most gracious about fitting us in, knowing the importance of the Amish Project. I just wish…"

He paused and smiled. "Well, you know how I felt about Quin. If only he could be here with us today."

"That's kind of you to say." Ella seemed a bit flustered. Perhaps the mention of her husband brought back too many memories.

She introduced Zach.

"Nice meeting you, Mr. Swain." After kissing Ella's cheek again, Underwood joined the director near the podium.

Ella smiled at a number of people who streamed into

the room. "You made points with Nancy," she said to
Zach. "But are you sure the commanding general would
be interested in the Amish Project?"

"He's a very philanthropic guy. His wife started a
craft fair with the Amish, and they both love kids, so
you never know. Plus I didn't want the director to ask
any more questions. I'd prefer her to think I'm here as
a friend and not as a CID agent."

"Thank you again, Zach, for protecting me. I'm losing count of the number of times you've saved my life."
Ella smiled at him, then turned her attention to the front
as the director was introduced.

Zach followed the introductions and explanation of
the preliminary work that had been done on the project.
But when the director mentioned various enzyme de-
ficiencies and how they played into the molecular and
physiological well-being of the children, he turned his
attention to their surroundings rather than the medical discussion.

He glanced at everyone who entered the room, and
searched the audience for someone, anyone, who looked
suspect. Ella was in danger, even in Atlanta, and he had
to be on guard to keep her safe.

When Nancy Vaughn finished speaking, she was
soon surrounded by many members of the audience,
individuals who probably wanted to offer congratulations or ask follow-up questions.

"Let's go," Ella said to Zach.

"Did you want to talk to anyone else?" he asked,
glancing around at the crowd.

She followed his gaze. Some of the people hurriedly
left the room, perhaps moving on to the next presen-

tation on the agenda. Others mulled about, chatting among themselves.

Ian Webb stood near the door. He smiled and headed her way. She extended her hand as he neared. "Ian, it's good to see you."

"Ella, a pleasure as always. The director mentioned that she had dropped an invitation to you in the post. I had hoped to see you, but you left Carlisle before I had a chance to stop by."

"I needed to move on with my life. I hope you understand."

"Be assured that I do." He glanced at Zach.

Ella made the introductions and again provided a reason for Zach accompanying her. "The military is interested in helping the Amish community where my clinic is located. I thought the symposium, and this talk especially, would shed light on the work being done with genetic diseases that impact Amish children."

Ian nodded. "Our hope from the onset has been to increase public awareness." He glanced at his watch. "I'm off to another lecture. I'll see you tonight?"

"We plan to attend."

"Till then." The Brit made his way from the room.

Ella watched him leave. "Ian was my husband's assistant," she told Zach. "I think he's a great guy, although Quin sometimes saw him in a different light." She smiled sheepishly. "As you've probably picked up from the comments I've made, my husband was faint on praise."

"Where's Webb from? I noticed his accent."

"Somewhere in the UK."

"The assailant last night had a muffled voice, and you mentioned an accent. Could it have been British?"

Ella shook her head. Zach had jumped to the wrong conclusion. "Ian is a good man," she insisted. "It wasn't his voice I heard."

"Are you sure?"

A chill settled over her. She couldn't be certain of Ian. Couldn't be certain of anyone right now.

Maybe coming to Atlanta had been a mistake, if danger had followed her here. She glanced at Zach, who had left her on the train platform to answer a phone call. Could he have returned unnoticed in the midst of the crowd? Could her protector also be her assailant?

She shook her head, unwilling to think such thoughts. What was wrong with her? She was seeing danger everywhere, even in a man who had warmed a place in her heart.

Not Zach. He was her protector, and he'd saved her life more than once. She owed him her gratitude and appreciation. But what about Ian? What motive would he have?

She thought of Quin's files. Was there something hidden that needed to be revealed? After she got home tomorrow, she'd unpack his office records and work her way through each scrap of information, looking for some clue as to why she was under attack. Until then, she needed to keep up her guard.

Zach took her arm and escorted her out of the room. Did she need to be on guard even around him?

"You need to eat," Zach insisted, as they left the symposium.

"I'm not hungry."

"Maybe not, but your body needs fuel, Ella. I would think a doctor would understand the importance of good nutrition. What would you tell a patient who refused to eat?"

"I'd tell them they wouldn't get well without nourishment, but I'm not sick."

"You're running on empty, and you've been through a lot. Stress can wear a person down as much as illness."

She sighed. "You're right, of course."

Stepping outside, Zach spied a sandwich shop on the next block. "Let's head across the street. It won't take long. Then we can catch a cab back to the hotel."

"You don't want to chance MARTA?"

"Do you?"

She shook her head. "A MARTA station is the last place I want to go."

"Then we'll take a taxi."

They both ordered a pastrami on rye and sweet tea.

"I never thought a Yankee would like sweet tea," Zach said with a laugh as she sipped from the chilled glass.

"And I wouldn't think a guy who lives in the South would order pastrami." Ella took another drink of tea and then asked, "So where's home for you?"

"Wherever Uncle Sam sends me. But I grew up in Mobile, so you're right about me being a Southern boy."

"Without an accent."

"I've moved around a lot in the military. Along the way, I dropped the drawl."

They lingered over lunch, as if neither of them wanted to go back to the hotel. Tonight would be difficult for Ella, Zach felt sure. He'd noticed her tension during the medical address this afternoon. Something was bothering her, although she had yet to share what it could be.

Ella glanced at her watch. "It's almost three o'clock.

We need to head to the hotel. The director invited us to a gathering of the research team in her suite, starting at 5:00 p.m. I'm not overly enthused about going, but I appreciate Nancy's thoughtfulness, and I need to attend." She looked at Zach. "You'll go with me?"

"Of course." He smiled and grabbed her hand, which was resting on the table. He'd intended the gesture to be a source of comfort, assuring her of his support and willingness to stand by her no matter where she needed to go.

But something happened as their palms touched. He felt it as surely as he felt the chair he was sitting on. A spark, an electric current, a jolt of power passed between them.

From the way Ella raised her gaze and inhaled sharply, it seemed she noticed it, as well. They sat, fingers entwined, as if time had stopped to give them this brief moment of connection.

Then their waitress interrupted them with the check. Ella hastily withdrew her hand while Zach paid the bill. He asked the server for the number of a local taxi service and made the call as soon as she provided it.

"Thanks for a delicious lunch," Ella said as they walked outside.

The serenity of their leisurely meal quickly evaporated as cars whizzed past them on the busy street. Zach moved protectively in front of Ella and kept his eyes peeled for anything that might look suspicious. A late model sports car carrying three older teens with long hair, tattoos and body piercings drove past. The bass on the vehicle's sound system thumped in the afternoon air.

Zach watched them pass and turn the corner. When they circled by again, he told Ella to step inside the restaurant, while he walked to the curb and stared at the driver.

The kid behind the wheel glared back before stomping on the accelerator and laying a black streak of rubber on the asphalt. Zach watched the car disappear from sight.

Relieved to see the punks drive off, he searched the block and focused on a man leaning against a storefront on the opposite side of the street. He had a folded newspaper under his arm, but made no attempt to read it. Instead, he pursed his lips and eyed Zach until the cab pulled to the curb.

Ella hurried from the sandwich shop and crawled into the rear seat. Before Zach slipped in next to her, he glanced again at the man across the street, who continued to stare at them.

"Do you know that guy?" Ella asked as Zach entered the cab.

"I've never seen him before. How about you?"

"No clue who he is or why he was watching us."

Watching you, Zach wanted to say, but he didn't need to alarm Ella any more.

The guy was midfifties, five-eleven, give or take an inch, probably 180 pounds, dressed in a flannel shirt and jeans. No reason to consider him a threat to Ella, except after what had happened, Zach didn't trust anyone. Not when her life was at stake. Everyone was suspicious, and everyone was a potential killer out to do her harm.

Chapter Sixteen

Ella hadn't expect Zach to look so handsome in his dress blue uniform. At some point, he had told her that CID special agents wore civilian clothes when working an investigation so that rank wouldn't interfere with any interrogations or questioning. She had thought the uniform rule would apply to their time in Atlanta, as well.

Instead he stood at her hotel room door looking bigger than life and twice as handsome as she remembered, even though they'd parted less than two hours ago.

"Blue becomes you," she said, struggling to find something to say that wouldn't give away the explosive emotions playing havoc with her heart.

"I hope you don't mind me wearing my uniform."

"I think it's the perfect attire."

He smiled and then dropped his gaze, as if taking in the little black cocktail dress she wore.

"I should have brought a bouquet of flowers to present to the beautiful woman who graced me with her presence tonight. As we often say around the office, you've made my day."

She laughed. "Is that a compliment?"

"Why, yes, ma'am, that's definitely a compliment, but if you have any doubts, let me rephrase my statement."

His eyes twinkled, making him look even more alluring.

"Dr. Jacobsen, you look stunning, and I'm humbled and honored to be escorting you this evening. If you're ready, ma'am?" He extended his arm.

She locked hers with his and laughed, feeling a burst of excitement that displaced her apprehension. Earlier she had fretted about what the night would bring, but Zach made her feel special and attractive. Something she hadn't felt for a very long time.

They walked arm in arm to the elevator and rode to the penthouse. "I'm more relaxed," she admitted. "The danger has passed, at least for tonight."

Zach nodded, although his eyes told a different story. He was still on guard and worried about her safety. He squeezed her hand as the elevator doors opened and they headed to the director's suite.

"Stay close." He tapped on the door. "If you feel threatened in any way, just tell me you're tired. That will be our code, and we'll leave immediately." He stared into her eyes. "Understand?"

She nodded as the door opened. The director glanced at Ella and then Zach, and hesitated for an instant before she invited them in. "Welcome. I'm so glad you both could join us this evening."

They followed her into the living room of the massive suite, where a number of people were gathered around a large table covered with trays of hors d'oeuvres.

"Tell the bartender what you and Ella would like to drink," Nancy said to Zach.

"Club soda with a twist of lime for me," Ella said.

"Make that two," he told the bartender.

Ross Underwood approached. "So glad you and Zach could be with us."

"I'm grateful Nancy included us." Ella accepted the drink Zach handed her. "You know Special Agent Swain."

Ross stuck out his hand. "The director said the general at Fort Rickman is interested in the health of the Amish children near your military post."

"General Cameron is interested in fostering good relations with all our civilian neighbors."

"Which I didn't expect from the military." The researcher turned abruptly back to Ella. "I hope you found the director's announcements today to be encouraging. She said you'd had twin patients with the same symptoms."

Ella nodded. "I called some months ago, when the children first came in for an evaluation. I wanted to ensure that Quin's treatment protocol, the one he established, was still the treatment of choice. Nancy said it was."

"How are the girls faring?"

"The results have been quite startling and so encouraging. With proper management, they should have a normal childhood and productive lives. Nancy said you're leading the team. Congratulations." The position Quin had held, although Ella didn't need to state what they both knew.

"Nancy encouraged me to take over after Quin's untimely death," Ross explained. "You know how upset I was. His were big shoes to fill, and of course, the work is never the result of any one person, but rather the efforts of the entire group."

A *tap-tap-tap* sounded at the door, and Ian Webb entered. He waved to the director, patted Ross on the back and then extended his hand to Ella and Zach. "Good to see you both again."

"We were just discussing Quin's contribution to the team." Ross brought the newcomer into the conversation.

"Your husband was a dedicated researcher," Ian told Ella.

"He loved his work, although something has troubled me." She stepped closer to both men and lowered her voice. "Quin had been upset shortly before his death because of some results he'd received. He said three sets of twins were involved."

Ross frowned thoughtfully. "We only had one set of twins as I recall, the Zook children." He looked with questioning eyes at Ella. "Are you referring to this study or to something earlier?"

"The last study Quin worked on. Surely you remember the twins. Quin kept pictures of the children in his office."

She turned to Ian. "Do you remember them?"

"I'd have to check my notes."

"Ross?" Nancy motioned to him from across the table.

"Excuse me for a minute."

Ian reached for a cracker from a tray, scooped up a large dollop of dip and popped it into his mouth. Soon afterward, his eyes widened and he reached for a second cracker.

"The dip's fantastic," he said. "A cream cheese base, garlic, onion, a dash or two of Tabasco and something else that I can't identify."

"It looks good." Zach grabbed a cracker. "I'll give it a try."

"The chef calls it a seafood spread," the bartender said as he handed Ian the glass of wine he had requested.

Ian turned to Ella. "Aren't you allergic to some type of seafood? Was it shrimp?"

She nodded. "Crab, but I stay away from shellfish of any kind."

"Then don't follow my lead," he insisted. "Nancy left the menu details to her secretary, who probably didn't know about your allergy."

Zach dropped the cracker he'd loaded with dip onto a cocktail napkin and reached for a piece of cheddar cheese instead.

Ella noticed the switch. "You don't like seafood?" she asked.

"My mother was allergic to shrimp. The doctor told me I could inherit her sensitivity. I've never been tested, so I just stay away from anything that comes from the sea."

Ian's brow furrowed. "You don't know whether you're allergic?"

Zach shrugged. "You don't miss what you've never had."

"Exactly right, my good man. Plus if you don't eat the dip, it leaves more for me." Ian laughed heartily as he fixed another cracker.

Nancy tapped her wineglass with a spoon, getting everyone's attention. "I just want to say a few words of thanks to this wonderful team that has worked successfully and achieved an amazing breakthrough in medical science."

She glanced about the room at the twenty or so scientists and guests who crowded around the table. "Your hard work and persistence even when the results weren't always positive, especially early on, made the difference." She glanced at Ella. "We lost a strong member of the team, and his death may have encouraged all of us to work harder."

Ella's cheeks burned.

"Each life is important, and the children who are being helped would not have survived without Quin's hard work and the treatment protocol he established."

The director glanced at the people gathered in the room. Pride was evident in her gaze. "Join me in a toast to the Amish Project. May this lead us to new break-throughs, so even more children can enjoy healthy, productive lives." She raised her glass. "To the research center and the successful completion of this project. May we never stop working for the betterment of mankind and the health of children, especially Amish children."

Everyone raised their glasses. Shouts of "Hear, hear!" echoed around the room.

Ross held his glass up again. "Join me in a toast to Quin Jacobsen and his significant contribution to the Amish Project."

Touched by Ross's thoughtfulness, Ella raised her glass. Zach stood next to her and followed suit. "To Quin Jacobsen."

"And now," the director said, "we need to proceed to the main ballroom to welcome our guests. As you know, the monies raised at this dinner will help cover the cost of care for many of our patients who lack insurance. The revenue will pay for their treatment and medication. Join me in welcoming the guests and thanking them for their contributions to our Healing Fund."

As the scientists finished their drinks and headed for the door, Ross approached Ella. "I am glad you're here today. I'm sure Quin would be honored, as well."

"Thank you for the toast, Ross. That was gracious and kind."

"I always admired Quin. He had a great mind and a gift for getting to the heart of a problem and finding a solution in a timely manner."

"Your words bring me comfort." Ella smiled with appreciation. "I'm grateful."

She and Zach took the elevator down to the third floor. They found their names on the seating chart posted outside the ballroom. They had been placed at one of the head tables, with some of the researchers. Ella was glad to see that Ian Webb would be with them.

Looking around the ballroom, she took in the ornate chandeliers and lovely flower arrangements. Many ladies wore flowing dresses, some decorated with sequins that glittered in the candlelight from the tables.

"Everyone looks so beautiful," she told Zach as guests streamed into the ballroom. The men were handsomely dressed, but no one looked as dashing as he did.

"You're the most beautiful woman here, Ella."

Surprised by Zach's comment, she felt her cheeks flush, although deep down, she was pleased by the compliment. Swept up in the moment as she was, the MARTA incident and break-in at her clinic seemed long ago.

"May I get you something to drink?" he asked.

"I'm fine. Just enjoying the grandeur."

"And I'm enjoying you. Should we considered this a date, even though *you* asked *me*?" His lips twitched with mischief.

She widened her eyes. "You *told* me you were accompanying me to Atlanta."

"Should I have stayed in Freemont?"

"No." She shook her head. "I'm very glad you're here."

Catching sight of a familiar face, she poked Zach's arm and pointed to the door. "Look who just entered the ballroom."

Zach's eyes flicked over the guests until he saw someone who made him pause. "The twins' grandfather, Mr. Landers."

"What's he doing here?" she asked.

"I'm ready to find out. Wait here, Ella."

She shook her head. "No, I'm going with you, Zach."

The older gentlemen looked surprised when they approached him. "I didn't expect to see either of you tonight," he said as a curt greeting.

"Sir." Ella extended her hand. Mr. Landers shook it and then Zach's.

"My husband was involved in the research team that first identified CED, the disease your granddaughters have," Ella explained. "I was invited because of my husband, and I asked Special Agent Swain to join me. How did you learn about the event?"

"Through the organization that raises money for children who can't pay for their treatments. My wife made reservations some weeks ago to attend tonight's dinner. Of course, with our daughter in the hospital, Lucy needed to stay with the girls. I'm here to make a contribution and to thank the research team."

He lowered his gaze. "Seems I need to thank you, Dr. Jacobsen, for diagnosing the girls' condition and for making me realize that I was wrong about Levi Miller."

"In what way, Mr. Landers?"

"I've always had hard feelings toward the Amish because they didn't accept me when I wanted to marry Lucy. It broke her heart to leave her family, but she did it because she loved me. Eventually, we moved to

Freemont to be close to Amish folks, although I never made an effort to get to know any of them. And I was especially hateful toward Levi. I forbade Mary Kate from seeing him when she was a teen. I might have saved all of us a lot of heartache if I hadn't been so bullheaded."

His eyes were filled with contrition when he looked up. "It was easier to see the fault in Levi, rather than accepting that I was wrong. It broke my heart to see Mary Kate make the same mistakes that her mother and I did. The Lord blessed us with the twins, but now my daughter's in the hospital and my son-in-law's got more on his shoulders than anyone should have to carry."

"How is Mary Kate?" Ella asked.

"There's a little improvement, but I'm still worried she won't survive."

Ella's heart went out to the troubled father. "Holding on to hope is important, Mr. Landers."

"Hugh's with her now. He'll head to the house later. The nurses said they'll call him if she takes a turn for the worse."

"How's his outlook?"

"Not good." Mr. Landers sighed. "He got into an argument with one of the doctors. A couple of the medics had to hold Hugh back so it didn't turn into something physical. The doc said he needs medical help, which only made matters worse. Hugh's discouraged and worried out of his mind."

That's what Ella feared.

"Do you think it's wise to have him with the girls, especially with his escalating outbursts? He's their father, but a lot has happened." She glanced at Zach, who picked up on her concern.

"He wasn't supposed to leave post," Zach said. "I'll

call his unit. He needs to stay in the barracks tonight. He'll be closer to the hospital and able to get to Mary Kate more quickly if there is a problem."

"That sounds like a good solution." Ella remained with Mr. Landers as Zach stepped into the hallway and made the call.

He returned and nodded. "The first sergeant will see to it. He's heading to the hospital now and will drive Corporal Powers back to the barracks."

"But will he go willingly?" Ella wondered.

She glanced from Zach to Mr. Landers, but neither man looked optimistic.

"I'll thank everyone now and head home immediately after dinner," Mr. Landers said. "You've got me worried about my wife and the girls. I've always had a good relationship with my son-in-law, but he came back a different man."

"Sir, why don't you call your wife," Zach suggested. "Tell her to keep her doors locked and the phone number for the Freemont police department close at hand. It might be overkill, but I'd rather be safe than sorry."

"You're right, Zach. That's good advice." The strain on Mr. Landers's face revealed how worried he was about his family.

Keep the girls safe.

The words flashed through Ella's mind. A thought? Or a prayer? If it was a prayer, would the Lord listen? And if He heard her, would He also respond?

Chapter Seventeen

Ella escorted Mr. Landers to the head table and introduced him to the director. While they talked, Zach went into the hallway and called Sergeant Abrams.

After explaining his concern about Corporal Powers, Zach added, "If you can, have one of your cars patrol around the Landerses' home. The first sergeant plans to keep Powers overnight in the barracks, but things can change. I wanted you to be aware of the situation."

"Thanks for the information. We'll watch the house. I wouldn't want anything to happen to those little girls or to their grandmother. Hate to think that their father would do something to harm them, but we've seen the results of PTSD before this. What time do you plan to return to Freemont tomorrow?"

"By early afternoon. I'll call you when we arrive."

"And I'll let you know if anything changes around here."

Zach disconnected and found Ella standing near their table. She shared that Mr. Landers had given the director a sizable check to help their research continue. "He embarrassed me by saying that I had saved his grand-daughters. I told him I wasn't the one to thank."

"You're too humble, Ella."

"The thanks goes to my husband and the members of the research team who made the breakthrough, which I mentioned to Mr. Landers."

She seemed more positive about her husband, Zach noted. Being back in the environment of researchers and physicians—her peers—probably gave her a renewed appreciation for what he had accomplished.

"Your husband must have been a brilliant physician," Zach said, feeling a tug of sadness. It hadn't been that long ago when Ella had allowed Zach to take her hand, had relied on him to keep her safe.

The director moved to the podium. "Ladies and gentlemen, if you would take your seats at this time, please."

Zach helped Ella with her chair and shook hands with the other people sitting at the table. They worked at the center, but in other areas of research, all except Ian.

Ella had mentioned the assailant's accent. While it seemed unlikely that the British researcher could be involved in the clinic break-in, Zach had learned long ago to keep an open mind.

Ian sat on the other side of Ella. Too close for Zach's comfort, but he could do little to change the seating arrangement.

The director tapped the microphone and the room quieted. "Ladies and gentlemen, I've asked Reverend Henry to lead us in an invocation."

The minister was tall and middle-aged, with a high forehead and long nose. "Father, we thank You for this gathering and for all that has been done in medical research to help children everywhere."

Zach glanced at Ella before he bowed his head. She seemed lost in prayer, and Zach wondered if he was wrong for not turning to the Lord.

God, I'm sorry. Forgive me for not making time for You in my life. Help me tonight to keep Ella safe.

Dinner was served following the invocation. Ella talked to Ian and occasionally tried to bring Zach into the conversation. She ate the salad and roll, but ignored the main entrée when it was served.

"You're not hungry?" Zach asked.

"We had a late lunch," she offered as an explanation.

Perhaps she wasn't hungry because she was enjoying the British man at her side. Ian seemed to be the life of the party and his accent became more pronounced with each glass of wine.

After the dessert was served, the director stepped to the podium again. "We have a special treat tonight. I know you're here to celebrate all the work done at the clinic. Because of your generosity, young boys and girls will have access to the medical care they need." The audience applauded.

"I'd like to pay a tribute to those involved in our latest project. Please, sit back and enjoy the program."

The lights dimmed and a photo of Amish children at play appeared on the large television monitors positioned around the room. A series of photos showed the research team. Some were bent over microscopes, others were at their computers and still others were in the Amish community talking to families. The photographer, no doubt understanding the Amish aversion to snapshots, had remained at a distance. The faces of the children were hard to make out, but their distinctive clothing and the farmhouses in front of which they stood pointed to their simple lifestyle.

Ella stared at the video and sighed at the photos of the children. She pointed to a man carrying a young child in his arms. "That's Quin."

Ian patted her hand. "I'm sure it's hard to watch."

Her eyes brimmed with tears. Zach flicked his gaze from her to the British researcher, who seemed overly zealous. More pictures of Quin flashed on the monitor.

The final photo showed him surrounded by children, looking happy and upbeat and not the negative person Ella had described.

The years of his birth and death were superimposed over his photograph, followed by, "With gratitude for the contributions Dr. Quin Jacobsen made to the Amish Project."

The applause was instantaneous.

Nancy Vaughn moved to the microphone. "At this time, I'd like Dr. Ella Jacobsen, Quin's wife, to join me onstage."

Ella gasped. She patted her cheeks and fought back more tears. Zach stood and helped her with her chair.

Ian stood in turn and hugged her. "Well deserved, Ella. We're so glad you're here this evening to receive the award."

"Award? I… I never expected anything like this."

Zach squeezed her arm, but she hurried away from him and made her way to the stage.

Ross gave her his hand and steadied her as she climbed the steps to join the director at the podium. Nancy greeted her with open arms, and the two women embraced for a long moment as the applause continued.

Ella brushed her hand over her cheeks, wiping away tears, and accepted the etched crystal plaque engraved with the caduceus logo of the research center.

The director kept her arm around Ella and spoke into the microphone. "It is my honor and privilege to present this award for the inspiration, dedication and hard work of Dr. Quinton Jacobsen, who led the research team in the early days and contributed a great extent to the breakthrough in childhood enzyme deficiency. Ella, I am so grateful that you could join us this evening so we could recognize your husband posthumously for his involvement with the Amish Project."

Ella gripped the award to her heart and leaned toward the microphone. "Thank you for this special honor for my husband." She glanced up. "I know Quin is looking down upon all of us and is appreciative of this expression of gratitude for his service. His work was his life. Thank you for recognizing him tonight."

Another round of applause accompanied Ella back to the table. Zach rose to help her with her chair, but she shook her head ever so slightly, grabbed her purse and hurried from the ballroom, still holding the award.

He excused himself from the table and hastened to catch up with her. She was standing in the hallway waiting for the elevator when he did so. Tears streamed from her eyes, and her grief seemed overwhelming.

Ella was mourning for a husband she still loved. Zach had been a fool to think that something could have developed between them. Her husband had died just eight months ago, hardly time for her to get over his passing.

The door to the elevator opened and they stepped in. Zach pushed the button for the seventh floor, handed her his handkerchief and then stood aside, hands folded in front of him, giving her space and a bit of privacy so she could continue grieving without him hovering too close.

The elevator stopped on their floor, and he walked her to her room, took the key from her hand and opened her door.

"We'll leave in the morning, Ella. What time shall I have the valet bring the car around to the front of the hotel?"

She shook her head. "I can't stay here. I need to go home."

"It's late," Zach reasoned. "You're tired." *And not thinking rationally*, he wanted to add, but seeing her troubled expression, he didn't voice his additional concern.

"I want to go home. There are boxes I need to unpack that belonged to Quin. There's a picture I want to find."

A picture of both of them, no doubt. As unsettled as she seemed, Zach knew going home was important to her.

"Give me fifteen minutes to change out of my uniform. Is that enough time for you?"

She nodded. "Knock on the door. I'll be packed and ready to go."

He hurried to his room, feeling heavyhearted. He'd made a mistake by getting emotionally involved with the doctor. He'd drive her home and ensure she was safe. Maybe he'd stand guard outside her clinic throughout the night.

Sergeant Abrams might have answers by now. Daniel Fisher could have confessed. Or perhaps Corporal Powers was somehow involved.

The end of the investigation was in sight; Zach could feel it as surely as he knew it was time to reel in his feelings and control his heart.

Once Tyler returned from his trip, Zach would ask

him to take over the case. Zach needed to return to post. He didn't need to cause Ella any more problems.

Before he entered his hotel room, he turned and looked down the hallway, thinking of when he and Ella had first arrived and the sense of connection he'd felt when he was with her. How had he been so wrong?

Letting out a stiff breath, he entered the room and closed the door behind him. If only closing the door to his heart would be as easy.

Getting over Ella would take time, but he would succeed. He had to. He had no other choice than to say goodbye to her and to what he had hoped would develop between them.

What Zach had hoped for would never be.

Not now.

Not ever.

Chapter Eighteen

Ella's heart was heavy as they drove back to Freemont. She stared into the dark night, her head turned away from Zach. She couldn't talk. Not tonight. Not after everything she had experienced in Atlanta.

The tribute to Quin had been unexpected. She'd set the crystal award at her feet in the car, unwilling to let it out of her sight. Quin deserved recognition, and she was thrilled the research team had honored him.

No wonder the director had been so insistent that she join them in Atlanta. Yet Ella was awash with mixed messages.

She thought of Ian, who had been so solicitous. He'd always been a friend to her. Quin had found fault with him at times, but her husband had been prone to finding fault.

Ross had seemed especially grateful for Quin's contribution. Even the director, who could be cold and unemotional at times, had tears in her eyes when she'd presented Ella with the award.

Yet Nancy hadn't mentioned Quin's name at the medical symposium. Perhaps she had saved her praise until the evening function to make the award more of a surprise.

Ella thought back over the last weeks of Quin's life. The comments he'd made concerning the treatment data played over in her mind. Something had bothered him. If only he would have been more forthcoming.

Zach coughed. She turned to glance at him. Even in the half-light from the car console, she could see that his face was flushed and a line of sweat rimmed his brow.

"Are you feeling okay?" The doctor in her became alert to the signs of some medical problem.

"I'm fine."

She touched his forehead and then pulled his hand to her cheek. "That's strange."

"I don't have a fever," he insisted.

"Maybe not, but something is making you flushed. Do you want me to drive?"

He shook his head. "We're almost to the Freemont turnoff from the highway."

"How's your stomach?"

He shrugged. "A bit queasy."

"The twins had a gastrointestinal virus the night of the attack. You could have been exposed at the clinic."

"The twins were gone by the time I arrived."

"Still, if you'd touched the bedding or if the virus lingered in the air... That type of bug is highly contagious."

"I don't have a stomach bug. It's probably fatigue." He rubbed his brow.

"You've got a headache?"

"A dull one, but nothing I can't handle."

"Men always try to be so strong."

He glanced at her with tired eyes.

"I didn't mean that as a negative comment," she was quick to add. "But it's the truth, Zach. I want you to lie down in my treatment room when we get to the clinic. You can't drive back to Fort Rickman tonight."

"I planned to stay at Tyler's house."

"You don't want him to get sick," she reasoned.

"He's out of town."

"As ill as you look, you shouldn't be alone. Are you sure you don't want me to drive?"

He shook his head again. "Here's the turnoff. We'll be at your clinic before long."

The drive through Freemont and then onto the road to the Amish community seemed to take longer than usual tonight.

Ella didn't like the way Zach looked. His face was pasty white and his breathing seemed labored. He held the steering wheel with one hand and rubbed his stomach with the other. A twenty-four hour virus was the most logical diagnosis, but she'd know more when she got him into her clinic and took his vitals.

Whatever was affecting him, it wasn't good.

"Turn there," she suggested. "It's a shortcut."

He shook his head. "I want to drive by the Landers place to make sure the twins and their grandmother are safe."

"Can you ever stop being a special agent caring for the needs of others?" Ella asked, hearing the sharpness in her tone, no doubt from worry.

"It's my job," he answered.

A job that was taking a toll on him, especially tonight.

He pulled the car into the Landerses' driveway. Ella

grabbed his arm when he started to get out. "Stay here," she insisted. "I'll run to the door and talk to Lucy."

She hated to leave him. "Are you sure you can make it to the clinic?"

He nodded. "Just see if the Landerses are all right."

Ella hurried to the door and tapped lightly so as not to wake the girls. "Mrs. Landers?"

"Who's there?" The grandmother's worried voice came from inside the house.

"It's Dr. Jacobsen."

The older woman opened the door, her face tight with concern. "Bob called. He said he saw you in Atlanta. He was surprised that you were attending the charity event."

"And I was surprised to see him. Are the girls all right?"

"They're fine."

"Did you or anyone else get the virus?"

"Thankfully, no, but then my husband always says I'm healthy as an ox."

Ella had to smile. "With everything that's happened, keep your doors locked. Corporal Powers is supposed to remain on post tonight. If he happens to knock at your door, call the police. Don't let him in. He's going through a hard time and needs to remain under observation."

"Sergeant Abrams called and told me to use caution. I hate to hear bad things about my son-in-law, but the officer reminded me that the twins' safety is the most important thing."

Relieved, Ella hurried back to the car. When she opened the door, she knew something was very wrong with Zach.

"You need to go to the hospital," she insisted.

He shook his head. "You're a doctor. I'm in good hands."

Ever the optimist and always affirming.

When they arrived at her clinic, Zach was nauseous and could hardly climb the steps to the porch. Unlocking the door, Ella noticed a note stuck under the mat.

"It's from Levi." She read the hastily written script. *"Sarah wants to visit her sister. We're going to Alabama for the weekend."*

Traveling in a horse-drawn buggy wasn't what she would recommend for a pregnant woman, but Levi could take care of his wife. Ella needed to focus on Zach.

She helped him into a treatment room and had him stretch out on one of the cots. He had a low-grade temperature with an elevated pulse. She gave him an antinausea medication and encouraged him to close his eyes.

"The medicine will make you sleepy. That's the best thing you can do now. When you wake up, you should feel better."

As he drifted to sleep, she thought back again to everything that had happened in Atlanta. The video and the information the director had provided didn't add up. Either the data had been transposed or Ella's memory was faulty.

The first night, Zach had said her husband's death could have something to do with the clinic attack. She'd thought that foolish at the time, but now she realized it could all play together. If only she could find the missing link. The box of Quin's things would be someplace to start.

Thinking of her Amish neighbors and their trust in the Lord, Ella clasped her hands and bowed her head. "Lord, direct my steps. This terrible turn of events needs to stop before someone else is hurt." She looked at Zach, with his flushed face. "Keep Zach in Your care."

Hurrying to the hallway closet, she pulled out a box,

rummaged through the contents and found the framed picture of the three sets of Amish twins.

The twins will provide the answer, Quin had said shortly before he left for Memphis.

She turned over the frame. On the back, he had written the dates when the children had started treatment. The Zook twins—two blond-headed boys—were the breakthrough case when Quin first realized they'd developed a successful treatment.

But the director said the Zook twins had come to the clinic three months after Quin had first seen them and two weeks after his death. Ella didn't understand the discrepancy in the dates. Nor did she understand why Ross had forgotten about the two other sets of twins.

Sitting at her desk, she clutched the frame to her heart, wishing she could clear away the confusion. Her fingers touched something wedged under the cardboard backing on the frame. Her pulse raced as she pulled out the staples that held the cardboard in place, and found a tiny flash drive.

With trembling hands, she inserted the device into her computer and opened the file. Pages of data that Quin had saved appeared, information that was supposed to have remained at the Harrisburg Genetic Research Center.

Ella scrolled through the results, her heart pounding. She was close to uncovering whatever had bothered her husband. Perhaps something that led to his death.

At the end of the last page, she read the final paragraph Quin had written. "I'm heading to Memphis this afternoon and am prepared to confront my assistant. The treatment of three sets of twins—the Yoder, Zook and Hershberger children—was mishandled. The protocol that I developed, which provided the fastest and most efficacious treatment, was not given to all the children. One child in each set of twins received a substandard and less effective medication, and those children have suffered serious complications. The mishandling of these three cases is criminal and was, no doubt, done to decrease cost and thus increase profits. I plan to get to the bottom of this problem, find the person at fault and notify the authorities of medical malpractice."

Ella thought back to the garbled voice she'd heard. A British accent. Had Quin's assistant tampered with or switched the medication each child was to receive? Did he know about the data Quin kept, and had he come after Ella in hopes of finding the flash drive?

Ella needed to call the director to warn her. "The data you presented today is inaccurate," Ella said when Nancy answered her cell.

After explaining what she had found on the flash drive, Ella added, "I remember Quin saying that Ian had been involved in the production of a low-cost treatment that had been rejected early on. Maybe Ian made the switch to compare his own product against the one Quin had developed."

"I don't understand."

Ella told her about the break-in and the attack in her clinic. "I called you some months ago and mentioned reading Quin's notes. Ian must have feared that I had information that would reveal his devious scheme to gain recognition."

"You talked to Ian?"

"Only briefly, before he transferred my call to your extension. I kept thinking about what you had said at the symposium, and the photos used for the tribute to Quin.

The dates they were taken appeared at the bottom of each photograph. I wrote down the dates you mentioned at the symposium this morning, and they didn't match. The breakthrough case was actually much earlier than you documented. It was when Quin first developed the treatment. Yet the data you used at the symposium— data Ian must have given you—incorrectly noted that the treatment was not developed until after Quin's death. It's Quin's work, yet the team is claiming the breakthrough as their own."

"You're sure about this?" the director asked.

"I've got the flash drive that has everything on it."

"Thank you, Ella. I've been suspicious that something underhanded may have been going on. I'll call Security here at the hotel to apprehend Ian."

"Be careful, Nancy. The person who came after me was armed and dangerous. Quin didn't take his own life. I'm convinced Ian killed him."

"He'll be arrested within the hour. Keep this confidential until he's apprehended. I wouldn't want anything to undermine the charity work that was done tonight. And again, thank you for being with us and for all Quin did for the research team."

Ella hung up, relieved that everything was coming to an end and that the truth about Quin's death would soon be revealed.

"Ella?" Zach's voice sounded weak.

"Are you okay?" She hurried to the treatment room.

His face was beet red, and he was gasping for air. "I…can't…breathe…"

She grabbed a syringe and a vial of epinephrine. "You're having some type of allergic reaction."

Had he inadvertently eaten seafood?

She filled the syringe, tied a tourniquet around his left arm and started to inject the medication.

A noise sounded behind her. Before she could release the tourniquet and completely dispense the epinephrine, someone grabbed her shoulders.

She screamed and fought against his hold. The syringe dropped from her hand.

Zach struggled off the cot and threw himself against the man who held her bound. The guy punched Zach in the chest. He doubled over, wheezing. His legs buckled, and he fell to the floor. His head hit the hard tile.

"No!" Ella threw her arms back against the assailant and kicked her legs. "He needs the rest of the injection or he'll die."

"You will, too," her captor snarled. "On the wooden bridge not far from here. You'll die like your husband." His hand tightened around her neck. "Where's the flash drive?" he demanded.

"I'll never tell you."

He cursed and struck her head. She cried in pain and struggled to get free.

"You can't get away with this, Ian."

"You're not even smart enough to know your killer."

She jerked, trying to see his face, but he held her tight against his chest and started to drag her out of the clinic. They passed a glass-fronted cabinet containing medical supplies. She saw her own reflection in the glass.

Narrowing her gaze, she gasped, never expecting to see the face of the man who wanted to kill her.

"Ross!"

Zach dug his way back from oblivion and gasped for air. He'd heard Ross and knew the bridge he mentioned.

Fall rains had raised the water level. Ella wouldn't—couldn't—survive in the angry current. Zach's heart pounded and his pulse raced. He had to save her.

After rolling to his side, he pushed himself upright. A red rash covered his hands and arms, and a metallic taste filled his mouth.

The syringe lay on the floor nearby, more than half filled with medication. The little bit he had received had opened his airway somewhat. Still, he labored to breathe.

Needing to inject the rest, he reached for the syringe, fumbling as he tried to grasp the slick plastic barrel. His fingers were stiff and swollen, the back of his hands splotched with hives.

Angry with his own clumsiness, he willed his limbs to work. Ever so slowly, he grasped the barrel and lifted the syringe off the floor. The tourniquet was still tight around his left arm. Blood seeped from the initial injection site.

Using his right hand, he held the syringe over his vein. His vision blurred. He blinked it back into focus, feeling light-headed as a wave of vertigo swept over him.

Determined to remain conscious, he clamped down on his jaw, slid the needle into his vein and pushed in the plunger. Heat coursed up his arm.

He thought of his mother who had died from an allergy treatment that should have saved her life.

Would the injection do harm or good? He'd know soon enough.

Please, God, help me survive so I can save Ella.

Chapter Nineteen

Buried alive.

That's how Ella felt, locked in the trunk of Ross's car. She forced down the panic that overwhelmed her and focused on getting free.

Ross was driving fast—too fast—over unpaved back roads. Her head crashed against the floor of the trunk with every bump and pothole. Lying in a fetal position as she was, her legs were crammed against her chest. Using her hands and feet, she pushed against the top of the trunk. If only it would open.

What had she seen on television about disengaging the wiring in the taillights to alert law enforcement?

She dug at the carpet that covered the floor and walls of the space where she was confined. Feeling a raw edge, she yanked with all her might. A portion of carpet lifted. She jammed her hand into what felt like a web of wires and tugged on anything that would pull free.

The car slowed to a stop.

Her heart lurched. Had Ross heard her?

She needed a plan.

Think. Think.

When he opened the trunk, she would kick him with both feet. He'd be thrown off guard long enough for her to crawl out and run to safety.

Zach's face played through her mind. He was dying at her clinic. Hot tears burned her eyes, but she couldn't cry. Not now. Nothing could interfere with her getting away from Ross. Only then would she be able to return to her clinic and save Zach.

Footsteps sounded on the gravel roadway.

Ella pulled in a deep breath.

The trunk opened. She kicked, catching Ross's chin. He gasped and took a step backward.

She scrambled out of the trunk, but he grabbed her before she could run.

"You deserve to die," he screamed, and slapped her face. "You're like your husband. He never cared about anyone on the team. He insulted us with his put-downs and negativity."

She fought against Ross's hold. "You tested your own treatment protocol on three children. Quin's was effective, and yours wasn't."

He snarled in rage. "Mine was cheaper. Cutting cost is as important as rapid recovery."

"Not when you're dealing with children's lives." She clawed at his face.

Incensed, he seized her hands. "No one died except Quin. You will, too. People saw you leave the ballroom, upset by the video. They know how distraught you've been since your husband's death."

"Distraught because I knew he didn't take his own life."

Ross wrapped his fingers about her neck. "They'll

think you've taken your life just the way he did. That's true love, to follow your husband into death."

Unable to breathe, she jerked a hand free from his grasp and reached for his eyes. He slapped her once, twice, knocking her to the road. Gravel cut her knees and hands. She crawled away from him on all fours. He kicked her. Air whooshed from her lungs, and she gasped with pain.

He kicked her again and again.

Unable to gain her footing, Ella curled into a ball.

She'd rather be beaten to death than die in the water. At least the police would know she hadn't taken her own life.

Grabbing her wrists, Ross pulled her hands behind her back. Pain seared through her arms and up her neck. "No!"

He dragged her over the gravel. The rough rocks scraped against her legs. She lost a shoe. Something sharp cut her foot.

"Help," she screamed, knowing there was no one to hear her. She wouldn't give up, not until every breath was taken from her.

Nearing the side of the bridge, he wrapped his left arm around her waist and shoved her against the guardrail. The glare from the headlights of his car blinded her. She heard the rush of water and looked down at the dark swell of the raging river.

A cry welled up within her, a plea so forceful it was as if her entire being was focused on three words that circled through her mind, words from scripture she remembered from her youth.

Save me, Lord.

The sound of an oncoming car made Ross hesitate

and gave her the motivation to keep fighting. Ella kicked her feet and connected with his shin.

He groaned, trying to lift her over the railing. She threw her head back, crashing against his nose. She made her body go limp, her dead weight forcing him off balance.

The sound of a car engine grew louder. Someone was coming to rescue her, but would he arrive in time?

Zach's head pounded and his eyes blurred. He was driving wildly and riding the middle yellow line, but no one else was on the road tonight. Levi was in Alabama, and Tyler was out of town. Zach had to rely on his own wherewithal. He had called Abrams. Two squad cars were on their way from Freemont, but they wouldn't arrive in time.

His hives had subsided somewhat, but his fingers were still swollen, and his mouth was as dry as cotton. At least his throat was less constricted and he could breathe.

Ross had mentioned the wooden bridge over the river. Zach took the shortcut along the dirt road that wound close to the Fisher home. The bridge stood at least fifteen feet above the river. If Ross hurled Ella into the water, she wouldn't survive. The current was strong and would quickly wash her body downstream.

Rounding a curve in the road, Zach spied headlights ahead. Accelerating, he raced to the bridge, screeched to a stop and leaped from his car. Still woozy, he stumbled toward the crazed researcher who was trying to shove Ella over the railing.

Tackling Ross with one hand, he grabbed Ella with the other. She collapsed to the ground as he punched

Ross in the gut. The guy hit back. Zach deflected the blow and struck him again and again.

Ross pulled out a Glock.

Ella screamed.

Zach lunged for the gun. The two men dropped and rolled, fighting for control of the weapon. Zach's eyes blurred, and a roar filled his ears. His grip weakened.

Ross angled the gun at his head.

Amassing the last of his strength, Zach twisted his opponent's wrist a fraction of a second before the researcher pulled the trigger. A round exploded. Ross grabbed his gut and twitched with pain, then let out a dying gasp, and his body went limp.

"Zach," Ella screamed. "Are you all right? Talk to me!"

But he couldn't respond. He didn't have the strength. Ella was alive. That was all that mattered.

Chapter Twenty

Ella turned at the sound of a car approaching on the far side of the bridge.

"Help!" She ran toward the oncoming vehicle and flailed her arms.

A late-model sedan braked to a stop. She gasped with relief. The driver's door opened, and a woman stepped to the pavement.

"Nancy?"

The director held a gun and aimed it at Ella. "Did you plan to escape? Don't you know that we need to get rid of you? Your husband proved to be a problem, and we got rid of him."

"You're working with Ross?"

Nancy didn't realize that her partner in crime was either dying or already dead, and Ella wouldn't be the bearer of bad news.

"Don't you see that our research and the work we do is more important than one man's life?" the director explained. "Quin stood in the way of us finding the most cost-effective treatment. He was convinced his own protocol was best."

"But it was," Ella countered.

"Only we needed to hold on to our capital, so we could help more children. If Quin had worked with us instead of against us, he would still be alive."

"He knew you were hurting children with subpar treatment."

"And he was so insistent that his protocol was the way to go. We eventually came to that same conclusion, but at a later time."

"After you killed him."

The woman shrugged, as if taking Quin's life had been inconsequential. "Now you're forcing me to kill you, Ella." She glanced around. "Where's Ross?"

Ella refused to answer.

The director's gaze narrowed as she glanced at where the researcher lay. "Is he dead?"

"Turn yourself in, Nancy."

"Absolutely not. All the better if I don't have to worry about Ross. He was always the weak link."

She was even more despicable than Ella had first realized. "You won't get away with this, Nancy. The police will be here in a few minutes."

"I'll say the special agent shot you and Ross, and make it look like you were out to do us harm."

Ella saw movement from the corner of her eye. Relief swept over her. Zach's eyes were open, and his hand was reaching for Ross's gun.

She needed to distract the director. "You sent Ross to my clinic to kill me."

"You said you weren't attending the symposium and charity dinner. But we knew you had information from your husband's data, records that should have remained at the research center. That was so like Quin, thinking he could bend the rules to fit his own needs."

"Someone pushed me onto the MARTA train tracks."

"Yet your boyfriend saved you," the director snarled. "You're like a cat with nine lives. Ross was a fool. He attacked the wrong person in your clinic, then tried to kill you a number of ways, including using his grandfather's rifle. He had hoped feigning an accent would throw you off track. Eventually, he decided the best plan was an anaphylactic reaction. He asked the hotel chef to add a light seafood glaze to the entrées served to the head tables. A glaze that was undetectable, but deadly for anyone allergic to shellfish."

The director's gaze narrowed. "But you didn't eat anything except your salad. We couldn't let you come back to your clinic and piece together the information. When you called about the flash drive, I was already en route here."

"You'll never find the data."

"If necessary, I'll burn down the clinic to get rid of the evidence."

Ella inched her way slowly around the front of the car. She put her hand behind her back and held up three fingers, not even sure if Zach could see them or if he would understand her plan.

Please, God, let this work, she silently prayed.

The director continued to talk about what she'd been able to accomplish and the children who had been helped through the research center.

"Your husband almost ruined all of that, Ella."

She held up two fingers behind her back.

"He was a good researcher, but he was expendable," Nancy continued.

One finger.

Pulling in a breath, Ella pointed behind the director's head and screamed, "Watch out!"

The woman turned, startled, expecting to see someone behind her.

Ella dropped to the ground and scooted to the far side of the car.

Half lying, half sitting, Zach raised Ross's weapon. "Drop your gun! CID Fort Rickman," he cried.

The director turned back and fired wide.

Grasping the weapon with two hands, Zach aimed and fired. The shot made its mark. The gun fell from Nancy's hands. She gasped, clutched her side and collapsed onto the road.

Ella scurried around the car, grabbed the director's gun and felt for her carotid artery. No pulse. She opened Nancy's jacket and began CPR.

Sirens screamed, and police sedans followed by two ambulances screeched to a stop on the bridge.

"We've got it from here, Doc." Two EMTS took over the compressions and worked to keep the director alive.

Ella ran to where Zach sat propped against the bridge. He tried to stand. "Don't get up. You're still dizzy," she told him. She waved over another team of paramedics. "This man needs medical attention."

They quickly got Zach onto a stretcher and lifted him into one of the ambulances. "You're not going without me," she said, climbing in behind them. "I'm his physician."

"Yes, ma'am."

Ella sat on the side seat next to the stretcher.

"I'm okay, Ella," Zach told her.

"Maybe, but we'll let the ER docs decide. And we're heading to the hospital at Fort Rickman."

"It's farther," he said.

"But they're not short staffed."

Ella couldn't let down her guard; she had to stay in control until she knew Zach was receiving the medical care he needed.

The ER doctor was waiting when the ambulance arrived. He raced alongside the stretcher, asking questions, as the medical team rushed Zach into the trauma room.

"You need to wait in the hallway, ma'am." One of the nurses closed the door, shutting Ella out.

Standing in the corridor, not knowing if Zach would be all right, was one of the hardest things Ella had ever had to do. She called Sergeant Abrams to fill him in, and was surprised by the information he shared.

When the door opened and the doctor invited her into the trauma room, she had to hold back tears of relief. Zach still lay on the stretcher, but his color had returned and he was smiling. She even saw a twinkle in his eyes.

"I'm not sure of everything that happened," the ER doc said. "But his symptoms point to histamine fish poisoning."

Ella nodded in agreement. "I talked to the police. Evidently a number of people at the head tables of a banquet we were at fell ill, eating entrées covered with a seafood glaze. The doctors in Atlanta called it scombroid food poisoning, which coincides with your diagnosis."

"How 'bout explaining what it is to the patient?" Zach asked.

"Basically, it's caused by spoiled fish," Ella told him.

"Bacteria breaks down protein in the fish and high levels of histamines are the by-product, which causes illness. Although usually not as severe as your reaction, Zach. Public health people in Atlanta are inspecting the hotel kitchen, but the problem could have occurred when the seafood was first shipped to market."

"Special Agent Swain mentioned his mother's allergy to shellfish," the ER doc added. "I'd recommend testing. An allergic reaction could have played into his quite significant response. In either case, the epinephrine helped to open his airway."

Ella was puzzled. "But I only administered a half cc at most."

"I injected myself." Zach held up his left arm and showed her the vein where a large hematoma had formed.

"My advice," the doctor said, "is to keep an EpiPen on hand." Turning to Ella, he added, "We want Special Agent Swain to stay here until his blood pressure returns to normal. If the lab work comes back without question, we'll release him in a few hours and you can take him home."

When the ER doctor left the trauma room, Ella stepped toward the stretcher and leaned over Zach. "I thought I'd lost you. You could hardly breathe, and I knew you were in severe distress."

"I feared Ross would hurl you off the bridge. You can't swim—isn't that what I heard?"

"I'm planning to take lessons."

"A good idea." He touched her cheek and wrapped her hand in his. "You're very brave, Dr. Jacobsen, and very smart."

"And you're always quick with praise." She smiled.

"Which is so…well, affirming. I'm thanking God that both of us survived."

"I'm sorry about Quin."

She nodded. "At least I know now that he didn't take his own life. Somehow it's easier to accept, this way, although it only shows how twisted the director and Ross were."

"Do you have any word on Nancy's condition?"

"I told you I called the police when I was in the hallway. Sergeant Abrams said she's critical, but will probably survive."

"And stand trial. What about Ross?"

Ella shook her head. "But there is good news. I asked one of the nurses to call ICU about Mary Kate's condition."

"Tell me she's better."

"How'd you guess? The RN told me she's turned a corner and is expected to make a full recovery. Her husband was with her."

"A lot has happened since that first night at your clinic." Zach touched Ella's hair and weaved a strand around his finger. "But in all the headache and struggle, something good occurred."

"Oh?"

"I got to know a wonderful physician who treats sick kids and makes them better."

"But I almost lost you."

"That wasn't your fault." He hesitated a moment. "I know you're grieving for your husband, but I hope someday you'll find room in your heart to love again."

"I don't think that will be a problem, especially if you're talking about a special agent who saved my life about—" Ella glanced up and pursed her lips coyly

"—hmm, maybe four or five times. I'd say that's the type of guy I want to keep around."

"I'd like to stay around." He pulled her closer. "For a long time."

Then she lowered her lips to his, and he did what she'd wanted him to do since the first night they'd met. He kissed her. His kiss was extra sweet.

With a contented sigh, Zach wrapped his arms around her and pulled her even closer. Then he kissed her again and again.

Pulling back ever so slightly, she wiggled her nose and smiled. "As a physician, I need to warn you."

"About what?" he asked.

"Kissing could cause your blood pressure to rise."

"But mine was too low." He feigned wide-eyed innocence. "Which means kissing would be good for the patient."

She laughed. "Good for the doctor, too."

As they waited for the lab tests to be run so Zach could be released, Ella snuggled against him. She never wanted to leave his embrace. So much had happened that had brought them together, and wrapped in Zach's arms was where she wanted to stay for a very long time.

Epilogue

Ella opened the oven, and inhaled the rich aroma as she basted the turkey with butter one last time. Then she glanced at the clock and wiped her hands on a towel. Everyone would arrive soon.

"I'm impressed." Wendy, her nurse, stood nearby and shook her head in amazement. "You're cooking your first Thanksgiving turkey for all these people?"

"I wanted to share the day with special friends. Thanks for joining us and for coming early to help."

After stepping into the dining room, Ella checked the table and admired the flower arrangement Zach had delivered ahead of time. The bouquet of mums and daisies interspersed with roses was gorgeous.

A tap at the entry caused her to giggle with excitement when she saw his car parked outside. "Happy Thanksgiving," she said, opening the door.

"Don't you look beautiful." Zach kissed her lightly on the lips as he stepped inside. Once she'd closed the door, he pulled her into his arms and kissed her again, much more decidedly.

Her toes tingled, and she had a hard time pulling out

of his embrace. "Wendy's in the kitchen," she finally teased, alerting him that they weren't alone.

"You're blushing." His eyes twinkled with mischief. "She's seen us kiss before."

"And I hope she sees us kissing many more times."

"Yes, ma'am." He gave her a mock salute. "I can make that happened."

Ella laughed and peered into a shopping bag he carried. "What did you bring?"

"Sodas and sparkling water, and some cheese and crackers to put out before the turkey's ready."

"Perfect." She motioned him into the kitchen. "Wendy can get those ready if you'll move some more chairs around the table."

The rest of the guests arrived and filled the house with merriment and laughter. When the food was ready, Ella invited everyone into the dining room, and Zach carried the turkey to the table.

Levi and a very pregnant Sarah sat across from Tyler and his fiancée. Their Amish neighbors, Isaac and Ruth Lapp, also pregnant and soon to deliver, sat on the far end with their son, Joseph. His blond hair and big blue eyes reminded Ella of the Zook twins, who had been the breakthrough case for CED. A new director had taken over the Harrisburg Genetic Research Center, and Ian was one of the lead physicians on staff.

Zach carved the turkey while Ella and Wendy brought the other dishes to the table. Sweet potato casserole, mashed potatoes, cranberry relish, summer squash and an array of breads, that Sarah had baked, filled the room with even more delicious smells.

"I'd like two helpings of everything," little Joseph said, his eyes wide and a smile on his sweet lips.

"Joseph, you are growing so big now," his mother chimed in. "But you need to eat one plateful of food before you ask for more."

"It looks so *gut, Mamm*."

Ella appreciated the boy's compliment and the artful way his mother had used affirmation to build up her son before she corrected him.

Glancing at Zach, Ella thought of the many times he had affirmed her, which was so opposite from Quin. Sarah's father had been faint on praise, as well. Concerned about the older man, she leaned closer to her neighbor.

"Sarah, have you heard from your father?" she asked.

"*Yah*, we received a letter. He is happy living in Alabama with my sister, and even his health is better. My sister said he is taking the medicine you prescribed."

"I'm glad. What about your brother?"

"He is working for my brother-in-law to pay off the debts he owed. There is a widow with a young child who lives nearby. She has been a good influence on Daniel."

Levi took Sarah's hand and smiled lovingly at his wife. He and Mr. Landers had reconciled their relationship, and Levi had had an opportunity to see the twins before Mary Kate and Hugh moved to his new military assignment at Fort Riley, Kansas.

The guests passed their plates, and Ella filled them high with the delectable assortment of food. Before they started to eat, Zach tapped his water glass to get everyone's attention.

"Ella asked me to say a few words of thanks. She and I consider all of you a blessing in our lives. Levi and Sarah are wonderful neighbors, and it won't be long until their baby is here."

"A very healthy baby," Ella said from her seat next to Sarah. "Why don't you tell them, Levi?"

"Dr. Ella got the results of the DNA tests not long ago. Our baby will be born healthy, without any of the genetic diseases we worried about."

"And on that happy note, let's bow our heads in prayer," Zach said. "Father, God, we thank You for Ella coming South to open her clinic, and for all that has brought us together on this special day. Thank You for the land across the street that I was able to purchase and for Levi agreeing to help me farm the property. Thank You for Amish friends, and bless Tyler and Carrie as they prepare for their wedding. God bless this food and those who prepared it."

He glanced up and smiled at Ella, causing her to blush with gratitude.

"And thank You for new beginnings," Zach continued. "For affirmation and love, for peaceful settings and for all Your blessings. Especially those we love who are here with us today. Amen."

Everyone ate their fill and then lingered at the table over dessert. Although Joseph had only one helping of the main course, he found room for two slices of pie.

After the guests left, Zach washed the dishes while Ella put everything away. Once the kitchen was tidy, they walked into the living room to the window that looked out upon the land Zach had bought.

"I don't want to rush you," he said, "but I'm feeling overjoyed today and so very grateful."

She nodded and rested her head on his shoulder as they both gazed at the rolling fields and the falling twilight.

"You're all I ever wanted in life, Ella, and I'm so thankful to have found you."

"I feel the same way, Zach. Being with you brings me total joy and happiness that I want to have continue for as long as I live."

He drew her closer. "Then maybe I'm not being too impatient."

He dug in his pocket and pulled out a small box. "I know you needed time, but I hope we've waited long enough. You'll have a lot of details to plan, so we won't be rushing into anything too quickly, but…"

He looked expectantly at her.

"But what?" she asked, her lips twitching in a coy smile.

"Will you marry me and become my wife?"

"I thought you'd never ask." She wrapped her arms around his neck. "Yes, I want to be your wife, and I'll go around the world with you, wherever you're stationed."

"How about right here? I'll get out of the army in another year. Levi can teach me how to farm. We can expand our property and, hopefully, have a family. I can help with the management and upkeep of the clinic, while you treat the children who need your care."

"Oh, Zach, that would make me so happy, but I'd be happy anyplace with you."

"I love you, Ella, and I always will."

"God knew what He was doing when He brought us together," she reasoned.

"That's why He's God," Zach said, before he kissed her again.

Twilight settled over the land and the stars twinkled overhead. A moon glowed in the night sky and showered the earth with shimmering light. Zach and

Ella moved onto the front porch and sat wrapped in an Amish quilt, watching the moon rise even higher over the horizon.

Nestled together, they talked about their future, about the children they prayed God would give them and about their life together, joined by love and surrounded by the beauty of God's bounty. Freemont, Georgia, and this Amish community would be their home, where they would raise their family and, with God's blessing, live happily ever after.

* * * * *

WE HOPE YOU ENJOYED THESE **LOVE INSPIRED®** AND **LOVE INSPIRED® SUSPENSE** BOOKS.

Whether you prefer heartwarming contemporary romance or heart-pounding suspense, Love Inspired® books has it all!

Look for 6 new titles available every month from both Love Inspired® and Love Inspired® Suspense.

Love Inspired®

www.LoveInspired.com

Love Inspired®

Save $1.00

on the purchase of any
Love Inspired®,
Love Inspired® Suspense or
Love Inspired® Historical book.

Available wherever books are sold, including
most bookstores, supermarkets, drugstores
and discount stores.

Save $1.00

on the purchase of any Love Inspired®, Love Inspired® Suspense
or Love Inspired® Historical book.

Coupon valid until December 31, 2017. Redeemable at participating retail outlets in
the U.S. and Canada only. Limit one coupon per customer.

52615144

Canadian Retailers: Harlequin Enterprises Limited will pay the face value of this coupon plus 10.25¢ if submitted by customer for this product only. Any other use constitutes fraud. Coupon is nonassignable. Void if taxed, prohibited or restricted by law. Consumer must pay any government taxes. Void if copied. Inmar Promotional Services ("IPS") customers submit coupons and proof of sales to Harlequin Enterprises Limited, PO Box 31000, Scarborough, ON M1R 0E7, Canada. Non-IPS retailer—for reimbursement submit coupons and proof of sales directly to Harlequin Enterprises Limited, Retail Marketing Department, 225 Duncan Mill Rd., Don Mills, ON M3B 3K9, Canada.

U.S. Retailers: Harlequin Enterprises Limited will pay the face value of this coupon plus 8¢ if submitted by customer for this product only. Any other use constitutes fraud. Coupon is nonassignable. Void if taxed, prohibited or restricted by law. Consumer must pay any government taxes. Void if copied. For reimbursement submit coupons and proof of sales directly to Harlequin Enterprises, Ltd 482, NCH Marketing Services, P.O. Box 880001, El Paso, TX 88588-0001, U.S.A. Cash value 1/100 cents.

5 65373 00076 2 (8100)0 12309

® and ™ are trademarks owned and used by the trademark owner and/or its licensee.

© 2017 Harlequin Enterprises Limited

LIINCICOUP0917

SPECIAL EXCERPT FROM

Love Inspired®

*When an accident strands pregnant widow Willa Chase
and her twins at the home of John Miller, she doesn't
know if she'll make it back to her Amish community for
Christmas. But the reclusive widower soon finds himself
hoping for a second chance at family.*

Read on for a sneak peek of
AMISH CHRISTMAS TWINS by USA TODAY
bestselling author Patricia Davids,
the first in the three-book CHRISTMAS TWINS series.

John waited beside Samuel's sleigh and tried
unsuccessfully to curb his excitement. He was almost as
giddy as Megan and Lucy. A sleigh ride with Willa at his
side was his idea of the perfect winter evening, especially
since he didn't have to drive. Lucy was the first one out of
the house. She quickly claimed her spot in the front seat
beside Samuel. Megan came out next and scrambled up
beside her sister. He'd never seen the twins so delighted.

Willa took John's hand as he helped her in. He gave
her gloved fingers a quick squeeze and saw her smile
before she looked down.

Samuel slapped the lines and the big horse took off
down the snow-covered lane. Sleigh bells jingled merrily
in time with the horse's footfalls, and Megan and Lucy
tried to catch snowflakes on their tongues between
giggles.

John leaned down to see Willa's face. "Are you warm

enough?" She nodded, but her cheeks looked rosy and cold. John took off his woolen scarf and wrapped it around her head to cover her mouth and nose.

"Danki," she murmured.

"Don't mention it. In spite of the cold, it's a lovely evening to go caroling, isn't it?" The thick snow obscured the horizon and made it feel as if they were riding inside a glass snow globe. The fields lay hidden under a thick blanket of white. A hushed stillness filled the air, broken only by the jingle of the harness bells and the muffled thudding of the horse's feet.

Their first destination was only a mile from John's house. As Lucy and Megan scrambled down from the sleigh, John offered Willa his hand to help her out.

"Was this what you imagined Christmas would be like when you decided to return to your Amish family?"

She shook her head. "I never imagined anything like this. Do you do it every year?"

"We do."

"You aren't going to actually sing, are you, John?"

He threw back his head and laughed. *"Nee,* but I will hum along."

"Softly, dear, softly," she suggested.

He wondered if she realized that she had called him "dear." It was turning out to be an even more wonderful night than he had hoped for.

Don't miss
AMISH CHRISTMAS TWINS
by Patricia Davids, available October 2017 wherever
Love Inspired® *books and ebooks are sold.*

www.LoveInspired.com